*Also By*

Alice Addy

*The Birdsong Series*

Tracks To Love

Sweetwater

Bonjour, My Love

It's Only The Beginning

*The Courage Series*

Missouri Legend

Arizona Justice

Pennsylvania Valor

*

Vernon Gunn liked his life. He was an Arizona Ranger and proud of it. It was all he ever wanted to be. No outlaw, no matter who they were or how dangerous, would slip through his hands. He figured his life would be just about perfect if it wasn't for a damnable, opinionated, and clumsy young woman bent on making him miserable. The hell of it was, he couldn't get her out of his thoughts or his dreams. She was soft in all the right places and so lovely to look at; she hurt his eyes. She was the type of woman that made a man yearn for more than a desk and a tin star.

Beth was blonde, beautiful … and on the run. Her flight from Richmond, Virginia to Tucson, Arizona, would lead her straight into the arms of the one man who would hold her future in his hands. He was a strong man with strong convictions, and more handsome than a lawman had any right to be, she thought. After he learned of her terrible secret, would his heart be moved enough to grant her freedom—or would he end her life at the end of a rope?

It's a harrowing time for the ranger and the lovely outlaw, but the hands of fate step in and take command of their lives. Unseen forces set the final stage, with an outcome no one could have foreseen.

*Riveting hot passion abounds in ARIZONA JUSTICE. Steamy!*

*

# Arizona Justice

## Vernon's Story

Alice Addy

This book is a work of fiction. Names, characters, places, and incidents are products of the author's imagination or are used fictitiously. Any resemblance to actual events, locales, or persons, living or dead, is entirely coincidental.

ISBN: 1481268996

ISBN-13: 978-1481268998

For my friend, Pat

Alice Addy

# DEDICATION

*To my wonderful family.*
*For giving me their support and sharing their ideas, I thank you.*
*You were willing to read my stories while they were still works in progress, and gave me invaluable advice. I couldn't have done it without you.*

CONTENTS

# CHAPTER ONE

*Tucson, Arizona Territory.*
*1865*

The tall Arizona Ranger stood defiantly in the doorway, blocking the light coming through from the outside. Standing with his feet planted far apart, his sharp green eyes quickly surveyed the small room and settled on the dangerous looking hombre sitting comfortably behind his desk, resting his huge boots on top of the most recent Wanted Posters. Both men stared … waiting for the other to make a move.

Ranger Vernon Gunn was first to break the silence. "Well? Where are they?" he bellowed. "Speak up. Where's my little sister and her children?" The ranger had clearly run out of patience.

The dark-headed man looked up and smiled slowly, tipping his hat back just far enough to reveal the sparkle in his brilliant blue eyes. "Easy, brother-in-law," he said in his soft country drawl. "Mary and the children were here, and she looked more beautiful than ever, but they were exhausted after that long stage ride. I took 'em over to the hotel and told her we'd all have supper together, after they'd rested a spell." He continued to grin, his eyes twinkling with merriment.

Ranger Gunn stepped into his office and shut the door behind him. Not being given much of a choice, he reluctantly sat down in a small, wooden chair, one that he normally reserved for the public's use. It was a little snug, he discovered, pressing up against his thighs. Maybe it was time to buy a new one.

It was disappointing that his sister, Mary Wilson, aka *Mary Williams*, wasn't here waiting for him. He hadn't seen her since he left Missouri for Kentucky, way back in '51. She'd been but a child, then. Now, she was married to this desperado, Daniel Wilson, only he was currently known as *David Williams*. It was said that she was deliriously happy and much in love with the man, the father of her three children. Vernon was anxious to confirm this for himself, and to finally get the chance to meet his little niece and twin nephews.

He liked Daniel, well enough, but the man had been in some serious trouble, back in Missouri, during the War Between the States. He was infamous in those parts and had a hefty price placed on his head—wanted dead or alive. However, he was a hero, too, and a legend to the folks living back in the hills. Dime novels had been written, exalting his courage and telling of his many exploits against the Union troops. It was his reputation that necessitated his leaving Missouri—permanently.

Vernon provided his brother-in-law with a change of identity and offered him refuge in the Arizona Territory. So far, it was working out real good, and Daniel had been able to arrange for his family to join him.

"How did Mary react when she discovered that you were alive and not killed back there in Texas? Was she angry with us?" Vernon inquired. He remembered his little sister had quite a temper when riled.

"She was surprised, that's fer sure," David chuckled, "but she was mighty happy, too. As soon as the shock wore off and I held her in my arms, it was as if we hadn't been apart. The boys were stunned and said nothin', but they'll come around. Little Sara—she looks so much like my ma—well, she cried. Hell, I cried a little, myself. They've had a rough time of it, but I hope to change all that. This was a good idea you had, Vernon. Again, I thank you."

"Well, if I know my little sister, that Cherokee blood of hers saw her through the hardest parts. She's tiny, but mighty. Pa always said she had grit and now I'm certain of it. Did you explain that you no longer go by the name, Daniel Wilson, and that she's gonna have to adopt your new last name as her own?"

David nodded and continued to smile. "I told her all about

the plan you came up with, and how only you and I know about the fake murder back in Texas. She understands and she simply wants to be able to get on with our lives. Besides," David's cheeks turned red and his grin broadened. "The last time I was with Mary, I guess I left her with more than just a kiss upon her sweet lips. You'll be an uncle again, sometime in December or January."

Now it was Vernon's turn to smile. "Well, I'll be damned. You sure do work fast, brother." He held out his hand and then changed his mind and put his arms around David's broad shoulders, giving him a good hard slap on the back. "This is great news all around, yessiree!"

David sighed as he observed the sun riding low on the horizon. At last, the day was almost spent and it was time to go and gather his family to meet up with Vernon at Lil's Fine Foods. He could barely contain his excitement. As he entered the hotel, his heart began to race, realizing that after months of being separated from his wife, paradise awaited him, one floor up. He ran toward the stairs, taking two at a time, hoping he hadn't kept his family waiting too long. They were probably all starving by now, he thought, and just as excited to go to supper, as he. Taking a deep breath, in a feeble attempt to calm his nerves, he turned the corner and approached room number twenty-three.

Quietly turning the doorknob, so as not to startle, David stuck his head in and called out. He noticed the darkened room was very quiet, except for the soft snores and sweet noises of sleeping children. It was a symphony to his ears. The big man silently entered the room and sat down in the chair next to the window, and took it all in.

He gazed at the two black, curly heads sleeping across the same bed, looking mischievously rumpled and tousled. His boys were so much like him. It would be worrisome when they were older, David mused. He found his *girls* asleep, side-by-side, all prim and proper under their yellow and green coverlet. They slept face to face—a mama protecting her lamb. Sara's riotess curls danced around her head, while Mary's black silken tresses spread out evenly, enveloping her pillow like a dark cloud. During all the horrible years of war, he had prayed for this one single moment. He was reunited was his family, at last. Life could get no better than this, he thought.

The room continued to darken, as the sun disappeared over the mountains, and still David sat watching his loved ones sleep. He knew he should go and find Vernon and explain, but he couldn't bring himself to get up and leave Mary and the children. They probably needed rest more than they needed food, he reckoned, and surely Vernon would understand. He'd arrange for them to take breakfast with the ranger, tomorrow morning, but for tonight, he'd sit and watch them sleep.

Meanwhile, Vernon sat patiently waiting at a blue and white covered table. Colorful flowers rested on the windowsills and the aroma of mouth-watering dishes wafted in from the kitchen, making Lil's the perfect choice for their reunion supper. He'd consumed a gallon of black coffee, while waiting for his family to appear. It had been many years since they'd been together, and he was eager to see Mary.

He glanced once again, at his timepiece. Had he misunderstood David? Suppertime was almost over and there was no sign of them. *What was keeping them?* He couldn't imagine. Then suddenly, Vernon smiled. *Well, of course.* How thick headed could he be? David had been separated from his wife for months. Slowly, Vernon rose from the table, tossed a dollar down, and left. He chuckled to himself. David wouldn't be showing himself tonight, he figured, and breakfast would be as good a time as any, for their long awaited reunion. Happily, the ranger strode down the street toward his office, whistling softly to himself.

Ranger Gunn liked his job. He'd done his fair share of enforcing the law, back in Kentucky—that is, until the war got all crazy. Eventually, he fought along side his brothers in gray. Now, at the advanced age of thirty-two, he was the law here, in Arizona. There'd been problems aplenty, with the Federal Troops and the Apache on the warpath, but in spite of it all, he liked being here, keeping the peace.

Vernon told himself he was content to be alone. The only family he had was his older brother, Melvin, now living in St. Louis, and his baby half-sister, Mary. He'd heard that Melvin survived the war by fighting on the side of the Union Army. Vernon couldn't understand his brother's choice of allegiance, but he'd forgive him. Mel was now going into business in St.

Louis. Mary had been orphaned while he was in Kentucky, but luckily, she met Daniel and married him, starting her own family. He'd suddenly gone from being alone, to being an uncle, and he was well pleased. Maybe he hadn't been as content with his old life, as he thought. It got a man to thinking.

Vernon watched David's face light up every time he mentioned his wife and children. Maybe he was truly missing out on one of life's greatest pleasures. But how could he ask a woman to share the uncertain life of a lawman?

Maybe someday he'd find the right woman and settle down. He knew he'd recognize her right off. The woman, of his dreams, would be small and dark, much like his sister. She'd be quiet and biddable and love to cook and take care of a house. His ideal mate would like nothing better than waiting on him, making sure he was comfortable and well pleased. She'd never question him. His word would be gospel in his own home. He liked his women soft and curvy, and on the short side. Her voice would be soft and soothing to his ears. When he found her, Vernon swore he'd act swiftly to make her his wife. *Nothing* would change his mind, once it was made up.

Ranger Gunn yawned and stretched his long, muscular arms above his head. For now, it was time for a little shut-eye. He locked up and retired to the bunk he kept, in the back room of the ranger's station. It wasn't much, but it was home and a sight better than sleeping on the ground. Maybe tonight he'd dream of her ... that one special little woman that would keep him warm at night.

* * *

"All right! All right! Keep your shirt on, I'm coming!" Vernon shouted, as he sat straight up in bed, trying to wipe the sleep from his eyes. "What's all the racket?"

He tugged on his pants and struggled to button his shirt. He didn't have time to put on his boots, but he managed to secure his gun and holster. "Oh, hell," he muttered, looking down at his stocking feet with his big toe protruding. He'd have to mend that, he grumbled.

The door was being struck repeatedly, and with such force; he thought it was nigh onto coming off its hinges. There'd be hell to pay for waking him this early, he grumbled to himself.

He pulled up the shade, letting it go with a loud snap, and

came eye to eye with a passel of smiling faces. They were all talking and shouting at the same time, making it impossible to understand a word. His fingers fumbled in his attempt to unlock the door—but finally—he met with success.

A cacophony of cheerful voices reached his ears, and arms and hands and fingers reached out for him. He was being attacked by a boisterous mob; a mob of the most precious human beings he had ever had the great fortune to meet. He recognized his sister, immediately; only she was more beautiful than ever. Along with her, was her little brood consisting of a charming, curly haired moppet and two identical twin boys, looking alarmingly, like their pa. He could see they made their parents very proud.

"Uncle Vernon, Uncle Vernon!" the voices squealed. "Let's have breakfast! Let's go eat! We're starving!" They were all pulling at him in different directions and dragging him toward the blinding light.

"You might want these, brother," a low voice said, as David presented Vernon with his boots.

"Yeah, thanks!"

Vernon couldn't stop laughing. He looked at the happy faces of both David and Mary, and felt such gratitude for the joy they were bringing into his staid and well organized life. This was definitely what he wanted for himself, he decided.

David hollered above the noise of his offspring, "If'n you all hadn't been such sleepyheads last evenin', you wouldn't have missed supper and you wouldn't be starvin' now," he chuckled. "Calm down. I wouldn't want yer uncle to think you had no manners, … And let the man put on his boots!"

Mary walked straight into Vernon's waiting embrace. He held her so tight, that for a moment, she couldn't breathe. He loved the way she felt in his arms, so warm and comforting. It was quite evident that the ranger loved his sister very much, and she returned those feelings. Both brothers had always felt the need to care for her, protect her from the hurt and slander of prejudiced people, but he knew she had no need of his protection any longer. She required only his love.

Mary looked up into her handsome brother's green eyes and whispered, "Thank you, Vernon. I will probably never know all that you risked for *Daniel* … I mean David … but I want you to know that I will always be grateful. He's my life. I love you so much." Tears threatened to overflow and make their way down her soft cheeks.

Vernon cleared his throat before speaking. "Oh, Little Bit, I've missed you so. I can't tell you how happy I am, that you're all here, safe and sound. I don't mind telling you, I was worried. Whatever I did for David and for you, I'd do it again without hesitation. There are some things, in this life, that a man must do, no matter what the law may dictate. I knew David was a good man because you loved him. So, I feel we're even. I saved David for you and he saved you for me." He winked. "Now let's eat before I have to arrest these wild heathens of yours, for disorderly conduct."

"Oh, Uncle Vernon. You're silly." Little Sara beamed up at him, as she placed her small hand in his and led him through the door and out into the sunshine.

* * *

After the most enjoyable breakfast he could remember, it was back to work for Ranger Gunn. He had just received another new batch of Wanted posters. Since the end of the war, it seemed like everybody had gone a little crazy and took to breaking the law. Somehow, all the bad ones ended up here, in the Arizona Territory. As his eyes glanced through the stack of papers, they all appeared to be the usual cast of characters—with one exception. Some guy named, Ryan Beaufort, was wanted for the murder of a United States Senator's son. It was a big deal and the senator vowed to leave no stone unturned. Described as tall, light haired, with a slim build, Beaufort could be one of a hundred men in Tucson, alone. Vernon wished the Senator good luck in his search.

Tucson was the new capital city of the Arizona Territory, and hopefully, the next state in the Union. The railroads were heading this way and stages arrived several times each day, from all directions. It was still a rough frontier town, but they had high hopes for it. Most of the Indians were peaceful and the weather was good. If a man was willing to work hard, he could make a good life for himself and his family.

Vernon stood up and stretched his tall, lean frame. He'd been sitting long enough. Peering through the small window, he spied his relief man crossing the street, walking toward the office. He reasoned it was time he took a look-see around town.

The door opened and Ranger Barclay entered. Barclay was slightly older than Vernon and figured he'd seen it all. You could read it in his friendly, but weary eyes. When in trouble, Barclay was a good man to have your back.

"Takin' off, Gunn?" he questioned, as he hung his hat on the peg beside the door.

"Yeah. My sister and her children finally made it in, yesterday. I think I'll go and look 'em up. Nothing new to report, here. You might want to check out this one poster, though. It seems a Senator's kid got himself killed back in Virginia, and the search for his killer is reaching far and wide. Some guy named, Ryan Beaufort, did it. See ya, later." He placed his Stetson on his head and walked out into the blinding light.

He squinted, looking up the street toward the stage office. It always took a minute or two for his eyes to adjust to the brilliant Arizona sun. As he stepped down off the sidewalk, he felt his large body impact with a small, soft object, knocking it to the ground. The object screamed out in pain.

"Whoa, take it easy," Vernon called out, as he grasped the young woman lying at his feet. "Are you hurt, ma'am?" He lifted her by her waist and set her onto her feet.

She wailed loudly. "I think I've hurt my knee. Ooh! I think it may be bleeding." She started to lift her skirts to inspect the wound, but stopped, when she noticed the big man staring down at her, smiling. She dropped her dress, smoothing the fabric down over her petticoats, then placed her fists defiantly on her hips. "You knocked me right off my feet, you big oaf!" she hollered. "Why don't you be more careful?" She continued to raise her voice. "If you'd only look down here, where most of us live, and not up into the blue sky, you might be able to avoid mauling people over!" She sniffled a few times, in spite of herself. Beth hated to show any weakness.

"Now wait just a darn minute, missy. You could look out for yourself a little better, you know. I was just stepping off the sidewalk, when you careened right into me. You pack quite a wallop, little lady. Lucky, for you, I didn't take a tumble on my backside. Where are you going in such an all-fired hurry, anyhow?"

Vernon was not amused and could feel his temperature climb. This girl was rude and creating a scene. She was in need of a serious attitude adjustment. The one thing he could not abide, was a bitter, screaming harpy, no matter how pretty she might be.

He still had his hands wrapped around her incredibly small waist, supporting her weight, when he noticed she was quite tall for a woman. He could practically look her in the eye. And what beguiling eyes, she had. They were the bluest he'd ever seen, with long, dark blonde lashes that curled up at the tips. She was slender and could be described as willowy. As his fingers took measure, he would not describe her as skinny, but gracefully proportioned. If she weren't yelling at him, he suspected she'd be quite beautiful. His eyes came to rest upon her lips, and he decided they were made for kissing, not yelling, and someone should inform her of that, he thought, ruefully.

Vernon also noticed the lovely young woman was dressed in widow's weeds and had dirt smudging her face. It was clearly obvious she had just recently arrived by stage.

There was always that *"newly arrived by stage"* look about people. They were always dusty, wrinkled, and plum worn out. Their eyes looked empty and they were invariably disappointed with their first impression of the dusty, frontier town.

Vernon tried to rein in his annoyance with the blasted female, as he was the law, hereabouts, and felt he should set the tone. Holding up his hand to silence her tirade, he said, politely, "Pardon me, ma'am. I'm afraid I misspoke. I apologize for running into you. May I see you somewhere, perhaps?" He smiled his most apologetic smile. Maybe she wouldn't be so cantankerous after she got some rest, he hoped.

"Ha! I wouldn't trust you to see me spit!" she retorted. With that, she turned on her heel to stomp away, only to have her knee buckle, causing her to collapse right there, in the middle of the street, in front of half of Tucson. The pretty woman closed her eyes in pain and mortification. What an entrance, she thought, as she covered her crimson face with her hands. It was useless to try to hold back the tears any longer. While she sat in the dust and sobbed, feeling like the biggest fool in Arizona, she felt small, gentle hands settle on her shoulders. She looked up and saw the face of an angel, with large, cinnamon-colored eyes, smiling down at her.

Mary said comfortingly, "Oh, my dear, are you hurt? I know the stage ride is backbreaking and this Arizona sunshine is something altogether new to get used to. I only just arrived here, myself. My name is Mary Williams. My eyes still have not adjusted to the glare, and I feel quite blind. Will you do me the kindness of coming with me to my hotel room? You can get cleaned up and I'll send down for tea. Please? I would love to have the company of another woman."

Elizabeth blinked back the tears and struggled to find her voice. She was very grateful to the petite, black-haired beauty. "Of course, Mary. I … I appreciate your offer, very much. My name's Elizabeth Painter," she said, gratefully.

The two ladies helped each other across the busy street and quickly disappeared into the hotel, leaving a very chagrined and embarrassed looking ranger standing on the sidewalk.

"Well I'll be a skunk's uncle," Vernon muttered, as he walked away. "Hope Mary knows what she's getting into with that little spitfire."

David and the boys offered to go down to the stage line office and fetch back Mrs. Elizabeth Painter's trunks, while little Sara napped. The tea arrived just as Elizabeth finished washing her face.

"I can't believe how much better I feel. I'm most obliged, Mary. You literally saved me, today. I was on my way to being a laughing stock."

Her savior giggled at the thought. "Please sit down and relax. You did have quite a day," agreed Mary, as she poured. "What exactly happened out there, if you don't mind me asking?"

Elizabeth groaned, remembering the fiasco. "I hate to recall it, but you deserve to know the truth, since it was you that came to my rescue. I had just stepped off the stage and was looking for the Hotel Doolittle, when suddenly, this giant of a man, jumped out from no where, and deliberately crashed into me, sending me flying into the dirt, where I turned my knee." She rubbed it gingerly. "Then, he actually had the audacity to ridicule me in public! I had been minding my own business when he trounced on me. There I was, lying helpless in the middle of the street, suffering in pain and feeling humiliated, while he continued to berate and yell at me, shouting at the top of his lungs. He's no gentleman, I can tell you. If he's an example of Arizona manhood, I should have stayed back East."

She took a sip of her tea. "Mmmm. Mary, this is very good."

Mary was surprised. She had met quite a few people, in the short time she'd been here, and they all seemed so nice. "Maybe he was new to Tucson. Did you get his name?"

"No, but I think he was wearing a star. He was really tall and hard muscled. I could feel them under his shirt." She turned pink. "I mean …uh …" Elizabeth struggled to curb her physical response to the stranger and took another sip of tea.

"He was a brute. He grabbed me and I was forced to defend myself. Oh, Mary … he had the meanest green eyes I've ever seen. They were beastly."

Mary started to laugh. "Forgive me, dear. Please, don't think I'm laughing at you, but my brother is an Arizona Ranger, here. He's six foot, three inches tall and has *gorgeous* green eyes. I think your assailant may have been my darling brother, Vernon Gunn." She continued to giggle, in spite of placing a hand over her mouth.

Elizabeth was wide-eyed with incredulity. "That can't be. This man was a rude, arrogant, bully. Your brother wouldn't act like that."

"My dear, he's just a man, and you never know how they'll act at any given moment. Please believe me when I tell you, if you knew him, you'd approve of him. He means everything to me. Perhaps one day, I'll tell you our story. It's a long one, but you'll learn how wonderful my big brother really is."

Mary placed her hand on top of Elizabeth's and gave it a slight squeeze. "In spite of everything, I do believe you and I are going to be best friends."

"I'd like that, Mary. I plan to stay here for a good long while. I'm the new schoolteacher. At least I think I am. After that scene in the street … "

Mary clapped her hands together. "That's grand. I'm anxious for my three children to start school as soon as possible. I've tried to help them along, but they've never had formal schooling."

Elizabeth was smiling now, too. "Maybe Tucson won't be as bad as I first thought. I'm really happy to have met you, Mary, even if you do have a brute for a brother."

Both women laughed.

"I need to find the Hotel Doolittle. Have you heard of it?" Elizabeth asked.

Mary wrinkled her forehead in thought. "No, I don't believe I know where it is, but I've only been here for three days, myself. I can ask my brother."

Elizabeth screamed, "No! I mean … I prefer not to bother your brother. I'm sure he is much too busy to be concerned with my problems. I'll ask the clerk downstairs. He'll know. It's about time I left, anyway. Thanks to the men in your family, I believe my trunks are all downstairs. Convey my gratitude to Mr. Williams and the boys, will you?" She stood and gave Mary a hug. "I know we'll be the best of friends, Mary."

The Hotel Doolittle was located at the far end of Main Street. Elizabeth wasn't at all positive she could find her way back to Mary's hotel, unaided. She had a tidy little room waiting for her, and she was given a written reference to present to Mayor Applebaum, for the teaching position. Everything was all as it should be.

Her room was small, but scrupulously clean. The bed had a new feather mattress that promised many nights of blissful sleep. A well-worn, but lemon oiled dresser stood against the wall for all her personal items, and an oval mirror hung above it on the floral papered wall. A multicolored rag rug covered the smooth painted floor. All in all, it was a very cheerful room and she was happier than she had been in months.

Beth requested a hot bath and a light supper to be delivered to her room. She'd face the world tomorrow, but for today, she wanted to attend to her wounded knee and rest a bit, before her meeting with the mayor. She'd need all her strength for whatever may happen, next.

Several hours later, Elizabeth met with the illustrious Mayor of Tucson. He held out his sweaty hand to welcome Mrs. Elizabeth Painter, the newest schoolteacher in town.

"I am certain, Mrs. Painter, that you'll be a most welcome addition to our fair city. The children are most fortunate to have you as their schoolmistress. I should have been so lucky to have had a beautiful woman teach me, when I was a young lad. Yes, indeed. I would have been a much better student," he chuckled, as he continued to hold her hand.

It was a most disagreeable experience and Elizabeth recoiled, slightly. She noticed his thick hands were clammy and he had the bad habit of slowly dragging his tongue across his bottom lip, while staring into her eyes. She tried to pull her hands back without offending the mayor, but he refused to let go. Suddenly, she felt the need to sneeze. Ordinarily, she would do her very best to stifle the urge, but she decided to let go with a rip-roaring KACHEW! Belatedly, she yanked back her hand to cover her mouth.

"Oh, pardon me, sir. I'm afraid I'm not yet used to the Arizona dust. I am quite embarrassed." She lowered her eyes, convincingly. Secretly, she was grateful for that sneeze. She'd have to keep it in mind for future reference, if she ever again found herself in need of breaking away from unwanted attention.

The mayor was startled, but not offended, as he pulled his handkerchief from his pocket and dabbed the moisture from his face. He would forgive her anything, as he could tell she was born with a delicate nature and was a true lady with a genteel manner. In fact, he thought he just might marry her, after her period of mourning ended, naturally. She couldn't do better than him. He was the mayor of this fine city and she could prove useful to him. He wasn't going to stop at mayor. Someday, he planned to be governor and she would make a marvelous first lady. She was superior to the riffraff he'd found here. He puffed out his chest, just imagining it. Yes, she was quite beautiful and he thought her deserving of the honor of being his wife.

"Good day to you, my dear. We will see each other again, soon." He smiled, showing his gums and his double chin.

Ignoring the urge to wipe her hand on her skirt, Elizabeth left as quickly as was practical. Mayor Applebaum was one to avoid, she decided. Her entire life was comprised of men to avoid. What was wrong with her? Her mother had taught her to behave as a lady and she thought she had succeeded at it. Her father loved her very much and practically doted on her, but he never let her forget that she was born from good, strong stock. She was raised to be useful and helpful and to be a good citizen. Elizabeth smiled. Just thinking about her parents, was bittersweet. She missed them, terribly.

Casually, walking down the sidewalk, thinking of her father

and recalling her happy childhood, Elizabeth passed the Jones Mercantile. She failed to notice the abrupt step off, until she suddenly felt herself falling through space. With her arms flailing in the air, trying to latch onto something—anything to break her fall, she was suddenly aware of two extremely strong arms catching her, and setting her upright on the boardwalk.

"There now, little lady. Twice in one day?" he cajoled. "Once again, I have saved you from catastrophe."

Beth heard just a hint of humor in the deep voice, and cringed.

"You seem to always be falling at my feet. Why is that, do you think? If you want to see me, little lady, you only have to ask," he chuckled.

Elizabeth's eyes narrowed and her lips flattened out in a thin, hard line, as she looked up into his magnificently handsome face. She was ready for a fight, but it would be more difficult than she thought, to avoid falling under his spell.

The ranger was grinning at her, and she had to admit, he was an extremely attractive man. He had perfect white teeth and the cutest dimple in his chin. She had the most absurd urge to put her finger to it. Mary had been correct about his truly gorgeous, green eyes. But there was something about him that irritated her. No matter how handsome he was, he had no right to laugh at her.

"Excuse me, *Mr.* Gunn," she said rather tersely. "I have no desire to see you now or ever." She spoke a little too harshly, she thought, and immediately regretted it.

"That's *Ranger* Gunn … *ma'am.*" he countered.

She had angered him and he proved to be as rude as she first thought. "Of course, Ranger Gunn. Thank you, once again, for saving me from harm," she smirked. "I don't know what I would do, if you were not always around to catch me." She bristled, setting her little black hat straight upon her blonde curls. "Now, if you'll excuse me … *Ranger.*" She tried to twist free from his grasp.

Vernon knew when someone was being smart with him, and she was most definitely being smart. "Just keep in mind, little lady, that I have more important things to do than follow you around, keeping you safe from yourself. I may not always be available at your beck and call. Try watching where you're going from now on, or I may have to hang a sign around your neck warning the citizens of a public danger."

Vernon let go of her waist and turned to walk away. Mad as she was, she sure was a beauty, he thought. Too bad he couldn't abide her.

"Well!" she exclaimed, indignantly. "I knew I was right and Mary Williams was wrong," she shouted back at the lawman. She brushed off her black skirt, corrected her black gloves, stuck her dainty, little nose in the air, and marched off in the opposite direction.

"What did she mean by that, I wonder?" Over his shoulder, Vernon stopped to watch the high and mighty woman stomp away, appearing remarkably similar to a skinny black crow. She'd been talking to his sister and there was no telling what those two women had been discussing, but he bet he came out on the bottom. He grumbled and shook his head in dismay. Whatever it was, it couldn't have been good.

Vernon stomped back to his office, feeling confused and angry as hell. Hopefully, he could lose himself in his work. Criminals … now that was something he knew a little something about. A man could never figure out a woman, but you always knew where you stood with an outlaw. Although, he had to admit, a female sure felt good in a man's arms. Damn it, anyway!

David walked into the Ranger's Office, shadowed by his two sons, Travis and Pete, exact miniatures of their pa.

Looking at the boys, Vernon thought how proud he would be to have sons like these two. Glancing up from his desk, he asked, "So what brings you boys in here, today? Can't you find some trouble to get into?" He winked at his nephews.

Travis spoke up, "Ma wants you to come to the hotel for dinner, tonight. Will you, Uncle Vernon?" The kid looked so hopeful, it would have taken a war to prevent Vernon from accepting.

"You tell your ma that I wouldn't miss it. I want to hear all about your plans. How about six o'clock?" He looked up at David.

"That sounds fine with us, Vernon. By the way, I wasn't supposed to say nothin', but I think Mary's tryin' to set you up with some gal. She wants to get you hitched. Says you'll be much happier, but I couldn't just let you walk in unprepared. Even though I'm the luckiest man on God's green earth, I don't much cotton to fixin' folks up without them a knowin' about it first. Don't know her name, so I cain't say much more. You still willin' to come for dinner?"

Vernon let out a long sigh. "Well, a man's gotta eat and I do love my little sister. Thanks for the warning."

David and the boys let themselves out. "Hey, Pa," Pete asked. "Who's this lady Ma wants Uncle Vernon to meet?"

"I think she's the new schoolmarm, son … your schoolmarm, to be more exact. You and your brother and sister get to go to school here, in Tucson, until we decide where it is we're a movin' to."

*"School?"* Both boys groaned, looking as if they might be sick. "We don't need no schoolin'."

David stopped in the middle of the street and took each boy by his shoulder. Starring down into their deep blue eyes, so like his very own, he calmly said, "Boys, you don't want to be ignorant all your lives. It's our intellect that separates man from beast. Someday, when the time is right, I'll tell you of my exploits durin' the war, and it was because of the education your grandpap and granny gave to me, that enabled me to survive against terrible odds. You must make the most of your minds. Study hard and never stop learnin'."

Both his sons stood a little taller. They were very proud of their pa and they knew what he said must be the honest truth. "Yes, Pa. We'll study real hard. We'll make you proud of us. Won't we Pete?"

Pete smiled and nodded his head, vigorously.

"Let's go, boys. Your Ma and little sister are waitin' for us and we don't want to anger them none. Part of your education is to know who has the *real* power in a marriage and a family. Men like to believe it's them, but in reality, it's the womenfolk that control it all. If they're happy, then they make their men happy. But if they're unhappy, woe is to us." He laughed and swatted both the boys as they all picked up the pace and hurried back to the hotel.

# CHAPTER TWO

*Richmond, VA.*

**MURDER! MURDER! MURDER!**

**The body of Lieutenant Mark Price, son of esteemed Senator Allenton Price, was discovered today in the alley off Broad Street, North. The victim had been dead for some time.**

**It is apparent that Lt. Price was viciously attacked with a large knife. He never stood a chance against the cold-blooded criminals responsible. After putting up a terrific fight, it is believed he was overcome by the overwhelming odds of more than three to one.**

**The Senator has vowed not to give up the investigation into the death of his only child. A reward of $10,000 is being offered for the arrest and conviction of those guilty in this most heinous crime.**

**Memorial service is private.**

Harry Doolittle read the notice for the third time. They were nailed up everywhere, including on the door to his little boarding house. The alley where the body had been discovered was more than two blocks away, but still the police and the private investigators had questioned him, repeatedly. He had nothing to tell them. He certainly would never tell them that he knew the true character of the illustrious Lieutenant Price.

With any luck, they would find some poor soul, guilty of other crimes, and pin the rap on him. He only wanted to be left alone. His boarding house didn't need the bad press this investigation was giving it. Perhaps, in time, they'd all just give up. Not bloody likely however, for just outside his window, Harry Doolittle spied Police Captain O'Hara talking with another officer. He was known to be a tough man and, it was said, he never left a case unsolved.

The bell above the doorway jingled, announcing the captain's arrival. Harry stood by patiently, once again, whilst the police officer grilled him with questions.

"Were you aware, man, that a witness saw the lieutenant enter your establishment a few nights before his body was discovered?"

"No, sir. I wasn't."

"We have witnesses that say you left the house early the following morning, leaving the front desk unattended. Is that customary?"

"Yes, sir. Sometimes I gotta leave to conduct business elsewhere."

"Come now, man. I know you know something. If you didn't see who did the deed, then you must have done it yourself. What I can't figure out is your motive."

Harry just looked at O'Hara. His questioning always ended the same way. He simply remained mute until the pesky police captain gave up and left. He had to protect his business and his friend.

Captain O'Hara sighed in frustration. His best leads always lead him right back to Doolittle, but he couldn't get him to spill. Who was the man the old boarding house proprietor was protecting? They had a name, but no one seemed to know who he was. Who was this Ryan Beaufort and where had he gone?

* * *

*Tucson, Arizona Territory*

David was on his way out to the Hotel Doolittle to pick up Elizabeth Painter for dinner, when he accidentally bumped into Vernon, crossing the street. He waved at his brother-in-law to get his attention.

"Sorry, Vernon, but I can't stop and jaw with you, just now, as I'm runnin' an errand for my wife. She sent me to pick up your date." He was grinning broadly, enjoying seeing the ranger squirm at the thought of meeting a woman.

He held up his hand as if to stop Vernon from speaking, and said, "Now, son, you needn't thank me. I'm willin' to help the cause anyway I can. You definitely need a woman." David laughed out loud, thinking he was one funny man.

"Shut the hell up, you dang fool!" Vernon snapped. "You'd think I never had dinner with a woman before. I'll have you know that the mothers in Tucson look upon me as a real catch. They've got me in their matrimonial gun sights and I'm always ducking behind walls trying to avoid them. So, you ain't as funny as you think you are. Who is this woman, you're going off to fetch? Is she pretty?"

David tried to look sincere. "Honestly, Vernon. I think she is second in beauty only to my Mary. The down side is ... she's real smart. Too smart for the likes of you, I'm a thinkin'." He slapped his hand on his thigh and hooted with laughter. David was in a real good mood.

"You know, Williams, I'm beginning to think I might have made a mistake in bringing you to Tucson. Maybe I should have let them Yankees have your sorry hide and string you to the nearest tree. My life was a lot more peaceful before you came along." He gritted his teeth and shoved his hands deep into his pockets.

"Now you know I'm just joshin' with you, Vernon. You're Mary's brother and there ain't nothin' I wouldn't do for her or for you. I tell you what. Why don't you take this here buggy and go on down to the Hotel Doolittle? Pick up the little woman, yourself. It'd give the two of you time to get to know each other, in private. It might make dinner more agreeable for ever'one."

Vernon thought over David's suggestion and found it to have merit. Perhaps that would, indeed, make it easier. If they met privately, they might not be so stiff and formal at dinner. "All right, brother. I'll go bring her back. What's her name?"

"Oh, let me think. I'm not quite sure. She's new in town. Well ... never you mind. She'll be waitin' for you in the lobby. Just say you're there to pick up Mary's friend for dinner."

"How do I let you talk me into these things, brother? You can't even remember her name? She'll think I'm as dumb as you!" he grumbled. With that said, he pushed David aside and walked on over to the buggy. "Dinner better be real good," Vernon warned, as he cracked the whip and took off for the other side of town.

Elizabeth was as nervous as a turkey at Christmas. She really didn't want to meet anyone yet, but because she treasured her friendship with Mary Williams, and this was important to her, she had agreed to dinner. She was waiting for Mary's husband, David, to pick her up in a black buggy. While waiting, she had time to fluff her hair, straighten her skirts, readjust her gloves, and pull her black shawl together. It was inconvenient having to wear all black, she thought, but it was necessary, and she had to admit, she didn't look too bad in the color. She smiled wistfully, remembering the beautiful clothes she once wore, but those days were forever behind her now, and she swore to make the best of her present situation.

Standing and fidgeting by the large window in the lobby, Elizabeth saw the arrival of the black buggy with a large man at the reins. His Stetson was pulled down low over his eyes. It made no sense to have Mr. Williams climb down to get her, when she was perfectly capable of meeting him there, so she turned around, in a swirl of black bombazine, and rushed to the doors. She pushed firmly, but it met with an immovable force and refused to open.

"What's going on?" she exclaimed. She pushed again—very hard.

"For God's sake, quit hitting me in the face and stand back so I can open the damn doors," yelled an angry and somewhat familiar voice from the other side. "What's your problem in there?"

*"Oh no. Please don't let it be him."* She closed her eyes and prayed silently. Elizabeth stepped back and allowed the door to open wide.

Vernon couldn't believe his eyes or his bad luck. Standing directly in front of him was his beautiful blonde nemesis. "For crying out loud, woman. I should've known it was you. Will you kindly tell me why you have taken it upon yourself to vex me so? What have I ever done to you?—No, don't answer that. I'm sure you'd make up something." He held up his hand to silence her. "Now kindly get out of my way, as I have come here to pick up a *real lady* for a dinner engagement, and you're delaying us."

That was the final straw. Elizabeth looked around the hotel lobby and saw all the stunned and disapproving faces. The ranger had humiliated her in public from the first moment she had arrived in town, and he was succeeding in doing it again. She couldn't fight it any longer. Her resolve began to crumble. Her bottom lip started to tremble and her chin quivered. Her eyes burned with unshed tears. Oh no, she was going to cry, in spite of herself, and in front of this horrible, terrible man.

In a tiny little whisper, she said, "I'm sorry for all the trouble I've caused you, sir." Then the floodgates opened and the tears surged down her soft cheeks, unabated.

Vernon stood frozen in time. He couldn't move or say a word. He was stunned just looking at her. She was breathtakingly beautiful and he was a bastard. She was the most glorious woman he had ever seen and he'd made her cry. She was all red and wrinkled, her nose was dripping and her eyes were swollen almost shut. A soft, golden curl fell over her brow and he was certain he'd never seen such perfection, in his entire life. While he stood there, like a lop-eared jackass, starring at her in all her magnificence, he failed to notice the small assemblage of hotel guests. Observing the little lady in black, sobbing from some cruelty the ranger had committed, a few decided to come to her aid.

A tiny old woman, closer to eighty years old than seventy, hobbled up to the big bully and struck him with her cane. "You are no gentleman, sir!"

Her friend was carrying a glass of sherry, and tossed it in the tall ranger's startled face.

"Now cut that out!" he sputtered. "You ain't too old for me to lock up, you know." Vernon had never been so disrespected. He snarled at the many onlookers, trying to convince them to stay away.

While wondering what he should do, a woman with a small boy timidly walked up to him and kicked him in the shins. Her little boy followed suit. "OW! Ow! Now stop that," he yelled. "I'm serious!" he huffed.

One glance, at the pitiful femme fatale, and he knew if he continued to stay there, in the lobby, his life wasn't worth a plugged nickel. She was obviously suffering a great deal of emotional pain and all the guests were blaming him. Vernon grabbed Elizabeth by the arm and attempted to move her toward the door. It was time for them to go.

"Now just where do you think you're a takin' the little lady?" A huge, well-muscled man with a broken nose stepped forward. He looked like bad news, but the lawman had put up with all he could endure.

"Get back, sir. I'm the law here, and I'm taking her in," he growled, as he continued to drag his captive toward the door. She was crying all the more now, afraid he really was taking her to jail. Beth was, in fact, crying so loud, that Vernon failed to hear the fist aimed directly at his jaw, but he did hear his teeth mash together.

"Damn!"

More than thirty people had gathered around the insensitive ranger, observing him manhandling the pretty widow. They shouted and threatened him with hotel objects, some making contact with his body—while aiming for his head, no doubt. They were shouting at him, calling him names. Suddenly, Vernon heard a friendly voice.

"Elizabeth, darling. What's going on here? My brother came to pick you up for dinner a half hour ago, and I discover a riot in your hotel? Who made you cry, sweetheart? You tell me and I'll have David straighten the ruffian out." Mary rocked Elizabeth back and forth in her arms, all the while, slowly heading for the door.

"Vernon, can't you do something? Find this troublemaker and throw him in jail."

The crowd mumbled and followed the women outside to the buggy. Many of the good folks were still armed with lamps, umbrellas, and canes.

Vernon rolled his eyes as he rubbed his bruised jaw. It promised to be a really long evening.

At last, when they were all settled in the buggy, Vernon noticed David was at the reins. He was chuckling to himself, but Vernon heard him, just the same.

"You think this is funny? You and I are gonna have a little talk, *brother,*" Vernon said, menacingly. "This was not amusing. I could have gotten killed."

David looked surprised. "Now, how was I supposed to know you'd insult your dinner date?"

Vernon seethed. "Shut up."

After arriving back to the Williams' hotel, Mary took Elizabeth up to her own room and let her freshen up before dinner. Mary had to convince her to join them, but in the end, the young woman agreed. Elizabeth thought she would be safe enough, if she concentrated on the children or on Mary. She would simply ignore Mr. Gunn, altogether.

As the two women descended the stairs, the men in the lobby took notice. They were both very beautiful and yet so different from one another. Mary was tiny and delicate, with lustrous black hair, a warm, golden complexion and exotic, cinnamon-colored eyes. She was a pure delight to the senses, a vision of sensuality.

Elizabeth was Mary's opposite. Tall and slender, her hair was the color of honey, all shiny and thick and it curled lovingly about her face. Her eyes were large and as blue as an Arizona sky. Her lips were full and softly pink. She was elegant and graceful, and practically floated down the stairs. She was innocence and purity, compelling a man to protect her with his life.

Two smiling men and a pair of twin boys, stood as the ladies approached their table. David was the first to speak.

"You both take my breath away, ladies. I'm certain that Tucson has never seen two more beautiful women." He lifted Mary's hand to his lips and winked. "Later, my darlin'."

Mary's heart skipped a beat. Her husband had the ability to fill her with desire, with just a wink.

"Mama, you are the most beautifulest mama in the whole world. I want to look just like you when I grow up," little Sara said, her eyes wide with wonder.

Vernon cleared his throat and said, "Sara, you are correct. Your mama is most beautiful, as is Mrs. Painter." He looked deep into her eyes and lost himself in their blue depths.

"Please forgive me for everything, Mrs. Painter. I've behaved badly, even though I didn't do so, deliberately. I'd like to start over, if you would allow."

Elizabeth let out the breath she had been holding. Maybe he wasn't so bad. He could actually be quite nice when he wanted to be, and he was so ruggedly handsome.

"Yes, Ranger Gunn. I think I would like to start over. And, please forgive me for all the times I brought trouble to you, even though I never intended to. We've just had a spell of bad luck, don't you think?"

Vernon smiled, turning on the charm. "Yes, ma'am. I think we surely have. Let's put all that behind us, what do you say?"

"I say, let's be friends, Ranger Gunn." She held out her hand and he gratefully lifted it to his lips.

David sat down and said, "Bout time the two of you made up. I'm starvin' and you two are still standin'. Let's order steaks with all the trimmin's, since my brother-in-law has offered to pay." He looked straight at Vernon and smiled. "Ain't that right?"

Everyone laughed, knowing full well that David had once again, gotten the better of his brother-in-law.

Gathering her courage, Elizabeth remained standing and said, "First of all, I would like for all of you to address me as Beth. Elizabeth is such a mouthful and I don't want us to stand on formalities." She looked directly at the ranger.

Vernon couldn't stop staring at her. She was all he had ever dreamed of. Like he said … when his perfect woman appeared, he'd know it. He forgot all about their squabbles and disagreements as an overwhelming need forced him to ask her a personal question. "That's a right pretty name, Beth. Do you mind telling me how long you're gonna mourn your late husband?"

Mary almost choked on a biscuit. "Vernon, that's improper. She has a right to her privacy and she may mourn for however long she deems fitting. Can we just order our dinner, now?"

Beth smiled as she took her seat. She didn't mind the handsome ranger inquiring about her past. In fact, if things were different, she would encourage his attentions. Sadly, things were not different and being what they were, she couldn't let him go on hoping for a relationship with her. She'd never be able to have a future with a good man. Marriage and children were out of the realm of possibility for her. She knew she had to discourage Ranger Gunn from hoping for more.

Sadly, she said, "That's quite all right, Ranger Gunn. I have only recently been widowed, less than three months. So you understand, I cannot even think of coming out of my mourning for a year and I will never marry again. I hope to stay in Tucson, but even that is uncertain at this time in my life."

"Oh. Forgive my asking, ma'am." Vernon felt like she'd punched him in the gut. He'd let himself imagine a future with the lovely young widow and now it was quite clear. She didn't feel the same about him.

Dinner was excellent and the company was totally enjoyable, even if Vernon was somewhat quieter than usual. He preferred looking upon the sky-blue eyes sitting across from him, to actual conversation. He noticed how her dimples flirted, every time she smiled. Her lips were plump and smooth as silk and occasionally, he got a glimpse of her small pink tongue. She begged to be kissed, to be tasted. Dark lashes, long and curling up at the very tips, blinked slowly, beckoning him to come closer. He yearned to stroke the satin smooth skin of her cheeks. Even her ears, he noticed, were perfect little shells.

He sighed, audibly.

"Hello, brother. Come back to us," David teased.

"What?" Vernon was startled back to reality. "Did you say something?"

David laughed. "Pardner, you're a real piece of work. You ain't heard nary a thing anyone has said since we sat down. Now, what do you suppose is on your mind, or should I ask … who?"

Mary had noticed Vernon's distraction as well, and knew without a doubt, the cause. Her big brother was smitten and it pleased her very much.

"Well, gentlemen. It's getting late, and the children and I must turn. I expect that Beth should be getting back, as well. This has been lovely. We must do it again, soon."

She reached for Beth's hand. "I'm so happy that you've come to Tucson. I'm going to need another woman to talk to." She placed her hands over her expanding tummy. "This little one will be here before I know it, and I'm not at all prepared." She giggled. Mary loved carrying her husband's children. With that said, she stood up, followed by her sleepy and very well behaved children.

David rose from the table and extended his hand to the two people remaining in their seats. He bowed, slightly, before Beth.

"Thank you, ma'am, for spendin' your evenin' with us. Your friendship means more to my Mary than you realize, and I'm grateful to you."

Turning to Vernon, he smiled from ear to ear. "Would you mind seein' to the welfare of our guest and makin' certain she arrives back to her hotel, safely? Can you manage to do that without causin' mayhem?"

Vernon was tired of the jokes his brother-in-law kept making at his expense. He didn't think the situation he was finding himself in was the least bit humorous. He glared back at David before reluctantly shaking his hand and replied, "I'll try my best."

With the goodbyes having all been said, the Williams family retired upstairs, to their quarters.

Beth and Vernon sat quietly for several minutes, before the waitress asked if they would require anything else? He looked questioningly at Beth. She shook her head and dabbed her lush lips with her napkin. He could have sat there all night, just reveling in her presence, but she broke the silence.

"It's been a wonderful evening, Ranger Gunn, even if it did start out a little rocky, but I need to go back to my room, now. I start teaching in the morning, you know, and I'm a bit nervous. This will be my first class and I want them to like me. Do you think they will?"

"Beth," he said dreamily, "I think they'll love you. Who wouldn't love you?" He heard a small giggle.

Beth was surprised and delighted by his comment. "I don't know about that, Ranger Gunn, but I hope I'm a good teacher. My own education is superb, but I have never taught children. Mr. Doolittle recommended me for the position and I don't want to let him down."

As Vernon paid the check, he wondered how a genteel woman like Elizabeth Painter would know a crusty old pioneer like Horace Doolittle? He guided her out to the buggy, placed his hands around her small waist, and lifted her onto the seat. She weighed close to nothing, he thought, and he'd be happy doing this little chore, every day, for the rest of his life. Vernon rushed around to the other side, climbed up and picked up the reins.

All too soon, they found themselves stopped in front of the

Hotel Doolittle.

Vernon didn't want the evening to end, just yet. He leaned over and looked into the beautiful face, so very close to his own. "Beth," he whispered low, "I know it's too soon, and you may not feel the same way I do, but… ."

"No!" Beth sat straight up, looking as if she'd been slapped. This is what she had feared. "This can't happen, Ranger Gunn. I definitely do *not* feel the same way. You can't let yourself be serious about me. I want to go in now, and I'd appreciate it if you would never bring this subject up again. You've ruined a perfectly wonderful evening."

Vernon felt as if he'd had the wind knocked right out of him. "But what did I do?" he pleaded.

Saying not a word, Beth turned very quickly and started to step down from the buggy, but misjudged the distance to the ground. Her hat flew off her head, her arms reached for the air, and the sound of a large rip tore through the silence of the evening, as she landed in a heap of black bombazine—right in front of the double wide doors.

Vernon rushed to her side and tried to help her up, but she didn't want his aid, as she was absolutely mortified at having, once again, fallen at his feet.

"Beth, let me help you."

She swatted his hands away and kicked out at him. "Leave me alone! Just go away," she cried. She was so embarrassed. Since meeting Vernon Gunn she had spent as much time down in the dirt, as she had on her feet. "Don't touch me," she screamed.

"Hey! Stop hitting me. What are you doing?" Vernon yelled.

Before Vernon knew it, the big double doors slammed open and a shot exploded just above his left ear. He stopped moving and threw his hands into the air, trying to come to grips with what was happening. Another shot rang out, splintering the wood rail, just beyond his shoulder. He dove behind the buggy, for cover, dragging a reluctant Beth with him.

"Hell!" he exclaimed. "Stop your firing. I'm the law!" the ranger hollered.

He peered between the wheels, trying to get an idea of who was doing the shooting. His weight was flattening the life out of Beth, but that couldn't be helped. He only wanted to protect her from the idiot with a gun.

"Put your gun down and step back inside, now," he ordered. Carefully, he peeked around the wheel again, but there was no movement he could see.

"You there," shouted the stranger with the weapon. "Let the woman go and stand up with your hands in the air and your guns in the dirt!"

Vernon had had enough. He ordered Beth to stay down. Slowly, he stood up and faced his shooter. "I'm Arizona Ranger, Vernon Gunn," he said in a slow and calculated voice. "You are sadly mistaken about what is happening here, friend. I order you to step away and holster your sidearm, or I will arrest you." He carefully lowered his hand to gently grasp the butt of his pistol. "This is no threat, stranger. It's a promise. You'll do as I say or I *will* shoot you dead. Decide, now!" He stepped away from the buggy, preparing to draw.

A terrified wail pierced through the night and a lady's voice pleaded from the dirt, below the buggy. "Oh, God. Will you men calm down? Somebody's going to get shot and it will be entirely my fault! No one is hurting me! Please just go away … both of you!"

The stranger holstered his six-shooter and asked, "Ma'am, are you a sayin' that this man is *not* forcing you to do somethin' against your will?"

From behind the wheel, the small voice, replied, "That is exactly what I'm saying. Please leave me alone."

"But ma'am, I saw that your dress is torn and your hair is comin' loose. You were angry and he was a grabbin' your body. Are you sayin' you were agreed to his actions?"

Vernon had heard enough and he was tired, through and through. "The lady is saying you misunderstood the situation and over reacted. She wasn't fighting my advances. She was not in distress. The clumsy woman simply fell out of the buggy."

Beth grimaced and tried to will herself to vanish. She'd never live this down.

A big woman, standing in the open door, was listening to their explanations. "Well, I never! Isn't that the new schoolteacher? She hasn't even started her new position, and already she's taking up with men. The mayor is going to hear about this, first thing in the morning, I can assure you." The woman's voice was getting louder, in search of a larger audience. "I carry a lot of weight in this town—"

"That's obvious," Vernon uttered under his breath.

"—and I will not tolerated a woman of loose morals to instruct our children. No, I will not!" The large and disagreeable woman flounced off; glorying in the smatter of applause she received.

The stranger tipped his hat toward the ranger and quietly apologized to him for interfering in his endeavors with the young woman. With his gun holstered, he returned inside.

"You can come out now, Beth," Vernon said in a low and ominous tone.

"No. Go away."

"Now don't behave like a child. It's late. I need some shut-eye and my jaw hurts. Come out!"

"No."

"I'm warning you. I'll come over there and get you, if you don't come out on your own."

"Don't you dare."

Vernon started around the front of the buggy, when the lady screamed.

"For God's sake, Beth!" Vernon yelled. "Don't do that! You almost got me shot the last time. Shut up!"

Beth was practically hysterical, now. "Please, just leave me here in the street, where I belong," she hiccupped. "I'm ruined. My life is ruined."

"Oh, for pity's sake, Beth. How much wine did you drink? You're behaving like a child."

"That's not very nice of you to say. I'll go back in after everyone has gone up to bed."

"Don't be ridiculous. You can't stay hiding under the buggy. Just walk in as if nothing out of the ordinary happened. Go straight up the stairs and get into bed. And don't forget to lock your door." He took two more steps toward the sad little thing, squatting in the dirt, and reached out. "Take my hand, honey."

Beth raised her impossibly blue eyes up to him and the look on her dirt-streaked face broke his heart. She looked so pathetic. He wanted to bundle her up in his arms and carry her away, but considering what had just happened, that probably wasn't a very good idea.

"I can't get up just yet, Vernon." She hiccupped again, and wiped her face on the back of her glove. Beth lowered her voice to a mere whisper. "My dress is torn."

Vernon smiled. This was the first time she had called him by his first name and it sounded so sweet to his ears. All his hurt and anger melted away. "What's a little tear, honey? You can just pull it together and no one will notice." He crouched down to her level and handed her his handkerchief.

She blew her nose and wiped her cheeks, then dutifully, handed the wet handkerchief back to the ranger.

"You don't understand. It is not a small rip and I can't pull it together. It's on my …well … It's on my backside. I think I'm totally exposed!"

He tried to stifle the laugh he could feel building deep in his chest. Trying to look serious, he put his fingers under her chin and said, "Let me see your skirt, Beth. I'll tell you if it's as bad as you think it is." He smiled, sincerely.

She nodded her head and turned slightly.

"Oh, wow," he exclaimed. "That's some tear, all right. That must be one hell of a nail on that buggy to cause that kind of damage. I can see right through your drawers to your skin!" He clapped his hand over his mouth, but it was out before he could stop it. He moaned. Oh why didn't he just shoot himself and get it over with? His mouth was committing romantic suicide.

"Is it really that bad?" It was evident by the hopeful look in her wide, tearful eyes that she'd thought she might have been mistaken.

"Yeah, Beth. It is. How about I wrap my coat around your waist. It'll look peculiar, but no one will see the *real* you."

She thought it over and decided there was nothing to be done about it, so she thanked the ranger for his assistance and wrapped his big jacket around her waist, where she proceeded to stroll like a queen into the hotel lobby. She glided up the stairs as if she was returning from a ball. Beth kept telling herself that these were all a bunch of small minded, poorly educated, frontier stock and she had more culture in her little pinkie than they had in their entire family tree. However, there was nothing she wanted more than to be one of them and belong in their community. Oh, well. Tomorrow promised to be another stressful day and she would need her sleep. She entered her room and locked the door and fell across the bed.

# CHAPTER THREE

Elizabeth Painter was awakened out of a deep sleep by a firm knock at her door. She thought she heard Mary's voice calling her and telling her to wake up. Why would Mary be at her door at this time in the morning?

She sat straight up in bed. "Oh, no! SCHOOL!"

Beth flew around the room, throwing together whatever she could find. She hadn't bothered to change out of her dusty and totally ruined dress, from the night before, so now it would take her longer to make herself presentable. She answered back through the door, " I'm up. What time is it? How long do I have?"

"You should have been there fifteen minutes ago," Mary answered. "Mayor Applebaum is waiting for you and he's not in a good mood. What happened last night after I went upstairs to bed? Did you and Vernon get into another disagreement?"

The door flew open and Beth grabbed Mary by the arm and started for the stairs. "Thanks for waking me. Let's hurry."

Beth's uncombed hair was crammed under the ugliest hat Mary had ever seen. Her shoes were untied and they looked as if they were on the wrong feet. Was that mud on Beth's cheeks?

"Whoa there, little lady. Unhand my wife if you please, ma'am."

David smiled as he placed his hands on Beth's shoulders to stop her body from its forward motion. "You do know that Mary's in a delicate condition and cannot be pulled or rushed down stairs?" His blue eyes were riveting, as he was quite serious.

Beth sucked in her breath. "Oh, I'm so sorry. You must think I'm a horrible and selfish person. I don't know what's wrong with me lately. I cry at the drop of a hat and I'm so grumpy. I forget things and I'm tired all the time. I've either no appetite or I'm famished. Look at all the trouble I've caused Ranger Gunn. Forgive me, Mary. Forgive me, David. Maybe you two should just leave me to stew in my own soup." Her bottom lip began to quiver.

David put his large arm around Beth and gave her a reassuring squeeze. "Now, now. You've had quite a time of it, lately, and Mary and I want to help you all we can. We want you to come to us when you need help and the goin' gets tough. So, since you're already really, *really* late," he smiled, "I suggest we walk slowly and carefully to the school house and take the lumps we got comin'. Sound good?"

Both ladies nodded and strolled casually down the stairs and out the door to the waiting buggy. Once settled, Mary looked at poor rumpled Beth and knew she needed help.

"May I?" she asked, as she motioned to the ugly little hat trying in vain to disguise the blonde disaster shoved beneath it.

Beth closed her eyes and nodded. She knew she must look a sight.

Mary wiped the mud off Beth's face and removed offensive hat. She braided and coiled her beautiful honey colored hair into a fashionable knot and tucked it neatly beneath Mary's own pretty bonnet.

"That's quite an improvement, if I do say so, myself," Mary giggled. "You have such lovely hair, Beth. Here, take my gloves, too, and bite your lips for color. No one will be able to guess you were sound asleep ten minutes ago." One last wipe of her cheeks and the lacing up of her shoes, and Mrs. Painter was ready to face her class.

"Looks like you got you a welcomin' committee," David muttered. "Some don't look too friendly."

The children were running circles in the play yard, while a cluster of parents stood listening to the lady, from the hotel, droll on and on about last night's events involving the new teacher.

"And there she was, admitting to carrying on with the ranger—and him being a single man and all. It's just unseemly!

I'm telling you, mayor, we expect you to do something. Discharge her! She's not fit to instruct our children." She pointed her pudgy finger toward the arriving buggy. "There she is … in that buggy with that half-breed."

Daniel heard the remark, and immediately, the muscles in his jaw seized and he knew if she didn't shut her mouth, woman or not, he'd put the bitch through the wall of the schoolhouse.

The feral look, the woman received from the man driving the buggy, caused her heart to practically stop. Never had she sensed such danger in a man. Her lips closed tightly as she turned away from his accusing eyes and sought protection from within the crowd.

"Calm yourself, Mrs. Pokelsnipe," stated the mayor. "I need to speak with Mrs. Painter before we take any action. Let's give her some time to get her bearings. I am certain she will be an asset to this city. However, I thank you for your diligence, Mrs. Pokelsnipe. It is good citizens, such as yourself, that keep me on my toes." The mayor grunted and turned away from the busybody to face the beautiful new teacher. She did not look as he expected, and for one moment, he was disappointed. It was apparent she was frazzled and her clothing looked thrown together, but she was still one of the loveliest women he had ever seen.

"I am so, *so* sorry for my tardiness, Mayor. I just simply overslept. I vow it will not happen again, sir." Beth was the image of a contrite young woman. It was obvious to everyone, that she was embarrassed.

Mayor Applebaum put his hands on her shoulders and gave a gentle squeeze. "Think nothing of it, Mrs. Painter. We all oversleep on occasion, and as I have heard, you had a rather tumultuous evening, last night." He kissed her cheek and whispered in her ear, "Just don't let it be repeated, dear."

Beth jumped back suddenly, feeling compelled to wash her face all over again.

"Now my dear, as the Mayor of Tucson, I announce school is in session. All you children go in and take your seats and let's get this day underway." The children cheered and quickly did as they were told.

After a less than auspicious start, class proceeded just the way Beth had hoped it would. The children were courteous and eager to learn. Some of them were very bright and quite inquisitive, and Beth had high hopes for them all. Mary's twins were exceptionally smart. They were intuitively bright—brilliant in fact. She wondered from which parent they inherited their superior intellect?

Beth's one concern was a precious little six-year-old girl, by the name of Lily. Lily was tiny for her age and the other children didn't want to play with her. They said she smelled bad. It was true that her clothing was none too clean, but there was more to it than just what she wore. She reminded Beth of Mary. Beth promised herself to take extra time with the little girl and see what could be done for her.

All too soon, the bell rang and her first class was dismissed. The children's cheerful faces glowed with excitement as they told their parents all about their first day. This was why people chose to teach, Beth thought to herself. There was nothing better than being appreciated and seeing all the potential in those happy, young faces.

That evening, Beth received another invitation to share dinner with the Williams' family, but to her disappointment, Vernon was not there. The conversation around the table centered on school, naturally. Sara had been so excited in class, that she could hardly contain her enthusiasm, bouncing up and down in her chair and holding up her hand at every opportunity. Pete and Travis had enjoyed the day, as well.

"We're the tallest in our grade," Pete boasted. Beth guessed that was somehow important to the twins and their pa. "And we knew everything we were asked," he added.

"That's correct, David. Your sons are quite intelligent, advanced well beyond their age, actually," she said quietly, so as not to sound too judgmental of all the other students. It was the truth, however, and she noticed that David was exceptionally pleased.

While they were finishing their pie, Beth mentioned her concern for Lily. The boys wrinkled their noses and even Sara made a bad face. It hurt Beth to the see the children's reactions. "There's something about her that reminds me of you, Mary. She's so pretty, but the other children ignore her … They say she stinks," she whispered into Mary's ear.

Mary's eyes grew enormous from the pain of an old injury

that she thought she had put behind her. David placed his arm, protectively, around her small shoulders. As her enormous eyes grew even larger, she appeared to have been transported back to another time—a painful time that left its scars indelibly etched in her memory.

David quietly explained. "Mary's pa was named Francis Gunn, a real nice man. I never met her ma. She died when Mary was born. Her name was *Fallin' Star*."

"Mama's an Indian. You're Cherokee, aren't you mama?" little Sara piped up. The pride she felt for her mother was obvious. "That makes me Cherokee, too," the little girl said proudly, as she took another bite of her pie.

David smiled at his clever daughter, then continued. "Mary wasn't allowed go to school with the other children, 'cause she was a half-breed. She was ignored by ever'one throughout the whole town." He began stroking Mary's back in wide, comforting circles.

"I must meet this child," Mary announced. "I *will* not allow her to suffer the way I did." Having said that, she took an enormous bite of the delicious pie and nodded her head once. The children and David knew that Ma had spoken.

Teaching school was Beth's saving grace. She loved it and the children loved her. She tried to make every day special for them. She endeavored to make history come alive for her pupils with cookies she had baked, resembling Columbus and the Mayflower. They drew pictures of the liberty bell and she told them all about Paul Revere's ride. More recently, she discussed the terrible War Between the States and how they must all learn tolerance.

At the end of the day, Beth realized how much she loved each and every one of her students. Hopefully, she would be able to stay in Tucson for many years.

As the temperatures cooled and the length of the days shortened, the whole town prepared to celebrate Harvest and Founder's Day. It was a long awaited holiday. Beth received several invitations to dine with friends. The Williams family, the Bennett family, and the mayor, all requested the honor of her presence for the holiday meal. She chose to dine with the Williams' family.

That morning, she dressed in her finest black dress, adding a small white and black cameo around her neck. It had belonged to her grandmother and she treasured it. She took a great deal of time with her hair, letting it curl naturally around her face and down her neck. Fancy ivory combs held the sides up and away from her face. She smiled at her reflection in the mirror. It promised to be a beautiful day.

Ranger Gunn arrived precisely on time. He bounded out of the buggy and rushed into the Hotel Doolittle, carrying a small bouquet of flowers. The ranger was all spruced up. He'd gotten a haircut and a shave and smelled real pretty. He snickered at his thoughts. Wearing a new shirt and pants, he'd polished his boots, dusted off his Stetson, and shined the star pinned to his black leather vest. He was ready to escort the lovely Beth Painter to dinner.

He discovered her sitting like a princess on a velvet cushion, waiting for his arrival. Vernon's face lit up like a pumpkin, when he saw her smile. She was perfection with her shiny golden curls crowning her angelic face. He knew, right then, that he was forever in love with her. But what was he to do about it? He walked up to her and offered his arm, which she readily took.

"You look might pretty today, Beth. Are you excited about all the grub we'll be eating?" That was a stupid thing to say, he thought.

She giggled. "As a matter of fact, Vernon, I'm quite excited."

Vernon just continued to stare with a dumb smile on his face.

"Are those flowers meant for me, Vernon?" Beth asked, coyly.

He looked down at the crushed bouquet he was holding in his fist. "Oh! I guess I forgot. These are for you." He held them out stiffly in front of him.

Beth giggled. "They were lovely, Ranger. Thank you."

"You're most welcome, Beth."

He stared at the broken stems and wilted petals. They were a pitiful offering, for sure. "Sorry," he muttered, as he lifted her high onto the seat.

Vernon walked around to the other side and stepped up, next to her. He continued to sit there, silently mesmerized by her presence, with the reins dangling loosely between his fingers, and feeling all sorts of stupid.

"Don't you think we should get going, now?" Beth prompted.

Vernon's face turned beet red from the neck up. In response, he jerked toward the horse and cracked the reins, high above the animal. He was certainly making a mess of things, he thought. "Get up!" he hollered, and the buggy lurched forward, down the street.

"You look mighty handsome, today, Ranger. Smell good, too," Beth said grinning, trying to lighten his mood.

Vernon ignored her well-intentioned comment, as he tried to concentrate on the road.

"I've decided to read part of the Pilgrim's Story to the children," Beth announced. "Hopefully, they won't realize they're getting a history lesson." She smiled at the ranger, waiting for him to respond.

"You can read to me any time you like," he finally said.

Beth blushed. "Why, Ranger Gunn. I think you're flirting with me. I take it, you've forgiven me for all the disasters I've caused you?"

Vernon grew serious, once again. He was scowling and thinking over his next words, very carefully. "Beth, I need to say something, and I know you don't want to hear it yet, and I know you don't feel the same way about me. But if I don't tell you how I feel … I'm going to explode."

She exaggerated a look of fear. "Well, I certainly don't want you to explode, Vernon. You might as well spit it out."

Pulling the buggy over to the side of the street, Vernon reined to a stop.

"Whoa, there!"

He secured the team and set the brake, then turned toward Beth. He took hold of both her hands, noticing how soft and elegant they were.

"Beth, darling. I'm thirty-two years old and not the kind of man to play games. I say what I feel and let the chips fall where they may. I've never said these words to another living soul. The most important thing in my life, until I met you, was my career. I wanted to be the best lawman in the West—still do. I've worked hard for that. But, one day, my whole world was turned upside down and changed forever by a graceful slip of a woman … a tall widow with golden curls. A woman so beautiful she stole my breath away. And that's a crime in these parts," he grinned.

"Oh, my … Vernon. You really mean these things you're saying, don't you?"

He brought her trembling hands up to his lips and kissed her fingertips. "I mean all this and much, much more. I'm lost without you, Beth. I have trouble thinking clearly, and in my line of work, that can be dangerous.

"I know you've been recently widowed and that I'm being premature, but I need to know if there's even a small chance that, after your time of bereavement, you will allow me to call on you?

"My heart beats harder and faster whenever you're around. I grow tongue-tied and make a mess of things—in case you haven't noticed—and I don't know how long I can continue on without knowing your feelings for me. I'm tormented with doubt and only you can bring me peace. Do you return *any* of my feelings?"

Tears filled her huge eyes. She sucked in her bottom lip to stop from losing control. Beth didn't want to cry in front of him, not again. "I do return your feelings, sir, but as you said, I cannot allow you to court me, just now. I must also think of my position. If I'm anything less than proper, I will lose my job, and those children are very precious to me."

Vernon nodded.

"I have a history, Vernon, and it's not a happy one. I'm not certain you would approve or understand. Do not make the mistake of believing me to be this paragon of virtue, for I assure you, nothing could be further from the truth," she sighed. "Let's ride on, please."

Vernon was puzzled by what she'd said. What kind of a past could she possibly have? He would think hard on all the little hints she'd let slip over the last couple of weeks. He was certain there was more to Mrs. Elizabeth Painter than first met the eye, but if she was in trouble and needed help, he'd be there for her.

Mary and David had convinced the hotel manager to allow them to entertain in one of the private suites. Their dinner was brought upstairs and laid out family style. In addition to Beth and Vernon, another couple and their little girl were present.

"Ranger Gunn and Mrs. Painter, I would like to introduce you to Mr. and Mrs. John Runyon and their daughter, Lily. I believe she's in your school, Beth."

Beth took the little girl by the hand. "Of course, she is. How are you, Lily? What a pretty new dress you're wearing." The child was scrubbed clean and fairly beamed at the compliment.

Everyone shook hands and started speaking at once. "Mrs. Runyon is Navajo and her Indian name is Summer Song." Mary explained. "Her white name is Jane. I was telling her that my Cherokee name is Robin's Song. I guess maybe, together, we could start a choir." They all laughed.

In very good English, Jane thanked Beth for all her hard work with the children and she promised to help Lily study hard. She was thankful that Beth was allowing her daughter to attend the school, along with the white children.

Beth was shocked that Lily's being half Indian would be an issue. She was an adorable and intelligent little girl, an asset to the classroom. She thought it was only her clothing and personal hygiene that was the issue. Apparently it was more.

John Runyon was from England and the children laughed at his funny way of speaking. He took it with good humor and said that he thought *they* spoke quite oddly. The children looked at one another with surprise. They didn't understand that at all. Before long, all the youngsters were playing together, just as if Lily had been a friend of theirs for years. That was the way it should be.

As this happy and appreciative group sat around the table to enjoy their bountiful meal, their thoughts turned to the loved ones they had left far behind.

Mary was grateful for reuniting with one of her brothers and she prayed that her other brother, Melvin, was happy and well. She missed her pa and Carolyn, but most of all, her heart broke for the loss of her daughter, Ruthie, buried back in Missouri. As she patted her tummy, feeling the new life stirring there, she was most grateful for her loving husband and her beautiful children.

David thanked God for his family. He missed his folks back home, knowing he'd never see them again, and that caused him considerable pain. But he was still alive, and for that, he was most grateful.

John and Jane gave thanks for good friends. Just knowing

that their lovely daughter might have a chance at a better life, filled them with gratitude.

Vernon stood and proclaimed loudly, " I thank heaven for my little sister and her happy brood of heathens." The children snickered. "I'm even thankful for the big galoot she married." He smiled at David's silly grin. "All in all, you're a mighty fine man, David, and almost worthy of Mary." These happy, smiling people were his family and he would gladly give up his life for them.

Then he glanced over at Beth and felt his heart swell with love for her. If it took the rest of his life, he would wait for her to return his love. "I am profoundly grateful to have all of you in my life." He smiled at Beth, and sat down, quietly.

The children wanted to eat, so their lists of things to be thankful for were short and very sweet. They loved God, country, and family.

Lastly, Elizabeth stood and gave thanks for good friends, the children, and for the family she had once known. She was reciting her list, when she suddenly felt a little woozy and the room started to sway. She reached out toward Vernon for support, and he was on his feet in a heartbeat. As she collapsed in his arms, he gathered her up and carried her to a bed.

"What happened?" Beth mumbled, after several minutes.

Mary replaced the cool washcloth on her forehead and said, "It seems you fainted, but don't worry, you didn't embarrass yourself. Are you feeling better, now?"

"Yes, I think so. I've never fainted before. I haven't been feeling well, lately. It must be the change in climate or something," Beth pondered.

Mary smiled at her, before saying, "Yes … it's probably *something*. Beth … is there any chance that you may be increasing?"

Beth was puzzled. "Increasing? What is that?"

"What is that?" Now Mary was the one confused. "You mean you aren't familiar with the term, *increasing?*"

"I've never heard it before."

Mary took one of Beth's hands and asked, "How long were you married to your husband?"

Again, Beth looked puzzled. "I don't know for sure."

"Oh Beth, help me out, here. I have reason to believe you

may be carrying his child. You might be pregnant, Beth. Is there any chance?"

Beth's hand flew up to cover her mouth, but she couldn't stop the bile from spewing forth, all over the rug. She retched over and over again. *It can't be true. Oh, dear God, no. This is a nightmare!*

"Darling, you poor thing. Lie back and I'll find something to help settle your stomach. Close your eyes and rest. Don't worry about the spot on the rug." With that, Mary ran from the room.

Beth dozed fitfully, her dreams filled with visions of torment and pain. She was scared, terrified of the tall officer. She ran and ran only to be caught by his strong and brutal hands. Oh, how she hated those hands. She was bleeding; she was hurting. *Please wake up.*

After dinner, the Runyons departed for home and Mary sat down with David. "I think Beth is going to have her husband's child, and she's terrified at the prospect. She's not the least bit happy about it. What do you suppose happened to her? Has she ever told you or Vernon how her husband died?"

David shook his head. "No. She's never mentioned him, as far as I know. I've never even heard her mention his name. With the two of you bein' women friends and all, I'd imagine she'd talk to you about him. Shouldn't she be missin' him or somethin'?"

Mary cuddled with her husband's arms wrapped securely around her. "Things aren't right. I can't put my finger on it, but I'm afraid my best friend is in trouble."

Vernon was worried about Beth too. She didn't look well when he caught her in his arms. Dinner hadn't turned out the way he had hoped, but now he just wanted Beth to feel better. What was ailing her, anyhow?

He stopped by the Ranger's Office to see if Barclay needed his assistance. As he entered, he noticed a new batch of Wanted posters scattered on his desk. "What are all these?"

Ranger Barclay answered. "It seems all hell's breakin' out in the Injun territories. Cochise finally joined up with his uncle and he's takin' revenge on all whites. We got farms and ranches burnin' all around us. A bunch of people rode in just today, askin' fer sanctuary. It's a sad thing when a man can't safely provide fer his own family."

This was all Vernon needed to know. "Well, I guess we'll get us a posse together and go up into those rocks and flush the bastards out. Can't let this go unchallenged. We'll, more than likely, be gone a couple of weeks. Damn it, anyway," he cursed.

* * *

*Richmond, VA.*

"I told you, over and over. The lieutenant wasn't a nice man. He paid for my services more than once, I tell you, and he liked it rough. If I wasn't cryin' or beggin' for him to stop, he couldn't finish. You know what I mean?"

Angie was a pretty girl—for her type. She made her living following the troops. The police had spoken to several girls and they all told the same story. Lt. Mark Price was sadistic and it sickened the police officer.

"Okay," he sighed, exasperated with the lack of evidence he'd received. "You can go, Angie, but be careful who you do business with in the future, or you might end up in the river."

The girl nodded and ran away as fast as her legs would carry her.

"Well, Sergeant," Captain O'Hara sighed. "We haven't made too much progress on this case. I'm thinking the victim roughed up some innocent woman and her husband, or boyfriend, took offense to it. He found the opportunity to do the lieutenant in, and did just that. Course, that ain't gonna mollify the senator. He's bound and determined to find the culprit, or see to it that I lose my job."

"What about that boarding house owner, Harry Doolittle? Did you ever get him to crack?" Sergeant Jack Brannigan asked.

"Nah. He's too afraid of the bad publicity it would bring his business. He just barely makes it, as it is. I'm sure he knows more than he's telling, but I don't know how to get him to show his hand."

"Maybe that's the secret," the sergeant pondered. "Maybe we should threaten to tell the press of our suspicions about his business. If he's truly afraid of the bad publicity, it might be enough to break his silence. Can't hurt to try."

For the first time that day, Captain O'Hara smiled. "Get it done, man."

Christmas was fast approaching and still no progress had

been made. The police stationed a watch, twenty-four hours a day, out in front of Doolittle's, trying to put pressure on Harry to tell them what he knew.

The senator was demanding they find more evidence in the case, putting pressure at the state level, on the entire department. As for Officer Danny Boyle it was unwelcome, indeed.

It was cold and miserable work, standing there, trying to keep his eyes and ears open for anything suspicious. His eyelids were nearly frozen over, and he was afraid if he closed them, they could possibly stick shut. Thinking of his mother, cooking her rich, Irish stew tonight, caused his stomach to rumble loudly, and his mouth to water. He'd be glad to put this night, behind him. To stay warm, he marched up and back, a small distance from the lobby doors. He flapped his beefy arms up and down, a bit. With his coat collar pulled up, as far as it would reach, and his cap pulled down, as far as he could force it, he was quite a sight. In fact, he didn't look much like a policeman, but more like a shopkeeper or a customer.

"Pardon me, sir. But ya look in need of a little warmin' up." A too thin, young woman purred from just inside the alleyway. "If you've got the money, I have the warmth ta' cheer ya."

Startled at the young woman's proposition, Danny Boyle stopped. He looked her over and felt sorry for her condition. It was freezing and she had only the thinnest wool wrap about her shoulders and he saw that her trim ankles were bare.

"Madam, do you not have somewhere warm to go to, tonight? Stay with family, perhaps?"

She shook her long, vibrant red hair. With tired eyes, big as saucers, she looked down, away from his kind face. "I have ta' earn more money before I can return to me room. My wee babe needs things that I can not provide." She started to weep. "Please sir, I need but just a wee bit for coal. Could I warm ya for half a dollar?"

Knowing he could lose his badge, but not caring much about that, at the moment, Danny came up with a better solution. "Do you know where Doherty Street crosses North?"

She nodded.

"My mother lives in the green buildin', on the third floor. Her name is Boyle, same as mine," he grinned. "I'm ta be there in two hours, for dinner … Irish stew. Could ya bring your child and meet me there?"

The pretty woman looked up at him in complete shock. "You want *me* ta' meet your mother and have dinner at your house? Do ya not know what I've been a doin' ta' earn money for me livin'? Your mother would not approve. But I thank ya, just the same. You are very kind." She started back down the alley.

"Stop! Wait! I know more about you than you think. It's almost Christmas, and I can't enjoy the season knowin' I didn't do all I could to help out a young mother, down on her luck. Please. It would make me happy, truly."

The young woman thought about it for a minute, then she peered into what little of his face she could see, and smiled. She gave a little curtsey. "Thank ya, sir. Seamus and I will be there with bells on." She giggled and skipped off. It was amazing what a little human kindness could do.

She was late. Danny felt like a fool. He had extended his hand in friendship, and she had obviously found better things to do than have dinner with a fiery red-headed Mick.

"Now, Danny, me boy, don't go a gettin' yerself all upset o'er this young woman standin' ya up. She may have met with a catastrophe. Ya never know. That should make ya feel better, doesn't it, son?"

Danny had to laugh at his mother. Being from Ireland, she had a funny and unusual way of lookin' at things. He didn't tell her what the lady did for a living. *That* unusual, his mother wasn't. Of course, since the woman in question had no intention of showing up, it was of no real concern.

Just as he was about to sit down and eat, he heard a slight scratching at the door. He waited to hear it again. Then he heard the wail of a baby out in the hall.

"Mother, I think our guest has arrived, along with a cryin' infant."

Danny rushed to open the door and discovered one of the most pathetic sights he'd ever seen. There stood the little red-head, holding a crying baby. Her face had once been scrubbed clean, but was now splotched with mud and dirty water. She had tried to restrain her glorious curly hair by pulling it back, severely, in a tight bun, giving her a pained and pinched expression. But it was her clothes that made Danny want to pick her up and cuddle her, to make things better. He knew the garments were her finest, but they'd seen a lot of wear and too many washings. Now they were simply fit for the rag bin ... the wet rag bin. She was soaked to the skin with mud and frozen slush. Her lips had turned blue and Danny bet her feet were numb with the cold.

"Saints preserve us," his mother exclaimed. "Outta the way, Danny boy. Let her in. She's obviously met with a *catastrophe*." His mother smiled as the words left her mouth. "Hand me that precious babe. He's a bonnie lad, if I do say so m'self. Just look at all that red fuzz. We're partial to red hair in this family." She took the baby to the big rocker and sat down with him resting up against her ample bosom.

"Danny, show the lady ta' my room and allow her ta' get cleaned up. She can use one o' my dresses ta' warm up in. Gracious, she's such a wee thing, they'll swallow her whole, but they're clean and warm," she said, as she continued to rock the babe, humming a little Irish tune.

Danny stepped aside and let the young woman come in. He held out his hand, directing her where to go, when it dawned on him, he didn't know her name. He knew her son's name was Seamus, but what was hers? As she followed him slowly down the hall, Danny heard the tinkling of a bell.

"Ma'am, what's that tinklin' I hear?"

She stopped and smiled, broadly. "I told ya. Seamus and I have arrived—with bells on." She giggled and turned through the door. "Thank ya mother for her generosity. I shall be out in a snap." Then, she closed the door in front of Danny.

"Son, I think we need ta' discuss a few things b'fore the pretty lady comes out."

Danny knew that tone of voice. His mother was to interrogate him in such a way that would make Scotland Yard envious. She knew something was up.

"Danny, who is tha' woman and who's the father o' this babe?"

Danny, not wanting to get in to it all, just now, shook his head at his mother and whispered, "Not now, Mother. She might hear and I wouldn't want to cause her any embarrassment. I know you've figured out her circumstances, for yourself, but she was desperate and I couldn't let her and her babe freeze, now could I?"

"No, boyo, I guess ya couldn't at that. But be careful, son. Don't lose yer heart ta' this one. Charity only goes so far."

When the bedroom door opened, a true vision appeared before Officer Danny Boyle. He thought to himself, that his mother's warning might have come too late.

With her hair all fluffed and toweled dry and her face pink with the scrubbin' of it, she looked fresh and sweet and straight from the Emerald Isle. Her fiery hair was a thing of beauty, hanging in shiny tight curls, all the way down her back. She had found a little pink ribbon to keep the tresses pulled back from her delicate face. Danny noticed a sprinkling of freckles across her nose and cheeks, and she had the most luscious coral lips he had ever yearned to touch. Her figure was too thin, but it held hints of a womanliness that had been there, only a short time ago. He was captivated with her.

"There you are," Danny sighed. His eyes were trying to take in all of her loveliness. He wanted to brand her image in his memory. On long, lonely nights, he would think of her and be warmed by her beauty.

Mrs. Boyle rose slowly from the chair and very gently laid the sleeping child on the settee. Placing pillows around him for safety, she turned and announced it was time to eat.

Everything was delicious and the conversation was relaxed and carefree. Katie O'Donnell told her entire story to the Boyles. She didn't seem to embellish or cover anything up. Danny admired her for that bit of honesty. So did Mrs. Boyle.

"Can I pack up some of this stew and soda bread for ya, Katie? My son's not too keen on left-overs."

Knowing that this food would last her for a week, if she were sparing, Katie gratefully accepted. "This has been an answer to me prayers—ya openin' yer home to us, the way ya have. May God bless all in this house. If there's anythin' I can do for either of ya, ya only have to ask."

Katie rose from the table to check on Seamus and found him fast asleep. She turned to look at Mrs. Boyle.

The old woman could not, in good conscience, let this young mother take her infant out in this horrible weather. "Dear, allow me ta' offer Danny's room fer the evenin'. The wee lad is dreamin' the dreams of the innocent, and ya aren't dressed warmly enough for this weather. If ya do not mind me askin', do ya have any other clothes to wear? Do ya own anythin' appropriate for winter?"

Katie knew that this was not the time for false modesty. "Nay. In all honesty, I do not, ma'am."

"Well, ya stay here, for tonight, and I'll see what can be done about yer situation, tomorrow. Is it a deal, Katie O'Donnell?"

Katie was bursting with joy and happiness. "Oh, bless you, bless you, Mother Boyle." Then the young woman started to cry.

The next day was like a miracle for Katie and Seamus. Mrs. Boyle was a force to be reckoned with, for sure. She found a childcare position for Katie, telling her employer that Katie was recently widowed and needed the employment—God forgive her for lyin', she muttered, as she crossed herself. She moved Katie and Seamus into a vacant utility room in her own building. It was tiny, but warm, and that was the first priority. Later, that day, Danny escorted Katie back to her corner of the alley, and gathered up her pitiful few belongings.

Walking back to Mrs. Boyle's, Danny and Katie were discussing his job.

"Usually, I like being an officer of the law, but currently the only case I seem ta' work is that murder case of the senator's son. We're at a dead end with the investigation and our best lead won't speak out. I'd love ta' be able to break this case open and make a name for m'self. It would lead to a promotion for me, I'm certain."

Katie hadn't heard of the murder. "What was the senator's son's name?"

"He was an officer in the army. His name was Lieutenant Mark Price."

"Faith and Begorrah," exclaimed a very surprised Katie. Her sparkling brown eyes grew huge and she stumbled a bit, in her step. "He was *murdered*, ya say?"

Danny noticed all the blood had disappeared from her cherubic face. She was shocked at hearing of the man's demise. "What's the matter, Katie? Did ya know him?" He prayed she did not—at least not intimately.

She thought for a moment and decided to tell Danny everything. She nodded her head slowly, reached out and took his hand, and pulled him along.

"I've met the man on several different occasions. Most of the time, I was successful at avoidin' him. He's a bad one, I tell ya. He likes to make girls cry, if ya know what I mean. Good lookin' he was, but he was just that mean, too. It's said that he did one girl in, and dumped her body in the river. I don't know who killed him, but I'm glad he did." She crossed herself. "You should stop lookin' fer this person, and let him be. I'm sure he had a very good reason for doin' what he did."

Danny listened, intently, to all she said. "You know, we have the name of the man who did it. Perhaps, you know him. We're looking for Mr. Ryan Beaufort."

Again, Katie stumbled, forcing Danny to catch her up and stop her from falling. *"Ryann?"* she shrieked. She grabbed Danny by the arm and turned him to look at her. "Ryann is not a man, Danny. Ryann Beaufort is a woman, and a very nice and proper one, too, she is. Ya can't mean *she* killed the lieutenant?"

"A woman? How do you know? Are you sure?" He couldn't believe what she was saying. They'd been looking for a man, for cryin' out loud.

Katie nodded. "She lived at the Doolittle, didn't she? I'd see her comin' and goin'. We talked a few times and she was always very nice to me, in spite of me situation and all. She *couldn't* have known the lieutenant."

"Can you describe her, Katie?"

She looked troubled. "Only for you, Danny. But promise me that you'll try ta' help her if they catch her?"

"Of course, darlin."

Katie noticed his term of endearment, and she was very pleased. "She's extremely beautiful and well spoken. I believe she was educated and raised proper, the daughter of a physician and a great singer, they say. She has long golden hair and the bonniest blue eyes. She's tall and slender. She didn't work the streets, Danny. She was a good woman."

Danny was excited now. "Thank ya, sweetheart. This may be the break we need in this case. I could kiss ya. In fact, I think I will." Danny grabbed her face and finally kissed those amazing lips of hers. This was turning into a great day, for Danny.

"Katie?" he whispered.

"Aye, Danny?"

"You're a good woman, too."

# CHAPTER FOUR

*Tucson, Arizona Territory*

Christmas was almost upon them, and the children were more active than usual. Beth tried to keep them occupied with their studies, but it took all of her energy. The little ones painted pictures of angels, stars, and the baby Jesus, while the older children built a manger for the church to use for their annual nativity. They also composed a song that they would present to their parents. In her precious free time, Beth tried to finish her gifts for all her friends. However, too much of her time was spent trying to find a solution to her current predicament. She had missed two monthly cycles. Mary's suspicion was correct. Beth was certain she was pregnant.

In Tucson, as in most other towns, the schoolmarm had to be single and with no children. Once the mayor heard of her problem, or the school board found out, she would be terminated. What would she do then? How would she support herself and her child? This was awful and she was at a loss as what to do.

"I'm certain she's with child, David. I need to tell Vernon. He hasn't said anything publicly, but I know he's in love with her … widow or not. He needs to know of her situation. Maybe he'll offer a solution. It would be nice to have my brother married to my best friend, and be as happy as we are," Mary said, hopefully.

David was more of a skeptic, and frowned. "I don't know,

Mary, darlin'. I know you mean well, but this is buttin' in where you ain't been asked. Maybe I should sort of test Vernon out a bit, run it around the barnyard. I could find out how he feels about a ready-made family."

Throwing her arms around her handsome husband's neck, Mary kissed his cheeks and said, "That's why I married you. You can do anything, and you're so very handsome, and smart, and—" She winked and pulled David to his feet, leading him to their bed. "—so good at everything you do ."

Much, much, later, David asked, "So, Vernon, your sister and I were a talkin' and she's a wonderin' what your intentions are toward her best friend, Mrs. Painter?"

The ranger laughed. "Well, David, don't be shy. Come to the point, why don't you?" He laughed good-naturedly, at his brother-in-law's obvious discomfort. "Isn't that getting a mite personal? Do you want me to answer truthfully or as a gentleman?"

David squirmed. "Truth, if you please. You know I have to report your answer back to your sister. She paid me well for the information." His eyes danced, as he blushed a deep shade of red, remembering the image of Mary, lying in the middle of their bed and wearing nothing more than a beautiful smile.

"You tell my sister, that I have finally met the woman I want to spend the rest of my life with—if she'll have me. Is that good enough?"

David slapped Vernon on the back and smiled. "Yeah, I think that's the perfect response. Mary wants you to come to dinner this evenin', around seven." Not waiting for an answer, he turned away and headed back toward the hotel. "See ya then," he hollered over his shoulder.

That afternoon, after class had been dismissed, Pete Williams handed the teacher a letter from his ma. It was an invitation to dinner. Ranger Gunn would be there and Mary had something important she wanted to ask Beth. It ended with a "please come".

Beth locked the door to the schoolhouse and started walking back toward her room at the Doolittle. The walk seemed to take longer every day. What was puzzling Mary, she wondered? It caused Beth some consternation, but she was excited, just the same, and looking forward to dinner. After all, she would get to see Vernon, again.

That evening, as the William's party sat around the enormous table, enjoying their dessert, they all tried to speak at once. The men were discussing the Indian problems, caused by cheating government agents, and thieving personnel. Cochise had slipped away from capture, once again, and he had sworn to kill all whites. After the holiday, Vernon would have to go out, one more time, in search of the elusive redskin. That worried David, and he volunteered to help him bring the Indian in.

"I thank you, brother, but you can't leave my sister at this time. Besides, she'd kill me if I allowed anything to happen to you, and I ain't ready to die just yet." The men both laughed, knowing this to be a fact.

Mary whispered to Beth, "Would you mind accompanying me to the ladies' retiring room?"

"Of course not, Mary. I need to visit there, as well." Beth smiled and helped Mary to her feet. She knew that Mary would deliver most any time, now. Perhaps she would have a Christmas baby.

Mary looked around the room to make certain they were alone. When convinced it was just the two of them, she sat Beth down on the cushions provided, and took her hands in her own. Speaking quietly, she said, "Beth, dear. I would like to tell you something I learned of, only today. I hope it will please you. My brother told David that you are the woman he wants to spend the rest of his life with. Were you aware of his feelings for you?"

Beth's heart leaped up in her chest. How wonderful, she thought, and how terrible, too. This was the talk she had dreaded. Her best friend would not understand her reluctance in allowing Vernon to court her.

"Yes, Mary. He told me of his feelings last month, but for reasons of my own, I can't allow his courtship. There are things in my past—terrible things, which he must not be made a part of. I'm not willing to lose our friendship over my earlier mistakes. So, you see, I won't encourage his attentions, even though it appears I'm truly in need of a solution to my imminent problem."

"The baby?"

Beth sighed. “Yes. I’m more than two months gone and I don’t know what to do. I can’t lose my position at the school. How will I feed us?”

“Are you happy about this child, Beth? You never mention your husband. Forgive me, but … he is the father of this child, is he not?”

Eye to eye, it was impossible to lie. “No, Mary. You see … I am not a widow. There was no husband.”

Mary sucked in her breath. She was stunned. Of course, she knew how this could happen to almost any woman—after all, it had happened to her dear deceased sister-in-law, Victoria. “Why did you deceive us, Beth? We would have understood.”

“You might like to think you would have understood, but in all honesty, I would never have gotten the job, here, in Tucson. I never would have met you, and your wonderful brother would never have looked at me, twice. In fact, the look on your face, just now, tells me that you are aghast, as well.”

Mary looked away for a moment, embarrassed that her shock shown on her face. She would never want to hurt Beth’s feelings. Turning back to face her friend, she asked, “What happened? I know you well enough to be certain that you were forced into a relationship or your love was unable to do the right thing by you. Perhaps he died before he could marry you? Tell me, Beth.”

Beth stood up and offered to help Mary to her feet. “No, dear. I have already divulged more than I should have. I will say that it is much worse than you can possibly imagine. Don’t worry about me, Mary. Something will turn up.” Looking more confident than she really felt, Beth escorted her dear friend back to their table.

Vernon and David came to their feet. “We missed the two most lovely ladies in Tucson. You were gone a long while,” Vernon said.

David’s concern for Mary was written all over his face. “Is everything well with you, darlin’? Should you retire, now?”

“Yes, David, all is well, but I am tired, and with the children bouncing around the room, I think it’s past time for us to call it a day.”

Mary turned to look at Beth. “Please know that you can always talk to me, dear. I love you like a sister and I want to help you in any way I possibly can." She gave Beth a hug and kissed her brother on his stubbly cheek. "You need a shave, sir," she teased.

The Williams' family left in a swarm of Christmas excitement and anticipation.

On the ride back to the Hotel Doolittle, Beth was uncommonly quiet. It had been a nice evening, spent with friends and family, and Vernon was concerned about her silence. Finally, he spoke up. "Beth, I know you must be in some sort of trouble. I could tell by your conversation with my sister. Obviously, if you wanted me to know the details, you would have told me, so I just want to let you know that I'll help you in any way I can. Nothing can be so terrible that I wouldn't help you. You believe that, don't you?"

"No, Vernon. That's not the truth. You may think it is, but it's not."

He pulled back on the reins, stopping the buggy in the middle of the street. "I say it's the truth and how dare you call me a liar. I'd shoot a man for accusing me of a lot less. I know this has something to do with your late husband. What did he do, shoot himself? Was he a bank robber? Tell me. It don't make no difference to me if he was a drunkard or liked to dress in women's undies. He has nothing to do with you. It only tells me that you're deserving of a good man, for a change."

"Fine!" she shouted. Beth couldn't pretend any longer. She was sick and tired of it all. "There was no husband … good, bad, or indifferent. I never married! Now are you satisfied? Tell me how you'll stand by me, now." Beth refused to look at him. She covered her face with her hands.

He didn't expect that, and was shocked at the revelation, but he knew that deep down, it didn't make any difference to him. She was the kind of woman that would not give herself easily, to just any man. She was not cheap. There had to be a good reason for her doing whatever it was she had done … and yes, he would offer for her, just the same.

He reached for her, and turned Beth's face up to his. "You silly woman. You precious, dopey, beautiful, and amazing woman. Of course, I love you still, and I'm relieved that you're not in true mourning. Now, there's nothing that prevents us getting hitched. In fact, I think right after I get back from chasing that damn Cochise, I'm talking to the preacher." He slapped the horse's rump and the buggy jerked forward, carrying a happy man at the reins and a very bewildered woman, sitting by his side.

It was December twenty-eighth and Vernon was preparing to leave, in hunt of Cochise. Ranger Barclay would hold down the fort while he was away.

"Keep things peaceful while I'm gone and don't go and do something stupid. Check the Wanted posters, look around a bit, and wait for me to return. I should be gone about a week, I figure." Vernon grabbed his hat, his rifle, and his coat, and left by the back door.

He'd said his goodbyes to his family, the night before, and told Beth to wait for him. He promised to be home in a week's time and he wanted to have dinner with her, in private.

Vernon loved to ride hell bent for leather on his black horse, Napoleon. The stallion was a magnificent animal, and a gift from David. Possessing a special gift with horses, and having knowledge of their bloodlines, David had chosen well for Vernon. Only the two of them, knew the history of his mount. The black horse played an integral part in the scheme that freed David from his past. The way David saw it, nothing was too good for the man who had helped him reclaim a future with his family. Now, with Napoleon flying across the desert rocks, Vernon hoped to finally bring peace to this part of Arizona and gain a family of his own.

The Navaho was the largest tribe in Arizona, and with the exception of occasional thefts and a few marauding expeditions, they were at peace with the white man. But it was the Apache-Mohave that caused Vernon to worry. They were the most bloody and warlike of the Apache tribes. The Chiricahuas were on the warpath.

The cavalry had been protecting the pioneers and miners out here, for some time, until the War Between the States broke out and they were ordered to move south to the Mexican border areas. That action left the rest of the territory defenseless against the Indians. Some of the warriors took advantage of this and hit the settlers hard. They killed and burned a wide path across the territory. Now, it was left up to the rangers to round up the renegades and bring peace to Arizona.

Ranger Gunn had been out, riding up into the highlands, when he spotted smoke coming from a clearing about a half mile away. "Oh, hell, Napoleon. This could be something real bad," he groaned. "Get up, there." He drove his heels into the horse's flanks and headed toward trouble.

Bad didn't begin to describe what he discovered. The cabin was still smoldering. Out in the yard, was the rancher with his rifle still clutched in his hand. He'd never gotten off a shot. About ten yards behind him, lay the man's son. The young boy had been shot and stabbed. It looked, to Vernon, like the boy had continued crawling toward his pa, when the killing blow came.

Vernon stepped off and led his horse through the gate, where he continued up to the house. He needed to search the ranch, and in doing so, he discovered what was left of this man's family.

"Oh, God, no. Damn it all," he growled. The man's wife had once been pretty and blonde, much like Beth. She was obviously with child. That child would never be born. Her belly was opened from breast to hip. It was disgusting in it's violence. Only a mad man could do this senseless act. Vernon swelled with rage and the desire to revenge this family overwhelmed him, as he cried out his need for retribution.

It was some time before Vernon had control of his emotions and was able to go in search of a shovel. Just before dusk, as the sun slipped behind the mountains, the ranger gave the family a decent burial. He swore to them, that he'd set off and not return until he found those responsible for this crime. He vowed to put them behind bars or see them hang.

Beth was afraid she wasn't much help to the old doctor caring for Mary. Her friend had been laboring with the birth of this child for nine hours. She was tired, but happy and optimistic. Her husband, on the other hand, was in a hopeless condition. Mary said that he had survived three births, but with every one, she was afraid that the stress of it all might kill him. She explained to Beth, that her own mother had died giving birth to her, and since she, too, was small, David fretted horribly. Bless him.

"Beth, would you mind going downstairs and holding David's hand for me? Not only is he incapable of watching the children, at this time, he can't remember to take care of himself, either. Make him eat, drink, and rest. Tell him…ooh, …oooh, … it won't be long, now. Thank …OOH!" she screamed.

Beth ran down the stairs, wild-eyed, calling David's name. "David. David! Oh, there you are. Mary's fine, but it won't be long now. She wants you to eat, drink and rest. Are the children all right? Oh, my," she shrieked breathlessly, as she rushed her words and looked wildly about the room.

"Compose yourself, Beth!" David said, as he jumped to his feet and rushed to put his arms around her shoulders. He was worried about his wife, that was true, but he was also concerned about the lovely blonde who looked dangerously close to collapsing. She was with child, also, and she looked none too stable right now. The last thing he wanted was another woman, he cared for, to be in need of a physician. "Breathe, honey. Mary'll have my hide if'n I let you fall apart. I've been through all of this before, and there ain't nothin' to get excited about," he said, not believing a word of it, himself.

Just as he was guiding Beth to the settee, the midwife, assisting the doctor, descended the stairs. "Mr. Williams," she calmly said, "you may come up now and see your wife and infant daughter." As she approached the stairs, a blur raced by her, taking three steps at a time. David was waiting impatiently for the woman, at the top of the stairs.

David was tall, muscular, with enormous paws for hands, and yet he managed to reach down and carefully pick up the most beautiful baby he had ever laid eyes upon. She looked just like her mama and her sister, Ruthie. Scalding tears ran down his cheeks, as he looked at his lovely wife. She knew what was in his heart—a deep gratitude that defied speech.

"She looks like you, Mary, and our Ruthie," he said in a hoarse whisper.

"I know, darling. The moment I first saw her, I knew. I felt it. My heart is so full. It feels like it may burst. Kiss me."

"Your wish, my darlin'." He gently kissed her waiting lips and then turned and kissed the tip of his daughter's perfect nose. This was little Rosa Etta Williams—Rosie, they'd call her.

Rosie was everyone's darling. She was the happiest and best

baby anyone could remember knowing. The twins were proud to be the big brothers, and now, Sara had her own little baby sister to help care for. She proclaimed Rosie to be almost as pretty as her mama.

David walked on clouds. He still remembered the dark times, back in Missouri, and this was all he ever wanted. He thought it was an impossibility, at the time. Now, with the help of friends and the will of God, this was his reality.

Beth shared in their happiness, and thought all would be perfect, if only Vernon would return to Tucson. She was worried. He'd been gone four weeks and there was no sign of him. Several search parties had gone out, but came back alone. Unfortunately, what they did discover, caused chills to run down Beth's spine. The Indians were killing and torturing the settlers and Vernon was alone, trying to put a stop to it.

Within a week, Mary was up and about, and feeling fully energized. She appreciated every moment spent with her husband and children. That is why, at dinner, she spoke to David about her brother.

"Darling, Beth and I are concerned about Vernon. It was foolish of him to leave in search of those outlaws by himself. I know he thought if he traveled alone, he could move faster and quieter, maybe take them by surprise, but he should have returned by now.

"David, there's no one better at tracking than you, especially over rocks. I don't want you to leave us, but I must ask. Would you go and look for Vernon?"

"Mary, it's amazin' how you continue to know my thoughts. I've wanted to ride out for some time now, but with you and little Rosie, the timin' wasn't right. I didn't want to bring the subject up, in fear you might worry, but you're right. I know your brother, and he wouldn't stay away this long 'less he was in trouble. If'n it's agreeable with you, I'll leave tomorrow mornin'. Now, give me a kiss and I'll take you up to your room. I feel the need to hold you for a few hours."

"This sure ain't Missouri, Dollar," David said to his horse. He often talked to his horse, as he was a very smart animal. "I don't see nothin' but red rocks. It's kinda purty, though. Maybe I should think about ranchin' somewheres out near here." His eyes were constantly scanning the horizon and his ears were listening for the smallest sound. "What d'ya think?"

The tracks were few. He came upon the scene where the Indians had attacked a couple of ranchers, but found no survivors, and it took time to do the right thing by the victims. Seeing such sights weighed heavy on a man. Whole families wiped out, never given a chance. He didn't understand it.

"Dollar, listen." David reined back. He strained his ears for a sound. Dollar stood motionless, absolutely silent. Horses—the sound of horse's hooves came to him from a distance. "Where are they?" he muttered.

From out of a box canyon, a black horse, wild eyed and lathered up, came tearing past. David turned Dollar and gave him his head. Dollar went in pursuit of the crazed, but tired, stallion. There were few horses that were as fast as his big palomino, but this black was almost. David knew without a doubt, it was Vernon's horse, Napoleon.

Dollar ran the big stallion to ground. His sides were heaving, trying to find his breath. David noticed the horse was also favoring his front leg. He'd been shot. Something had spooked this animal, to the extreme, and he had no time to waste if he wanted to help his brother. He calmed Napoleon and put a light dressing on the leg. It would have to do, for now.

Quietly, David approached the entrance to the canyon, not knowing what he would discover hidden within its walls. There was the faintest smell of wood smoke, in the air, and he could hear far off laughter. He tied up the horses and proceeded on foot, skirting the walls of the canyon, trying to blend in with the rocks. He could make out ten, maybe twelve horses tied at this end of the camp. "Not very smart," he whispered to himself. There didn't seem to be any lookouts, and that was odd, he thought.

A few dirty and dangerous looking individuals came into view. They looked to be Mexican or maybe Apache. David wasn't familiar with the different people living out here. Whatever group they belonged with, he knew they were bad and it would take considerable effort and some good luck to find Vernon ... if he was here ... and if he was still alive.

David did his best to locate his brother-in-law and was starting to have doubts as to whether he'd find him, when he heard one particularly ugly varmint mention the lawman. It had to be him. Vernon was definitely being held in the canyon.

Much of what was being said was in a language David didn't understand. He was beginning to think that fighting the Yankees had been a whole lot easier. Looking around, he noticed that it would not be too difficult to climb to the top of one of the canyon walls and start some boulders rolling down into the camp. Problem with that was, he didn't have any control over who got flattened. But he was absolutely certain that, from up there, he could fire down upon them and take half of them out in less than a minute. That would be the plan. Not much of one, but hell, he was just one man.

He'd been right. Being overly confident, the targets were out in the open and just waiting for him to pick them off, one by one. "Mistake number two," he mumbled. They were feeling too safe in their hidey-hole. Thankfully, David was well prepared. He wore two six-shooters and carried his rifle. He wouldn't need anything more.

Patience was his gift and he was a crack shot. Whatever he aimed at, David hit. He picked out his first victim and located the second and the third. He gently squeezed the triggers on both pistols and watched the outlaws hit the dirt in complete surprise. He fired so rapidly that the men, down below, never located the direction of the bullets. They ran around looking for their weapons and places to hide, but found nothing to protect them from the hail of bullets cutting into them. They were outgunned and obviously outmanned.

As quickly as it had begun, it was over. Not a sound came from the camp. David went around to the canyon entrance and entered slowly. Always looking for the one that might have gotten away, his eyes constantly moved back and forth, taking it all in. It had been too simple. Then he saw something move, near the back of the encampment. At first he was alarmed, thinking it was one of the desperados, but it didn't come any closer. He noticed that it appeared to be a man tied to a post. With his pistols drawn, he started to walk faster and then broke into a run.

"Vernon," he shouted, over and over again. "Vernon, it's me. I've come to fetch ya' up and take ya' home." When he finally got close enough to see his brother-in-law clearly, he winced at what he saw, and was afraid he might get sick. Vernon looked more dead than alive. Not an inch of what David could see, had been spared the savage's torture. Vernon was covered in blood and it looked as if he had several broken bones. David wasn't convinced his brother-in-law would survive the trip back to Tucson.

Beth was worrying herself sick. She had no appetite and she couldn't sleep. David had been gone too long and her school lessons were no longer enough to fill her days. She knew that no matter how hard she tried to deny it, she desperately loved the ranger. After what had happened to her, back home, she thought she would never fall in love or be able to return a man's affections, but with Vernon, there was no question. She wanted him to possess her, body and soul. She could imagine a future with him. Now she prayed that she would be able to tell him so, face to face. He had to return to her. She wanted to tell him about the baby. She knew she might lose him, but her pregnancy was not something that she could keep hidden for long. Would he be willing to care for another man's child? Beth thought he would. She prayed he would.

Rubbing her hand across her tummy, she could feel the slightest swelling, now. Except for Mary and David, no one had any idea of her condition. Currently, her job was secure and she was saving every penny. Her dresses were cut loose on her slender frame, offering her months of concealment. She just needed Vernon to come home, safely.

"You older children, please help the younger ones with their sums. Class will be—what's going on outside?"

There was quite a commotion out in the street. The children ran to the windows and Beth walked to the doors, opening them wide. She noticed a buggy coming toward the schoolhouse, at a very unsafe speed. As she stepped out onto the steps, she saw David was at the reins and she knew.

"Class is dismissed, children! Go directly home," she shouted.

The buggy had barely stopped before David jumped down and lifted Beth up onto the seat. "Vernon's in a bad way, Beth. Don't know if he's gonna make it, but he's askin' for you. Will you be all right?"

Too stunned to speak, she simply nodded.

David quickly gave Beth the highlights of the past couple of days, omitting some of the atrocities he had witnessed. They arrived at the doctor's house and he helped her in. Mary was already there. Beth noticed Mary's eyes were red and swollen. "Oh, dear God, don't let me be too late," she prayed.

David took her gently by the elbow and escorted her to the closed door. "Before you see him, you need to know that he looks real bad. Do not swoon or scream. He needs your strength now. Can you do that for him?"

Again, she simply nodded.

The door opened and she felt as if she were floating across the floor. There, on the long table, covered in a clean sheet, was her beloved, all torn and ripped apart, mangled and broken, fighting for his life. Her heart lurched in her chest and a lump filled her throat, but she was determined to be strong for him.

She wanted to reach out and touch him, but she didn't want to cause him additional pain. He had suffered grievous wounds, everywhere. Looking down, she noticed his big feet sticking out from beneath the short sheet. They were not as raw as the rest of what she could see, so she reached out and grabbed his big toe.

"Hey, Ranger. I'm glad to have you back."

He opened one eye and succeeded in smiling, though somewhat feebly. His breathing was irregular and came in short pants, but he managed to whisper her name.

"Please, you don't need to talk, I know what you're thinking. 'What does this crazy woman want of me, now?' Well, I'll tell you. I want you to get well. We've a lot of things to talk about, you and I, and I have a very important question for you, but it'll have to wait until you're all fixed up. Oh, Vernon, I've missed you so much. I've been so stupid. You and I have much to make up for."

Again, he smiled. Vernon loved looking at Beth, even if it was with just one eye.

She gave his toe a little wiggle and gave him the sweetest smile he'd ever seen.

"I'll be just outside, darling. You rest and get better." She left the room and closed the door, and immediately her legs gave way. Her strength had evaporated and she welcomed the blackness, quick to envelope her.

David caught her and gently laid her down on the sofa. “Mary, what do we do? Should she see the doc?”

Mary was looking Beth over, carefully. “No, I don’t think that’s necessary, and I don’t trust the good doctor to keep his findings to himself. It could cause her more problems than she has already. I think it’s best if we take her back to our hotel and keep an eye on her, there.”

Beth opened her eyes and read the concern on Mary’s face. “I’m sorry. Please, don’t be alarmed. I know I’m healthy. It’s just that Vernon … Oh, Mary, he looks so bad, it breaks my heart.” She started to weep; great sobs escaped from deep within her chest. “He was tortured! Tortured!” Her small shoulders shook uncontrollably. “Who would do such a thing?”

David was frantic. This couldn’t be good for her or her unborn child. “Mary, we’ve got to do somethin’.”

“No, I don’t think so, dear. We should let her cry and get this out. She has a lot trapped inside her, and I think this might be just what she needs. Beth’s been strong for so long, and she’s felt like she was all alone with her problems. Let’s stay with her and keep an eye on her, but let her cry all she wants.”

Mary did a little crying, herself. Several hours later, Vernon’s condition had not changed and David was now concerned for Mary. Their daughter was less than one month old and she needed her mother and Mary still required extra rest. He decided to take her home and he’d come back to sit with Beth.

While David was gone, Vernon’s condition changed. The nurse, looking grave, came out to get Beth. “He’s asking for you, miss,” she sniffled. She held the door open, and then disappeared, leaving the two people alone.

Beth didn’t know what to expect. She had never been so frightened in her entire life. Carefully placing one foot in front of the other, she reached Vernon’s side. She tried to smile, but it was a futile attempt, as a fat tear rolled down her face and dripped off her stubborn, little chin.

Vernon looked up at her with his one good eye. “Wow, do I look that bad, honey? You look as if you’re afraid I might take a bite out of you, or something. It’s me. I’m the same Vernon, just not quite as pretty as usual. Are you feeling all right?”

She couldn't help it. She started to cry all over again and then started to apologize for the tears. "Oh, my darling, sweet Vernon. I am so sorry. They all told me not to cry, to be strong, but I feel so bad and I'm so scared. I love you more than anything and I can't stand the thought of you being in pain. You look like you hurt all over, and—"

"Wait a minute. Did you just say you loved me?"

"Of course, I said I love you. You know I love you, Vernon."

Vernon would have smiled if he could have managed it. "So once I'm healed, you gonna make me a happy man and marry me?"

Beth wanted to marry this man more than anything in the world, but she knew she had to be honest with him, first. "I love you, but I think we need to wait until you're much better before we talk about marriage. There are some things about me that you don't know and I can't marry you without telling you everything." Her voice was shaking. This would be a big risk to take, she knew, but if she wanted to find true happiness in this life, it would only be with Vernon Gunn.

She smoothed his sun-streaked hair back off his forehead. He was so handsome. His nose was still straight. Thankfully, it had not been broken. His lips were usually wide and firm, but it was the dimple in his chin that she noticed. It forced her imagination to work overtime. Currently, his lips were split and swollen, his chin was raw and bloodied, but she knew the dimple was still there, waiting for her kiss. She looked up into his eyes, and noticed he was fast asleep. His breathing was more regular now, and she could relax. Vernon was going to be just fine. She knew he'd get better. Very quietly, she kissed his forehead and slipped out the door.

When she came out of the room, she discovered David there, waiting for word.

"He's going to be just fine, I think. He's talking and making sense, planning for the future. Right now, he's sleeping."

David saw how weary she was. "Beth, Mary and I would like for you to come and stay with us for a few days. You'd be much closer to Vernon and we'd be able to keep an eye on you. What do you say?"

Ordinarily, Beth would have put up a fuss and her pride would win out, but she didn't have the strength, at the moment, to refuse. “Thank you, both. I’m really tired and I’d like to stay close by. I appreciate your offer. Could we leave now?”

David smiled, “Sure thing, little lady. Allow me.” He held out his arm and escorted the pretty schoolmarm over to the hotel for some well deserved rest.

# CHAPTER FIVE

"What do you mean, they shot my horse? Is Napoleon okay? He's the best dang horse in Arizona and there ain't one of them damn renegades worth half his weight. If they weren't already dead, I'd kill 'em," he swore.

"Hey, calm down pardner," David pleaded. "Napoleon is healin' just fine. In fact, later on today, I intend to take him and Dollar out for a little exercise. Those two get along real nice—for stallions," he chuckled. "Back there, in Texas, Dollar got to spend a lot of time with Napoleon. I hitched them together, and Dollar led him away to safety, where they waited for me to show up. They're damn smart animals. You know, maybe I am as good with horses as the legend says I am." He laughed, thinking he was quite clever.

Vernon was smiling, too. "Don't go believing all them stories about yourself, or you might find your butt in trouble, again. Remember, *he* is *dead*."

"Don't worry about that. I just wish I could get a message to my ma and my brother, Midge. They've been mournin' their loss for some time now, and I sure would like to spare them that, if I could," David lamented. "Don't know what happened to my brother, Logan. Sure hope he didn't get hisself killed in the war."

Vernon knew this was hard on David. "Wait a while longer, give it some more time, and then maybe we can figure something out. It'll all work itself right, eventually. You know that."

Deciding to change the subject, David turned the conversation around to Beth.

"Have you asked her to marry you again?"

Vernon grinned big and slow. "We briefly touched on the subject when I was first brought back, but I promised her I'd wait until I was healed before I asked her again. She has it in her head, that when I find out about her secret past, I'll refuse to marry her. I can't seem to dissuade her. So, when I walk out of here, I hope to walk into her life, forever. You gonna come to the wedding?"

"Are you kiddin'? Mary wouldn't let me miss it. But you know, we're a thinkin' about movin' out of town, just as soon as I can find the right place to raise my horses. I've been lookin' near Red Rock. It's mighty purty and it has sufficient water. They need a deputy there, so I've applied for the job. What do you think?"

Vernon didn't know what to think. He'd grown accustomed to having his entire family living in town, and he liked it. For too many years he'd been alone and he didn't want to go back to that lonesome existence. Also, there was still the problem with the Indians. He shook his head.

"Do you think it's safe enough for Mary and the children, out there? You won't always be around if you take the deputy's job. After what I've seen, I'm afraid of them living that far from town, and maybe having to defend themselves."

David appreciated and understood Vernon's concern, but he was being very careful with his family. "I have it all worked out in my head. I know the kind of men I want to hire to work the ranch. They won't be just your ordinary sodbusters. No, they're gonna be good with a gun and they'll be honorable men. I might even take a couple of family men. That would give Mary and the children comp'ny. When I build the house and the outbuildin's, I'll place them in strategic locations. I'll make my family as safe as possible, but they can't live here, in town, for the rest of their lives.

"I need to do somethin' with my life, and Mary longs for a ranch and a house with a garden. My boys deserve to grow up like I did, learnin' and carin' for critters. I want them to be strong and brave, reliable and trustworthy men. These are things they'll learn out there, on a ranch. Could somethin' happen?

Surely—just like an accident could happen right here, in town. I appreciate your concern, Vernon, but rest easy. I'll take good care of mine." He patted Vernon on the shoulder in an attempt to reassure him.

There was a small knock at the door and a feminine voice asked, "Vernon, are you decent? Can I come in?"

Vernon's whole face lit up. "Whooee! You better come on in, sugar. I need to see you right now." He winked at David. It had been weeks since he had held Beth. Both his arms had been splinted and carefully wrapped, but today, one hand was free.

Beth floated through the door and straight to Vernon's side. He turned and grabbed her around the waist, pulling her close, so he could kiss her properly. It made no difference that David was standing there, watching the whole thing. Vernon laid his lips against her forehead, and then, giving her waist a little squeeze, he remarked, teasingly,

"What have you been eating over at that hotel? You've put on some weight while I've been stuck in this here bed. It feels good, though. I like some meat on my woman."

Beth stood straight up and stepped several feet away from his embrace. Her face blanched, just before she turned her head and avoided looking at him, altogether.

David cleared his throat and looked straight at her, eye to eye. He waited for Beth to say something. When she didn't, he said, "I think the two of you need to have that talk now. I'll leave you to it." He turned and quietly left the room, shutting the door behind him.

Neither Beth nor Vernon was willing to breach the ensuing silence. Just as she was about to bolt out the door, Vernon asked, "Sugar, what did I say? Speak to me. I feel this is really important and I want you to tell me what it is I'm missing. David obviously knows something that I don't, and I suspect he learned it from my sister. Don't you think you owe me the courtesy of telling me what's going on?" He patted the edge of the bed, beckoning her to his side.

Slowly, and ever so timidly, Beth took the tiny steps needed to bring herself up next to the ranger … the man she loved so very much. She stared into the dark depths of his emerald green eyes, trying to find the answers she needed. He loved her. Of that, she was certain, but she wasn't as certain of his reaction to what she had to divulge to him, now.

She traced the side of his face with the tip of her finger. Signs of the injuries, he had sustained a month ago, lingered, but he was still just as handsome as ever. Her mouth watered, thinking of touching his warm lips with her own. She yearned to feel the strength of his arms surround her, in a loving embrace.

It was now or never. Beth closed her eyes, leaned in, placing her lips on his. They were firm and welcoming. He moved his tongue across her mouth, tasting her sweetness, and looking for entry.

As she parted her lips, just the smallest degree, Vernon rushed in to take dominance over her mouth. His tongue caressed hers and explored the inner sides of her cheeks. He tasted wonderful, so masculine and clean. As his tongue moved inside her mouth, his hand explored up and down her spine. He was reclaiming her as his own.

Just as suddenly, Vernon pulled away. He was flushed and his entire body ached with unfulfilled passion for this woman, but now was not the time. He struggled to hold her at arm's length. "Elizabeth Painter, tell me," he demanded. For several minutes, he stared at her, not allowing her to evade him any longer. By the strength of his willpower alone, she capitulated and confessed everything.

"Vernon, I've lied to you. I've lied to everyone here, in Tucson. Mary guessed my secret long before I knew, myself. There never was a husband. I'm not a widow. There was some trouble back in my hometown and I needed to get away, so I thought about coming West. I needed to think of how I'd support myself, and I figured I could teach school. I have a superior education. I speak three languages and I have knowledge of ancient civilizations. I can play the pianoforte, the harp, the violin, and I daresay, any other stringed instrument you place before me. Just don't ask me to sing." She grinned.

"The one requirement of all school teachers is that they must be single, or widowed, and preferably have no children. Now, don't think me vain, but I know I'm not unattractive, and I needed to discourage the attention of men. Therefore, being a widow filled my needs. I wore black and men left me alone, that is, until I met you.

Vernon blushed. He was guilty, as charged.

"You have always been a gentleman, and I appreciate that."

Vernon started to say something, but Beth held up her hand to silence him. She continued. "Everything was going according to plan. I was happy here and I simply adore Mary and her family. I think, or at least I hope, you know how I feel about you. Tucson's growing on me. Unfortunately, as I discovered several weeks ago, the city of Tucson isn't the only thing growing on me." She cleared her throat and took a deep breath.

"Vernon, I'm not as proper as you thought, not nearly good enough to be your wife. I'm not an innocent. In fact, it appears that sometime, in early summer, I'm going to have a baby." She waited, not daring to breathe, but watched his face, intently, for a reaction.

Vernon sat motionless, trying to understand what it was that she just said. His Beth had known a man, *not her husband*, before him and now was pregnant with his child? His stomach rolled over. He thought for a moment he was going to be sick. He continued to stare at her. She appeared the same as she always did … just as beautiful, with her golden hair and her soft blue eyes. But she was a liar. How could she have lain with another man and not have been married to him? Did he rape her? Were there others? If so, how many? Did she even know the identity of the father of her child?

Beth knew something was terribly wrong. She tried to explain, to make him understand. "I know it sounds bad, but—"

Vernon shot to life with a roar. "Get the HELL out of here, you lying piece of … I don't want to see your disgusting face again. Pack up your things and find someone else to play the fool. I'm tellin' you to get outta Tucson before I get outta this bed." He turned his face from her and Beth knew it was his final word. It was over, just that quickly.

She couldn't let it all end this way, not without trying to explain, "No, Vernon. You've got it all wrong. I … I didn't …" But what could she say? The truth was far uglier than anything the ranger could possibly imagine.

Seeing Vernon's back turned towards her, hearing his deafening silence, she found she couldn't breathe. It was if she'd been struck by lightning. Beth tore from the room and ran out into the street, blinded by the pain directed at her heart. She ran with tears obstructing her vision, paying no heed to the traffic crossing her path.

Mary had just stepped down from the Jones Mercantile, with little Rosie in her arms, when she heard the scream and the racket from a team of horses pulling a full wagon. Boxes and wooden crates flew across the intersection. The horses were rearing and trying to break free. A woman on the sidewalk screamed before she fainted. Someone had been run down by the wagon and Mary had a terrifying premonition. Carefully, she turned toward the chaotic scene. There, with her delicate body lying motionless and her face pressed into the dirt, Mary discovered her friend.

"David!" Mary shouted, at the top of her lungs. She grabbed a cowboy, still on his horse, and ordered him to go get the doctor. Without any hesitation, he raced off at top speed. When Mary told you to do something, you didn't argue.

David came out of the store with the other children in tow, and quickly surveyed the scene. "You boys take Sara back to the hotel," he shouted. "There's been an accident and I have some things I need to take care of."

The boys grabbed their sister's hand and obediently, headed away from the scene, walking straight back to the hotel.

David ran to the center of the street where he saw Mary holding Rosie in one arm and kneeling, talking to someone lying injured.

He looked down and saw Beth. "Oh my God. Is she …?"

Mary was crying. "I think she's alive, but I don't know if the baby was injured," she whispered. "What do we do, David?"

He had to think about it. "Let's see what the doc says about everythin'. He's bound to find out about the babe. I'm glad Beth told Vernon, first. She was tellin' him, just as I left. I don't think we should say anythin' to him until we know what's what. Worryin' won't help him none."

Beth was starting to come around. Moaning, she tried to sit up, but David ordered her to stay still. She wasn't clear on what was happening around her. Her mind was all fuzzy and mixed up. All she knew was that she wanted Vernon.

"Vernon?" she whispered, softly.

"No, darlin'. He's still mendin' back in his room. You lie still and let the doctor examine you and make sure you and the little one are okay. I'll go on over and talk to Vernon for you."

She was confused. What more was there to say? He hated her. He hated this baby and now, she might lose the baby too. She started to cry. She needed somebody to love her. She'd been alone for too long, and had been hurt over and over again. Vernon was supposed to be the one to change all that, and now she had ruined that, too.

"No, don't talk to Vernon," she begged. "I need to get up."

She pushed David and Mary out of her way, and tried with all her strength to sit up. She wobbled and her stomach heaved, but she insisted she be allowed to stand and continue on her way, back to her own room, in her own hotel. Her eyes pleaded with David for strength and he, begrudgingly, helped her to her feet. They slowly proceeded to walk back to her hotel.

As he practically carried her, David growled his objections. "I think you should see the doc, Beth. You're injured. I don't like this one bit. Mary'll have my hide if I allow something to happen to you."

Onlookers were shocked. The schoolteacher was dirty and covered with scrapes and bruises. Who knew what might be broken? She could have been killed, they muttered. They thought she was clearly being unreasonable—maybe she was suffering from a blow to her head. The doctor had to run to catch up with the contrary woman.

"Nonsense," she insisted. "My head is fine." As the darkness suddenly overtook her, Beth collapsed into David's arms, just outside the hotel doors.

Mary was far behind, not being able to run with the baby in her arms.

"Open the doors!" David yelled. A young man, sitting on the porch, jumped up and ran to help. Once inside, David made for the stairs, throwing orders over his shoulder. "Get some hot water, some clean towels, some whiskey and my wife!"

The hours passed and still, Beth hadn't awakened. The doctor had followed them to the hotel, thankfully, and announced she was not seriously injured and her baby was doing as well as could be expected. It was perplexing to him, however, that she had not yet awakened. He left orders for Mary or David to contact him first thing, if her condition worsened. He left perplexed, scratching his head.

"Well, darlin', what do we do now?" David asked. "You

can't stay here all night. Our children need you and you're not that strong, yourself. It isn't proper for me to stay here, alone. We need to find a woman to sit with her. Got any ideas?"

"I've been sitting here, thinking about that very thing. I must get back to our room and our children. I miss them and I know they must be frightened.

"Oh, David, have you sent a message to Vernon? I forgot all about him. How's he going to react to all this and our not telling him, first thing?"

David looked concerned. "I imagine he's gonna be none too happy with us. Now that he knows about the baby, he's gonna be doubly worried. Frankly, darlin', I don't know how much we should tell him. He's not as recovered as he thinks he is. After we arrange for a woman to come and sit with Beth, I'll see you back home, then I'll traipse on over and have a talk with your brother. Damn, but when it rains, it pours. I'm afraid to ask what's next?"

He shouldn't have asked. Mr. Doolittle had a lady friend that, he said, would be happy to oblige and sit with Mrs. Painter. He'd give Robin the message and he promised she'd be right over. David agreed and walked Mary back to their hotel.

The children had gotten hungry while their parents were away, and had requested that their dinners be brought up to their rooms. That was not acceptable to Mary and David. However, the real problem was *what* the little scamps had ordered for their dinners. Mary discovered all three of her little darlings, lying across their beds with their little tummies distended and hard to the touch. Sara had been sick several times, and the boys were just getting by, moaning as if they were going to die. Remnants of pie, half-eaten cakes, cookie crumbs, and all manner of sweets were spread out on half-empty trays. They had consumed quite a decadent feast and were now paying the price.

"Oh dear," Mary sighed, as she surveyed the shambles. "This is going to be a long night, dear. I'll take care of them and you take care of Vernon." She stood on her toes and kissed her husband's lips. "Hurry home, sweetheart. I'm going to need some loving after all this," she cooed, as a grinning David took off at a trot.

On his way over to Vernon's, David kept running the name, Robin, over and over in his mind. It sounded vaguely familiar.

The only Robin he knew, was a gal at the Fancy Garter Saloon. She was a pretty thing, all curly haired and big bosomed. Surely, she wasn't a friend of Doolittle's … not a saloon gal! Aw, hell. If Mary found out, she'd tie him to a rail.

David finally reached Vernon's room. He knocked on the door, but didn't wait for an invitation to enter. He just walked in. "Hey brother. How you feelin'? You look none too good."

Vernon pulled himself up to a better position, so he could take on his good-for-nothing, poor excuse of a friend. He smiled a strange sort of grimace before he welcomed David. "Come in and close the door behind you, *brother.* I'm right glad you stopped by. There's a few things I want to say to you."

David looked sheepish. "Yeah, I know. I should have come over here and told you sooner, but I've been real busy and I wasn't sure you should know everythin', right now."

"What the hell do you mean you were busy? Too busy to tell me the most important thing in my life? You son of a bitch! You should've made time to tell me! How long have you known? Who else knows?" Vernon was trembling with rage.

David couldn't understand why Vernon was so angry. He expected him to be slightly put out, but he was past hostile. "Most of Tucson probably knows by now, but so what? Now, you know, too."

Vernon bellowed, "You snake! You sidewinder! If I could get out of this damned bed, I'd beat the life out of you. By gum, I'll do it, yet!"

"Look, you might want to pull back on your anger a notch or two, brother. I don't take to men … *any man* … threatenin' me. I was busy and that's all there is to it. I thought you'd be grateful, you selfish skunk! I was afraid of how you'd take it. Hell, you haven't even asked how she's doin'. Don't you care?"

"Why the hell should I care, you yella' varmint," Vernon spat. "I'm gonna tear you limb from limb."

"That's it. I don't take that from no man. In fact, as you well know, *brother,* I've killed men for less. Mary and I'll be leavin' at the end of the month. Hopefully, you'll still have your sorry ass stuck in this bed. I don't understand you anymore. I think maybe you've gone loco. She's too good for you, you know. You aren't the man I thought you were, Ranger." David spun on his heels and slammed the door so hard, the number fell off the other side.

Vernon was seething. How dare David come by just to gloat. He'd known Elizabeth was pregnant, without benefit of marriage, the whole time, and he had allowed him to stay in the dark until he fell in love with her. *And all of Tucson knew?* What business was it of theirs? Did they all think he was a fool and would take another man's leavings? Why did Mary take part in this lie? … this … masquerade? He thought he could trust her above all others. The really pathetic thing, about all of this, was the fact that he had, indeed, fallen in love with Beth Painter, and he loved her yet. No one was more heartbroken than he.

How could he have been so wrong about her? He was convinced she loved him. After all, hadn't she told him so? What was she doing, right now, he wondered? Had she gone to Mary's or had she gone back to her hotel?

Vernon's fury soon gave way to feelings of guilt. As his thoughts became clearer and as sanity started to rule his emotions, he began to recall all the disgusting and horrible things he had said to Beth, and he grew ashamed. She'd come to him of her own free will, and she had had the decency to tell him everything, before their relationship proceeded to the next step. She'd been honest. He knew that she hadn't deliberately tried to deceive him. He had pursued her, even though she insisted there was something in her past that he wouldn't be able to forgive. Then he went and proved her correct. He was an imbecile.

Tomorrow, he would get up out of his bed—with help, if need be—make his way down to the Hotel Doolittle, and apologize to Beth. He prayed it wasn't too late and it would be possible to salvage their broken relationship.

A knock on his door brought Vernon back to the present. It didn't sound like David's fists pounding and he was in no mood for company.

"I'm sleeping. Go away!" he growled.

The door flew open and a tiny termagant stormed in. Mary was furious. With her hands fisted on her hips, she marched to within inches of Vernon's face.

"What's wrong with you? Did those Indians steal what little sense God gave you? Why on earth are you yelling at David? He spent hours caring for her, you know. You're ungrateful, and

I am ashamed to be related to you, right now." Her beautiful eyes started to tear up, as she spoke. "I love you as much as anyone in this world, Vernon Gunn, and to think that you don't care whether Beth lives or dies, or if her baby survives, is appalling!"

Suddenly, as if her hand belonged to an unseen person, she felt it swing out away from her body and strike her brother across his astonished face. The crack of its force was formidable. Never had she struck a man with such anger.

Just as she turned to leave, her brother grabbed her hand and yelled, "Stop!"

Had he heard her correctly? "Did you say Beth was in danger of dying and maybe her child, too? But from what? Did she suddenly fall ill?" His eyes were wide with alarm and his face had lost all its color, in spite of the glaring red handprint to his cheek. Obviously, he had been taken by surprise by his sister's remarks.

"What? Don't you know what happened after she left here?" Mary asked, incredulously?

"I don't know anything. What happened to her?" Vernon was in a state of shock. He couldn't understand what was going on. He speculated he wasn't thinking too clearly. What had David been talking about? "Tell me."

Mary tried to comprehend what the two men had discussed. Obviously, Vernon and David had suffered a major misunderstanding. "Let's take this one step at a time. Did Beth finally tell you about the baby?"

Vernon gritted his teeth, still hurt by the revelation. "Yes."

"Well, when she left here, she must have been so happy, that she wasn't paying attention to the traffic in the street. She didn't hear the wagon approaching and was struck down. David picked her up and carried her to the hotel. The doctor said, given time, she'll recover and, God willing, the baby, too. When David came to tell you about her accident, you verbally attacked him, and I don't know if I'll ever forgive you. He stayed by her side for hours, Vernon. For hours!" She sniffed with fury. "I stayed with her, too, instead of caring for my children who, by the way, got sick while I was attending her." Okay, she knew that was a half-truth, but it was an effective tool to make her point. "What is wrong with you?"

"Oh my God, Mary. I had no idea. I'm such a blasted fool. Beth wasn't happy when she left here. In fact, I'm pretty certain she was in tears. I accused her of some terrible things when she told me she was pregnant."

"Oh, no, you didn't," Mary interrupted. "If you weren't so pathetic, I'd strike you again."

Vernon grimaced, as he unconsciously rubbed his jaw. His baby sister packed quite a wallop. "I was still angry at her, when David came in to tell me she'd been run down, I guess. I made the mistake of thinking he came here to see how I was feeling about her being with child, without the benefit of marriage. When he told me he'd been too busy to tell me sooner, I jumped to the wrong conclusion and thought he just hadn't bothered to take the time to tell me she was pregnant. I knew nothing of her accident."

He ran his bandaged hand through his hair. Tears of regret and humiliation ran down his face. "No wonder your husband was so surprised by my rage. I need to apologize to David and to you, but most of all, I need to get down on my knees to Beth. I really didn't mean all those horrible things I said to her. It was just my male pride talking. Do you think she'll forgive me?" His green eyes looked so sad, Mary softened, somewhat.

"Don't count on it. This is a serious dilemma you've gotten yourself into, brother. You know how long it took for her to trust you, and in five minutes, you ruined it all. It may take a bit more than you getting down on your knees. As for David, he doesn't hold a grudge … but I do. *Never* be this careless with other people's feelings again. All right, Vernon? Swear?"

He nodded and crossed his heart.

"Then my visit is complete. I still love you, but you've got some making up to do." She bent over and kissed his cheek. "If you want to see Beth, I'll ask David to assist you tomorrow, after lunch. Good night, dear."

# CHAPTER SIX

Beth hurt all over, but she refused to open her eyes. Life was too painful for her to face, at the moment. How could Vernon say such vile things to her? She hadn't expected him to react with such condemnation. He was not the man she thought him to be. Perhaps it was better to know how he truly felt, before she got too involved with him. Trouble was, she already loved him and didn't want to face a future without him. Her heart was bleeding and she didn't care if she lived or died, so … she simply refused to open her eyes.

"Come on, pigeon. I know you're comin' round. I can see your eyelids a twitchin'. You 'ad a scare, you did, but now, it's all over and it's time for you to wake up."

Beth heard the oddest voice. It was kind of Irish, but not quite. She couldn't place it, precisely. Who was speaking to her in such a strange manner? Curiosity got the best of her. Very carefully, she lifted one eye … ever so slightly … so she could peek through the smallest of cracks. Who was this strange person?

"Now, there you go again, duckie. You're a peekin'. I can tell. It takes a gal smarter than you to pull one over on Robin. Open up them baby blues."

Beth had always been obedient, so she did as she was told and opened her eyes. Standing in the middle of the room was the most amazing looking woman she had ever seen. She was petite in height, but made up for it with her over abundance of womanliness. Her bosoms were enormous and practically falling out, up and over the top of her corset. Her bottom was as round as a hassock and her skirt revealed her legs, practically up to her knees! Being held in place by green feathers, bright yellow curls swirled and twirled all over her head. That hair couldn't be natural born, Beth thought. Her eyes were framed in kohl and her lips were shiny red. Her style of dress, or undress, as Beth thought of it, clearly announced her profession. She was a saloon girl, and no doubt, a very good one.

"There you are, pet. Did you get a good look at me? I know I must look a bloody sight, but I didn't 'ave time to finish gettin' dressed 'fore old Doo called me over 'ere to keep an eye on you. I work over at the Fancy Garter." Incredibly, her chest seemed to swell even larger, with pride. "That's a saloon, in case you 'adn't 'eard. A real nice little dive, it is, too. They treats a lady like a lady. Maybe you could get a job there, if you lose your position at the school?"

At first, Beth thought Robin was being hateful, until she saw the look of total honesty on her face. This young woman meant what she was saying about the Fancy Garter. She really liked it there, and thought that Beth might like it as well.

"They'd get you out o' those widow's weeds fast enough, and the men might like the slender type, for a change. With some paint on your face and a nice dress like mine, you could be a real looker. Take my advice, duckie, and don't spend another minute cryin' over that man o' yours. He ain't worth it. None o' them are. Robin says there are men aplenty, just waitin' for a pretty woman to swish her bum." She laughed a bawdy laugh and gave her ample hips a shake.

Beth liked this strange woman instantly, even if she shouldn't. She could just imagine the reaction of the mayor and the ladies of this fair city, when they saw her carrying on with Robin from the Fancy Garter.

"I'm Elizabeth Painter and I teach school here, but I'll think about your offer. A change of jobs might be just the thing I need." She smiled her warmest smile at the saloon girl. Beth thought that if her reputation got totally ruined, so what? In a few months, she'd be ruined, anyway.

"Well, Miss Painter, I've got to get goin' … now that it looks like you ain't gonna die anytime soon." She grinned. "Come look me up, if you need anythin'." She winked at Beth, grabbed her thin wrap and sashayed out the door.

"I wonder if she knows?" Beth whispered to herself. She placed her hands across her tummy and suddenly everything was clear. She didn't care who knew about this child. It made no difference in the scheme of things if she was married, widowed, or not. This living child was hers, all hers, and she was in love with it, already. Vernon, the Mayor, and anyone else not approving, could just go jump in the lake. She didn't care.

She sat up carefully, and proceeded to wash her face and brush her hair. Tomorrow was another day, and she was going to face it head on, on her own terms, and Mr. Gunn could just go to hell. He could leave Tucson, if he didn't want to see her again. She was stronger than he knew.

The next afternoon, David walked into Vernon's room pushing the biggest wheelchair, Vernon had ever seen. "What do you think you're gonna do with that contraption?"

"Well, you don't think I'm gonna carry you all the way to the Doolittle, do ya? Stand up and see if you can get your butt into this here chair."

Vernon was embarrassed as all get out, but he couldn't lift himself off the damn bed. He'd been flat on his back for several weeks and he was simply too weak. "Forget it," he grumbled. "I'm not much of a man, at the moment, and I won't let her see me like this. I ain't got the strength of a piss ant." He threw himself back against the pillows and looked away from David.

"So you're just gonna give up and lay there, sulking like a baby. Do you want to see Beth or not? Do you want to apologize for actin' like a jackass or not? If'n you do, I suggest you try again. Hell, Ranger, I suffered more than this, fightin' those damn Yankees, back in Missouri, and I *never* gave up. Did I tell you about the time I nearly froze to death? Damn it, I've been burned out, froze out, tied up, and shot. And you're willin' to lie back in that soft bed and let the best thing that ever happened to you, just walk away? I'm disappointed in you, brother. It do appear like Mary got all the gumption in the Gunn family." Having said that, David pushed the chair toward the door.

"Wait a minute. Bring that ugly thing back here. If you help me, I might be able to pull myself up." Vernon's face was beet red with humiliation, but he needed to make things right with

Beth. "And don't mention any of this to my sister," he growled. "A man's gotta have some pride."

David hid his grin, thinking about his little wife and the tongue-lashing she had given her big brother. Without saying another word, he bent over and put his arms, gingerly, around Vernon's ribcage, and lifted him up from the mattress. The ranger really was as weak as he'd said. David was shocked at his condition. His ribs were still bandaged, so the effort that went into getting him on his feet was quite painful.

To break the tension in the room, David threatened, "If you tell anyone that I put my arms around you, *in bed*, I'll deny it—right after I shoot you."

They both, laughed.

The sidewalks in Tucson could have used some improvements. The only alternative, the two men had, was to travel right down the middle of Main Street. With it being the top of the afternoon, everyone was out and about, taking care of business. However, the people all stopped whatever it was they were doing, to watch the comical scene unfolding before them.

The ranger was hiding his face, the best he could—as if people didn't recognize him and the big shiny star pinned to his chest. The handsome man pushing him from behind, was tipping his hat to everyone; smiling and saying, "How do" to all the folks around. It was obvious that David Williams was enjoying this walk immensely, and all the attention they garnered.

The last straw came when the dogs started barking loudly, and running circles around the traveling twosome. Vernon had had about all he could take. If he'd had his pistol on him, he thought, he just might have to shoot something … or someone, as he looked up at the joyful expression on his brother-in-law's face. David was having too much fun at his expense, once again. Thank God, the Doolittle was just another half block away.

By the time they approached the doors of the Hotel Doolittle, the two men found themselves accompanied by an assortment of mangy mutts, a few children, several town drunks, and one very blonde saloon gal. It looked like a damn parade, grumbled the ranger. But for the people in town, this little adventure had turned into one of the highlights of the year.

Vernon, gritting his teeth, ordered David to just get them inside, "Now!"

But David had other plans. He decided he was going to get back at this man for having been such a rude s.o.b. the day before. He smiled real wide and walked slowly around the chair, to face Vernon.

Scratching his head, he looked a mite perplexed. "Now, brother, I don't know as how I can lift you and this here chair, all by myself," he shook his head. "Nope. I don't reckon I can. You just sit tight while I go in and see if I can scare up some help." He looked up at the odd assemblage and pointed to the pretty saloon girl, with the wild yeller' hair.

"You, miss. What's your name?"

She sashayed over to the two handsome men, knowing full well who they were and why they were there. She sidled up alongside David and purred, "Robin, sir. What can Robin do for you?"

David was a little shocked by the woman's brazen behavior and stepped back. Clearing his throat, he asked, "Robin, will you keep my friend comp'ny, whilst I go in and get some assistance with his chair? He's a weak cripple, you know, and cain't do nothin' fer himself." David grinned, playfully.

"Well, o' course, pigeon. You're so good-lookin' and all, Robin would do *anythin'* you asked of her." She winked, provocatively.

Then turning her attentions to Vernon, she placed her hand on his forehead, and whispered, "You're in good 'ands with Robin, you are. I can make you feel so much better. Just relax, guv'nor. Ain't nobody lookin'," she whispered. Of course, she knew half the town had turned out to stare and she thought it served the varmint right. He was the man that made nice Mrs. Painter cry.

"David, for God's sake, don't leave me out here," Vernon pleaded. "Not with her," he whispered under his breath, his eyes darting back and forth toward the provocative woman.

David took one last look at Vernon, and smiled from ear to ear. The ranger was so uncomfortable he was shooting smoke out his ears. The wider David grinned, the more embarrassed Vernon looked. For his own safety, David stepped into the lobby and closed the door behind him.

Slowly walking over to the front desk, he inquired if Mrs. Painter was in her room. He knew it wouldn't be proper for him to just start up those stairs. His ma had taught him better.

"Nope, she ain't in," the crusty old proprietor muttered.

"Well, do you know when to expect her?"

"Nope, didn't say."

"Do you at least know where she went?"

"Nope, and if I did, I wouldn't tell ya'."

David was growing tired of this game, he played, with the crusty old clerk. "Look, you idiot. I brought a grievously wounded man, *by wheelchair*, to see her, and we're not leavin' 'til he does."

The clerk sighed and turned back to his duties, disregarding David, altogether.

"Have I lost my touch?" David whispered to himself, as he turned away and started back outside to rescue Vernon from the clutches of the friendly Robin. In the past, men quaked in their boots from just one arched brow from him. Bad desperados were known to cross the street, to the other side, when he strode down the sidewalk. As he pondered all this, he was taken by surprise when the hotel doors flew open and in stomped Beth.

"Hey, beautiful. I was hopin' you'd show up soon. You look right as rain, sweetheart. Mary will be pleased to hear it. Did you see who I brought with me? He's out on the porch, dyin' to speak with you. He feels just awful about the misunderstandin' you two had." He waited for her to reply, expecting her to be happy and grateful to him for bringing the man she loved, to her door.

However, Beth didn't look none to friendly, he thought. Something wasn't as it should be. "Beth, are you still mad at Vernon? He was all mixed up and didn't know what he was sayin. He wants to fix this. I think it was the pain talkin'. He's in awful pain, Beth … in here," he said, dramatically laying his hand over his heart. Did that work, he wondered, or was he laying it on a little too thick?

"David, you can go bat those big blue eyes at someone who cares. I would appreciate you wheeling that snake back to the rock from whence he came. I have no interest in anything he has to say and I don't particularly care about anything you have to say, either. From this day forward, I am a widow, understand?

I'm going to have my deceased husband's child. That's all anyone is entitled to know. Later today, I have a meeting with Mayor Applebaum, where I know I'll more than likely lose my job. But you see … I have viable alternatives to marrying a rude and hateful man. The Fancy Garter will take me on until I'm too large, and then, when the baby is old enough for a sitter, I can resume my duties there—that is, if I choose to stay here, in Tucson. Mr. Gunn did order me to leave town, you know.

"Now, go out there and roll him back to his room … that is, if you can peel him away from Robin. He seems to have taken quite a shine to her."

Suddenly turning around, Beth furiously tossed her head, causing her blonde curls to come tumbling out from beneath her hat. She grabbed handfuls of her skirt and flounced up the stairs, never once looking back at the man she left standing in the parlor, with his mouth hanging wide open. The sound of her slamming her door, resonated all the way down into the lobby.

It took a moment for David to recover. "Damn," he muttered to himself. "I thought Mary had a temper." Then he chuckled, softly. Vernon would never find his life dull, that was for sure.

It wasn't nearly as much fun pushing Vernon back up Main Street, as it had been parading him down, thought David. For one thing, neither one of them was very talkative. The day had not gone well. Even the laughing crowds had disappeared. If it weren't for the one old dog, with a missing ear, trailing behind them, they would go unnoticed. They sure were a pathetic lot.

Vernon was truly depressed at the day's outcome. He'd had high hopes. Now, the only thing he had to look forward to was his work. He'd been out of his office for almost two months, considering he'd gone out in search of the outlaws prior to getting ambushed and tortured. Tomorrow, he'd attack the Wanted posters, from his bed. He was still man enough to do that.

Ranger Barclay was more than happy to bring the paperwork over for Vernon to attend to. He'd been feeling overworked and under appreciated, lately. "Well, Vernon, after lookin' at all these, ya might wanna stay in yer sick bed fer a little longer. At the very least, I think ya might want to think it over before ya repeat yesterday's performance. Yer the talk o' the town, ya know. Sorry I missed it." He chuckled in spite of himself. "I heard tell that Robin has taken a real likin' to ya." His snickers quickly grew into outright laughs, making it necessary for him to wipe the traitorous tears from his eyes.

Vernon was not amused. "What do you mean by that remark? Get the hell outta here," he shouted. He stifled an indignant *humpf*, as the man left the room, still laughing.

Vernon was livid and feeling real sorry for himself. He vowed it would be a cold day in Tucson, before he played the fool, again—no matter how beautiful the woman. Not even if she smelled of sunshine and was softer than a summer breeze. No! Never again, would he make a fool of himself over a woman—unless she said she forgave him and loved him as much as he loved her. No, never.

While idly thumbing through the posters, Vernon found one that caught his eye.

"Well, I'll be damned. Ryann Beaufort's a woman!" He laughed at all those ignorant officers in Richmond, looking for a man and wasting all this time. They'd never catch him—her—now. She had about six months on them, and a person could disappear in a lot less time. He read the particulars of the case, again. She was wanted for an especially violent murder. She was tall—built like a man, no doubt—and probably looked like one, too, he thought. The senator had sworn not to give up until she was apprehended. Well, Vernon would keep his eyes open, but what were the chances she'd show up in Tucson?

"Call me Arthur, my dear. You could use my influence in this town. If I say you are to keep your job, then you shall keep it. I am grateful that you felt comfortable enough to come to me with your problem." The mayor reached out and took Beth's hands in own, caressing them, slightly. His fat thumbs massaged her wrists, trailing little circles, higher and higher up her arm. "You can show me your appreciation by going to dinner with me … often."

He smiled, and Beth found it to be very unpleasant, to say the least. The curling of his lips revealed too much gum and odious yellow teeth. The sour and distasteful smell of his breath was nauseating. What had the man been eating? The thick oil, encapsulating his thin hair, completed the picture of a totally repugnant man.

It could have been her delicate condition or maybe she just didn't admire the mayor's hygiene, but Beth's stomach tightened into a knot and lurched upwards, forcing her to run from the table with her hands covering her mouth.

She splashed cold water on her face and started to cry. So, this was going to be her life. Men, like the illustrious mayor, were going to be trying to get to know her better, by giving her little tokens of their esteem, or by doing small favors for her, since she was a damsel in *real* distress.

"Damn you, Vernon," she said, to herself. "This is all your fault. I loved you." She knew there would never be another man for her and that was a lonely prospect.

For days, Beth and Vernon carried on, pretending the other did not exist. They both stayed to their own part of town. Tucson was big enough to allow them some privacy, from one another, but the people of the town, took notice of their obvious avoidance. The whispers and the gossip naturally reared its ugly head.

One morning, while in the classroom, a beautiful little girl stood up and complimented her beloved teacher. All the students liked Mrs. Painter and Becky was a particular favorite of hers.

"Yes, Becky, what would you like to say to the class?"

Smiling sweetly, with eyes sparkling innocently, she stood up proudly and announced in a loud voice, "My ma says you're graceful, Mrs. Painter." She continued smiling and sat down.

That was odd, Beth thought. "Thank you, Becky, and thank your mother too."

Becky's older brother, Bob, stood up, looking embarrassed. "Excuse me, ma'am, but she didn't say, *graceful*, exactly." He looked at his little sister. "Ma was talking with Mrs. Albers and agreed that Mrs. Painter was *disgraceful*. It don't mean the same thing, you little ninny."

Becky looked as if she might cry. "I think she's graceful and very pretty, so there!" She stuck her tongue out at Bob.

"Oh, my." Beth didn't know what to say, but she felt as if she had been slapped. She couldn't ignore this, so she asked Bob, "Would you ask your mother to come and see me, soon? I need to know what I have done to offend her."

"Don't worry yourself too much, teacher. The entire town's

talkin' about ya. You know, your condition and all," he whispered. The boy looked a tad uncomfortable.

"Well, I don't understand, but I must speak with your mother, just the same. Please ask her to see me?"

"Sure thing, ma'am, but you ain't gonna like it. She's on a real rant, just now."

After school dismissed, Beth began her daily walk home. This time, however, she noticed how people, that used to smile and say howdy, were now staying to the other side of the street, away from her, and not one of them had acknowledged her passing. She was being shunned and she wasn't certain as to why. No one in town knew she had never been married, except for Vernon and the Williams, and she knew Mary and David wouldn't utter a single word. That left only Vernon. He must be trying to shame her into leaving. Beth felt a sharp pain cut across her chest. Did he actually hate her that much? Well, two could play his despicable game. They'd just see who'd leave town, first.

Beth decided to kill everyone with kindness, if needed. As she walked home, she held her head high and pretended she didn't notice the cruel actions of her neighbors. In fact, when she encountered someone, she made it a point to say hello or good afternoon, forcing herself to smile. It was a long walk home.

She was passing Jones Mercantile, when the Grande Dame of Tucson, Mrs. Calliope Bigsby literally bumped into her, almost knocking her off her feet. The lady started to apologize, until she discovered whom it was she had run into.

"I'm so … oh, it's you. Well! I didn't see you. You really should be looking where you are going, young woman. You could have hurt me. The sidewalk belongs to everyone, you know." She turned aside, preparing to walk around Beth, when Beth responded.

"Of course, you're so right, Mrs. Bigsby. I pray you're not hurt. I know you have that problem with your neck. How is it feeling nowadays?"

Shocked that Mrs. Painter would remember her bad neck, and actually take the time to comment on it, stopped Mrs. Bigsby in her tracks. "Yes, well," she cleared her throat. "It feels better, now that the weather is starting to warm."

Beth smiled her prettiest and continued on, "I hope I did nothing to make it worse. You see, I wasn't watching where I was going, as I have so much on my mind. With you, being a married lady and all, you'd understand the problems I suffer." Beth took out her hanky and dabbed at her eyes. "I don't know what I've done, but the whole town has turned against me, just when I need the friendship of the good women here, more than ever." She placed her hands over her tummy. "I know nothing about what I am experiencing or what I have to look forward to. Sometimes, I'm so scared. Please forgive me, ma'am, for my clumsiness." A huge tear made its way down her cheek.

She smiled, once again, and turned to leave, when Mrs. Bigsby placed her bejeweled hand on her arm. Beth noticed there were tears filling the old lady's eyes.

"Don't worry, my dear. I'll get to the bottom of all this nonsense, and I'll set it right. This Sunday, after church meeting, a few ladies of Tucson will gather in my home. Please come, and I'll see what we can do." She nodded and turned in the other direction.

Beth had made a conquest. She figured she only had to do that a couple hundred more times and all this nonsense would be behind her. For now, she was tired and needed to get off her feet.

Robin took it upon herself to keep an eye on the good-looking ranger, for the pretty lady. Today had been her day off, so she decided to pay Ranger Gunn a visit. She carried a food tray, from the Fancy Garter, to his room. Their cook was a reasonably good one. With her hands full, she was forced to kick at the ranger's door. How was she to know it wasn't securely latched and that it would fly open at the slightest nudge?

Inside, standing very close to the man sitting in the chair, a beautiful woman was massaging his shoulders and talking softly in his ear.

"Ahem!" Robin announced. "I'm 'ere, duckie, and I brung you your dinner. It smells right good, it does. Would you like Robin to feed it to you, like I did last time, precious?"

She'd never fed him before, but she didn't like the way this beautiful lady's hands were rubbing all over Beth's man. "Get away, girlie. Robin gives the back rubs to the Ranger." She placed the food tray down on the bed, walked over to the chair, and with one thrust of her ample hip, bumped Mary almost to the floor.

"Robin! What do you think you're doing, busting in here, unannounced like this, and practically attacking my sister?" Vernon demanded to know.

With her eyes as big as eggs, Robin looked like she wanted to crawl beneath the carpet and hide. "Sister, you say? Oh, Gawd, Robin made a terrible mistake, she did. She mistook this lovely lady for a *special* friend o' yours. Robin 'ad no way of knowin' she was your sister! Please forgive her, guv'. Robin'll leave right now."

"Oh no you don't. You get back here," Vernon shouted. "I want to know what exactly is going on here? People are acting queer around me, and I haven't the slightest notion why. I know the whole town knows about Mrs. Painter refusing to see me the other day, but that's not sufficient reason for the buzz that's going around. You know something, woman, and I demand you spill it, or I might have to do some digging in your past and see what I come up with."

"That's blackmail, Ranger. Robin doesn't think she likes you very much, after all." She waited a few seconds before she started talking. Looking at Mary, Robin asked, "Can I speak freely in front o' you, Miss?"

"Yes, of course." Mary answered. "Beth is my very best friend and I love my brother, as well, even if he can be an ornery galoot."

Robin snickered behind her hand. She liked the ranger's sister. "That's good enough for me. You see, Mr. Ranger, I got to know Miss Elizabeth after her accident. She's precious, she is, and I don't mind lettin' you know, we're friends. For reasons of 'er own, it seems she loves your sorry 'ide, and I don't know what you said or did, but you near broke 'er 'eart. She don't trust you now, and she's out to prove to you that she don't need you none." Robin shook her finger at Vernon. "With all them vicious rumors goin' around town, you've made life miserable for 'er, and it might prove to be too much for 'er to bear. I thought you were a real man, Ranger, different from the blokes I see at the saloon, but you disappoint Robin. You're just a common wanker, after all." The tough saloon gal looked close to tears.

"What rumors are you talking about? How am I making it difficult for her? I haven't left this room but just a few times. Our paths have never crossed."

"Well, dovie, that's just the problem. The whole town knew you was sweet on the schoolteacher, even if she was in mournin'. That was bad enough, but you two were discreet. So, out of respect for you and 'er, they said very little and looked the other way. Now, suddenly, she's in a delicate condition, and you two are no longer speakin'. The tongues are waggin', sayin' it might not be 'er late 'usband's babe at all, and that you've refused to face up to your responsibilities. Now, Robin don't believe it, mind you, but who listens to Robin?"

Vernon was on his feet. His head was splitting with anger. "I believe you, Robin, and I'm gonna beat the hell out of the next person who even hints at such a slanderous suggestion about Mrs. Painter. We've *never* been improper. I just enjoy her company." He turned to Mary. "Invite Beth to dinner."

Robin smiled with satisfaction. Her job was done, here. "Don't forget the food tray, guv'nor. It really is good and you need to put some meat back on those bones. Oh, by the by, I wouldn't wait too long to stake a claim on the lovely schoolteacher, cause from what I gather, at the Fancy Garter, the men are startin' to line up with their offers. Offers of *all* types, I might add. Well, toodles, you two." Robin wiggled her fingers over her shoulder and departed.

"Remarkable woman," giggled Mary.

Vernon sat back down in a daze. "This has proven to be quite a day."

"Thank you, sir. I am honored by your offer, but I am not seeing gentlemen during this period of my bereavement." Beth had repeated this to men, over and over, during the past week, but they continued to come with their offers. Some gentlemen were interested in marriage. They were young and some were old. Most had children needing a mother. Some of the less respectable offers came from drunks and gamblers, taking bets on whether the young schoolmarm would say yes to them and their plans to help her over her loneliness. Therefore, it was a relief to receive an invitation she could accept.

"David, I would be most happy to have dinner with your family. It's been difficult, lately, and I need to relax with friends. Thank Mary for me. Is ... is *he* going to be there? Tell me true, please."

David couldn't lie to her sweet, sad face. Impending motherhood agreed with her, for her loveliness had only increased, as of late. "Yes, Beth, he's been invited. In fact, he suggested the dinner. Vernon feels real bad about the things he said to you, and he wants you to hear him out." David hesitated. "I think you should. All men are stupid when it comes to women. You should know that by now. Mary's had to put up with her share of ignorance from me."

"So she's told me," Beth happily informed.

David grinned, and cleared his throat before proceeding. "I can tell you it's all true, but love wins in the end. That's what's important—isn't it, Beth? Love?"

Beth wanted to see Vernon again. In fact, she dreamed of him every night. When she felt like giving up, she imagined his handsome face, smiling at her, telling her to be strong. She couldn't even remember the hateful things he had said to her the last time they spoke. However, she was aware that he no longer loved her and was not willing to care for her and her child. She fought with her pride, before answering David.

"Tell Mary, I would love to have dinner. I've missed her and the children so much. I imagine Rosie has grown quite a bit since I saw her last." She smiled wistfully, thinking that soon, she would have a little baby of her own to love and care for.

"Tell Ranger Gunn that I will listen to him, and afterward, he will listen to me." She continued smiling, but it wasn't altogether pleasant. Behind it was a stockpile of volatile emotion and that made David a mite uneasy.

"Okay, then. Is tonight too soon?"

"It's perfect. I eat dinner every night. Thank you for your thoughtful invitation." With a slight smile of appreciation, Beth disappeared back through the schoolhouse doors.

# CHAPTER SEVEN

Dinner was nice. Beth had missed Mary and her family very much over the past few weeks. She recalled how happy their friendship made her when she first arrived in town, and how very important it had all been to her.

With her dark past well hidden, Beth hoped it was still possible for her to have a promising future with a wonderful man—a man that caused her pulse to beat rapidly whenever he entered the room. He'd be a man capable of inspiring her to dream very naughty dreams, while alone in her bed. Vernon was just that kind of man, and she continued to hope that someday, he'd take her in his arms and carry her off to paradise.

Sara tugged incessantly, on her mother's sleeve. "Mama, mama, can I tell now? Can I tell?" She was wiggling so, Beth was afraid she might fall off her chair. "Pleeease?"

David laughed. "Well, darlin', it looks like we're gonna have to make our announcement soon, before little Sara here, starts screamin' in the dinin' room."

Looking adoringly at her husband, Mary agreed. "Yes, dear. You tell Beth and Vernon our good news."

"Please, papa, hurry and tell, so I can tell them the REAL good news!" Sara insisted.

Everyone was taking delight in the childish exuberance of little Sara. Something was thrilling her, for sure.

David stood up and clinked the side of his water glass with his spoon, getting everyone's attention. "I saw this done once, in a fancy restaurant in Springfield. Always wanted to do it, myself." He grinned, slightly embarrassed.

Clearing his throat, he said, "I've decided to take the Deputy's job in Red Rock. With the money Mary received, from the sale of our farm, back in Missouri, I bought the perfect place for us to start our ranch. It's between Red Rock and here, so's it ain't too far for you gals to see each other, now and then. I'm already talkin' to some men interested in goin' and helpin' out with the ranchin' and such. Two have signed on and they're good men. One has a wife and two daughters." He glanced at Vernon, wanting to reassure him of Mary's safety, away from her brother's watchful eye, in Tucson.

He looked at Beth. "Mary's been talkin' to Jane Runyon about comin' along with us. Lily's just a little older than Sara, and with Jane bein' Navajo and all, she has a lot in common with Mary. She wants to spend more time with the little girl. It's good for ever'one, we figure. We'll be leavin' the first of the month."

David's announcement left Beth and Vernon stunned. He sat down and waited for his brother-in-law's response.

Vernon was quiet as he mulled over this "good news". He didn't like it one bit, but he knew it had to happen one day. He saw the hopeful expression on his sister's face and knew he needed to be happy for her. She, obviously, wanted this very much.

"Even though I expressed my concerns to David, I want you to know that I'm confident he's doing the right thing, and I know that you'll be very happy out there, on your ranch. I know what the raising of horses means to all of you, and the boys are of an age when they need to be learning life skills. Just be careful and watchful. This is still a young territory and, as I found out, it can be extremely hostile."

He took Mary's small hand and brought it to his lips. "I'll miss you, little sister. I just got you back."

"Oh dear, I think I'm going to cry," Mary sniffled.

"Mama, *now* can I tell Uncle Vernon and Mrs. Painter that I'm getting a puppy? Can I tell them, now?" Sara had been as patient as any little girl with a big secret could be. She looked up at her mama with eyes large and pleading. She had absolutely no idea she had just let the "pup" out of the bag.

Everyone was laughing. "Yes, baby. You tell us all about

your puppy."

Sara stood, taking her milk cup in her hand, carefully—so as not to spill—she lightly tapped it with her spoon. Looking toward her pa, she grinned impishly. "I have a *'portant 'nouncent* to make."

Beth covered her mouth with her hand, in an attempt to restrain her giggles. Vernon was red-faced and about to bust with laughter. Sara's brothers were chuckling aloud—until their pa shot them a scolding look.

Sara stopped and looked toward her pa for support.

"You go on, honey. We're all listenin'."

The little girl took a deep breath, and began again. "We can't have a puppy here—cause the hotel won't let us," she grumbled, "and I had to leave my Buster on the farm, and papa's promised me another puppy when we move to our new house. I got a box ready and everything … honest. I want a girl or a boy, and he doesn't have to be big or nothing, but real smart. This puppy is going to be mine and maybe Rosie's, but she's still a baby and can't play with puppies yet, so I'll teach him everything, and mama says if the puppy is good, he can sleep in my room." She sat down, smiling, feeling very proud of herself. It was a speech well delivered.

Vernon grinned at his precocious niece. "You can breathe now, Sara. I think that sounds like a fine idea and I might know just the pup for you." He winked at David.

"Robin mentioned that an old dog came by the Fanc—uh—the establishment where she's employed," he cleared his throat and quickly looked at Beth.

She showed no sign of censure, but mouthed "Thank you," silently.

"It seems an old dog came by last month, with two tiny pups. The girls have been feeding them. Bart, the piano man, has taken quite a shine to the mama dog, but he can't keep all three and the girl's can't keep the pups, permanently. If you'd like, I could come by tomorrow and escort you ladies over to the … or … maybe I could bring the pups to you? Yeah, that would definitely be better. What do you think, sweetie? You want to look at those pups?"

"Oh mama, oh papa! Could I? Uncle Vernon is the best uncle in the whole town," she squealed. "Can I see the pups tomorrow?" She stood up and began jumping and twirling about in circles.

David nodded.

Sara was beside herself with happiness, as she ran over to her Uncle Vernon and threw her chubby arms around his neck. As he leaned down to her level, she gave him a sloppy, apple pie covered kiss, on his cheek.

"The best uncle in the whole, entire town? Well, I'll be," he chuckled.

Vernon felt heaven was almost in his grasp. He yearned to have a beautiful and loving woman, waiting for him everyday, standing by his side, and a sweet child looking up at him with love in her eyes. Undoubtedly, that woman was Beth, but unfortunately, he'd been a very stupid man.

Much later, after the Williams' family had retired, Vernon and Beth sat nursing what was left of their coffee. "Would you like more, Beth, before I see you back to your hotel?" Vernon couldn't stand the thought of saying goodnight and was willing to delay the inevitable for as long as possible.

Beth looked … *really* looked at Vernon, and suddenly she felt so very foolish. Their disagreement had been serious, and he had said some truly horrible things to her, but in his defense, she had sprung a baby at him, from out of nowhere. Perhaps they could try again.

"No, I think I've had enough. Thank you, Vernon."

He noticed she had used his Christian name for the first time in weeks. He stood, offered his arm to her, and said, "Then, let's be off, my lady."

It was a warm starry night, a night made for lovers. They walked slowly, in silence, down the partially hidden sidewalks of closed-up Tucson. With the exception of the saloons, all the businesses were shuttered and the lights put out. Both, Vernon and Beth, were uncertain their new truce would hold up through conversation, so neither chose to speak. Beth was, however, aware of how close Vernon's body was to her own and how his legs would sometimes brush against her skirts. She could feel his body's heat through the sleeve he offered her, and she could smell his masculine scent.

In a voice barely above a whisper, Vernon said, "Beth, I need to talk to you. I need to apologize for everything and I can't do it justice out here, on the street. It's not proper, I know, but would you consent to come to my room? I'll keep the door ajar, if that would make you feel better. Please, darling. I promise you won't regret your decision."

A chill ran up Beth's spine. Her breathing picked up rapidly. This could be what she had been waiting for, all her life. "It's quite all right, Vernon. I want to speak with you, too. I have some apologies of my own to make. Please, lead the way, sir." She smiled hopefully, and stepped off the sidewalk to cross the street, caring not one whit if they were seen by half of Tucson.

The moment she entered his room, Beth knew her life would be forever changed. There was no need for apologies. She definitely loved Vernon, and she believed him when he professed his love for her. Now was the time for truth with no more games. She quietly closed the door behind her and locked the latch.

"Sweetheart," Vernon exclaimed. Surprised by her actions, and overcome by his strong feelings, he reached out and turned her toward him, grasping her face in his hands, he guided her lips to his. He'd been thinking of kissing those soft, pliant lips, all evening. He longed to taste her and fill her mouth with his tongue, taking possession of it. The kiss was warm and solid and it worked its magic. His tongue teased her lips until they parted, inviting him to explore.

Vernon heard Beth's moan of pleasure and it only served to fire his blood even more. She splayed her hands through his hair, and luxuriated in the feel of its soft, thick curls tangling around her fingers. His hair was shiny and smelled of the clean outdoors. She was afraid she might swoon from sheer pleasure.

His hands roamed up and down her slender back, exploring all her curves. He discovered Beth was built in an elegant fashion, but strong. Carefully, he brought his hands around to the front of her dress and felt the gentle swell of her breasts beneath the fabric.

Vernon drew back to observe her. Beth was innocently sensual. Even though she had been with another man, he could sense this was as if it was her first time. It was confusing, but he knew it to be the truth. His eyes slowly drifted down from her lovely face, past her collarbone and on down to the twin soft mounds of her breasts. He longed to see them, to gently roll her nipples with his fingers, but he would have to wait. After all, she was with child, and there were things that she probably shouldn't do. Kissing her face, her hands, and maybe caressing her lovely long legs would have to be enough for him.

"Vernon, kiss me, here." Beth had unbuttoned the top three buttons on her dress, revealing her soft creamy skin. "Please, don't be frightened of my condition. That is … if you want to touch me and you don't find me too ugly."

Vernon's face registered shock at her comment. Not because she wanted him to continue kissing her, but that she could possibly think he would find her anything less than perfection!

With a growl, he buried his face in her neck and breathed deeply, taking in her divine scent. Kissing was hardly adequate to sate his lust. He kissed and nuzzled her neck, making her sigh with contentment and giggle with joy. "Beth, darling. I want you so much. I know you're not ready, but I've been looking for you, all my life, and I don't want to let you walk away from me, again."

Beth felt his hands drop down past her waist and cup her bottom, pressing her body close to his. She felt his body harden and grow with excitement. To her surprise, she was eager to receive his love.

"Darling, I want you to love me. I want you to take me now, and make me yours," she pleaded.

Vernon stopped his hands and looked deep into her amazing blue eyes. "Are you certain, sweetheart? Should I make love to you when you're with child? Don't forget, until today, you weren't even speaking to me." He smiled, wickedly, but he was sincere. "You need to be certain. Once I claim your body, I'll never let you go."

"I may not have been speaking to you, Vernon, but I was always dreaming of you and of your touch." She unbuttoned his top shirt button and smiled seductively, as she placed her lips against his fevered skin.

How could he resist?

"I'll be very gentle, darling."

He kissed her gently, at first., then the kiss turned hot and fierce as he dragged her into his arms and breathed in her alluring scent. She was warm and soft in all the right places, and caused his heart to race with excitement.

He slipped her dress off her shoulders, letting it fall around her waist, and feasted his hungry eyes upon her creamy white flesh and her twin, plump mounds. With trembling hands, he untied her chemise, baring those breasts—and what breasts they were. He gasped in awe, at first sight. Never before, in his entire life, had he seen two more magnificent breasts—and he had not lived the life of a monk. They were firm and full, perfectly rounded, and topped with cherry pink nipples, begging to be suckled and tasted.

"You're exquisite," he sighed. He couldn't resist running his tongue over their pouty peaks, tasting them and marveling at their ability to pebble under his efforts.

Beth pressed herself against his face, craving more … much more. "Yes, darling, kiss me, love me—just like that." She was enraptured by his touch. Her wits were dulled, but her senses were heightened to the point of aching.

Vernon replaced his lips, with his hands, and gently squeezed and massaged her breasts, just enough to make her squirm. They felt heavy and lush, in his hands, and only increased his desire.

Returning his mouth to hers, he discovered she tasted like dessert.

"Enough, Beth," he growled, stepping back, pulling her chemise back up over her shoulders. "I'm only human, for God's sake."

Beth felt absolutely bewildered. Why had Vernon stopped, when she was enjoying herself so much? This was what she wanted, what she had dreamed of, and now he was stopping? Didn't he want her in the same way?

"What's wrong? Why don't you want to go on? I want to, Vernon. Oh how I want to." She rubbed up against his chest, begging for his attention. With smoldering eyes, she conveyed her intent.

Vernon turned away and sat up on the edge of the bed, trying to regain his wits. Raking his hands through his hair, he looked like a man who had just lost a fight. He was in agony, but he knew that Beth deserved nothing less than him using as much restraint as he could muster. He didn't want to rush her into anything.

"Beth," he began, his voice low and intimate, "I need to say some things I want you to know that I love you … even more, now, than before we entered this room." He grinned, mischievously. "Please, don't misunderstand me. I want you so much, I doubt that I can walk at present, but I also want you for more than just this." He waved at the bed.

"I want you to marry me and be my wife. I want you and the baby and everything that goes along with it. It was a terrible mistake for me to overreact the way I did, at the news of your condition. I misjudged you, and that was wrong."

Beth sat down next to Vernon and laid her head on his shoulder. "You're doing fine, Vernon," she purred. "Continue on."

"Yes, well, when I thought you'd been married, I knew you'd been with another man, but I guess I chose to ignore that. I wanted to pretend to be your first. When I discovered you'd never been married, but were with child, my stupid male brain came up with all kinds of inappropriate scenarios. My mouth ran off with my good sense."

Vernon looked into Beth's face, and saw such breathtaking beauty and innocence, there. He marveled at how delicately lovely she truly was, and he knew that it wasn't just her physical beauty that attracted him to her, but her inner beauty, as well. A huge lump formed in his throat, making it difficult to speak.

"In my whole life, Beth, I've never felt about anyone the way I feel about you. You amaze me and humble me. I know I don't deserve you, but I swear, I won't let you get away a second time. I'd gladly die for you. Your happiness and the happiness of our child will be top priority with me, from this moment forward." He lifted her hands to his lips and kissed the tops of her knuckles and, turning them over, he kissed her palms, sending bolts of quivering sensation up her arms, directly to her heart.

Beth was softly crying at his poetic words. "Oh, Vernon. I never want to hear you apologize for that awful conversation, again. I didn't react appropriately, either. I should have stayed and tried harder to explain, but it was so difficult. Let's not revisit that day, ever again."

She tilted her head and sought his lips, once again. She wanted to remain with him, in that kiss, forever. His strong arms wrapped around her and brought her in close, making her feel safe and protected from whatever evil may come. In that moment, Beth knew she was where she should be, locked in his arms.

Vernon stood and reached down and offered to assist her to her feet. "I need to get you back to your room, now, my lady. Tomorrow, I'd like to tell David and Mary about us and invite them to a wedding … if you agree?" His extraordinary green eyes begged her to accept his proposal. How could she say no?

"Yes, please do, darling. I'd like for us to marry before they leave Tucson. Is that possible?"

"Whoopee!" The ranger let out with a loud shout. He didn't care how many people he may have awakened. They should all know that Elizabeth Painter had agreed to marry his sorry hide. "Not only is it possible, darling … but I *insist* on it."

The very next morning, Beth addressed her students. "Children, I am sorry to say that by the end of the month, I will no longer be your teacher. I'm marrying Ranger Gunn." The children moaned at the announcement.

"I am sure your new teacher will like you and appreciate you as much as I do. Please honor me by being on your very best behavior for her. She'll be scared, just as I was, and will need your help. You were so nice to me, and I know you'll be nice to her. I love each and every one of you. You'll always be welcome to stop by my house for a visit." She began to sniffle. Saying goodbye was harder than she had expected.

Becky stood up with tears in her enormous eyes. "You're not graceful anymore, Mrs. Painter. Please don't leave cause you're mad at mama." Her bottom lip began to quiver.

Beth rushed to Becky's side and she took the child into her arms. "Oh, no, no, sweetheart. It has nothing to do with any of that." She gave Becky a tight squeeze, before returning to the front of the class. "You see, I love Ranger Gunn very much, and he wants me to marry him and share his life. It makes us both, most happy. This is a good thing."

Lily, who had finally been accepted by the other children, was happy for the teacher. Soon, she was moving to a ranch and live with Sara and her brothers. Sara and Mrs. Williams had taught her how to clean herself properly and had shown her how to care for her new dresses. She was happy now, and she wanted to thank her teacher for everything. Timidly, she stood and smiled at Beth. "Thank you, ma'am. You are my friend, forever."

Beth could feel her tears at the back of her eyes, as they threatened to spill over.

A tall boy, in the back of the room, stood and quietly said what Beth knew many of the townspeople were thinking. "You're gonna have a babe. He gonna care fer it?"

She cleared her throat, and stiffened her spine. "That's really between Ranger Gunn and myself. However, I will tell you—so that you may tell your ma—that we'll be a very happy family."

School was dismissed and Beth couldn't wait to get to the hotel and meet up with Mary. They had wedding plans to make. She didn't really know how they were going to plan a wedding, with her being "widowed" and with a bun in the oven, but she absolutely *refused* to be married in black.

Mary immediately grasped Beth's hands. "I am so terribly happy, I can't begin to tell you how much. Finally, I'll have a sister, and you're just the very one I want. How lucky is that? I want you to know, I think my brother is the luckiest man in Arizona, with maybe the exception of my David," she giggled. She led Beth over to the settee, to get her off her feet, remembering when she was pregnant, how quickly she tired.

"The first thing I want to say is … I *refuse* to let you marry my brother while wearing widow's weeds! We need to go to the mercantile and pick out something appropriate, and with all the trimmings. Do you sew?"

"Of course, don't you?"

Mary looked a little embarrassed. "I embroider fancy flowers, and that's about all. I'll do all the trimmings, if you can sew the dress. Will that work? We have only two weeks!"

Beth was incapable of sitting and taking it easy. "I'm so excited about marrying Vernon, I could stay up all night and have my dress ready to wear by morning!" The two women laughed, heartily. It was turning out to be a wonderful day.

The ladies spent what was left of the afternoon, sitting in the hotel lobby, enjoying little cakes and glasses of cold lemonade while they made their plans. Flowers, a guest list, and a cake, if they could find one, were to be discussed. It was all so pleasant, until the honorable Mayor Applebaum decided to stop by for a visit.

Upon seeing the two lovely ladies, he puffed out his enormous chest and stroked his greasy hair back from his face.

"There you are. The two most beautiful women in Tucson, and I find you both, gathered together, under one roof. How fortunate." He slithered over to where the two women sat, trying to ignore his arrival.

"My dear, dear Beth." He reached for her hand, but not before she succeeded in tucking it in her pocket. Clearly annoyed, he asked, "What's this I hear about you getting married? Say it isn't so, fair lady." He whispered, in a menacing tone, "I thought you and I had an understandin'. Mr. Gunn might be interested to know of all the evenin's we spent together … alone." He smirked while raising one brow.

"How dare you … you skunk!" Beth jumped to her feet and stared at him, eye to eye. "You can tell him anything you choose, but he'll consider the source, and spit in your beady little eye! You're a polecat dressed up like a politician and you're not good enough to shine his boots—or mine either, for that matter. Good day to you, Mayor!"

Applebaum grabbed Beth by her upper arm in a tight, bruising grip, showing surprising strength. "Madam! Beware of whom you anger and of whom you make an enemy. I can be of great assistance to my friends, and I can be quite treacherous to those I choose to punish." He glared daggers at the bold young woman.

Placing her small hand firmly upon the mayor's pudgy fist, Mary pressed her nails just hard enough to get his attention, and spoke volumes with her flashing eyes.

Without saying a word, he dropped his hold on Beth. Perspiration popped out on his forehead. He knew all about the half-breed's husband, and he didn't want to rile him. He was a politician, after all, not a gunslinger. The mayor, wisely, took two steps back.

The two ladies rose with their noses in the air, looking as if something in the room smelled offensive, and quickly left the premises. Together, they stomped off down the street toward the Mercantile, and find refuge from the irritating little man.

"You were amazing, Beth! You really told him a thing or two," Mary giggled. "I'm so proud of you, and Vernon will absolutely howl with pleasure. David and I never did like that man. He's a pompous ass. Did you notice how he was perspiring? His hair absolutely reeks. Is that bear grease on his head? What an awful little toad, he is."

"*You* were the amazing one, Mary. I saw your eyes. I sure hope I never give you reason to stare at me, like that."

"It's a Cherokee thing."

They both laughed. Beth reached out for Mary's hand and the two women continued on down the sidewalk. Now, the true fun could begin.

"Look over here, Beth," Mary called out. "These ribbons and lace are beautiful and very fine, indeed. Look at all the colors! Oh my, this blue would look heavenly with your eyes. You know, I always wanted blue or green eyes, instead of these brown ones. They're so common," Mary lamented.

Beth was taken aback. "Common? Your eyes? Obviously you haven't spent much time staring at yourself in a looking glass. Your eyes are truly unusual with their cinnamon coloring. They flash with hints of red, gold, and copper flakes. I've never seen any others quite like them. I bet if you ask your handsome husband what he thinks about your *common eyes*, he'll laugh his head off, right before he kisses you senseless for being so silly." She chuckled at the thought of it.

"Look at these bolts of fabric, Mary. They're lovely. I'm surprised that Tucson has this quality available to it."

Beth turned to the owner of the store and said, "I must compliment you, Mr. Jones, on your inventory. It's just as nice as the stores back in Richmond. You deserve to be commended, and I will shop here often."

"Richmond? You're from Richmond?" Mary asked innocently. "I always wondered where you were from, but you never said, and I didn't want to pry. You know, occasionally, you have this soft southern drawl to your diction. It's lovely."

Mary walked over to look at the fabrics Beth had been admiring, but Beth was no longer seeing their beauty. She'd said too much. *How could she have been so careless?* She needed to be more careful. All this time, she had avoided telling anyone where she lived prior to moving here. She prayed nothing would come of this information … not now. Not now, when she was so close to getting everything she wanted.

Mary suggested the rich, royal blue, thin wool. It was soft, lightweight, and would last for years. Beth would be able to remove some of the wedding finery from it and wear it to many dressy occasions in the future. "What do you think, Beth?"

"What?" She'd let her mind wander. "Oh, yes, that's pretty. I'll buy that one," she muttered, unenthusiastically.

Mary was puzzled by the sudden change that had come over her friend. What brought it on, she wondered? They had been discussing Richmond, when Beth went pale and lost her desire for shopping. Mary would discuss it with David. Something was not right, and she learned back in Missouri, if it didn't feel right, chances are, there was more to it, than met the eye. She loved Beth and wanted her to be happy, but she loved her brother, as well, and he deserved to know of any trouble, that Beth may be involved in, or if there was something she was running away from. Hopefully, it would prove to be nothing.

By suppertime, when they all gathered together around the dining room table, Beth was feeling much better. Sara was excited and eager to tell everyone about her new puppies.

Vernon's coloring deepened as he gazed at all the smiling faces staring back at him. "It seems that Sara couldn't decide which puppy deserved to be taken home, and she got so fretful about leaving one behind, that David and I gave in. We decided that both of the girls should have their own best friend. Of course, Rosie doesn't know a puppy from a guppy, but that makes no difference. It made my niece real happy. So, that's the way of it."

The women tried to stifle their laughter behind their hands, and abruptly turned their faces away.

"*My* puppy is the smartest one," Sara piped up. "He's fat with a black nose and eyebrows. His ears stick up and his tale has a white tip on the end. He's mostly red and papa says he's going to grow really, really, big." She giggled to the point of choking on her cookie and had to take a drink of milk.

"I want a really big dog. He's a boy puppy, so I'm gonna call him Bear! Don't you think that's a good name, Uncle Vernon?"

"Yep, he looks like a big red bear to me. Tell everyone about Rosie's puppy, Sara."

"Oh, yes," she said excitedly, clapping her little hands together. "She's a girl puppy and she's Bear's best friend. She's red too, only she has a pink nose and her ears are floppy. She has a black tip on her tail and three white feet. Rosie's gonna love her very much. We'll sleep with them in our beds, huh Mama?"

"In your beds?" Mary's eyes grew round. "I don't think so, darling. Maybe on the floor, next to your beds, would be acceptable. What are you naming Rosie's puppy, dear?"

Sara's eyes lit up and she announced proudly, "FANCY GARTER!"

Vernon spewed his coffee down the front of his white shirt, the twins fell out of their chairs and went rolling across the floor, while Mary's usually composed face was horrified at the pronouncement. She looked around the dining room to see who might have overheard.

David was laughing so hard, tears were rolling down his cheeks. Oh how priceless these moments were, he thought. His daughter was always a surprise and such a blessing to their family.

Beth, trying to keep her composure, looked at Sara glowing with happiness over the beautiful name she had selected so carefully, for her sister's pup. "That's truly a special name, Sara, but it's a mouthful for little Rosie to say. Would it be all right if she called her dog, Fancy?"

Sara wrinkled her forehead, while deep in thought, and then after thinking it over, she nodded. "Yes, I think that would be fine, if she whispered her *real* name to the puppy, now and then." Problem solved.

The children retired early, with the boys taking Sara's chubby hand and leading her up to their rooms. Rosie was fast asleep in her Uncle Vernon's arms, and he couldn't have been happier. Vernon discovered he was quite relaxed holding an infant, and decided it was all in preparation for his own little bit of humanity, coming into this world.

Beth was staring wistfully at the man she loved, when he broke the silence.

"The funniest thing has been happening at the Ranger's Office. While I've been out, lollygagging around, the Wanted posters have been pouring in. There was this murder, committed months ago, and the police were looking for a man by the name of Ryan Beaufort. Turns out, after all the posters had been sent to every ranger and sheriff's office in the country—here's the good part—it seems the man turns out to be a woman!" He shook his head as if he couldn't believe it. "If that don't beat all.

Them folks in Richmond don't know a man from a woman, I reckon." He laughed. "That wouldn't happen out here, in the Arizona Territory."

Mary glanced over at Beth, and saw her friend looking as if she were going to get sick at the table, and became alarmed. "Darling, you're obviously not well. Close your eyes and relax. Vernon, dampen the napkin in your water glass and place it at the back of her neck. David, pay the bill." Mary quickly gathered up their things and began to move Beth to their private rooms.

"No, I'm better now. Please, don't make a fuss. I just need to lie down." Beth looked up at Vernon's concerned face. "Take me home? I'm sorry for all this trouble."

"Of course, sweetheart. I'll take you, right now. Was it somethin' you ate?"

Vernon stood and gently gathered Beth in his arms. She felt his strong muscles flex with great strength as he picked her up and carried her out to their waiting wagon. Something told her she needed to store this feeling away in her memory, because very soon, her world would once again, come crashing down around her. She started to cry.

Vernon saw her to her door and kissed her gently on her lips. "Love, is there anything I can do for you? You seem to be more distressed about something, than actually ill. Did I say something or did David?"

"Not now, Vernon. It's more horrible than you can possibly imagine, and I simply haven't the strength to talk about it now. But I promise you; I will not force you to marry me. You must know the truth, and the whole truth, of who I really am and the circumstances that brought me here. It's most important that you know the dark secrets I keep to myself, before we wed—but I need to lie down now. Please, darling. Give me just a little more time?"

Vernon trusted her. He'd never again, make the mistake of jumping to the wrong conclusions. If the woman he loved, needed more time, then he'd see that she received it.

He nodded his head. "Sleep on it tonight and we'll discuss it tomorrow. Just remember I love you and nothing you've done in the past is going to change that. Sweet dreams, angel." He kissed her once more and watched her disappear through the door. After he heard the lock click into place, he turned and left, worried about what tomorrow might bring.

By the time Vernon got back to the hotel, David and Mary had retired to their rooms. He decided to take a moment and check on things at the Ranger's Office. He'd been there maybe fifteen minutes before David and Mary surprised him. It was very late for the two of them to come over to talk, and he knew it must be pretty important if they were willing to leave their children alone, at the hotel.

"Barclay, why don't you take a rest and go on out for a walk-about? Stop for a meal or a drink. Come back in about an hour." Vernon didn't have to ask twice. The ranger was gone in a flash.

"This is a surprise. What are you two doing here at this hour? Did you want to collect my half of the check?" He tried to lighten the moment, but he felt like they were going to tell him something he didn't want to hear. "Well, go on. Spill it. I ain't got all night and neither do you. Barclay'll be back soon."

Mary sat in a chair against the wall, obviously wanting to hide from what she was afraid might be the truth. David sat in a chair directly in front of Vernon's desk; always preferring to face problems, head on. "Can we look at that murder poster? The Ryan Beaufort poster?"

Vernon searched through the tall stack on his desk and pulled it out. In fact, he found three different versions and noticed the reward increased with each successive printing. "What's this all about, pardner? There ain't no picture. Just a description."

"Dear God, Vernon, I hope nothin'. I hope we've jumped to some ugly and unfair conclusions. I'd rather you be mad at us for speculatin', than to have it pan out to be factual.

"Mary was with Beth today. Beth let it slip that she was from Richmond. When she realized Mary took notice, she went pale and lost interest in what they were doin'. If you think about it, she's tried very hard to keep her past hidden, even from the three of us. She's mysteriously found herself with child, but wasn't married. She reacts strangely when people mention the father of her child. Beth gets nervous at the talk of the Wanted Posters, and if you remember back, she got upset and almost swooned when she first heard the name, Ryan Beaufort. There's more here than first meets the eye, and it deserves some investigatin'—for both yer sakes." David waited for Vernon's response.

Vernon brought his hands together under his chin. He needed to think. His sister and brother-in-law were well intentioned, he knew, but did he dare risk alienating Beth, once again, by delving into her past? He didn't know what to do, but much of what David said, had caused him to wonder. Hell, if he were honest with himself, he'd admit he'd been thinking along those same lines, for quite some time. Only tonight, she had admitted there was something very serious in her past that might prevent their marrying.

Letting out a long sigh, Vernon looked up at his family. "Beth and I are riding out to the Rockland's tomorrow. We're gonna take a lunch and talk about all of this. I'll get the answers I need. We'll hash it all out, if we have to stay there 'til nightfall. Then, after I'm satisfied, you two will be satisfied, as well. Yes?"

Mary was the first to agree. "Yes, oh yes, Vernon. We love Beth and we want only what's best for both of you."

"Good, 'cause I do, too."

Vernon waved them out and rested his head on his desk.

# CHAPTER EIGHT

It promised to be a glorious day. The air smelled clean and fragrant under a brilliant blue sky sprinkled with white wispy clouds. The birds swirled their patterns high into the sky, waiting for the updraft to carry them higher still. The sun smiled down on Tucson, this day, and upon all its inhabitants.

Vernon arrived promptly at ten o'clock in the morning to take Beth for their picnic out among the magnificent painted rocks. He wanted to share with her the vivid colors of the desert. He hoped she would appreciate the awesome grandeur, he so admired. Vernon loved Arizona and he wanted her to love it, too.

When Beth descended the stairs, it was quite obvious, to Vernon, that she'd had little sleep the night before. Looking pale, with red and blue smudges under her sad eyes, she attempted to smile. It broke his heart to know that something was troubling her so. Beth was a fragile, gentle soul, and he wanted to protect her, always. Smiling, he approached and offered her his arm.

"I know I look a fright, Vernon. I apologize," Beth whispered low. "I do want to spend the day with you." She cleared her throat, looking quite frightened. "I want to spend the rest of my life with you, but you may find that impossible after hearing what I have to tell you, today."

Vernon felt her shiver in his arms. "For right now, angel, let's enjoy this beautiful day God has made for us. It's a long ride out to the Rocklands. Let's relax and think only of our wonderful future together," Vernon said, trying to reassure her. He placed his hands around her waist and carefully lifted her up onto the buggy. "I love you, ma'am. Don't be frightened."

Vernon walked around to the other side, hopped up and took his seat next to Beth. Picking up the reins, he snapped them and the bay jumped to, taking them off at a low and leisurely pace.

As Vernon spoke of the desert, Beth started to see it through his eyes. She agreed with him, when he pointed out the beauty of this rugged and barren land. It really wasn't barren at all. He drew to her attention, the magnificent cacti blooming all around them. They were so colorful and pretty, but dangerously prickly. There were great expanses of grasslands with purple mountains rising up in the distance. He pointed out snakes, lizards, and all sorts of critters with whom she was unfamiliar. A particular favorite, of Vernon's, was the bird that ran swiftly across the sand. One of the things that struck Beth was the fact that so much of this wilderness was beautiful and deadly at the same time. The prettier it was, the more lethal it seemed to be.

Some of the rock formations were blood red, while others were swirled with tans and shades of cream. Beth had to admit, the view was magnificent. They rode on for several hours, never speaking of the reason for this outing, but simply enjoying each other's company and the glorious scenery.

Eventually, they came upon an area close to the river, shaded by small trees dotting the landscape. Imposing cliffs with rock shelves hung out over the gurgling waters and creek beds, creating a tunnel effect. It looked cool and secluded, and very inviting.

"This is it, angel. We'll stop here, have our lunch, and rest a bit." This was where he would ask her to reveal her secret. "If you want, you can stick your pretty little feet in the water, down by the creek. It'll help you cool off some." He grinned like a naughty little boy. "I promise I won't look." *And if she believed that ...*

Vernon helped Beth spread out the blanket, and placed the food basket over to one side. He slowly moved his hands across her shoulders and gently coaxed her to lie back, beneath him.

"Oh Beth, my sweet angel. I've wanted to do this all morning." Vernon leaned down and tasted her soft lips. She eagerly anticipated his kiss and opened her lips automatically.

His tongue tangled with her own, feeling the smooth interior of her mouth, sampling her sweetness.

The ranger's large hands began to explore the silky flesh found just inside Beth's bodice, when she suddenly pulled back, took a deep breath, and stopped him in his tracks.

"Stop, Vernon. Please. If you continue to kiss me, I'll never find the strength to do this. It's the hardest thing I've ever had to do in my life, but I love you too much, and it must be done.

"Just as you had the right to know about the baby, and the fact that I wasn't married to his father, you have the right to know the circumstances surrounding his conception. You also need to know what resulted from that union—but I warn you—it's ugly and violent and you may never speak to me again, but that's the risk I must take. It's the biggest gamble of my life. You have to know everything before I can marry you.

"Sit back, Vernon, darling, for this is a long and ugly story. After I've told you everything, you'll have a big decision to make, and I want you to know, whatever you decide, I will support that decision and I will always love you."

"I was born, Ryann Beaufort, in Richmond, Virginia and lived there all my life, until last September, when I was forced to leave and hide from all who knew me.

"My father was the best man I ever knew. He was honest and loyal, a truly decent man. He was a physician, but never became a rich one. You see … he cared too much for his fellow man to worry about money. My mother would often times scold him, when he refused payment for curing a sick child, knowing the parents had little food on their table. In the meantime, we would be eating bread and cheese, ourselves." She smiled, remembering. "But it was a wonderful childhood. I loved my parents very much.

"I learned so much from the two of them. My father taught me math, science and even history and Latin. My mother was musical and made sure I understood music and appreciated it as much as she did. She had been a great singer, until she met my father. They were devoted to each other, to the very end.

"One horrible night, a fire swept through the hospital. My father refused to leave until all the patients had been safely removed. He made it out. My mother was waiting for him with coffee and a clean coat. They were embracing, happy to be alive, when the wall, they were standing in front of, collapsed on them." Beth caught her breath, and tried her very best not to sob. "They died in each other's arms, and left me very much alone."

She paused, staring at the massive rock formations surrounding her, perhaps expecting to draw upon their strength. It was difficult recalling the pain and desolation she felt, at such a vulnerable age.

Vernon couldn't tell what she was thinking, but he decided to give her time to continue with her thoughts.

Still staring off into the distance, Beth continued. "I was fifteen and unprepared to live on my own. We didn't own our home and soon the bank asked me to find a relative to live with. Of course, I explained, I had none. Therefore, I was forced to look for employment. Luckily, the Colonel's daughter, at Fort Clark, needed music and voice lessons, of which I was more than qualified to teach. The fact that I was a young lady was a benefit, as well.

"The war had just started and I was terrified. A very nice man, the brother of Horace Doolittle, actually, owned a little boarding house close to the hospital. He knew my father. I asked him how much a room would cost, and he lent me a pretty one, for almost nothing. He told me he owed my father more than he could ever repay, and the least he could do for him, was to give me shelter." She sniffed, wiping her eyes on her sleeve. "Harry is a good and loyal friend.

"Things were going ahead, the way they do, day in and day out, when the war started to turn against us. The town was in a panic most of the time. The Colonel's daughter no longer needed voice lessons. He was gone on a campaign when he took a musket ball to the head. I needed to find other employment. There's not much for a young girl to do, in time of war. I did whatever would pay the rent … rolling bandages, carrying food trays, helping in the hospital, in any way I could. They paid me in Confederate dollars, and it wasn't much. We almost starved." She took a breath.

"Weren't you in the war, Vernon?"

He nodded. "I never enlisted, but as my brother-in-law discovered, a man isn't allowed to sit out a war. It will find him no matter how hard he tries to avoid it. I fought in Kentucky, along with our boys in gray, but I never enlisted. I knew it was a lost cause. The first chance I got, at the end of '64, I headed for the Arizona Territory. I refused to die and be planted back there, when a life awaited me out here. What did you do after the war, angel?"

"When I was a little older," Beth said, "I did some nursing for the soldiers. I continued to live at the Doolittle, in Richmond."

She shook her head slowly. "Just think. I still live at the Doolittle." She giggled softly, to herself.

"Men started paying attention to me. They said I was pretty and they wanted to court me. I didn't have the time or the inclination, but I did go to a dance at Fort Clark, once. A girlfriend of mine, Libby, begged me to go with her. She loaned me a dress and fixed my hair. I must say, I was surprised when I saw my reflection in the glass.

"It was a purely, magical night. The young officers were all so attractive and polite—even if they were Yankees," she grinned. "I met a lot of ladies that I would have liked to have known better, but one lieutenant, in particular, paid more attention to me than all the rest."

Vernon's stomach tensed. "Lieutenant?"

"He was tall and handsome in a ruthless sort of way, with dark hair, dark eyes, and a neatly trimmed, black mustache. I always wondered about his dark coloring, as his father is fair, like me. I remember he was muscular with strong features and cruel lips. He leered at me, all evening. He danced me around the room several times, always acting the gentleman, until it was time for us all to leave. He offered to escort me home. When I refused his offer, he insisted and would not be dissuaded. He gave me his jacket, for the weather had turned cool, and he took me in his carriage to my home. The way he stared at me, made me extremely uncomfortable, but he didn't do anything overtly threatening.

"I was surprised to see him waiting for me, the next evening, downstairs in the lobby. He offered to take me to dinner. I politely refused, but he insisted, and took me by my arm and led me, once again, to his carriage. He tried to kiss me on the ride back, but I had never been kissed and I certainly didn't want my first kiss coming from a man I didn't like. I was successful at turning my face away to avoid his lips.

"As we pulled up in front of the Doolittle, I told him not to return. I was not interested in seeing him again. As I stepped over him to leave, he grabbed my arms, digging his nails into the flesh above my elbows. He was still smiling, but his lips had grown thin and hard as he hissed, *'We'll see about that.'* I was frightened of him, and that seemed to excite him even more."

* * *

*The lieutenant reluctantly let Miss Beaufort out of his carriage. No matter what she'd said, he would return and see to it that she paid for her haughty attitude. Who did she think she was? He was the son of a U. S. Senator. She was a pretty little chit and nothing more.*

*"Good evenin', Missy. You look a little worried. Is there anythin' old Harry can help you with?"*

*Ryann shook her head, too upset to speak. She covered her arms with her shawl, so he would not see the purple welts she knew would be visible. She vowed she would never see that awful man again, so there was no use in getting anyone else involved in her problems. The young woman ran up the stairs and locked the door.*

*After stripping off her dress and underthings, Ryann scrubbed her face and her arms until they glowed red. She felt the need to purge his hateful touch from her body. Donning her softest nightgown, she crawled into bed, feeling a little better. Ryann would just have to be careful not to run into the man, in the future. Surely, he would give up, in time.*

*Several days went by, uneventfully, and for that, she was thankful. She began to relax and let down her guard. "Mr. Doolittle, I would like to walk to the library before it closes. Would you watch for my friend, Libby, and ask her to wait? I promise not to be long, as I only want to drop off this book."*

*"That ain't no problem at all, Missy. You be careful now."*

*The library wasn't far, but Ryann was woolgathering on her way. She was recalling seeing President Lincoln, when he came to Richmond. He was much taller than she had thought he would be, and he looked so very weary. Even though she approved of Jefferson Davis, as president, it was good to see Mr. Lincoln, and she remembered he had kind eyes. Just ten days later, he was killed, shot by an actor in Ford's Theatre. How sad, she sighed.*

*Ryann had just passed the Tobacco Emporium when two very strong and hurtful hands grabbed her from behind. She shrieked as the man placed one hand across her mouth and whispered in her ear.*

*"Shut the hell up or I'll drag you into this alley and break your lovely, little neck ... and it's such a pretty, delicate neck. You're coming with me, my dear, where we can get to know each other better."*

*Ryann recognized the voice as that belonging to the lieutenant. She struggled, but she was no match for his strength. She was terrified, but couldn't scream loudly enough to draw anyone's attention. The sidewalks were almost abandoned and she knew she had no choice but to go along with him. Maybe if she didn't fight him, he would let her go.*

*The brutal man twisted her arm up behind her back, while he forced her to his waiting carriage. Her arm felt as if it were going to break. For the first time, Ryann noticed how his carriage was totally enclosed, giving them too much privacy. He snapped the reins and tore off down the street, heading out of town.*

*About a half hour later, she discovered they were in a rural section, with no people, no shops, not even any houses within sight. Ryann's fear intensified. The lieutenant turned off the road and headed down a seldom traveled, dirt path. At the end of the path, was a shack, in deplorable condition. Her abductor drew up the reins and the carriage stopped. The man reached in and grabbed Ryann by her arm, pulling her out and shoving her to the ground.*

*"Well, pet. Now I'll show you how to treat a lover. If you don't do exactly as I say, I can not be held responsible for your punishment." He chuckled a strange and crazy kind of snicker. He was clearly mad. With his boot, he kicked the heavy wooden door open and dragged her inside, leaving her on the filthy floor.*

*He went directly to a small, dirty table, and retrieved a small brown bottle from his pocket. Turning his back to Ryann, he swallowed some of the contents. A minute passed before he turned back around with a new sense of vigor.*

*"You're so pretty and sweet. I like my women sweet." He*

*smelled her neck, and then with obvious approval, he dragged his tongue up the side of it, licking all the way to her ear. "No sluts for me. I like my women innocent. I know you want me to teach you how to be a real woman, don't you, pet?" He forced her face to look up into his, bruising her cheeks with his calloused thumbs.*

*Ryann noticed his eyes had become strange and glassy and his breath smelled odd. She'd seen such eyes, while working in the hospital. He forced his thumb into her mouth, rubbing along the inside of her cheek. It tasted dirty and sour. He groaned with pleasure. Then, he pressed his lips against hers with such force he hit her tooth, cutting her lip.*

*This was not the kiss that Ryann had dreamed about, all her life, but an assault on her. She gagged when he forced her to open wide while he rammed his fat tongue deep into her mouth, almost to the back of her throat. She had the urge to bite down, but suddenly, overcome with laughter, he released her.*

*"That was your first kiss, wasn't it? Did you enjoy it? No matter. You will, in time. You see, I've taken a liking to you, and I intend to see you as often as I can. If you don't cooperate, I'll just take you, as I did today, and no one will ever see you again."*

*The lieutenant grabbed her by her hair and jerked her off balance, causing Ryann to fall to her knees, in front of him. Still smiling, he said, "It isn't wise to fight me, girlie. It actually excites me more and sometimes I lose control. You wouldn't like that, I assure you. I really don't want to hurt you, I just want you to cry out a little, and maybe be just a bit afraid. Don't ever forget. I'm in control of whether you live or not."*

*Then, suddenly, he let her go, allowing her to fall the rest of the way to the floor.*

*Ryann noticed her knees were bleeding. Walking over to the table, the lieutenant poured himself a drink from a glass decanter. It was obvious the man had used this shack before today. Had he brought other girls here? Ryann wondered. If so, what did he do to them? She began to tremble violently.*

*"Now, stand up and unbutton your blouse. I want to see those titties," he commanded.*

*Her eyes grew wild with fear. She couldn't remove her top. She wouldn't do that. With shaking hands, she covered her bosoms instead, gripping her blouse more tightly together. Ryann didn't expect the sharp sting that landed across her face and brought tears to her eyes.*

*"Come now, pet. No false modesty, please. I know you want me to see them, to taste them. Now! I want to see them, now!" he screamed. The lieutenant rushed over and grabbed her blouse by the neck, yanking it down in one swift movement. The buttons flew across the small room. He reached in and ripped her chemise open, leaving her breasts totally exposed.*

*"Little, aren't they?" he scowled. "I like 'em bigger and darker. Oh well, I guess a man can't have everything. At least, you're a virgin. You are, aren't you?"*

*Ryann didn't know how she wanted to answer him. If she said the wrong thing, he might hurt her even more than he already had. She stammered the truth, "Yes ... yes sir, I am."*

*"Come here!"*

*She slowly stepped toward him, noticing the strangeness of his eyes, almost diabolical. He grasped the hem of her skirt and threw it up, catching it with his other hand. He swiftly put his free hand inside her drawers and touched her private woman's place. Ryann screamed in shock. His fist tightened on her soft mound, causing extreme pain.*

*"There will be no more of that, you little cry baby. I'm going to touch you in any manner I see fit, and you have nothing to say about it. Remember? Now spread your legs for me. I want to make sure for myself that you're what you profess to be. You must be untouched."*

*After feeling her feminine spot and squeezing her breasts to the point of pain, he released her and announced that he had an engagement. He was going to return her back to her hotel.*

*The lieutenant cupped her chin in his nasty fingers and forced her to look at his face, closely. "Listen to what I say, pet. I'm taking you back, now. I trust you not to say a word to anyone about our little rendezvous. If you tell that senile old man about me, or what we do here, I'll have him killed and it will be your fault. The same can be said about that stupid, Libby. Don't make that mistake. You can't hide from me and you can't go to the authorities. My father owns them." He snorted, loudly. "At least he's good for something."*

*He pulled her clothes together and provided her a shawl, with which to cover herself. She had no idea who it had belonged to, and that frightened her all the more*

*Once out in the carriage, they travelled extremely fast, back to the heart of the city. As the carriage pulled up in front of the Doolittle, the lieutenant grabbed Ryann's chin and forced her face up, toward his own. Caring nothing for her pleasure, he brutally kissed her mouth, bruising her lips and making her cry out in pain.*

*"Don't make me mad, Ryann. I am not a nice man when I get angry. You won't see me for a couple of days, pet. I must ride out with my company, but I'll return in time to escort you to a gathering of officers and their wives and fiancés. As you are mine, I will take you. Do something about your wardrobe and hair. I don't like being embarrassed. Now, get out—and remember—not a word."*

*Ryann ran through the doors, not stopping to talk to the friendly Harry Doolittle. She clutched the shawl so tightly, her knuckles turned white ... neither was there a drop of color on her face. She ran for the stairs and didn't stop until she was safely inside her room and the door was securely bolted.*

*Harry wasn't blind. Something bad had happened to this precious girl. He hadn't seen her leave, and he didn't catch the identity of the man who let her out of his carriage. The carriage, however, was plenty identifiable. It was a strange one. He would look into it. Harry knew Ryann had seen that Army lieutenan,t a time or two. If he found out that some damn skunk had taken advantage of Missy Beaufort, he'd call in the police. It was up to him to protect her ... and protect her, he would.*

*Ryann was up all night, vomiting into the chamber pot. She'd never been so scared in her entire life, and she had no idea where to turn for help.*

*For two days, she refused to leave her room. Mr. Doolittle brought up her meals; after she told him she was too ill to go down to the dining room. Libby called twice, but Ryann couldn't take the chance that the evil officer would carry through with his threat to hurt her best friend, so she refused to see her. What was she going to do?*

*Saturday, after lunch, Ryann was startled by a knock at her door. She'd been dozing, trying to catch up on some badly needed sleep. "Yes?" she asked, drowsily.*

*"It's me, Missy. There's a gentleman down in the lobby. Says you're goin' to an event at Fort Clark this evenin'. He's brung you a gift. I'll leave it out here, fer you. He says to tell you, he'll pick you up at six o'clock, sharp. Shall I tell him you're too ill? I can get rid of him fer you."*

*"No! I mean, don't talk to him ... I mean ... tell him I'll meet him at six. Please be polite, Mr. Doolittle."*

*Only after the old man left, did Ryann slowly open her door. There was an enormous box sitting in the hall. She brought it inside, and quickly bolted the door.*

*The box just sat there, on the bed, looking ominous and threatening. Ryann couldn't take her eyes from it. Its wrappings were expensive and concealed the vile nature of the gift. She had been shaking violently for the last hour. He was back. The monster had come for her. What was she to do? How could she get away from him? Maybe if she went to Fort Clark and confided in another officer, he might leave her alone. Yes, that's what she would do. He'd never endanger his military career for her. She felt some relief, and curiosity made her open the box.*

*Inside, were many layers of tissue paper. It was beautiful paper. Only the finest clothing from France was wrapped in such a manner. She gasped when she saw the lovely creation folded neatly in the bottom of the box. It was a white gown with lace and sparkling crystals sewn onto the bodice. It was truly fit for a princess. Also enclosed, was a card. Written in a masterful scrawl, was a message from the Mad Lieutenant, as she was now beginning to think of him. "Wear this, my pet. You'll be the most beautiful one there. You'll make me proud. Don't forget your hair." It was left unsigned.*

*Ryann looked at her mother's mantel clock. It was four in the afternoon, leaving her only two hours to dress. With her plan firmly in mind, she dressed quickly and found she was anxious to see it through. This time, tomorrow, he'd no longer be a threat to her or her friends.*

*At promptly six o'clock, Ryann was downstairs waiting in the lobby for the lieutenant. The dress fit perfectly and she'd managed to draw her hair up, allowing some curls to cascade behind one ear. She thought she looked quite nice, but when she saw the look of disgust on his face, she knew she had failed.*

*Lieutenant Price smiled, but his eyes were threatening and promised retribution. Leaning his face close to her ear, he whispered, "I thought I told you to fix your hair. You chose to disobey me, and you will be punished. It was important to me that you not embarrass me in front of my friends."*

*He politely offered his arm and gently led Ryann to his carriage. He acted the gentleman, even though she knew he wasn't pleased.*

*Old Harry took notice of the young officer. He saw the way the man claimed Ryann for himself, and noticed the fear in her eyes. This man was the controlling sort and had a look of danger about him. Harry would wait for her return.*

*The formal affair was quite wonderful, actually. The officers and their ladies looked so handsome and so very beautiful. There was music, and flowers and lots of food. The men all laughed, demonstrating their camaraderie with one another.*

*As wonderful as it all was, it was necessary for Ryann to get off by herself, if she were to find help. However, the lieutenant seemed to have other plans, and never let her step away, not even for an instant. Several wives approached them and asked if Ryann might join them in the ladies' retiring room? That's when women talked and got to know each other.*

*Lieutenant Price, looking love-struck, patted her arm and declined to give his permission. "I cannot possibly be separated from my fiancé for even those few minutes, ladies. You understand." He smiled, turning on his considerable charm, and making the ladies practically swoon. One lady even told Ryann how fortunate she was to have such a caring and loving man.*

*This was not going according to plan, Ryann thought. Real panic was growing inside her. The dance was drawing to a close, and it was almost time to leave. The lieutenant had never let her step away, even for a moment. She'd have to say something in front of him. She closed her eyes and prayed.*

*"Major Struthers, I have a problem." She winced as she felt the lieutenant's nails dig into her flesh. The heat from his body was scorching her side, but she bravely, continued on. "Lieutenant Price is under the false notion that I am going to marry him. I ... "*

*The lieutenant laughed loudly and pulled her closer to him.*

*"Now dear, don't bother the major with our little disagreements." He smiled apologetically at the older officer. "We can't agree on a wedding date, sir, and she is, therefore, saying we may not marry at all. Women! What do you do with them, sir?"*

*"No!" she screamed. "No, sir. I am deathly afraid of this man. He's cruel and violent to me. Please, save me, sir." Her eyes registered extreme fear, and she pulled back from the lieutenant's brutal grip.*

*The major noticed her extreme reaction. "What's going on, lieutenant? This girl is genuinely afraid of you. What do you say for yourself?"*

*"Sir, I would like to speak with you in private, if I may. Please, sir."*

*The major glanced around and decided that was probably a wise decision. Looking at Ryann, he said, "Dear, I would like for you to come with us. I'll protect you, if you are nervous."*

*The three of them quietly exited the ballroom and found a private alcove where they could talk freely. "Now, lieutenant, explain yourself. It had better be good, for this young woman is truly terrified to be alone with you."*

*The lieutenant took his time. He had the ability of a chameleon, being able to change the look of his face and countenance, on demand. He appeared contrite and slightly embarrassed for his fiancé. He whispered his answer to the major. "This is a very delicate matter, sir. My beautiful fiancé and I were caught up in a moment of passion and we could not stop ourselves. I'm sure you know of what I am speaking. She had never been with a man, naturally, and I am larger than most. It was quite painful for her."*

*He stopped and looked so sorrowful at Ryann, she almost believed his lies. "I apologized, over and over again. It broke my heart to have caused her such pain, but she is being unreasonable. I promised her it would not be painful again, but she doesn't believe me. We wanted to be married before we made love, but we were foolish. I still wish to marry her, sir. Now that she has been compromised, I must marry her. Talk to her, sir. Convince her of my love for her," he pleaded.*

*Ryann knew he had won. Who wouldn't believe him? She was just a hysterical virgin, having lain with her handsome fiancé and now regretting it. What was she to do?*

*"Sir, I need to go to the ladies room while you two men speak with one another. May I be excused?"*

*"Of course dear. Take your time. You need to compose yourself, as I believe you are somewhat hysterical, just now. We'll wait for you in the ballroom."*

*Ryann gave a little curtsy to the major and ignored the lieutenant. She had to put as much distance, as she possibly could, between the two of them, and as quickly as she could. She was on foot, so she hoped to find a good hiding place, a place where she could stay until he had given up looking for her.*

*She ran down the steps and across the parade grounds. She looked for safety behind the animal livery. She ran to the smokehouse, but it was locked. She found the laundry locked, as well. There was a root cellar, not too far away. She ran as far as her slippered feet could carry her. With great relief, she discovered the door was not bolted. She lifted the door and ran down the steps, dropping the door behind her. It was dark and damp in the cellar, and exactly what she needed to hide from the Mad Lieutenant. She squeezed behind the furthest most rack of potatoes and forced her breathing to calm to a steady in and out. She would not give herself away. She waited.*

*"Ryann ... Oh, Ry ... ann. Come out now, dear. It's time for us to leave."*

*She heard his soft footsteps padding across the dirt floor. She'd been hiding for hours, and now, he had discovered her whereabouts. How? What had given her away?*

*"I can smell your scent, you silly goose. Don't you know a man always knows that special fragrance? The intimate scent of his woman?" He stepped closer.*

*Ryann closed her eyes and held her breath. Maybe he was just guessing that she was here.*

*"Ahhgh!" Ryann screamed, as strong hands reached out from the darkness, and closed tightly around her neck, squeezing the very life out of her. She struggled in vain to breathe, as her throat began to swell and catch fire under the assault. The lieutenant placed his thumbs on her windpipe and applied intense pressure.*

*Spots began to form in front of her eyes, and a strange calm settled over her. Ryann could feel herself drifting. He was going to kill her now. She felt consciousness slowly ebb, as her knees buckled, and she slipped quietly to the floor.*

* * *

*Ryann opened her eyes, feeling groggy and her fiery throat was so swollen she could not speak. She looked around, but didn't recognize where she was. It was not the dirty little shack. This was a nice room. It could be in any hotel or maybe a private home. How did she get here, she wondered? Then she noticed something else. She was unclothed under the sheet. She wore not a stitch. As she struggled to sit up, he came in, and stood at the foot of the bed, grinning.*

*"You were extremely naughty last night, my dear. Why did you have to embarrass me that way? We could have had a nice evening ... just you and I ... but no. You had to make up lies and try to get me in trouble with my superiors. That was very bad. But it's all right, pet. I'll get my revenge on you, and it shall be sweet. You see, right after I left Fort Clark, without you, I went straight to your hotel and asked your nice, Mr. Doolittle, if he'd seen you. I told him you left the dance early, without my protection, and I was concerned for your safety. As far as anyone knows, you behaved impetuously and now you are missing. So I guess I'll just keep you here, for a couple of days, or until I tire of you. It will be our little secret. We'll have fun. You'll see."*

*His hand reached up and undid the first button on his shirt. It was so entertaining to watch Ryann's discomfort increase, as each button revealed a little more of his chest. She could not turn away. He was proud of his muscular physique. He boasted a manly chest covered with a fine net of black hair. His stomach was flat and his hips were narrow. He'd been wounded below his waist, but it was not noticeable. Women thought he was handsome, in the extreme.*

*The lieutenant unbuckled his belt and then unbuttoned his trousers. At that point, he walked over to Ryann and threw back her covering. She closed her eyes, feeling the humiliation of him seeing her naked body. She tried to wiggle enough to provide some coverage, but discovered her ankles were tethered to the bed.*

*"What are you going to do to me?" she asked, horrified.*

*"I'm going to pleasure you, my pet." He slowly proceeded to*

*remove his pants and then came around to her side of the bed. Grasping his male member, in his hand, he ordered her to open her mouth.*

* * *

*It was three days before the lieutenant allowed Ryann to leave. Of course, he recited the same warnings, as before. Don't tell anyone or they would be killed. Don't act suspicious, and she must wait for him to come to her, again. He was not finished with her.*

*Ryann tiptoed silently, into the hotel, hoping that Mr. Doolittle wouldn't hear her. But luck wasn't with her. She gasped, in alarm, as frightened as if he'd been a bear. What was she going to say?*

*The old man did not miss the fear in her eyes or her pathetic overall appearance.*

*"Howdy, little Miss. We've been mighty worried about you. Everthin' all right?"*

*She nodded, not trusting herself to speak. There was the very real danger that she would collapse in front of the old man, putting his life in danger. She was emotionally damaged and physically broken. She couldn't face him, at that moment. Ryann ran up the stairs, taking two at a time, and bolted her door.*

*"That rotten bastard. I'll see that he never touches her again," Harry muttered to himself. "He's hurt her fer sure."*

*Disrobing soon after returning to her room, Ryann threw everything into the woodstove and set it afire. Standing before her looking glass, she stared long and hard at her naked body. She was covered from neck to knee, front to back, with bruises, welts, scratches, and several small burns on her buttocks. Her breasts were covered in vicious bite marks. Her own face was practically unrecognizable. It was puffy and red, with scratches down both cheeks. There was no doubt; she would have to stay in her room for days, before being seen in public.*

*She proceeded to rinse her body off with a cool wet cloth. The Mad Lieutenant had bathed her, but it had only made her feel dirtier. As she tried to lend some comfort to her injured body, with the soft wet cloth, she noticed how the spot between her legs hurt. He had been rough with her, not caring that it was her first time, making her bleed profusely. He took pleasure in the pain he caused her, and bragged about his larger than average size. Sniffling, feeling her eyes fill with unshed tears, Ryann gently placed the cool wetness there, and let it lay upon her irritated flesh, undisturbed. What was she going to do? She started to weep.*

*Twice more, Price came for her. Once, he actually slipped by the desk unnoticed, and dashed up the stairs. She refused to unbolt the door, until he threatened to hurt the people she cared about. Reluctantly, she lifted the bolt and allowed him entry.*

*She knew it would be bad. He had that odd, crazed look in his eyes again, and that awful, sick smell on his breath. He bolted the door and threw her down on the bed. Taking a long knife, out of his coat sleeve, he placed it under her chin.*

*She started to whimper.*

*"That's it, pet. Beg for mercy, and maybe I'll let you live. I'm getting just a little tired of you, you know. You're meek and you give in, all too soon. I want you scared and fighting! He took the point of the knife and ran it down the front of her dress, neatly slicing through several layers of fabric, and leaving a pink trail running down her flesh.*

*"For the love of God, why are you doing this to me? I've never lied to you or done you harm."*

*"Because I want to. I don't like you much. You're a haughty little bitch and you think you're too good for the likes of me. But the truth is, you're just a slut. Exactly like all the rest of 'em. You lead me on, letting me believe that you're something special, but in the end, you're all the same. Now, roll over and put that little bottom of yours up in the air!"*

*She screamed into her pillow, but it did no good. He was a horrible monster and her life wasn't her own. He did what he wanted with her.*

*Later, as he was getting dressed, he decided to leave Ryann with one last thought. "You see this knife, pet? I killed more than a few Johnny Rebs with it. It's tasted a lot of Virginia blood and maybe it will taste it again ... I'll have to think on it. For now, I'm leaving. I know this will make you very sad, but I have to lead my men out for a couple of weeks, and I won't be able to love you, for some time. For that, I'm truly apologetic, but I promise to make it up to you when I return." He smiled a hideous grin, imagining his homecoming, no doubt. "I have something very special planned. It won't kill you, or I don't think it will. You might even enjoy it." He laughed, his eyes crazed by unknown demons.*

*Suddenly, Lieutenant Price grabbed her shoulders and planted a kiss, firmly on her mouth. Then, he did the most unexpected thing. With a sincere look of regret shining in his dark eyes, he murmured softly, into her ear, "I'm truly sorry for all this, pet. If things had only been different—" And then he quickly left, slamming the door behind him.*

*Ryann almost believed him.*

# CHAPTER NINE

*"I'm sorry about this, Mr. Doolittle, but I need to move on, and I thought I would look for work out West. There is sure to be a need for nurses, out there, now that the war is over. I appreciate all you've done for me, here, but I need to go and I need to go this week."*

*Harry could see panic, not excitement in Ryann's eyes. "Missy, I'm gonna come right out and ask it, and I don't want you to fib. Are you a leavin' on account of that lieutenant feller?"*

*Her eyes got as big as saucers. "No. Where did you get that idea? I just need to leave, that's all, and I have to be gone before—" She stopped. "Please don't ask any questions. He's a very dangerous man, and I don't want you hurt. Please promise me you won't tell him about this conversation ... and whatever you do ... don't let him know I told you that I had to disappear before he came back. He'll do terrible things, if you interfere."*

*"That's just as I thought. Dammit! He's been scarin' you and mistreatin' you too, hasn't he? That polecat! I otta' tell his commandin' officer about him. That'd fix him good."*

*"Oh, no! You mustn't. He'll kill you. I think he's killed before. In fact, I'm certain of it." She laid her small hand on top of Harry's in a sign of friendship, and left the lobby, returning to her room. There were plans to make and she needed to hurry.*

*Ryann made a list of all the things that she had to accomplish before he returned. She needed cash. Looking around her room, she made a mental note of what she had that was of any monetary worth. It broke her heart, but she would have to sell the last few remaining possessions she owned, things once belonging to her mother and father. There was the mantel clock of course, and her father's silver watch fob. She couldn't part with the watch.*

*Her mother left her a gold broach, a gift from a French marquis, when she toured Europe. Being a successful singer, she had been given many priceless pieces of jewelry, but sadly, Ryann had sold most of it, already. There was still a matched set of ruby earrings and a rope of pearls that she thought would bring a good price. She would give most of her clothing to the poor, for she needed to travel light. She would sell her father's beloved books to the library. They were always in need of good literature. As she rubbed her hands over their leather bindings, she reminisced about the days when her father would sit reading in the parlor, while her mother sang an aria from the kitchen. These beautiful old volumes were precious to her and were well-loved friends. As her list of items grew longer, her heart broke a little more.*

*It took the better part of two days to sell everything, but Ryann was pleased with the amount of money she'd accumulated. The sum was much greater than she had expected. There was money to buy a train ticket as far as St. Louis. From St. Louis, she would travel, by stage, to Texas, and once there, she'd decide on her final destination.*

*The next item on her list was informing the hospital that she was quitting her job. Hopefully, word of her leaving would not get back to Fort Clark before she was well away.*

*Lastly, it was necessary to settle her debts. She owed Harry twelve dollars for rent. He would put up a fight against accepting it, but she knew if she left it on her bureau, he would eventually find it, and it would be too late for him to return it to her.*

*Maude, at the bakery, had, more than once, given Ryann a few buns when she didn't have the coin. In addition to the buns, Ryann would discover a sweet treat tucked into the bottom of the bag. Hidden beneath the rolls, would be a cookie, a small bit of cake, or some other delectable delight. She never forgot the woman's kindness to her, and wanted to thank her for her generosity. She would give her five dollars.*

*Ryann was still paying the seamstress, down at the Harrison Arms, for the dress and undergarments she had ordered last month. She needed to pay the balance owed. That still left her with quite a bit of money and she figured she would need it when she got to wherever it was she was going.*

*Five days had come and gone. Ryann figured the lieutenant should be away for at least another six days. That provided her with more than enough time to escape his evil clutches. First thing, in the morning, she would go to the train station and pick up her schedule and her ticket. Then, nothing would stop her.*

*Ryann couldn't believe her good fortune. Everything had gone according to plan. She'd soon be on her way, and safe from him. She could breathe easier, now, sitting on her bed with her ticket and train schedule in her hands. She trembled with excitement. Never had she been out of Richmond. Her father often spoke of traveling, but he could never leave some poor soul suffering, while he took a rest.*

*Leaning her head back and closing her eyes, she could just imagine what magnificent sights she would see. First, she would go north, to Washington, and from there, head west. She'd see Ohio and Indiana. In a day or two, she would cross the great Mississippi River and find herself in one of the busiest cities in the country, St. Louis, Missouri. They had everything there and she was going to see it all.*

*The clocked ticked by, and soon, it was time to go downstairs and meet with her friend, Libby. She, like Ryann, had to work for a living. Ryann wasn't certain what it was she did to earn her money, but she didn't care. Libby was sweet and trustworthy and a true friend, indeed. She helped many girls, forced to live on their own.*

*Feeling happy and carefree for the first time in months, Ryann decided to wear her hair down in a casual fashion. It was, perhaps, a style more appropriate for a younger girl, but today, she felt younger than she had in a long time and she was going to wear it in curls down her back, held up and away from her face with a beautiful pearl comb. It had belonged to her mother and she could not part with it. After brushing her hair to a high shine, and dressing in her new, pink-flowered dress, she was ready to take on Richmond, and sadly, say one last goodbye to her best friend.*

*It was an emotional meeting for both women. They had a lovely lunch in a small café, but neither woman could eat much. More than once, a tear would fall. Ryann promised to write and let Libby know where she had finally settled. Maybe, when things had calmed down a bit, Libby would be able to come out for a visit. The thought of that excited them both.*

*All too soon, it was time to leave. With an onslaught of fresh tears and sincere promises to keep in touch, the women parted company. As she walked away, Ryann took one long, look over her shoulder, and tried to ignore the feeling of apprehension rising up inside her. She smiled one last time, at her friend, and returned to the hotel.*

*Upon arriving back at the Doolittle, Ryann noticed Harry was not at his desk. He really needed someone to help him run the boarding house, she thought to herself. Occasionally, the old man had business that forced him to leave the hotel unattended. Oh, well, she couldn't think about that now, she had to finish her packing. Ryan ran up the stairs, unlocked her door and froze in her tracks.*

*Dear God, it couldn't be.*

*Sitting on her bed, looking quite angry and disturbed, sat Lieutenant Price. In his hands, he waved the train schedule and her precious ticket, taunting her. Ryann stumbled backwards, the wooden door jam catching her fall.*

*"Going somewhere, pet?" he snarled. "Do come in and tell me all about it." He patted the bed, next to him, obviously wanting her to sit there, beside him.*

*Ryann started to shake. "No, it can't be," she whispered to herself. Her whole body was weakening. She opened her mouth to scream, but not a sound came forth. There was, after all, no one to hear her cries. Her eyes were swimming in tears as she shook her head back and forth, in disbelief. Back and forth, back and forth, the motion of her head moved violently—until Ryann started to lose hold on reality. The room started to swim, and she felt her knees begin to buckle, as her head struck the edge of the door. After that, she knew nothing.*

*When Ryann opened her eyes, she instantly recalled the horror at discovering the Mad Lieutenant in her room. He knew all her plans. What was she to do now? Without moving her head, she forced her eyes to look about the room. She was still on the floor, and she could feel a sticky substance at the back of her head. It hurt so badly her stomach threatened to heave. She figured she must have struck her head when she fell, and she was still lying where she had collapsed. She could hear his quiet and insane laughter. The officer was enjoying her misery and pain.*

*Noticing Ryann had regained consciousness, the lieutenant ceased his amusement, and had to take a breath before speaking. "I must admit, Ryann, you are entertaining. Too bad I'm running out of patience. While you were taking your nap, I took the liberty of packing your things. You're correct in assuming you're leaving, but your destination has been revised." He slowly tore the train ticket in half and in half again, letting the pieces flutter to the floor, as leaves in an autumn breeze.*

*The room grew cold, as his evil intentions were revealed. "I'm taking you somewhere quiet and remote, Ryann. A place where we won't be disturbed for days or even weeks. It will be delightful for me ... if not for you. Finally, I can do all the things I've wanted to do, and I can take my time about it. No one will be the wiser, since you've already said your goodbyes, and no one will be looking for you. This is absolutely perfect. I feel as if I should be thanking you for all your careful preparations." He smiled a dark and treacherous grin.*

*"Now, get up. We have to leave. Who knows? You might stay there ... permanently," he hissed.*

*In a very small voice, still quivering from shock, Ryann refused to do as he demanded. "No. You're crazy and I want you to leave me alone." She was crying now, on the verge of hysterics.*

*Before Ryann could react, he grabbed her by the hair on her head and forced her to her knees. He twisted the golden locks around his fist and pulled very hard. Ryann was sure her hair was going to rip from her scalp.*

*"There you go again, pet—disagreeing with me. I've told you and I've shown you that your stubbornness only garners you more pain. Why do you insist on being difficult? I know you like a little pain, but really, pet. Next time I punish you, it might be too much for you to bear. It might kill you." He wrinkled his forehead for a moment and actually looked dismayed at the*

*thought of her dying. Anyone, seeing his sympathetic performance, would believe him to be honestly saddened by the whole situation she'd found herself in ... but that was only temporary. Just as quickly, his eyes grew black and void of any sympathy for her, filled instead, with a look of total evil.*

*"Do as I say, if you want to see your friend, Doolittle, sitting back at his desk."*

*"Oh, my God! You didn't hurt him, did you?"*

*"I told you what would happen if you continued to defy me. I know your little friend, Libby, as well. In fact, I think I'll pay her a visit, next."*

*He paused for several seconds, as if he was planning something in his warped mind. A truly frightening smile crossed his features. "Yes, I think I will. Before I kill you, I'll bring Libby to you and let her watch you die—slowly," he giggled. "Then I'll have her just where I had you." He slapped his thigh. "This is working out splendidly." The lieutenant was absolutely giddy.*

*He grabbed up Ryann's bags, both of them, and looked around the room for anything he might have missed. Satisfied he left nothing of value behind, he grabbed Ryann by the arm and forced her through the door. Instead of going down the main staircase, he turned and took her down the back way and out the servant's door. No one would know he'd been there, and the beautiful young woman would have just disappeared, not to be seen or heard from, ever again.*

*Waiting for them in the alley, was his dreaded carriage, looking more like a conveyance of death than a coach for travel, Ryann thought. Funny how she hadn't noticed it's ominous presence before. She knew her fate was sealed and she was too tired to continue the fight. It was, what it was, and he was much stronger than she—not to mention he was as mad as they come. Ryann knew she'd never return to this place again. She'd never see her friends, but at least they'd be alive and well. It was an unavoidable fact. Lieutenant Price was going to kill her, at long last.*

*As always, Price drove his own carriage. He was in a good mood this day, and very talkative that evening. Everything had gone better than he'd even dared to hope. He took great delight in describing all the dangerous and perverse things he was going to do to his captive. Each act was more heinous than the other. Many, he'd done before, causing much pain and degradation. All were disgusting and considered abnormal behavior. While Ryann knew little about the physical relations between a man and a woman, she knew his likes were clinically insane and that he was unable to perform in a normal relationship.*

*She sat back, trying not to listen to his excited rantings. Maybe she could will herself to die. He was clearly a lunatic and anything would be preferable to his torture.*

*Ryann closed her eyes, shutting out the evil ramblings of a mad man, and forced herself to dream of a man who would deliver her from all this. He'd have a kind face and a quiet disposition. Goodness would radiate out from him. He'd be strong and love her deeply.*

*Unfortunately, it wasn't going to happen in time for her, but she dreamed it all the same. Instead of being frightened of all men, or sickened by the physical relationship between a man and woman—as some women might be after being subjected to this kind of pain and perversion—Ryann still believed in the goodness and purity that could be found between a loving couple. Her father had been gentle and caring. She saw the look of adoration in her mother's eyes every time she gazed upon her husband. That's what Ryann wanted for herself. She wanted to find that kindness and comfort in the arms of her own chosen man. She would try to hold on to that thought, until the end came to claim her.*

*After leaving the main road and enduring, for quite some time, the painful tosses and jostling caused by the deep ruts carved into the rough trail, Lieutenant Price pulled back on the reins and brought the carriage to a halt. There it was. Ryann recognized it, immediately. Even through the approaching darkness, she saw the ugly abandoned shack that would, more than likely, be the last place she would ever see. She closed her eyes and said a silent prayer for her safe delivery.*

*"Here we are, pet. Now the fun can begin, but I'm beat. Before I can pleasure you, we need to sleep. Grab your bags." He stepped down and left Ryann to get down the best she could, grappling with the bags.*

*He walked the horse and carriage around to the back, to keep them from being seen from the road. That was totally unnecessary, Ryann mused, as they hadn't seen anyone for miles.*

*She opened the door to the abandoned structure and was immediately assaulted by the painful and disgusting memories of all she had once been subjected to. The revulsion she felt, surged to the back of her throat as she bent over the firewood box and heaved. She vomited all over the wood and the hearth, and still she kept heaving.*

*"For Christ's sake! If you're gonna puke, do it outside, he shouted, as he stepped out for some fresh air. "Clean this mess up or I'll make you do something that may even sicken me"*

*Holding her stomach, Ryann looked around the room, desperately searching for water, but there was none. She found a water bucket and started out the door to refill it.*

*"Where do you think you're going?"*

*"I need water to clean the floor, to please you. I know the smell disturbs you." She waited for permission.*

*"All right. The creek is just over there, but I swear to you, if you do anything that I do not approve, you won't live to see the morning."*

*Ryann knew he wasn't bluffing. She quickly filled the bucket and grabbed some wildflowers growing around the water's edge. They were odiferous enough to help cover the stench of her sickness. She ran back to the shack, sloshing the water all over her dress.*

*Once inside, Ryann got down on her hands and knees and cleaned the mess as best she could. The Mad Lieutenant watched from a crooked little chair placed against the wall. Ryann noticed that he, once again, took out the small brown bottle and drank from it. He leaned his head back and closed his eyes. What was in that bottle, she wondered? He was never without it and it seemed to exacerbate his penchant for causing her pain.*

*"Take off that smelly, wet dress and put it outback to dry and air out. The stench makes me sick. Take off your underthings, as well," he ordered, in a low and quiet voice, never bothering to open his eyes.*

*So ... it was to start. She did as he commanded. Totally naked and completely exposed to this man, she continued to clean the floor and hearth. When finished to his satisfaction, she sat on the bed, waiting for his next demand.*

*The time she spent captive, in abject horror, dragged on from one day to the next. Ryann lost track of the days of the week. It made no real difference, anymore. She was scratched, bloodied, black and blue ... but she was still alive. She was terrified from moment to moment. No matter how she racked her brain, she couldn't see an escape. There was nothing for her to use against him and he never let her out of his sight, even for private necessities. But one day, everything changed.*

*The lieutenant had tied her to the bed, many times. He would often leave for five minutes or an hour, doing whatever it is that a sick and sadistic lieutenant does—that is, until this day. Ryann had been tied securely to the bed since dawn, and it was now twilight. The need to relieve herself had become overwhelming, but she didn't dare have an accident in the bed, where he would lie. What if something bad had happened to him? she wondered. Many times, she had prayed for misfortune to fall upon him, saving her from his cruelty, but what if he never returned? Who would release her? As it grew darker and darker, her fear and hope grew substantially, until, finally, the door opened and revealed a tall man's silhouette.*

*"Did you miss me, pet?" The voice was his, only he sounded almost happy. "I bet you have to go pee, isn't that right? Well, let me untie your hands and feet and you can make a run for it. How's that sound?"*

*Ryann didn't know what to think of this sudden change in his personality. He appeared almost normal.*

*"Y ... yes, thank you," she stammered, meekly.*

*He continued to observe her from the doorway, but she didn't care; for it was sheer bliss to finally relieve herself. Still naked, she ran back to the shack and slipped in behind him, through the open door.*

*Again, that night, he had his way with her, but it lacked some of the deliberate brutality he had displayed before. He went to sleep early, after tying only her hands to the bed. For once, he even shared the blanket. Ryann laid there for hours, wondering what had brought about this obvious change in his mood.*

*Early, the next morning, before the sun shown over the horizon, the lieutenant was up and dressed. He awakened*

*Ryann and told her to go outside and relieve herself again, as he didn't know how soon he would be able to return. She did as instructed. He then retied her hands.*

*"I might be back in an hour, and then again, if I find you've misbehaved, I could stay away for weeks. No one will find your shriveled body, Ryann, and you'll have died from thirst, weeks earlier. Hell of a way to die. Or ... I could sell you to some friends I have." He yanked hard on the ropes, making certain they were all good and tight. "They're kind of a rough and crude type, but you might like it. Depends on how much they're willing to pay."*

*The lieutenant enjoyed threatening her, watching the fear grow in her beautiful blue eyes. She was quite a beauty, he admitted to himself, with the bluest eyes he'd ever seen and the most kissable lips he'd ever tasted. It was a shame that she was a cheap whore like all the others.*

*Price walked over to the water bucket and dipped a pie pan into it; filling it with the cool, clear liquid. He laid it next to Ryann on the bed. "I'm feeling generous this morning, pet. Here's some water you can lap up like a dog. Careful not to spill it on my side of the bed, or there'll be consequences."*

*Just as he approached the door, he stopped and turned around with one final warning. "You might want to keep your toes off the floor and away from the wall ... rats you know. They bite!"*

*Whistling, as he stepped away from the shack, he saddled his horse and rode away, leaving Ryann with a lot to think about. He stayed away, all day. Then, once again, just after dark, he returned.*

*Ryann never questioned his coming and going. He'd made it abundantly clear that he didn't like it and there were always consequences. However, this day, Ryann was certain she had figured it all out. Of course! Lieutenant Price was reporting for duty, back at Fort Clark. He couldn't spend all his time guarding her. Tomorrow, if he left early, she would find some way to escape her bondage, even if she had to entice one of his fictional rats to gnaw off the ropes. She smiled. At last, she had a plan.*

*The lieutenant must have had a tough day, as he ignored Ryann completely, and fell quickly, asleep. He'd been too tired to even remove his clothes and, of course, eating was out of the question. It really didn't matter to Ryann. She no longer had a need for food. Turning on her side, she closed her eyes and, for once, slept soundly throughout the night.*

*When she opened her eyes, he was gone, and the pan of water had been refilled and rested beside her on the bed. Now was the time, she thought. Ryann started with the ropes around her wrists. She worked feverishly at her bindings, until her fingers bled. She tried to pull the knots with her teeth, but they wouldn't give way. In her efforts, the mattress slid off the bed and onto the floor, making it all the more difficult to remain in an upright position. If her plan wasn't successful, the lieutenant would surely notice her attempts at escape, and she'd pay a terrible price. Ryann was on the verge of hysteria, when suddenly, the door burst open, and she screamed!*

*"Oh Missy! What's that bastard done to ya?" Doolittle was by her side, working the ropes as quickly as his old fingers could move.*

*"Doo? How did you find me?"*

*"I'll explain everythin' on the way back to the house, but first, let's get you outta' here."*

*Ryann was crying so hard with relief, that she had forgotten she was stark naked. She threw her unfettered arms around the old man's neck and kissed his face multiple times. "Oh, Doo. You've saved me. I'm not going to die!" She was crying so hard, she couldn't catch her breath.*

*"Missy, we ain't got time fer hellos." The old man looked around the room, and through the window, he saw a pink dress, thrown over a bush. He stood up and rushed outside to the back of the shack, retrieving the dress. Shielding his eyes, he handed it to Ryann.*

*"Please, Missy, slip this on, quick. We don't know how long he'll be gone."*

*In less than one minute, they were running out the door toward his wagon. Doolittle had to assist Ryann up onto the seat, as she'd lost a great deal of weight and body strength. "Damn," he muttered under his breath, "you're as weak as a kitten. Hold on tight," he ordered, as he cracked the whip over the team. "We're runnin' fer our lives, now girl."*

*On the long trip back to Richmond, Harry Doolittle attempted to explain how he came to find her. "I been a waitin' fer him to come by. Never did trust him around you, but you insisted you were all right. Then, one night, you came in and I saw them marks." He spit into the dirt, alongside the wheel. "A man ain't a man if he lays a hand to a woman, I always say. I knew when you surprised me about leavin' town that you were runnin' from him. Cain't say as I blame ya none. He's a bad'un. After I got back from the Post Office, I waited fer you to come down to the desk. When you didn't, I got curious and went up to yer room. He should'a locked that door. It would've kept me out fer at least the night. When I walked in and saw the blood on the floor and all your bags were gone, with the train ticket torn to shreds, I knew he'd grabbed ya."*

*Doolittle looked over at Ryann with an apology written all over his tired old face. "I'm sorry, Missy. I shouldn't have gone out and left ya all alone."*

*She put her hand on his arm. "Oh, Doo, there was nothing you could have done to keep him from getting to me. I tried everything I knew to avoid him, but he's crazy and determined. He led me to believe he had you, and was going to kill you. He threatened Libby, as well. I couldn't let that happen." She smiled up at her friend.*

*"First thin' I did, was to visit the fort. Fer two days, I hung around, tryin' to hear somethin'. He was out on maneuvers with his men and they weren't expected back fer another day or two, or at least that's what I was told. I asked a lot of questions 'bout his character. Oddly enough, he's got the respect of ever'one, there." He shook his head, not understanding how that could be the case.*

*Doolittle was getting nervous as they approached the intersection to Fort Clark. "Missy, if we should meet up with this varmint, afore we get home, you reach into my pocket and pull out my pistol. Have ya ever shot a gun?"*

*"No, but believe me, I would have no problem shooting him right out of his saddle. He's never going to take me again." The look of resolve was firmly established across her ravaged face. She wasn't bragging ... it was fact.*

*"I saw him ridin' in with his men early one mornin', just a couple a days ago," Doolittle continued. "I was somewhat perplexed. How could he have taken you, when he hadn't been*

*around? Then I heard some privates grumblin'. It seems the young lieutenant hadn't spent the last week with his men, at all. He came up with some lame excuse and left them to the leadership of a sergeant and a couple of corporals. Morale ain't been too high under their orders, but now that they're back with Lieutenant Price, things should get straightened out."*

*"I think I was that special matter he had to attend to, Doo. He was with me every moment, of every day, for a week. Then early one morning, he just up and rode out and didn't return until the end of the day. It took me another day to figure out what he was doing and where he was going. It gave me a window of time to make my escape. That's what I was trying to do when you discovered me today. I figured, he was at Fort Clark with his men. That gave me about ten hours to get out of those ropes and run for freedom. Thank God, you showed up when you did. I wasn't making much progress. I probably would have lost a tooth, gnawing on those ropes," she giggled.*

*Doolittle looked down and noticed her bloodied fingers and torn nails. Her wrists were bruised and scraped raw. "Sorry I didn't get there sooner. I followed him to that damn shack, the night before, but I had to wait fer him to leave. I couldn't risk him harmin' ya anymore than he already had. I knew you was still alive, cause he kept comin' back there. This mornin', I gave him enough time to get to the fort, afore I rushed in to save ya." He grinned, looking slightly embarrassed. "I didn't want him to turn back around, fer some reason, and find an old man fumblin' with the ropes and kill us both. Some rescue that'd be." He snickered at the thought.*

*"You did everything just right, Doo." Ryann smiled. She felt relief for the first time in weeks.*

*Richmond came into view. Thankfully, they were almost there and safety was close at hand. The horses were lathered and looked ready to drop, but continued their fast pace. Poor animals, Ryann thought. She would order a special helping of oats for them when they got back, and would make sure they were rubbed down properly. They were, after all, heroes too.*

*Doolittle pulled the horses around to the back of the hotel and jumped down spryly, for an old codger, and offered his assistance to Ryann.*

*"At last, a true gentleman," she teased, as she held out her*

*damaged hand.*

*Harry rushed her inside and took her directly to his rooms. "Now, you stay here, with that there door bolted. Don't leave it fer no reason, no matter what you may hear. I don't want to leave you, but I need to get yer tickets to get you outta' town. I shouldn't be gone more than an hour. I sent a telegram to my brother, Horace, out in Tucson. He owns a hotel, there. That's where yer a goin'. He says he'll see to it that you get the schoolmarm job and you can live there fer free, 'til you get on yer feet. He's a good man, Horace."*

*Ryann was beaming. "Oh, how wonderful." She kissed his stubbled cheek. "Tucson! It sounds magical. I thank you so much. I know I'll like Horace, if he's your brother. Good men must run in your family. You're my hero, Doo."*

*"Aw shucks," the old man blushed, and stepped out. Through the closed door, he said softly, "Bolt the door." He waited until he heard the bar slide into place and then he left the building.*

*For the first time in days, Ryann allowed herself to relax. She might not die, after all. She looked briefly into Mr. Doolittle's shaving mirror. Her face was not too marred. If she could find a brush and get control of her hair, she could perhaps pass unnoticed on the train. She didn't look her best, but it could have been so much worse. Most of her wounds were covered by her dress. She sadly examined her pretty pink dress with the lovely flowers on it. It had been new, when she wore it last, and she had felt so young and carefree. But that seemed a lifetime ago. Now, the dress was dirty, slightly smelly, and ripped in a number of places. Ryann tried to remember if she left anything to wear in her wardrobe, back up in her room? She couldn't remember if she had, but ... she did remember her money hidden in her drawer, next to the bed. Doolittle hadn't said anything about that, and she seriously doubted he had taken the time to look for it. He would have assumed the lieutenant had taken everything. She really needed that money.*

*"How long has Doo been gone?" she wondered. "If I run up the stairs, I can be back down here, all locked in tight, in less than five minutes. The Mad Lieutenant is still at the fort. Dear Lord, help me," she prayed. With her mind made up, she unbolted the door, looked both ways, and ran up the stairs.*

*Luckily, the door was unlocked, as she no longer had her key. She hadn't thought of that. Carefully, she opened the door and looked in, before entering. It was safe. She closed the door behind her and bolted it. Running over to the wardrobe, she found her oldest dress. It had been too worn to give to charity, but it looked divine to her now, and it was soft and clean. She unbuttoned her ruined pink dress and remembered that she had no undergarments. "Well, that can't be helped," she murmured, aloud. She carefully picked up the old garment, preparing to pull it down over her head, when the door she had bolted, crashed open, and the man she most feared in the world, stood there, glaring at her, with the fires of Hades burning in his black eyes.*

*"Hello, pet," he growled, as he grabbed her by the neck. His eyes traveled up and down her body as he took in her nakedness. "How nice ... you were waiting for me, and I thought you were running away," he said sarcastically.*

*He pushed her down on the bed and quickly unbuttoned his pants. "I saw the old man leave in a hurry, and I knew what you were up to. You're such a little imbecile to believe you can outthink me. At least, God gave you beauty. Oh well, after I take care of you, this one last time, you'll have no need for brains and it won't matter if you're no longer pretty. I'm real sorry, pet, but I warned you ... repeatedly. This is how it is going to end. Later, I'll meet up with your savior. He's lived a long and dull life. Nobody will miss him."*

*He forced his kisses on her face and neck, biting her just enough to draw blood, trying to make her cry or beg for mercy. He pulled her head back by her beautiful blonde hair, but Ryann refused to show pain in front of this monster.*

*"It's a shame really. You always taste so good," he sighed. His thumb found it's way to her delicate white throat and he started to exert pressure, slowly cutting off her air supply. "You were my favorite."*

*Her eyes narrowed, as she glared back at the perverted face, before her. "Not this time," she whispered. Ryann had never really fought back physically before, but she knew she had nothing to lose. He was going to kill her. The large man was unprepared, when she threw her body weight against him and dove for the drawer, next to the bed. In it, was her father's knife. She had started sleeping with it close by, for just such an emergency as this. Feeling the smooth handle under her fingers, she grasped it as tightly as she could. When the lieutenant turned to see what she was doing, Ryann brought the blade around and stuck him between his shoulders, burying the small blade up to the hilt.*

*"Arrggh" he screamed. "You damn nasty slut!" He stood up and tried to reach for the knife, twisting at odd angles, but couldn't quite grab it. He danced in a macabre fashion, contorting his body enough to make grasping the handle, possible. Then he did the most unusual thing. He started laughing. He laughed and laughed, to the point of tears. "I can't believe you had the guts to do this, pet." He continued to laugh. "You sometimes amaze me, Ryann." Blood was blooming over the back of his shirt.*

*Ryann jumped up and grabbed for her old dress. Not taking the time to put it on, or even to retrieve the money hidden in the drawer, she dashed for the open door. The lieutenant had kicked it in with his massive boots, splintering the wooden frame. For a brief instant, Ryann shuddered, imagining what those boots could do to her skull. He had once threatened to do just that. She made it to the hallway, when his hand reach across and covered her mouth, from behind. She felt her body being dragged back into the little room by her already bruised neck. She kicked and fought bravely, but to no avail.*

*"All I have to do is turn my wrist and I can snap your neck like a twig ... but what would be the fun in that? I want to see you beg me for your life, Ryann. I want it to hurt, and most of all ... I want to be able to take my time."*

*He cupped her chin, gently, "So lovely, it is a shame," he whispered. Then, he slapped her. He slapped her again and again, taking delight in the physical damage he was inflicting. He formed a fist and struck her in the cheek, just under her right eye.*

*"Look how quickly it swells," he declared. "You're so delicate." He marveled at the rapid bruising of the soft flesh under his thumb, as he gently touched her cheek. "I guess you can't look, just now." He then struck her across her ear.*

*Stars were floating before Ryann's eyes and she found she wasn't able to utter a sound. Her mouth filled with her own blood and the taste of it caused her stomach to recoil. As her eyes were closing, his fists kept up the relentless attack upon her face. He was unmerciful in his punishment of her.*

*"I told you, repeatedly, to be good, but you were not a good girl. You didn't believe I'd punish you for being disobedient. Now, you will know I always tell the truth." He hit her again, but with slightly less force.*

*Thankfully, he was tiring from his own loss of blood, and the extreme amount of energy he had released upon Ryann, had depleted his strength. He tossed her weak and pathetic body to the floor. If she wasn't dead now, he'd see to it before he attended to the old man. But—first things first. He had to get the damn, annoying knife out of his back.*

*He had an idea. He staggered over to the wardrobe and put his back into the door jam. Positioning the knife handle into the crack, he was able to shut the door with his hip, causing it to grip the knife handle. Taking a deep breath, he lunged forward and the small knife fell to the floor. He stood there looking at the offending object. It was insignificant, but it had caused him a great deal of pain.*

*He bent over and grabbed Ryann by her chin. Holding the knife in front of her eyes, he threatened, "This tiny thing can't kill a man, you stupid bitch, but it hurts like hell. I should cut off your nose and see what you think, or maybe stick your eye ... but why bother?" He tossed the inconsequential knife onto the table. "I'd rather play with you some more, before I break your lovely neck, but I need you to wake up, first."*

*Ryann was unconscious and the lieutenant found there was very little pleasure in killing someone when they didn't realize what was happening to them. "Right after I take care of Doolittle, I'll come back for you and we'll play one last time," he said almost cheerfully.*

*He turned toward the door. Lieutenant Mark Price, son of Senator Allenton Price, never heard the woman rise up, behind him. He didn't feel the small knife slice through his neck, until it was much too late. Yes, the knife was small, but it was very sharp, and it cut deep—extremely deep. He collapsed at Ryann's feet, looking up at her with a look of total incredulity.*

*His mouth moved to form the word, "How?"*

*He couldn't believe that this little slip of a girl had finally gotten the better of him. Just before his eyes closed for the final time, he smiled up at Ryann. For one brief moment, she recognized the look of thanksgiving as it flashed across his face. His torment was finally over. He breathed his last breath and his soul was given up to God for judgment. The man appeared different. He was a man at peace.*

*Ryann continued to stand there, blood dripping from the small knife she still held tightly in her hand. She was nude and she didn't care. What had she done? A man lay dead at her feet—an evil, dangerous man—but a man, nonetheless.*

*Thus, was the scene Harry Doolittle came upon when he discovered Ryann was no longer in his apartment. He saw her face, its delicate beauty hidden behind hideous cuts, purple bruises and swellings. Her nose may have been broken, he couldn't be sure, for blood covered her face. Her soft lips were unidentifiable. Shock and rage surged through the old man's body as he noticed she was, once again, nude, and held a bloody knife clutched tightly in her trembling hand.*

*Harry gently guided Ryann back into the room and took the knife away. Spying the dress on the bed, he pulled it down over her head. Ryann sat down and tried to come to grips with what had just occurred. She knew she was safe and the mad lieutenant was dead. She turned her eyes upon Doo, and saw her precious friend was alive, and once again, taking care of her. That's when she made up her mind not to be a victim any longer.*

*"Doo," she mumbled. Her lips were so misshapen she couldn't speak clearly. "Let me help."*

*He smiled sympathetically and looked around the room. Then, an idea came to him. "Can ya walk?"*

*She nodded.*

*"Good. It's time fer ya to leave. Don't worry about nothin', here. I'll take care of all this." He motioned to everything around the room. "Go down to my apartment and stay there. I'll get ya some more clothes. Is there anythin' here, you need?"*

*She pointed to the drawer next to the bed.*

*"In here?" He opened the drawer and saw nothing.*

*She continued to point and nodded her head.*

*Doo pulled the drawer out and discovered an envelope at the back of the table. He reached in and discovered it contained a great deal of cash. He handed it to Ryann and smiled broadly. "Well, all righty then. Looks like one problem's solved."*

*Obediently, she went downstairs, all too grateful to leave the horrific scene behind her. She hid, while Doo sealed off her room, the best he could. Fortunately, the boarding house was practically empty, and he was confident that the room would remain undisturbed.*

*Harry Doolittle had a special lady friend who'd been a widow for many years. He knew she'd never thrown out her blacks. When he asked for a few dresses, she was more than happy to give them to him, with no questions asked. She also included a pair of black gloves and a large, black veiled hat.*

*He promptly returned to Ryann. "Yer now a widow, right and proper. It's a perfect disguise. No one will look too close at yer face, 'specially if yer veiled, and the men will leave ya alone. You'll be safe on this trip, and it's a long one, Missy." He handed her a schedule. "I got you tickets on a few different trains and coaches, just to mix'em up a little. Don't write me or telegraph me. I'll know ya made it safe, by what my brother says. I'm right sorry, but I had to tell him everthin' I knowed. He won't say nothin' to nobody. You need to change yer name, but don't tell it to me. I cain't tell what I don't know." He winked at her.*

*He cleared his throat and his voice sounded a little hoarse. "Missy, I ain't never had no children of my own, but I'd sure like to think of you as my daughter, if'n that don't offend ya, none. I know'd yer father was a right good man and a fine doctor. He was my friend. If you'd allow an old man his fantasy, I'd be much beholdin' to ya."*

*Ryann began to cry. "Oh, Doo. You've saved my life. What more could any father do for his child? I love you. You may think of me in any way you wish, and I know my father and mother are smiling down at you from heaven, thanking you, as well." She put her thin arms around him and laid her bruised cheeks on his shoulder. She whispered, "Thank you, Doo."*

# CHAPTER TEN

*Tucson, Arizona Territory*

Beth sat quietly on the pretty blanket Vernon had provided. She waited for him to say something, but he didn't utter a sound. She knew she was hoping for too much. No man would be able to look at her, once he knew of her violent past. She knew that he would see her as damaged and dirty in ways beyond imagination. A man could only forgive so much and he'd never be able to forget what he'd heard. She was wanted for murder and Vernon would have to take her in. Her breath caught, as she prepared for his reaction.

For the longest time, they sat side by side, neither one daring to disturb the peace of the moment. Finally, Vernon stood up and looked down at her. She looked up into his face and saw his tears. Incredible pain was etched across his handsome features. He looked like a man who had just lost his closest and dearest friend. The ranger was clearly devastated by the decision he must make.

A single tear ran down Beth's cheek.

Vernon held out his hand and she took it, longing to feel his warmth, once more. She stood and faced her love, trying not to collapse with the dreadful truth she knew he must deliver. She held her wrists out in front of her, in anticipation of the cuffs he would snap into place.

Vernon took a step closer and captured her arms. He could feel her trembling body, and knew she was terrified of his reaction to her story. He had trouble finding his voice. It was difficult to say the words he needed to say to her, but necessary. He could not ignore her confession.

He cleared his throat. "Sweetheart … I had no idea. Oh, my God, darling … if you hadn't already killed his worthless hide, I'd have to go to Richmond and do it myself. Come here, angel."

He gently pulled her quaking body into his embrace and provided a safe haven for her to vent her emotions. Ryann had not wept so hard since the death of her parents. She couldn't believe that he still loved her. To her surprise, Vernon wasn't repulsed by her or even angry with her.

"Out here, we look at the world a little different, I guess," he whispered. "Each one of us has his own story to tell, some good and some not so good; but this harsh and beautiful land allows us to start anew. Hopefully, we are blessed with a better beginning. It's true for David and Mary, and it's true for me and you."

She hiccupped a few times, before being able to ask, "So you aren't going to arrest me, Vernon?"

"Darling," he laughed. "You lovely, silly woman. Arrest you? I should give you a medal for bravery in the midst of unimaginable danger. You're an amazing woman and I admire you and love you more than I can say. I'm surprised though, that you allow me to touch you intimately, after suffering so much at the hands of that maniac. I'm worried that I might unintentionally scare you. You'll stop me, yes?"

"Vernon, I never lost my dream of finding true love. When I found it with you, I realized a physical relationship was a part of that dream. I know you'd never hurt me or do something I found distasteful. Please, don't worry about that and don't treat me special. I am *not* damaged goods. I'm a survivor."

The two lovers stood there kissing and holding one another, reveling in the comfort each provided the other. They lowered themselves back to the blanket and continued their embrace. Both needed reassurance that, soon, all would be right again and their future would be secure.

As the sun settled low in the sky, it turned the rocks a myriad of colors, each more striking that the next. The reds seemed redder and the oranges were more vivid than ever before.

Yellows glowed in the sunset, indicating it was time to head back home, to Tucson.

Vernon helped Beth pack up, and they climbed up into the buggy. On the trail back, they had plenty of time to think about all that had been revealed and the problems it presented.

"What will you do about the Wanted posters, Vernon?" Beth asked.

He thought about it, before giving her his answer. "First, I'll keep only the most recent, and I'll keep it buried under the stack. No one will see it, but me. It says I'm to look for a Ryann Beaufort. Don't know anyone by that name, do you?"

She smiled. "Nope."

"I ain't a very smart ranger, cain't put two and two together, no how." He grinned, being sarcastic. "Then, I'm going to have a short chat with Mr. Horace Doolittle. I want to let him know that I owe him and his brother a great debt, one that I can never totally repay. If it hadn't been for Harry, I shudder to think …"

Beth kissed his cheek and took his free hand. "I know, darling. I know."

"I know you love Mary, and so do I, but now is not the time to inform anyone else of this history of yours. The less they know, the safer you are … and *you*, angel, are my primary concern. We're going to be married in just one week's time and I won't have any ghost from the past, raise his ugly head and ruin it. Got it?"

Ryann giggled. "Yes, sir."

"That's what I like—an obedient wife." He leaned over and gave her a big wet smooch on her cheek.

"Now, tell me about this little bundle we're gonna be adding to our family tree. Considering what you went through, how do you feel about it? Truth, if you please."

Beth could see he was serious and concerned. She sat up, away from Vernon's side, and placed both hands on her baby bump. It would be understandable to resent the child, but she just didn't.

"This baby is mine—all mine, but if you wish, I will share him with you. He wasn't conceived in love, but he'll be raised with more than his share of it. I need this little one, Vernon, to help make things right. His goodness will offset all the bad and unthinkable things that happened. When I look at this babe, I'll not once, remember the pain, but I'll think only of the miracle of his birth. If the baby is a girl, I want to name her for my mother."

"If it's a boy," Vernon interrupted, "I'd like the honor of naming him for my father, Frank. Would you allow that?"

Instantly, her enormous blue eyes fill with tears and a flood surged down her face. Beth grabbed Vernon around his midsection, almost pulling him from his seat. "I love you so very, very much, darling. Frank, it is, and he'll be one lucky little boy to have you for his papa." She hugged him as hard as she possibly could. This was her dream. It had finally come to pass.

Beth and Vernon's wedding day arrived right on schedule, and none too soon for the ranger. Never before had the birds sang quite as sweetly as they did that day. Flowers of all kinds graced the little church located at the far end of town, and never before had there been a happier bride and groom.

Mary and Beth completed the wedding dress in record time, and they were proud with the results. Shades of ivory lace, over the palest blue wool, fell from a high-waisted design, caught up in the back with a blue bow. It was quietly elegant and concealed Beth's tummy, admirably. In Beth's beautiful golden hair, she wore her mother's pearl comb, and in her new reticule, she carried her father's watch. She borrowed her lovely, ivory lace gloves from her best friend, Mary. Horace and Harry Doolittle gave the bride an ornate pearl broach that once belonged to their mother. They were both honored to have her wear it and keep it always. Her new pearl earbobs were a gift from Ranger Vernon Gunn.

David and all his children were in attendance, along with Mr. Doolittle and Robin, from the Fancy Garter. She was a favorite of little Sara's. The mayor sent his regards and his regrets. His absence made the day even more perfect. Mr. and Mrs. Jones, owners of the Jones Mercantile, sat in the third row and Calliope Bigsby sat just behind them, along with some of the most socially prominent women in Tucson. The Grande Dame was putting her stamp of approval on this union and no one would dare cast aspersions. Beth was pleased to see a few of her students, and their parents, sitting in the pews, as well. The wedding was small, but their friends were all there and smiling, ready to witness the joining of two special people, very much in love.

The person Beth was most anxious to see stood tall, at the end of the aisle, awaiting her arrival. She felt her heart skip a beat as her eyes traveled forward and settled on the ruggedly handsome face of her soon-to-be husband. His sandy colored hair curled over his collar, just slightly, daring Beth to run her fingers through its silkiness. With eyes as green as grass, a smile to light up the room, and the sexy dimple in his chin, Beth had never known any man to be quite as attractive. His best feature, however, was his huge heart. In that, he was very much like her father. Vernon Gunn was a man of honor and goodness. He was loyal and trustworthy, brave and tender. He was all of the best things this world had to offer, and soon, he would be all hers.

Vernon caught his breath as his beloved stepped into view. He watched, awestruck, as a golden vision floated down the aisle toward him. Tall, gracefully elegant, and totally divine, Beth was lovelier than the angels in heaven, he thought. And he knew her to be strong and courageous, a woman of true convictions and just the lady he wanted to be the mother of his children. He loved her more than he thought possible.

Upon hearing the preacher ask if she would take this man, Beth grinned and practically shouted, “I will.” The little church rang with the laughter.

When the preacher asked Vernon the same question, the big man was so overcome with emotion that he could barely squeak his answer, “I will.” Once again, the little congregation reacted to his response by giggling and showing their approval.

Love surrounded them. People cheered and applauded and some shed a few tears. This was a happy day and it wasn’t over yet. The preacher announced, that after the ceremony, the wedding party and their guests were all invited to the Hotel Doolittle, where a wedding breakfast, fine enough to serve a king and his queen, was being prepared. The children were wild with excitement, knowing they were going to share in such a feast, and they imagined there would be lots of sweets.

Vernon and Beth laughed heartily, when they walked out of the church and saw their buggy. One glance at David’s red and slightly embarrassed face, and they knew he and his adorable children had been busy. Sara was giggling and hiding behind her mother's skirt, while the boys stood, tall and proud, alongside all their hard work, and laughed at their own mischief.

There were all sorts of items hanging off the thing. There were old shoes—donated by the boys—cans, ribbons, and flowers attached to every possible square inch. It was quite a site and the bride and groom were touched by the contributions, as well as the considerable amount of effort that went into the decorating.

Sara walked up to Beth and timidly pulled on her sleeve. "Mama and I tied the flowers. I told her you would like them best. They're pretty, like you, Auntie Beth," she whispered. The little girl was so proud of their handiwork.

Beth leaned over and kissed Sara's cheek. "It wouldn't be nearly as beautiful without the flowers. Thank you, darling."

The hotel looked beautiful and the food was sumptuous. After everyone found his seat, David figured it was time to make the wedding toast. He stood, clanging the side of his glass with his spoon, to get their attention. He looked over at Sara, and smiled. She had her glass and spoon ready, waiting her turn to clang.

"Vernon, Beth. Congratulations on this miraculous event. I never thought I'd see the day that some gal would lasso this ranger. He was a tough one, but her aim was true. Now, fer the rest of his life, she'll be callin' the shots and makin' him jump through all the hoops." He laughed, along with the rest of the men. The ladies just stared at him. "Uh oh, I guess maybe I stepped outta' line, cause my boss is givin' me that look that you'll soon get mighty used to, brother." He looked at Mary and winked. "But it's the best life a man could imagine, bein' married to the woman of his dreams.

"So, Mary and I would like to give the two of you a little gift. Fer five days, you're gonna stay at the Capital Arms, in their bridal suite. Take my advice," he looked conspiratorially at his wife and grinned, "Have *all* your meals delivered to yer room. You won't have to leave the room fer five whole days."

The room exploded with applause. It was all good-natured fun, and Vernon and Beth blushed with anticipation. As they were thanking everyone, the clanking of another glass got their attention.

Little Sara was standing on her chair, with her glass and spoon in hand. "Uncle Vernon and Auntie Beth," she exclaimed loudly and clearly, above the celebratory noise. "I want to give you a puppy for your present, but I can't give you Bear or Fancy Garter, though."

Everybody giggled at the pups' imaginative names, especially Robin.

"But don't be sad, cause I'll keep looking so you will have something to play with, cause I know you only gots each other to play with, now."

Beth turned bright pink, once again, and walked up to the precious little girl. She put her arms around her and squeezed tightly. "Sara, you are the sweetest child I know, and if I ever have a little girl, I want her to be just like you. Thank you for your lovely gift." Then, she kissed her.

Sara beamed with pride. She looked around the room and discovered her brothers, over on the side, eating huge pieces of chocolate cake. She smiled like an angel at them and then stuck out her tongue, while putting her fingers in her ears. Yes, she was quite the little lady.

After several hours, the lively reception dissipated and most of the guests returned to their homes, happy and full of wedding cake. Mary and David were the last to say goodbye and wish the newlyweds good luck. Their little family had just gotten bigger, and they were all very happy about that.

Beth and Vernon thanked Horace Doolittle for more than just hosting the wedding breakfast. He knew what they meant, and nodded, dabbing at his eyes. Then they packed up Beth's things, for she would not be returning to her little room at the Doolittle.

Vernon loaded up the buggy and they cheerfully headed on down the street to the Capital Arms Hotel. It was high time they started their honeymoon. Beth's whole body was quivering with excitement. Finally, this man was her husband and she would love him forever. She was Mrs. Vernon Gunn—Elizabeth Gunn—and she wasn't alone anymore. Within minutes, she planned to show her husband how much she loved and appreciated him. She had a lifetime of love stored up in her and she was going to give it all to him.

The Capital was breathtaking, Beth thought, with its crystal chandeliers gracing the lobby and the dining room. Men and women, in black and white uniforms, were stationed around in different areas, waiting to be of some assistance to the guests. The carpets were deep blue with floral borders and the comfortable furniture, placed artfully around the lobby, was covered in gold damask and cream-colored velvet. Never before had Beth or Vernon seen such opulence.

Vernon eagerly guided his bride up to the marble front desk and announced their arrival. "We have a reservation. The name is Gunn." Vernon waited impatiently for the clerk to look up the name, but the man seemed to be in no hurry. They waited. *What is the problem?*

"It could be under the name Williams. Try that," Vernon suggested. It seemed to take forever to locate their reservation, and then the clerk looked up at Beth and smiled from one ear to the other.

"You two, have the Bridal Suite!" he happily announced to everyone within a thirty-foot radius. "Congratulations!" Everyone applauded and shouted their best wishes to the impatient couple.

Feeling slightly embarrassed, the newlyweds just wanted to go upstairs. Vernon waved his hat at the crowd beginning to gather around them, while Beth stood by and smiled prettily.

Men started to line up in front of the happy bride, pulling money out of their pockets. It was the kissing line. They offered the bride a dollar for each kiss. It was a silly tradition, but harmless. However, some men had more money than was proper, Beth thought. She looked up at Vernon, silently pleading for his help, when suddenly the ladies encircled the groom and led him to the center of the room. There, they proceeded to walk slowly around him, with each lady stepping forward and stealing a kiss from the handsome groom. Everyone was happy to participate in welcoming the newlyweds.

This was all very nice and had been fun, but it was, after all, their wedding night—afternoon—and Vernon decided it was past time to make a stand. He pulled Beth up to the third step, and from the elegantly curved staircase, he announced to one and all, "Thank you very much. This has been right nice and thoughtful of all of you, and my bride and I appreciate your good wishes. It is, however, getting late and we wish to retire now. Good night." Vernon gave them a quick smile and turned his back to his audience.

Beth giggled as she felt his strong arms suddenly lift her off her feet and swoop her up the stairs. They were soon out of sight, but could still hear the happy laughter from down below.

*Getting late, indeed.* It was almost three o'clock in the afternoon and the young couple needed to retire. With good humor, the crowd began to disburse, many remembering what it was like to be newly married and so much in love. Some of the older couples were holding hands and looking endearingly into one another's eyes, still in love that way.

"Vernon, you can put me down now, darling. I'm much too heavy for you to be doing this," Beth laughed.

"You're as light as a feather, Mrs. Gunn, and I'm as strong as an ox. Watch this." With one arm, he held her securely against his body, while he unlocked the door with his free hand. "Your chamber, my lady." He carried her over the threshold and quickly deposited her to her feet. He was clearly breathing hard.

Beth started to laugh, once again. "You are such a man. I told you I was too heavy. Come here and kiss me … when you get your wind."

She didn't have to ask twice. Vernon was more than willing to kiss her now and kiss her later. He had dreamed of this moment since shortly after meeting her. What a time they'd had in the beginning, he remembered. And to think, it all came to this end. Life was a curious thing.

The newlyweds stood in the center of the room, their arms intricately wrapped around the other, holding on tightly as they allowed their long awaited passion to finally overtake them. Vernon buried his face in the thickness of Beth's golden hair and breathed in its clean, sweet fragrance. His wife smelled of sunshine and wildflowers and aroused woman. He kissed her eyes, her nose, her silken cheeks. Her luscious lips beckoned him, and all the while, his hands explored the curve of her slender back.

Beth moaned with pleasure. It felt divine being held in such a manner. She wanted all this and much, much more. She surrendered easily to her husband's hands and urged them to caress her body, front and back. She returned his kisses with a hunger she had never experienced before. With her tongue, she teased his lips, begging for entrance into the lush warmth of his mouth, wanting to savor the taste of him.

"Oh Beth, I've never wanted anything as much as I want you. I love you so." Vernon nibbled on her neck and ears, causing her to giggle. "I'm going to make love to you now, and every day, from this day forward. I want to give you pleasure."

One by one, Vernon pulled the pins from Beth's carefully coiffed hair, allowing them to scatter on the floor. After he removed the elegant comb, placing it gently on the bureau, he stood back, mesmerized by the vision standing before him.

Beth ran her fingers through her hair to loosen the curls. As they spilled over her shoulders and down her back, her golden tresses glowed with a heavenly light. Thick and heavy, it was magnificent, and quite the most beautiful hair Vernon had ever seen. His fingers itched to stroke the great length of it. He craved to immerse his face in its softness. It was then, he remembered, there would be time for him to enjoy his wife to the fullest. She was his for all eternity.

With trembling fingers, he turned his attention to the many buttons on her beautiful blue dress, taking great care not to harm the garment. As the buttons came undone, the fabric slowly revealed the creamy flesh hidden beneath. Her shoulders were perfect, down to the small dimple in each one. Her slender neck flowed into her shoulders in a most provocative manner, making it impossible to deny himself a little nibble. Another tug, and the bodice fell to her waist, exposing the briefest of camisoles. The thin fabric did nothing to hide the perfect twin mounds straining to burst forth at any moment. Clearly visible, were two large, pink nipples perched upon the upper tip of each breast. Vernon felt his mouth water. He remembered seeing Beth's breasts once before, and had never forgotten their beauty, but they had grown even lovelier over the past few weeks.

Vernon was perspiring heavily. It was time for him to claim his wife, but she was still trapped in yards of blue wool. In his eagerness, he struggled with the fastenings, but was unsuccessful. Finding it more complicated than he ever could have imagined, Vernon looked to Beth for help.

Beth laughed. "Most brides don't have to accommodate a baby bump, darling. I'll help you." Her fingers deftly unfastened the buttons and the underskirt fell away, in short order. She daintily stepped out of her dress and stood before her husband in nothing more than her wedding chemise, stockings and drawers. Feeling quite silly, Beth tried to cover herself.

Vernon was a happy man, and he was smiling so broadly he thought he'd burst. Standing in front of him was his golden goddess and she had professed her love for him. *Was he a lucky man or what?*

"Angel, come here," he growled softly.

Beth walked into his arms.

Vernon laughed at his bride's eagerness. He could smell the light musk of her arousal, making it extremely difficult for him to contain his own enthusiasm. However, now was not the time to rush things. He'd waited too long for this night, to speed through it now.

Her beauty overwhelmed him and caused his heart to race. He saw the splendor of her uncovered breasts, with their two cherry ripe nipples just begging for his attention. They appeared a bit larger and heavier now, than when he first saw them, but that didn't change the fact that they were still perfect.

"My God, Beth. They're flawless," he gushed, as he looked admiringly, from one to the other. "May I taste them?" He looked up at her, waiting for permission.

"Please, do. Put your lips on them and suck them into your mouth. Make love to them," she begged.

At the touch of his lips on her pink, swollen nipple, Beth cried out in delight. She could feel the erotic sensation of his kiss and suckling clear down into the depths of her stomach. It was overpowering. Soon, a warm moistness seeped between her legs, and she felt the need to be filled. Pressing his head tightly against her, Beth moaned, "I never knew anything could feel so wonderful." Her whole body began to tremble.

While licking and attending to the right breast, Vernon placed his hand upon the other one and gently massaged it, causing Beth to squeal with delight. His teeth pulled gently on the nipple, fanning her internal flames to burn even hotter.

His hand wandered down across her stomach, and slowly, he slid it under her drawers. His long fingers needed to feel the moist curls surrounding her womanhood. It was almost his undoing. Gently, his fingers stroked her in a circular motion, teasing the small bud. He took great pleasure in feeling the silkiness and the wetness of her femininity increase simply by his touch.

Vernon sat up and untied Beth's drawers, pulling them down over her curvy bottom and letting them puddle around her dainty feet. He pulled a stocking down one long and incredibly shapely leg and kissed her ankle, working his way up her calf and behind her knee.

"Oh, that's delightful, darling," Beth sighed.

Vernon looked up at her and winked. Then, he removed the second stocking and kissed her leg, as before, only he didn't stop at the knee. He kissed the inner part of her thigh, and then very slowly, he forced her legs to separate and he placed a kiss on her thatch of golden curls.

"Vernon!" Beth shouted, her eyes wide with surprise. She didn't know men did things like that. "Why did you do that?" She didn't understand.

"Sweetheart, I intend to kiss every square inch of your beautiful body and taste every inch too, so don't be surprised when I sneak down here and fill my mouth with your sweetness. You're glorious and your body is a feast for my manly appetites. Is that going to be a problem?"

"No, I guess not. It's just ... just new to me, that's all. You're so tender and loving. I guess I'm a bit embarrassed."

"Anything we do in the privacy of our bedroom is perfectly normal and acceptable. We love each other and I'll never hurt you. This is the way it will always be with us. It's the way it always should have been, angel. Let me love you the way you deserve to be loved."

Beth relaxed, took a few breaths, and smiled, coyly. "Vernon, I'm naked. You're not. See anything unfair about this?"

He laughed. "I can take care of that in a hurry."

He tried. In his exuberance, he managed to pull off his shirt, along with half its buttons. He quickly unbuckled his belt and yanked down his trousers, only to get them stuck over his boots. His tie wrapped around his neck, threatening to choke him, and his underthings knotted around his legs.

"Damn it!" he grumbled.

Beth started laughing. "Just how long have you been undressing yourself, Vernon? Need some help?"

"Very funny."

"It is," Beth responded, as she bent over and pulled at a boot. With some effort, it finally came off … along with a sock. She then pulled on the other boot, pulling Vernon clear off his feet, causing him to fall forcefully on his butt. Tears threatened to spill down her cheeks, as Beth was now laughing all the harder. "Let me at that tie before you strangle yourself." She carefully loosened it and slipped it over his head. Her big husband looked so funny in his underthings, all tangled up, just like a little boy. In fact, she was so caught up in his charming fumbling, that she didn't notice his sly grin.

Vernon was enjoying the show too. Beth would be surprised to find out she was the subject of his amusement. He wasn't taking notice of his own predicament. No, Vernon was watching his voluptuous and very naked wife bending all over him, trying to help him get his clothes off. She was oblivious to the erotic picture she was searing into his brain. Never would he forget how she looked, just now, bending over to pull off his boot, or reaching above his head trying to slip off his tie, allowing the tips of her breasts to brush up against his forehead. It was sheer bliss, he thought. He was in heaven.

Finally, after having dealt with the clothing issues, the newlyweds stood back, looking at each other. Both feasted their eyes on the other's nakedness. It was odd, but satisfying. She was gorgeous, Vernon knew that, and Beth knew he was an extraordinary example of masculine beauty. What were they waiting for?

Smiling at his bride, Vernon picked her up and very gently laid her on the bed. He stood there, for a moment, looking down upon his wife. He studied her from head to toe, and enjoyed every silken inch. Then he slid in next to her, loving the feel of her soft, sweet scented skin against his own. His arm reached around her, pulling her closer. Placing his hand on her tummy, he slowly and lightly circled it, imagining the child being kept snug within, and a lump formed in his throat.

"Sweetheart, I'm in unchartered territory, here. I want you real bad, but I need to think of the child. Is it safe?"

Beth smiled serenely. "There's nothing you'll do that will endanger my babe. We trust you."

"Don't you mean, our babe?" Vernon leaned over and spread a row of kisses over the slight swell of her belly. The baby chose that moment to turn.

"Feel that?" he asked, excitedly. "That's amazing. Does it hurt when he rolls like that?"

She chuckled. "No. It feels wonderful. Soon you'll get to feel his kicks. They can be powerful, but it's comforting to feel those, too. Now, Vernon, make love to me, please. Show me you love me." Beth sighed as she pulled his face down to hers. She smothered him in kisses, making it difficult to breathe. She was desperate for something more.

Vernon's hand traveled lower, parting her long legs, making his entry into her body, easier. She was wet and ready for him.

Beth was aware of his thick shaft, pulsing against her thigh. She closed her eyes, waiting for him to possess her.

He positioned his hard and engorged tip at her entrance, and proceeded slowly, going deeper, filling her, sinking further into her wet heat. Going slow was heavenly torture for him. She was hot and slick inside and so very tight. It was hard to believe that he was not her first. He looked down into her shining face and took joy in the brilliance of her sky blue eyes. She had the look of a woman overcome by passion and being well pleased by the man she loved.

"Angel," he gasped, as he thrust himself deep inside her, until there was room for no more. Vernon was large, and that worried him, but Beth seemed to be comfortable with him. He began to pump inside her, slowly at first, and then after a few minutes, he couldn't restrain his ardor one second longer. Faster and harder, he thrust. Beth clawed his back in raw desire and her mouth opened in ecstasy. Her lips were hungry, ravenous for a taste of her man.

He thought his heart would surely burst with joy. Never before had it been like this.

A sense of impending release overcame Vernon, and he knew it could not be held off for very long. He needed to bring Beth with him. "Darling, let yourself go. Feel my love inside you. Let your body reach its climax. Now, sweetheart, now. Feel me move." He pumped harder and harder as sweat gilded his body. Just as he thought he might not be able to refrain from reaching his own release, he felt her body stiffen and start to quiver from within.

Beth's eyes opened wide, questioning what was happening to

her? She felt a deep tightening sensation in her lower regions. An urge to reach an unknown summit was overwhelming. Each nerve cried out for release when, suddenly, she shattered into a thousand little bits, crying out her husband's name. Light exploded behind her eyes and her body convulsed, squeezing Vernon tightly, while still inside. Beth was carried away by the tremendous sensations of it all.

Vernon cried out, "Angel," just before he exploded his seed into her. He pumped and pumped; releasing every thing he had into his wife. He collapsed beside her, both breathing heavily and taking in the moment.

"What was that?" Beth inquired after a few minutes.

"That, my darling, was the first of many earth-shattering climaxes for you. That's what making love is all about. Have you never experienced fulfillment?"

Beth shook her head.

"A woman should experience as much pleasure as any man. Did you experience pleasure?"

She smiled a sly and slightly wicked smile. "Husband, if it was any more pleasurable, I would have died from it. You promise I will feel that again?"

He leaned over her and kissed her slightly swollen lips and growled, "Is it too soon to find out?"

They made love several times, that afternoon. Each time, he treated her tenderly, with respect and admiration—but mostly with love. She was his everything and he needed her to know it. She had suffered so much and he vowed she would never know that kind of pain again. In every way, she had been an innocent.

Vernon was sleeping soundly, his breathing constant and reassuring. Beth could not believe her good fortune in meeting this amazing man, and at a time when she felt her life could be over. Her heart swelled with joy at the mere thought of him, bringing tears to her eyes. Her eyes lovingly traveled over his strong and muscular body. She marveled at the strength and perfection of him. Lightly running her fingers over his chest, she noticed a number of scars. They were, no doubt, the result of the torture he'd received not so long ago, at the hands of those despicable outlaws.

On his abdomen, she noticed several unusual scars, dark red in color. They were small rectangles, about four to six inches long and approximately one half inch wide. *What caused those?* Just as her hand began to trace his rib cage, she heard a small snicker.

"What? Are you pretending to be asleep?" she accused.

Vernon laughed. "For crying out loud, woman. A man needs a little rest if he's to keep his wife satisfied. There you go, tickling me while I slumber." His green eyes twinkled. "I am quite ticklish in a few places, you know."

"Where?" Beth asked, mischievously.

"Ha! I'll never tell you. I don't trust you, woman."

He reached across and grabbed her, pulling her tightly against his chest. "I guess you need to be taught a lesson. A man needs his sleep." His fingers found their mark as he tickled her under her arms, causing her to laugh hysterically!

"Stop! Stop. I can't breathe! The baby! Don't forget the baby!"

It was as if she had thrown a bucket of ice-cold water on Vernon. "Oh my Lord, how could I've forgotten? Are you all right, sweetheart?" The man appeared terrified.

"Sucker!" Beth shouted, as she rolled over on top and pinned his arms down to his side. She was merciless as she ran her fingers around his ribcage, forcing him to laugh until he was crying.

"Give? Say uncle! Say it!" she demanded.

"Okay … uncle!" Vernon yelled.

Beth stopped her fun, her chest rising and falling with each breath. She pushed a curl back from her forehead and waited for Vernon to speak. It felt good and deliciously wicked to be victorious.

"Lord, woman. Who did I marry? You're quite the bully, you know."

Beth suddenly looked very sorry and quite contrite. She stuck out her lower lip in the cutest pout Vernon had ever seen. He knew he would never be able to get his way with her. She owned him, body and soul, and he smiled, thinking it was an exquisite surrender.

"I'm sorry, husband. Forgive me?" she whispered low.

Vernon looked at this woman-child he'd married. Beautiful, did not do her justice. He stared reverently at her … just as her hands started to touch her breasts. He couldn't believe his eyes, as she very softly, caressed her bosoms, running her fingers lightly over her nipples, causing them to harden. Vernon licked his lips—his mouth was so dry he couldn't swallow. His innocent angel was seducing him.

Her nipples pebbled under her soft touch. Then she grasped the tips and pulled slightly, causing them to swell and grow larger. Beth leaned her head back, tossing her golden mane, and sighed loudly. She found she enjoyed being the temptress.

That was it! Vernon couldn't take any more. His body was going to explode if he didn't find relief inside his wife, and at this very instant. He grabbed her and pulled her down on top of him.

"Ride me, precious. Ride me hard!" He placed his hands on her hips and guided her down onto his swollen shaft, burying himself deep within her.

Her body throbbed in response. "Oh, Vernon. This feels so ... so amazing." Beth discovered she loved being in control of the speed and the forcefulness of their lovemaking. She rode him well—too well. Vernon found it difficult to hold off his release.

What he saw, hovering above him, was every young man's dream. This woman was his fantasy in living flesh. With her golden hair falling down around her creamy shoulders and onto his chest, with her perfect breasts heaving back and forth, beckoning him to take a taste of their fruity nipples, he found he was in paradise. Her sex tightened around him. *Thank goodness*, he thought to himself. She was on the verge of her own fulfillment; he wouldn't have to hold out much longer.

Beth bucked and pressed herself onto him, rubbing harder and harder until they exploded together, spasm after glorious spasm, sharing the ecstasy of fulfillment. She collapsed on top of Vernon, their bodies covered with the sheen of perspiration.

After some time had passed and their hearts had returned to a normal rhythm, they lay together, curled around one another like contented cats. Vernon spoke up. "Well, little lady. I guess I don't have to wonder if you can ride a horse. I think you could teach me a few tricks of your own." He smiled with admiration for his new bride.

He brushed a wet curl from Beth's neck, enjoying the way it sprung back into a tight coil. "Is it time for your bath?" He had fantasized about running his hands over her wet soapy body for some while now. It was time he treated his wife to some special attention … and himself, as well. His eyes shone with excitement, just at the thought of it. "May I?"

"You're such a romantic, Vernon. Of course, you may bathe me, if I can return the favor. I would love to run my hands over your wet muscles. Order the water extra hot."

Vernon insisted that Beth be the first into the tub and she gladly complied. She laid her head back and closed her eyes, totally relaxed as her husband soaped his cloth and gently started bathing her shoulders. He slowly worked his way down, pausing for a while to play with her breasts and nipples. Vernon seemed to be a bosom buddy. He delighted in their weight and size and the way they filled his hands. He especially like the way they tilted up, and were capped by delicious pink nipples. From her breasts, his gaze traveled down to her belly, round with child. He gently swabbed the precious mound. It was awe inspiring to know that a small human life was being protected and cared for within that lovely body—and truly miraculous.

Vernon lifted her legs, one at a time, and started sudsing her pretty little toes and her feet. He remarked on how lovely they were. He soaped and massaged his way up to her hips and continued on to her most private place. With a wicked smile, he proceeded to soap and lather her feminine parts. Carefully, he slipped one finger inside, soon joined by a second. In and out, and all around, his fingers undulated her sex.

First, Beth gasped, not expecting his touch, but quickly, it was followed by a smile. "Mmmm, feels divine," she cooed.

Her body was warm silk inside and it grasped Vernon's fingers, tightly. He reasoned he had to stop or they would be back in the bed before he knew it.

"You're done, lazy girl. Now it's my turn," he declared happily.

He reached down and lifted her from the tub. "Don't bother to dress. I want to watch you, while you bathe me." He winked.

Beth knew what he liked to watch, so she slowly dragged her breasts around his face and shoulders, while she washed his curly hair. He had such nice hair. It was incredibly soft and a very pretty color.

Then, there was that dimple. Beth couldn't help herself.

From the time she first met him, she had been held spellbound by the charming cleft in his chin. Since falling in love, she had kissed it many times, even ran her tongue over its surface, but now, she wanted to play with it. She sudsed her finger and placed it directly over the dimple. Grinning, she bored into it; delighting in the tiny suction she could create. She kissed it, licked it, and blew on it; having so much fun that Vernon had to call a halt to it. In her exuberance, she hadn't noticed his face was covered in lather from her soapy breasts and he could barely breathe. She laughed at his predicament, but agreed to move on.

Creating a mass of bubbles, she ran her hands down his strong back. His hard muscles felt like granite beneath her hands. She noticed old scars from a whip and a few round scars that could have been from bullets. *What has he endured*, she asked herself?

Moving on around to his chest and stomach, she couldn't help but admire his masculine torso. His shoulders were broad and his chest was finely sculpted. His nipples were flat and begging to be licked. She delighted in hearing her husband groan, as she put one in her mouth and suckled it deeply. He tasted of soap and of great strength—if that had a flavor. She worked her way down to his belly button. It was of a perfect size and partially hidden in his curly, sandy hair. His stomach was flat and his hips were narrow. She would never tire of touching his body.

The last thing Beth needed to wash was his manhood. It had grown considerably while she had been bathing him. Soaping the cloth, she reached under the water and grasped him firmly in her hands.

"Holy Cow! Beth." He shouted, as he sat straight up, sloshing water onto the floor. "You can't do all that to me and then just grab me that way. I'll explode in your hand! You've got no idea of the effect you have on me, but I'll tell you now. I'm just a man who's besotted with his beautiful wife, and you're going to have to cut me some slack, or I'm sure to die from desire."

Vernon jumped to his feet and stood there, water dripping from his massive frame. "Hand me a towel and you go stand over there—way over there." He pointed across the room. His face shown the strain he was under as he tried to take control of himself and the situation. "I think it would be wise if we took a little stroll and enjoyed what's left of the sunshine. What say you?"

"Of course, dear. If that's what you *really* want to do. I just wanted to lay around and cuddle and get all sticky again, but if you'd rather go out—" Beth sat down on the bed, wiggling her round little bottom on the sheet. She was enjoying herself, immensely.

"I guess I can pleasure myself a bit, before we go."

Vernon threw down the towel and lunged for the bed and his sexy wife. "God, Beth. You'll surely be the death of me." Then he proceeded to take possession of his wife, kissing and smiling and having the time of his life.

# CHAPTER ELEVEN

As the two lovers rested, Beth found herself so enthralled with her husband that she could not take her eyes off his naked form. She needed to know everything about him and the life he led before they met. He was a man of experience—which she knew for a fact, as his flesh bared testimony to his many trials.

"Darling, tell me about your scars. I know you were hurt seriously, just a while back, but I don't understand what could have made them all. It looks as if you've been shot more than once." The concern she had for her husband was evident in her blue eyes and Vernon could see she was frightened of what she may hear.

"It's nothing for you to worry about, angel. Being a ranger can be dangerous work, but it isn't always. Most of the bullet holes came from the war in Kentucky. The last time I was shot, I woke up and asked myself, what the hell am I doing fighting in Kentucky, when all I ever really wanted was to come out here and find a woman like you to love? So, I lit out. It wasn't desertion, 'cause I never signed up. I just felt I needed to help our boys out a little, even though it was obvious that they couldn't possibly win and it would end badly for us all.

"I've been stabbed once or twice breaking up disagreements in the saloons. I even had a pitchfork drove into my thigh by a jealous wife. She was aiming for her cheating husband, but stuck me instead. Damn, but that hurt. It was one sharp pitchfork." He chuckled, thinking back on it, while unconsciously rubbing his thigh.

Beth still had some questions. "What are those whip marks across your shoulders and those strange red stripes on your stomach?"

"Those, my darling, are best left to be explained later. You're correct in assuming they're from my last run in with those renegades, but it's not acceptable conversation on our honeymoon … and to be quite honest, I can't revisit it, just yet. I'm sorry, darling."

"They tortured you, didn't they?" she asked, knowing the truth.

"Yes."

"I'm so excited, Vernon. Where will we be living? Not behind the Ranger's Office, I hope. I can't raise a child there." Suddenly, Beth looked scandalized just thinking about the dismal prospects of their possible living arrangements.

"Now sugar, would I have married you and then have no place to put you? What kind of a husband do you think I am? There's a couple of rooms above the Fancy Garter that I thought—Ouch!" he hollered.

Beth was laughing as she struck his arm, lightly. "You're a mean man, Mr. Gunn, teasing your sweet little wife when she's in a most delicate condition." She batted her eyelashes at him.

"Delicate condition? You pack a pretty strong wallop for a *delicate* little wife, Mrs. Gunn. Come here, so I can teach you a lesson." Vernon reached out for Beth and drew her close so he could kiss her sweet, sweet lips. "Yes, honey, I do believe your lips are sweeter than candy." He smacked his lips loudly, causing Beth to roll with laughter at his silly antics.

"Seriously, Vernon. Where are we going to live?"

"I've been given it some thought, for some time now. Guess you'd been in town a month or so, when I started thinking about hitchin' up with you. I knew when I asked you, you'd never *really* refuse me." He grinned. "So, I started looking for a nice little place appropriate to start our lives together. Right before Christmas, Emma Taylor, a nice old lady I met when I first came to Tucson, passed away in her sleep—God rest her soul. She was quite elderly and left no family. For years, she taught piano, hereabouts. I went to her funeral and the preacher made mention of her house.

"The long and the short of it is … I bought it. Lock, stock, and barrel! It's yours and mine and the kid's. It's a real nice house, honey. Maybe not as nice as the one you grew up in, back in Richmond, but for Tucson, it's right nice. The baby will have his own room, with one to spare." He smiled at the thought of someday, filling both those bedrooms. "It has space for a garden and even a few chickens and a milk cow, if you want. Unfortunately, the piano had to stay with the house 'cause it was too big and heavy for anyone to move." He smiled real big. "I can't wait to hear you play it, sweetheart."

Tears flowed down Beth's cheeks. To think, she now had the love of her life, a baby kicking happily inside her, and a new home with a piano! Life didn't get any better than this.

Like a small child, Beth wiped her tears on her sleeve before gazing up at the man she loved. "Can we have a party, Vernon? I've never given a party before, in my whole life, and we have so many good friends now. Can we?"

"Sure thing, angel. We'll tell Sara, and give her a glass and spoon, with which she can announce it to all of Tucson. Oh yeah, that reminds me. Knowing Sara, we need to prepare for a pup real soon," Vernon chuckled. "She's something special, that girl."

April first was fast approaching and the Williams' were preparing for their move. It just about broke Beth's heart to see them leave. She had grown to love the children almost as if they were her own. If it hadn't been for David and Mary, she and Vernon would, in all probability, not have gotten married to each other. The Williams' were more than family—they were their best and truest friends.

Finally, the last of the wagons was loaded up with the new furniture David had purchased. He insisted Mary have the best of everything. Beth sat on the porch of the hotel, rocking little Rosie in her lap.

"Rosie," she sighed, as she nuzzled the infant's soft black hair and watched her blow tiny milk bubbles. "I'm going to miss you terribly." The child was Mary in miniature. How different she would be the next time she held her.

The older children, along with the two pups, were as wild as little Indians and raring to go. They had been confined in the wagon all morning. Vernon helped Mary up to the wagon seat, reluctant to let go, and David gave Beth a tender goodbye kiss on her cheek, before he climbed aboard to join his wife. You could see the happiness radiating out from him. Once again, he would have a ranch to call his own.

"Now, don't ferget. Yer comin' fer a visit, real soon."

David tipped his hat at his brother-in-law and his new wife, and cracked the whip, causing the team to lurch forward, sending them were on their way. Everyone waved and shouted their goodbyes, as their eyes filled with tears of happiness.

"Good luck," Beth hollered out. "Keep in touch." Her heart was already breaking … "We'll miss you." She was crying, now … "Come back, soon," she whispered, as the wagon rolled out of sight. "Good bye," she sobbed, to herself.

Beth stood there, staring off down the road toward a small speck on the horizon. The family had long disappeared. She sniffled and hiccupped, then slowly turned back toward the sidewalk, where she saw Vernon watching her. Just the sight of his handsome face made her heart flutter with joy. She looked up into his intelligent green eyes and took comfort in knowing her place was here, with him.

A brilliant smile replaced her tears, as she walked up to him and wrapped her arms around his waist, laying her head against his chest. "I love you, darling," she sighed.

"Well, little lady, I've got a surprise for you."

"A surprise? For me?" Beth hadn't received many surprises in her life—at least not many good ones. "What is it?" she asked excitedly.

Vernon laughed. His wife reminded him of an adorable child, eagerly anticipating a present on her birthday. Her innocence melted his heart. "Pretty lady, I have arranged to have three entire days off to spend with my bride. We've got some settling in, of our own, to do. I've got a bankroll burning a hole in my pocket. What would you say to three days of shopping?"

He waited for her reaction.

Beth thought it over, taking her time. Frowning and chewing on her bottom lip, she gave it serious consideration. She liked to shop, but three days of it? She had better plans.

"Well, Vernon. If we get started right this minute and shop until you beg to call a halt to it, do you think we can finish it up today?"

This was not the reaction he expected. What wife didn't want to go on a three day shopping spree? "What do you have in mind?"

"Sweetheart," she said, with a slight tone of exasperation in her voice. "We've been married less than two weeks and you want to spend *all* that time *shopping?* Can't you think of a better way to spend our time together?" Beth looked at him, as if he didn't have the sense to come in, out of the rain, then gave him a soft bump with her hip.

"Ahh ..." Her meaning registered. He grabbed her hand and pulled her down the sidewalk at a slow run. "Let's go!" he shouted, gleefully.

Within three weeks, Vernon and Beth were completely settled in. The house was cheery and comfortable and ready for Beth to give piano lessons. She placed notices in some of the stores and, of course, in the lobby of the Hotel Doolittle. She took a few over to the schoolhouse and passed them out to the children. They were very happy to see their favorite teacher, and she was glad to be reunited with them. The new teacher was older, but extremely nice, and she had taken over Beth's class with very little effort.

"Please stop by to say hello, anytime, Mrs. Gunn. I've heard such nice things about you from the children," Miss Browning said. "Do you teach music lessons to adults, too?"

Beth liked her, immediately. "Certainly. I even give discounts to adults in the field of education." She smiled and winked.

It was nearly noon and Beth had only a couple of notices left to distribute. Her tummy was rumbling and she thought about walking over to see if Vernon could have lunch with her. Maybe they'd share a sandwich. As she drew closer to the Ranger's Office, she noticed a group of men standing just outside the doors. Curious, she walked up and inquired what was going on?

"Ranger Gunn got into it, at the livery. Some stupid coyote said somethin' not too flatterin' about the his wife havin' a papoose from some other feller—her not bein' all she said she was—and not fittin' for the womenfolk around here." The stranger stopped speaking as he looked into the face of the lovely lady. She appeared to have been struck hard by what he had just said. It was then he noticed her rounded belly.

"Oh, I'm sorry, ma'am. It weren't nothin' I believed. He was a hothead and probably drunk, to boot. Don't you pay him no account. The ranger took care of it, right good and proper … Arizona style. We call it justice." He tipped his hat and skedaddled down the boardwalk, not wanting to face the pretty lady's husband.

Beth charged ahead, pushing her way through the open door. When her eyes adjusted to the dim light, she saw Vernon leaning back in his chair, allowing the doctor to attend to the injuries on his face.

"Oh, my God, Vernon!" she cried. "What's happened to your pretty face?"

Beth was serious, but the term, *pretty*, had Vernon and the old doc chuckling.

"This here ranger's still just as purty as a picture, ma'am," the old man replied. "A few more scars won't make no difference, one way or the other."

Looking at Vernon, through her tears, Beth had to know the truth. "I heard that you got into a fight with a man over things he said about me. Is that so, Vernon?"

His face clouded up. "Don't listen to all that talk. It wasn't anything."

"I know better, darling. I've heard women whisper behind my back and I've seen some of their accusing glances. Not everyone in Tucson is as accepting of me as our friends. Promise me you won't do this again."

"Don't worry about that. I'm on probation for the next six months. If I do something stupid before then, I'll lose my badge." He was serious. This was, after all, everything he had always wanted to do and now, because of her, his dream was in jeopardy … or at least that's what Beth believed.

"I'm finished for the day. As soon as this old saw-bones finishes stitching me up, how about you and I go over to the Blue Owl and having some lunch? I'm starving and I can hear your stomach growling, from here. Gotta feed my son, you know." He grinned.

"Oh, Vernon. You're wonderful and I love you so." Beth beamed with pride.

A few days later, while Beth was picking up some fabric to

make baby clothes, Mr. Jones informed her that a big box had arrived all the way from Chicago. "You want to send Vernon down to get it?"

"What's in it, Mr. Jones?"

"Now, how'd I know that? You women are all alike. You get a big fancy box from Chicago or New York and you can't wait 'til your man brings it home to find out what's in it." He snickered. "My wife is the same. Can't surprise her, no way, no how. She tears into everythin'. Now, you go on over and tell Vernon he has a box to pick up." The storekeeper winked at Beth, just before he turned and stepped away.

*A big box for me?* She smiled to herself as she excitedly started off down the street. Maybe, if she pleaded real hard, he would tell her what was in it.

Upon entering the small office, she noticed her husband sitting with his head down, studying the papers on his desk. "What's so important that you don't notice your wife entering your workplace?" she teased.

"Oh," Vernon replied, noncommittally. "It's just regular work … notices and such. What brings you here in the middle of the day?" He finally looked up, while carefully shuffling the papers, placing those on top of the pile, under the bottom, and out of sight. Beth could see the strain on his face.

"Mr. Jones says he has a big fancy box waiting for you to pick up at the mercantile. It's for me, he says." Beth sashayed around the room. "It is, isn't it? You're going to spoil me, Vernon Gunn."

"Ha! You're already spoiled, so it don't make no difference how much I give you, from here on out. Besides, it really isn't so much for you as it is for the baby." His cheeks colored. "I saw it in a catalogue and thought, since I don't have much time off and I don't have the right tools, why make a cradle when I can buy the best one they sell?"

Beth clapped her hands together with joy. "Oh, Vernon, a cradle? You're so sweet. Will you bring it home with you, tonight? Will you set it up in the baby's room?"

"Sure thing, angel. Now, you be careful and get on home. I've got work to do, here. Gotta pay for that cradle." His eyes crinkled with good humor as he smiled, briefly, and then returned to his papers.

"Vernon," Beth said softly. "It's really happening, isn't it?"

"What's that, angel?"

"We're going to have a baby and be a real family soon, aren't we?"

Once more, Vernon's gaze settled upon his wife. He admired her loving and gentle nature. Life could be so unfair, he thought. "Yes, angel. We're having a baby, and I consider myself the luckiest man alive. I only hope I can make you as happy as you make me. Now go home, woman, and get some rest. I won't be long, I promise."

The paper he'd been studying so intently, when Beth came in, was a notice from Washington. Senator Price was appealing to all law enforcement officers to come to his aid in the arrest and conviction of his son's killer. The man was relentless. The notice said the murderer was a tall, blonde woman, of loose morals. Being rather pretty, she was more than likely trying to pass herself off as a woman of good breeding. There were rumors that she had obtained a train ticket to St. Louis and had gone west from there. Her name, Ryann Beaufort, may not be the name she is using. Her last known address was the Doolittle Boarding House in Richmond, Virginia.

"Good God, the Doolittle." Vernon didn't know what to do with this new information. It couldn't be passed off as a coincidence. *No one must see this*. He tore it in half and stuck it in his pocket. He'd been a ranger for long enough to know when they were closing in on their man, and this sure felt like that. Only, this wasn't a man … it was Beth, and he swore he'd do whatever it took to protect her and their child. He needed to talk to Horace Doolittle.

"Have you talked to Harry?" Vernon tried not to be too obvious with his questioning. He knew that Horace needed to protect his brother. "I received a notice just today and it bothers me a great deal. It seems that this *person* they're looking for, last lived at his boarding house."

Horace avoided talking about his brother's involvement in the trouble back east. Harry had been watched and tormented by the police, for months. Most of his boarders had moved out, not willing to be questioned and harassed every time they left or entered the premises. He wasn't certain how long he'd be able to hold out. The two brothers were trying to come up with a plan that could get Harry out to Tucson and yet not give away Ryann's location.

"Thanks fer lettin' me know, Ranger. We've almost got things worked out, but we still need another month," Horace said. He looked around to ascertain that they were alone. Leaning over, he whispered, "Tell Beth, Doo is worried. People are askin' the girls, that worked close to the boardin' house, a lot of questions. Oh, yeah, tell her that her friend, Libby somethin' … has left town."

Vernon thought about that and said, "Thanks, but I don't think I'll pass that message on. I can't have her worried just now. The baby is due in another month and it can't do her any good. I'll take care of everything. If you hear anything you think I should know, will you get word to me?"

"Sure thing, Ranger. I'm mighty partial to that little gal o' yours, and Harry would have my hide if I let something happen to her."

June 1st, and Beth was miserable and cranky to the extreme. Vernon walked quietly around her. She was too hot and her ankles were swollen. Of course, she couldn't see them for herself, but she took his word for it. Nothing fit comfortably because she was so huge. However, what made her crankier than anything else was the fact that she had gotten too unattractive for her husband. Vernon never made love to her anymore and she was pouting. He still kissed her, but she felt his heart wasn't in it.

"Vernon … what are you doing now?" she whined.

"Exactly what I was doing the last time you asked, … sweetheart," he sighed. She was driving him a little mad. His heart went out to her, but every five minutes it was the same thing. If he suggested they take a walk, she thought it was too hot. If he suggested she take a nap, she said she wasn't tired, only bored. She didn't want to eat, drink or leave her chair. What was he supposed to do for the next few weeks? Did Mary behave this way, he wondered?

"Honey … I'm bored."

Vernon stood up suddenly, knocking his chair over backwards. He marched out onto the porch, prepared to finally have it out with her—until he saw how pitiful she looked. Once again, he lost the battle.

Her hair had partially come undone from its pins and was hanging damp around her slender neck. Not only had her shapely ankles swollen to twice their normal size, but Vernon noticed her wedding band looked uncomfortably tight. Her eyes were filled with tears and her nose was red and running, from crying so often. His angel did indeed make a pathetic picture.

Yet she looked up at him as if he was her knight in shining armor. Guilt forced him to clear his throat before speaking. "Darling, you look so sad. Come with me and let me try to make you feel better." He held out his hands.

It took Beth two attempts just to stand, but she finally succeeded. Vernon noticed how she waddled across the floor in front of him. Two thoughts entered his mind. "Bless her dear heart … and … thank God women had the children!"

He guided Beth to their bedroom where he proceeded to undress her. Slowly, he unbuttoned her dress and threw it aside. He then lifted her damp chemise up over her head. He could tell she was uncomfortable with him seeing her standing nude in just her stockings. Beth was aware the light was bright enough for him to take notice of all her flaws. She tried to hide behind her hands.

"No, no, sugar. There's no point in hiding yourself from me. I've memorized every hill and valley of your glorious body. Don't you know how magnificent you are?" He pulled her hands down, exposing her plump round breasts. He bent to lay a soft kiss on the tip of each one. Looking up at her, he grinned broadly, showing his pleasure with her.

"Sit here, on the edge of the bed, angel. Let me roll down your stockings. It will make you cooler. In fact, why don't you skip wearing stockings for the rest of the summer? They look terribly hot and uncomfortable. I think you should skip the chemise as well. Arizona is like a furnace in the summertime and you're not used to it. Besides, once our child arrives, you'll be getting in and out of that bodice every hour or so." He winked and licked his lips. He couldn't help it. Every time he thought of his wife's breasts, his mouth watered. Their child was a lucky little guy, he mused.

"Now, my wife. I want you to lie back and allow your husband to tend to your wants and needs. Let me cool you off some."

Vernon walked over to the bowl and pitcher and poured a cool stream of water over a clean cloth. Lifting her arms, and starting with her fingertips, Vernon took the cool wet cloth and dragged it up and down the length of Beth's arms. She sighed with pleasure. It was pure heaven. He cooled her forehead and brushed the hair up off her neck. Beth's nipples puckered when the cool water ran in small rivulets over her ripe breasts. Vernon grinned, as he couldn't stop there. He needed to taste the swollen tips and suck them gently into his mouth. Soon, he figured, those lovely orbs would be off limits to him … but not yet.

Beth was enjoying this interlude more than anything she had experienced in quite some time. It was amazing how her husband could read her mind and know instinctively, just what she needed. She closed her eyes and let the feeling of ecstasy overtake her.

Vernon moved on to Beth's tummy. It surprised him whenever he saw how large his wife had grown. How could a woman's body do this, he wondered? It was hard and rather lumpy. The child rolled around much of the time, and kicked from all sides. He knew she was having difficulty sleeping, but rubbing her stomach seemed to calm the child inside.

He ran the cloth slowly down the inside of her thighs, and took particular pleasure in cooling off her woman's parts. He got a good close look and made sure he didn't ignore anything.

"Angel, I would like to sample your sweetness, now. Would you mind if I take just a little time to taste your wares?"

Beth laughed at his formality. "Please do, sir. All I have, is yours," she joked.

The moment his tongue touched her, Beth writhed with pleasure and called out his name. The sensation was electric. His mouth searched her out, exploring her inner folds, stroking and sucking until she thought she might swoon from desire. She craved to have him fill her. "Please, Vernon. I need you, darling. I need to feel you inside me."

Vernon smiled and kissed his way back up to his wife's lovely mouth. Knowing he could not love her the way she preferred just now, the attention he gave her with his mouth and fingers would have to suffice. "Soon, angel, but for now, we must be patient. You like this, don't you?"

"Yes," she purred. "I like it very much."

Vernon was pleased by her answer. It was damn near impossible for him not to make sexual demands on his wife. Lately, he felt like a starving man. The fragrance of his wife's arousal acted as an aphrodisiac to him, and her taste was ambrosia to his tongue. He continued to cover her with kisses and intimate caresses, until she rested on the brink of orgasm.

"Beth, is it safe for me to bring you to fulfillment?"

"If you don't, I'll never speak to you again," she shouted.

Vernon laughed and worked his tongue around her little nubbin, creating magic, and driving her over the edge. Feeling her body shiver and tighten around him, he knew she had been released from her sweet torment.

Afterward, he sat up and looked at his wife. She had the face of a woman well satisfied and at peace, for the moment. His work was complete. He had finished cooling off her legs and feet, when he noticed she had fallen fast asleep. Quietly, Vernon stepped back, pulled the curtains to darken the room, and silently left with a rather smug smile on his lips.

The next week was blisteringly hot. The animals sought whatever shade they could find and most folks stayed off the streets whenever possible. Beth, oddly enough, was feeling much better. Her baby was sitting lower and gave her more breathing room. She took Vernon's advice and wore only a dress and slippers. Of course, she never let anyone see her dressed so informally.

Mrs. Jones came by every evening to check up on the young mother-to-be. She nodded to Vernon and patted his hand. "It won't be long now, son. You're going to be a papa real soon."

A frisson of fear ran up Vernon's spine at the mere thought of it. Was he really ready for the responsibility? It was too late for cold feet, but he felt like running and hiding until it was all over.

Early one morning, when Vernon first arrived at the ranger's station, he discovered new Wanted Notices had been delivered during the evening hours, the night before. It was imperative that he saw them before anyone else had the chance. Within minutes, he had thumbed through the top five or six when he heard the sound of gunfire, out in the street.

Drawing his pistol, Vernon threw open the door, and looked

up and down the boardwalk for the disturbance. Four men were running from the bank and mounting their horses. By the looks of them, they'd made quite a haul, with each one carrying a heavy bag.

"Stop!" Vernon shouted, as he drew a bead on the man riding the lead horse. Aiming true, Vernon fired off a shot and the outlaw flew off the back of his horse. The two men behind him rode over his inert body, not caring for anything but getting away. Vernon stood out in the street, bravely facing the two oncoming horses and fired off two more shots.

One man fell, but the other was only wounded and it would take more than a bullet in this thigh to stop him. In one swift move, he reached around, grabbing his partner's horse and rode straight for the ranger. Vernon spun out of the way, just in the nick of time. Firing from behind, he struck the robber in the upper shoulder, but still, the outlaw rode on.

Vernon looked around desperately for a horse at his disposal. He shouted at two men standing on the sidewalk. "Where the hell's the sheriff?"

"Killt!" answered one man.

"Aw, hell," Vernon spit. He ran for the painted gelding tied off at the rail, and swung up into the saddle. Digging his heels into the horse's flanks, he took off after the wounded man. He'd gotten all three of them; two killed and one severely wounded. Then, suddenly he reined the horse to a stop. *Not three! It was four!* "There's four of them. Shit!" he growled.

He turned the horse around thinking that the wounded man couldn't go too far before getting some medical attention. It was that fourth man that worried Vernon. He rode full out, back toward the bank.

The street was deserted. Slowly, he guided the horse down the center of town. Following the tracks leaving the bank, he knew the man had come this way. He continued to walk the horse down Main Street, looking right and left. The tracks veered to the left, just past the Doolittle. He followed, feeling the hairs on the back of his neck rise up. Quietly, he entered a narrowing of the road. He knew it could be a trap, but why wouldn't the robber hightail it out of here, instead of hanging around trying to kill him? Who had a grudge against him?

Suddenly, his blood ran cold. He spurred the horse to a run, racing for home. Before throwing himself off the saddle, he heard Beth scream. Rage overcame his good sense, as he threw himself through the parlor window, rolled and came up to his feet with his gun blazing. He fired straight into the bastard holding Beth hostage. She fell to the floor and he kept firing. Vernon fired long after the bullets and been spent.

Strong hands pulled him back and took his gun. He allowed the hands to guide him to his chair. Looking up and seeing reality for the first time in minutes, Vernon recognized Ranger Barclay, his friend.

"Beth," he said weakly. "How's my wife?"

"Doc's with her, now. She appears to be shaken up, but unhurt … thanks to you. How you doin'? You want to clue me in on what happened here?"

Barclay pressed a glass of water into Vernon's trembling hand. He drank and began to speak. "I heard the shots coming from the bank. I shot three men as they were riding away with the loot. I was feeling pretty proud of myself—going after the wounded man and all—when I remembered it was four men that robbed the bank, not three. One had split from the others and had perhaps gotten away. It wasn't until I followed his tracks that I started to suspect this might have been personal. I had a good idea he was headed for my house … and Beth."

He drank some more water. "Are you sure Beth's okay?" His voice was still shaking.

Ranger Barclay nodded.

"I couldn't take the chance that he'd hurt her, so I just lost my mind a little and jumped through the window glass. Damn good thing I did, too. He had her by her throat and was aiming for the door." Vernon started to tremble. He couldn't stop the tears that began rolling down his face. "What would I have done, Barclay, if he'd hurt her? I can't even think about it without gettin' sick."

"Take it easy, Vernon. Beth's fine and you did the right thing. Did you know him?"

"Oh, yeah. I knew him," Vernon growled. "The bastard was Manuel Ortiz, brother to the varmint I killed out in box canyon. Raoul Ortiz was a S.O.B. and he deserved to die. So Manuel's dead then? I killed him?"

"Oh, he's dead all right. About six times dead. Remind me not to get on your bad side." The ranger grinned. "Why don't you take the next couple of days off and spend them with your lovely wife. I ain't got nothin' to do. I'll fill in for you."

Vernon stood up and gave Barclay a hug. "Thanks, pardner. I'm not doing too well, at the moment. Feel a little shaky. I do appreciate your offer." Then he walked off, needing to check on his wife, for himself.

The couple spent all the rest of that day and night, asleep, held in each other's arms. Late, the next morning, Beth stirred. She looked at her sleeping husband and was filled with admiration of his bravery. He had come charging in, with no regard for his own safety, and saved her from harm. Vernon was a real hero, her very own knight in shining armor. She got up on one elbow and kissed his beautifully sculpted lips.

Vernon's eyes fluttered awake. "Good morning, sunshine," he whispered, as he stretched his long body. "How are you doing this fine morning?"

"I'm feeling wonderful, thanks to you." Placing her hand on her stomach, she smiled, "We both are. How did you guess what was happening? You know, he was waiting for you to come through that door. You never would have had a chance."

"I heard you scream, angel, and I couldn't think of anything but getting to you as quickly as possible, and that just happened to be through the window." He grimaced at the thought of it. His body felt the burn of hundreds of little cuts all over it. "I guess you could say, you saved my life, as well. When I heard you scream …" Vernon didn't have the words to finish his thought. It was all too horrible to imagine.

"Mr. Doolittle and Mr. Jones came over earlier and boarded it up. We have a lot of good friends, Vernon. After this baby comes, and it cools off some, I still want to have that party. Can we?"

Vernon laughed. "We both almost get killed yesterday, and today, you're dreaming of throwing a shindig?" He shook his head. "You're an amazing woman, Elizabeth Gunn, and I thank my lucky stars, every day, that you married me. Now, give me a kiss."

Beth lay in Vernon's arms, reveling in his strength. She traced her fingers around his chest and down the center of his stomach and back up again. It was divine to lie there like that, feeling as if they had all the time in the world to enjoy each other's company. She knew of course, that life would soon intrude upon their little piece of paradise. Might as well face it head on, she thought.

"Darling, I heard you tell Ranger Barclay that you knew the dead man. He was involved in your capture, wasn't he? Will you tell me what happened to you, out there in that canyon? It might help you get past it, you know. It might ease your nightmares."

"Beth, it's ugly, but if you really want to know, I'll tell you … but only this once."

# CHAPTER TWELVE

*Six months earlier*

"Well, Napoleon, I'm beat and we haven't found a damn thing. I think tomorrow we'll turn back and go home to Beth. I miss her something fierce and I still have to get her to agree to marry me. Get up, now." Vernon spurred his horse forward, across the difficult terrain.

There had been no signs of Indian activity for the past week, and not much else either. There was evidence that marauders were out causing havoc, but he couldn't get ahead of them. He'd go back to Tucson and regroup. With fresh horses and fresh men, maybe they'd make some progress. He and his horse, Napoleon, were just plum done in. They rode slow and easy, waiting for the sun to set, so they could make camp and head back home at first sunrise.

Suddenly, Vernon caught some movement out of the corner of his eye, just as he heard some scramblin' behind the rocks. He heard the report, just after a slug hit him in the shoulder, knocking him back in the saddle. Reeling from the pain, he managed to turn Napoleon away and run for safety. Damn it, he knew better than to ride right into a stinkin' ambush.

Napoleon, given his head, fairly flew up the side of the hill, with bullets barely missing their mark. Faster and higher he climbed, with Vernon twisting and firing over his shoulder. He struck one man and watched him fall to the ground. They were going to make it. Vernon needed to reload, just when he heard

Napoleon cry out and start to stumble. The horse couldn't keep his footing as blood poured from his leg, and Vernon couldn't keep his seat. He fell under the flying hooves, barely missing having his head opened like a ripe melon. Napoleon made it out of the canyon … but he did so, without his rider.

Vernon managed to crawl behind a boulder. This wasn't over yet, he thought, as he took aim on another rider. He squeezed the trigger and the big Indian fell back with the look of surprise in his lifeless eyes. It seemed that time stood still. The more men he wounded or killed, the more appeared to take their place. His ammo was running dangerously low. Four bullets was all that stood between him and the eight or nine men bearing down on him. He could do the math and it wasn't good.

The men were shouting in Mexican. Damn it. Vernon didn't know a word of it. He promised to change that when he got home … if he got home. Just as he took a bead on the man he suspected to be the leader, pain exploded in his gun hand and the pistol flew out of his grasp. The battle was over.

The big Mexican rode up to him with his pistol aimed at Vernon's head. Sneering, with cruel black eyes and rotten teeth, he commanded, "Surrender, now, Ranger?" The man understood English.

"Do I have a choice?"

"A man always has a choice, senior, but it isn't always a pleasant one. You've been following us and making us run. I don't like to look over my shoulder and being forced to run. Now, we stop, Si?"

"What's your name?" Vernon demanded.

The outlaw just laughed. "I will tell you everything you need to know, gringo, and nothing else. Shut up now, or Raoul will shut you up, permanently," he said, looking over at a tall, thin and dangerous looking man. The man smiled big at Vernon, letting him know that he would enjoy causing him enough pain to shut him up.

"Tie him up and walk him behind our horses, amigos. Keep an eye on him!"

The outlaws half-walked and half-dragged Vernon for two days. They laughed at his distress. He was given no food and only enough water to keep him alive. It was clear to Vernon that he was being kept alive for either ransom or for their enjoyment.

He wasn't sure which, but prayed for the former. The bullet had passed through his shoulder, but he could tell by the heat building up around the wound that it was getting infected. He knew that the bullet, he received in his hand, had broken a couple of bones, as it was impossible for him to make a fist.

The evening of the third day, they made camp in a small box canyon. It was obvious the outlaws had hidden out there before. Vernon was stripped of his shirt and his arms were tied to a tree in an ominous embrace.

After getting settled in and fed, the men relaxed and decided to play some cards. It seemed their captive hadn't yet suffered enough to please these heathens, so they placed a whip on the table. Whoever won the hand got possession of the whip—the higher the score, the more lashes they were allowed. They whooped and hollered, obviously excited about inflicting more pain on the big ranger.

Sure enough, after the first hand, a pockmarked Indian grabbed up the whip and flayed it across Vernon's smooth flesh. He relished his winnings as he struck again and again, slicing deep into muscle.

Vernon refused to cry out, but he couldn't will himself to stay conscious. The searing pain cut across his back incessantly, carving it into raw pieces of meat. He tried to fill his mind with visions of Beth, picturing her golden hair and her brilliant blue eyes. He tried valiantly to mask his pain with thoughts of her loveliness, but in the end, he succumbed to the blessed blackness.

Raoul threw a bucket of water on the unconscious ranger, after the men had exhausted themselves playing their kind of cards. The blood still ran down his back, but he never opened his eyes. Reluctantly, the ranger was left to embrace the tree for the rest of the night. If he was still alive in the morning, they would feed him, so they could play with him again.

"Hey, hombre! Wake up. I thought rangers were supposed to be tough. You cry like a woman," the man snarled. Vernon felt the toe of the man's boot strike his side. He heard the rib break. Still, he refused to scream or give them any satisfaction.

"Drink and eat," a young man whispered to the ranger, while he cut his leather bonds. "We must leave soon. You stay. Be back." He sat down and watched Vernon drink and eat. After

Vernon had consumed the bread and vile tasting soup, the Apache warrior retied his hands behind his back, pulling the leather strips down between his legs and securely tying them around his ankles. Hogtied in such a manner, Vernon could not even roll over. He was powerless, but thankfully, he was left alone to think and plan his escape.

The outlaws returned several hours later. Wherever the men had gone, earlier in the day, it had put them in a foul mood. Vernon noticed that one white man did not return. While he was observing them getting ready to eat and bed down for the night, he noticed the Mexican leader, Manuel, staring at him with hate filled eyes. *What was the man planning for him, tonight?* Vernon closed his eyes and waited for the inevitable.

"Hey, you … Ranger! Wake up and see what we have for you. The man pulled a bloody scalp out of his saddlebag and threw it at Vernon. It was long and blonde, covered in blood. It was a woman's scalp.

Vernon felt his stomach heave. He couldn't help himself. With nothing in his stomach, he dry-heaved over and over again, causing excruciating pain to radiate out from his broken ribs. With each gut-wrenching purge, the ugly man laughed harder and harder.

"You can relax, Ranger," he spat. "I am not going to scalp you, however your pretty curls would make me a nice coup. No, I am going to allow Silver Wolf to show you how the Apache can make a man cry for death, a thousand times. You might find it interesting." He laughed again.

"Silver Wolf! Strip this man out and peel him. Si?"

The Indian nodded. He grabbed Vernon by the ropes and led him to the center of the camp. All the men stood around, waiting for the night's entertainment to begin.

Silver Wolf staked a naked Vernon, spread eagle on the ground. He pulled out his knife and spoke softly, so that only Vernon could hear. "Make friends with the pain, white man. It is the only way."

Vernon was only partly aware of the agony spreading across his midsection. It burned … it tore at his skin. His nerves were laid bare by Silver Wolf's knife. The Indian sliced small strips of skin off his stomach, and held each piece up for inspection. Vernon was being skinned alive. He could hear the shouts and insults coming from the men, around him. Shutting his eyes and willing the pain to disappear, he thought he had screamed aloud, but it was only the pain he heard in his mind. His teeth cut through his lips, causing blood to run down his chin.

"Beth," he whispered, "my angel ..."

"Cease!" ordered Manuel. "This is no fun. The bastard's stronger than we had thought. Where are the screams and the curses? This gringo can't even die well!" He got up and spit in Vernon's face. Then taking the knife, he sliced a stripe down the center of the ranger's chest, just to see if it would bleed. At last, too tired to care anymore, he bent over and cut the ties that held Vernon to the ground.

"Tie him to the pole and we'll let the buzzards feast on him, tomorrow. Tonight, I'm riding out to see a little senorita, I met today. She don't know it, but she will make me a very happy man, before she dies." His lips turned up in a crooked smile as he strode over to the horses.

"Raoul, you are in charge. Keep watch!"

No sooner had Manuel disappeared from view, than Raoul decided to have some fun of his own. He enjoyed inflicting pain—as long as his victim couldn't fight back. Basically, he was a coward. He walked over to Vernon and gave him a good strong kick to the groin, just to get his attention.

He slapped Vernon several times and then, using his fist, he pummeled his face and upper chest. He swore when the ranger's blood splattered across his clean shirt.

"You dirty, filthy lawman. I will see that you do not live long enough for the sun to roast your skin." With both hands, he grabbed Vernon's head and slammed it hard into the post—but not before he'd pinned the ranger's badge onto his bloody flesh.

Everything finally went black for Vernon. His last thoughts were of his family and his desire to spare them pain. Soon, the blessed darkness settled over him and gave him respite from his agony.

# CHAPTER THIRTEEN

Beth sat motionless with her mouth hanging slightly ajar. Silent tears had been running down her cheeks, for some time now. "You were terrorized and tortured, the same as me. That's why you're so understanding of how I feel." She laid her head on Vernon's shoulder so that he wouldn't be a witness to the horror and revulsion she felt at what he'd revealed to her. Her eyes glanced over to the star pinned on Vernon's vest. *So that's what caused the terrible puncture wound above his heart.*

"My poor darling. I wish I could kiss it and make it all go away."

"Thank you, angel, but that's about all I remember anyway … that is until David Williams rode in, with his guns a blazing, and saved my sorry ass. I was barely conscious, but I could hear the shooting and the fear in the voices of my captors. They went loco, running around and accomplishing nothing but getting themselves shot. Manuel was lucky enough to get away, though … until he broke into my home and grabbed my wife." His voice cracked with emotion.

"God, Beth. When I think of what could have happened to you and our child."

She wrapped her arms around him tightly and cooed in his ears, "Hush. Don't think about it, now. It's over and you saved me, darling. I knew you would. We're all fine now, and our lives, together, will be long and happy. You must believe that, sweetheart."

Vernon lifted her face to his and kissed her long and hard—

right up until they heard the knock at the front door.

"What was that?" Vernon asked.

"Somebody's at the door, silly. You're dressed more than I am, you go."

"Aw, now who'd bother a man when he's a resting in bed with his gorgeous wife at his side?"

"Yer good-lookin' brother-in-law, that's who. Get dressed and get out here. The whole family has come a visitin'," David shouted through the door. Beth was certain the neighbors could hear.

"Oh, Vernon! Help me. Mary and the children are here. Hurry, hurry!" Beth pleaded.

"Mary, I'll be right out," she shouted. "Make yourself at home. I think Vernon made lemonade this morning. Help yourself!"

"Vernon made lemonade?" David chuckled quietly.

Vernon tried to find something to wrap his very pregnant wife in, besides her nightgown. She'd been living in it for the past couple of days. And where was her slippers and hairbrush?"

"Hurry, Vernon! Hurry!"

"I'm trying, Beth! Give a man a chance!"

A soft knock at the bedroom door announced Mary's arrival. "May I intrude?" she asked, as she stuck her head into the room.

Vernon stood up straight, and sighed, "Thank God. Please come in and help me get my difficult wife dressed for meeting company."

Mary smiled at her handsome brother, usually so in control of every situation. He looked worn out and completely at a loss as what to do. His hair was pointing every which-way and he could have packed his entire wardrobe into the saddlebags beneath his eyes.

"Vernon, dear, why don't you go out and keep David company, while I finish what you started?"

He didn't need to be invited twice. Vernon was through the door before Mary could complete her sentence.

Beth watched her husband run out. "Well, that didn't take long. I guess he couldn't wait to get away from me," she grumbled. Looking up at Mary, Beth rolled her eyes, causing them both to break out in great peals of laughter. "Men are such little boys."

It took more than a half an hour, but finally Beth made her appearance. Vernon was surprised at how pretty and serene she seemed. Mary had worked a miracle. The lady's came in and were immediately swamped with happy children. Sara was jumping up and down and wiggling like a little worm. This familiar activity indicated to Beth that her niece had a secret, and was having a hard time keeping it to herself.

Travis and his brother, Pete, spoke first. "Pa said we're all to go get ice cream. We would like you to come, too, Aunt Beth."

Vernon agreed that that was a fine idea. He and Beth needed to get out and get some fresh air. He expected his wife to balk at the idea, but he'd turn on the charm and gently coax her out of the house.

Just as he began to tell her that she needed her exercise, Beth, Mary, and little Sara were already on their way out the door, giggling like school children—oh, yeah—*one* actually was a child.

"That was easy enough." Vernon muttered to himself, as he kicked a small pebble off the porch. *What have I been doing wrong?* Those women made it look so easy.

The entire family sat in the Sweets Parlor, laughing and catching up on all the news they'd missed, while consuming a vast quantity of ice cream. After finishing her soda, Sara made her long awaited announcement. To gain everyone's attention, she stood on her chair. Sara liked being the center of attention. Clearing her throat, the little girl announced, "Auntie Beth … oh, and Uncle Vernon too."

Everyone laughed, except Vernon. He was clearly put out at his wife's sudden popularity, while he was relegated to being an afterthought.

David leaned over and whispered, "Get used to it, brother. The women in our families run our lives." He smiled, knowing he and his brother-in-law wouldn't want it any other way.

"I finally gots your wedding present," the little girl said, excitedly. "But I'm sorry I couldn't find a puppy. I looked everywhere … honest." Then she smiled broadly. "I gots you something just as good, though. Her name is Snowball and you'll love her a lot. You can make baby clothes with her, and socks, too. She's tied to your back door. She's a baby lamb!"

Vernon looked at Beth and smiled wickedly. "I like lamb,"

he said, softly. For that bit of information, he got an elbow to his stomach.

Sara waited patiently for their response.

Beth and Vernon both stood and thanked the Williams' family and especially little Sara. "I think that Snowball will be perfect for our family, Sara. In fact, I think Uncle Vernon will make her a little bed, right in our parlor. How about that, Uncle Vernon? You will let us keep Snowball in the house, right?" Beth was full of mischief, today.

"Sure. Sure. Anything you say, *dear*." Vernon sat down and crossed his arms over his chest. "Humpf."

The day passed, splendidly. Everyone had stories to tell and questions to ask. It was decided that as soon as the baby and Beth were able to travel, the Gunn family would go for an extended visit to Red Rock.

It was getting late, when David announced he was going to put his family up at the Doolittle for the night, and they would start out for home, in the morning. It had been a joyous reunion but he had a ranch to run, he said, cheerfully.

Beth loved Snowball. The lamb was snowy white and all curls. She had the biggest eyes and the pinkest little tongue. Beth had not been serious about keeping the lamb indoors, but it had been delicious fun to torment Vernon about it. She loved to have fun with him and he was ultimately a good sport to her teasing. It had been a wonderful day, but she was tired and her back ached dreadfully, forcing her to retire before her husband.

Vernon sat out on the porch mulling things over in his head. He'd taken several days off from his job, but he needed to get back to it, first thing tomorrow. There was something he'd forgotten to do, something important, and it had bothered him since the day of the bank robbery. But, try as he might, he just couldn't recall what it was he'd been doing.

"Vernon." A tiny voice reached out to him from inside the house.

Beth must need a glass of water, or her back rubbed, he thought. It had been bothering her the last couple of nights.

"Vernon, please."

"Coming, coming. You need some water, honey?"

"No, I need some towels."

*What does she need towels for?* "It's too late to be bathing, dear."

What was his wife up to? He slowly walked into the bedroom and froze in his tracks. Standing in the center of the room, was his beautiful Beth, her nightgown soaked to the skin. He looked over to the bed and saw the bed was soaked as well.

"What did you do? Where are we gonna sleep?" he scolded, as he put his hands on his hips, looking at her as if she had been a disobedient child.

"Vernon, the baby is coming," she whispered. "Would you go and get Mary and the doctor? And … Oooh … please hurry."

Vernon continued to stand there. His feet had taken root to the floor and he'd suddenly been struck deaf and blind.

"Vernon! For pity's sake, go get me some help!" she screamed.

That brought him out of his stupor, and the soon-to-be father flew out the door and ran all the way to the Doolittle for help. David told Vernon to keep calm. After all, women had babies every day. David managed to relay that message to Vernon, just as the two men took off, at a run, heading toward the doc's house.

"Couldn't we have saddled a horse?" David complained, as he kept pace, step for step, right alongside Vernon,. He wanted to be near, in case he had to catch the man. From the moist pallor of his skin, Vernon looked as if he might pass out, at any moment. Never had David seen a father so fearful and anxiety ridden.

He'd tried talking to him, but Vernon wouldn't listen. "Come on now. Beth's healthy and she's got the doc and Mary with her. Ain't nothin' for you to worry about. Look at Mary … tiniest little thing I ever did see and she's had five babies, all born healthy. Come on now and sit a spell. I'm plum tuckered out chasin' after you."

Just then, Mary burst through the bedroom door and shouted at the men.

"Where's my water? I need that boiling water now! Land's sake, Vernon! Your baby's gonna be here before you get that water to boiling. Now, run!" Looking at David, she shouted, "Help him, David. You've done this before."

"Well, not exactly, dear. I was always where he is now, and I don't remember much."

"I don't CARE! Get moving and get me that water!" She stormed off and rushed back into the room and closed the door.

The two men stood motionless for a moment, and then they both turned, at the same instant, and ran to the kitchen, knocking into walls, bouncing off the table, and overturning chairs. "Water! Where's the water?" one of them shouted.

Vernon was carrying the pitcher of extremely hot water down the hallway, when he heard Beth's voice calling his name.

"Vernnnnnn".

It was almost his name. He frantically looked for a place to set the pitcher down, so he could run to her side, when the doc came out and carefully took the water from his hands.

"Won't be long now, son," he said, as he rushed back, leaving Vernon and David standing useless, once again.

David tried to ease Vernon's fears. "It'll be at least four or five hours yet. The first one takes a long time and little Rosie took two days to finally get here. You've got lots of time to get ready." He slapped his brother on the back. "Let's go back and sit a spell. You got any checkers?"

Suddenly, there it was—just a tiny squeak, but Vernon had never heard that sound before. He looked to David for confirmation. David shrugged his shoulders.

There it was again, and it was immediately followed by a loud wail that echoed through the entire house. The baby was here and he didn't sound none too happy about making his arrival. The wailing continued and got louder with each successive cry. *It had to be a boy*, Vernon thought.

He was on his feet. "How come nobody's come out to tell us? What's wrong, do you think? Should I go in?" Vernon was panicked.

"Nah, they got a lot a work to do in there, yet. I'm sure Beth wants to look her best fer ya, and they want to check the baby, first. Get him all cleaned up. This is great, huh? Beth sure didn't waste any time." David was smiling from ear to ear. "I'm an uncle. Hey, you're a pa," he said, as if he just thought of it.

With eyes as big as half-dollars, Vernon shook his head. "I swear … never again. I don't plan to do this, *ever* again. Women were made to have babies, but men were not made to wait it out. Nope, never again."

David laughed. "Yeah, that's what I said right after the twins was born. Good luck, brother."

The doctor and Mary came out, both looking happy and relieved. Walking up to Vernon, the doctor said, "I didn't arrive none too soon. It sometimes happens like this. First delivery or not, the baby just decides to come on and there ain't a thing nobody can do to stop it. I figure that gal of yours is made for birthin' babies. Congratulations, Ranger. I'll go on home now and try to get some sleep yet. You can settle the bill when next I see you. Good night to all."

Mary reached out to Vernon's hand, tears of happiness filling her beautiful brown eyes. "Oh darling, she was so brave and so good. She didn't scream at all, until right at the end. She's the most amazing woman I know. Kiss her for me and kiss that precious son of yours, too. He'll be the light of your life, I promise. Go on, now. She's ready to see you. I'll drop back by, first thing in the morning, and give you a hand. She'll need help for the next week to ten days. Sara and I will come by and help you." She stood on tiptoes and gave her brother a kiss on his stubbled cheek.

"Come on, husband. Take me home and put me to bed. I need a back rub and some special lovin'." She winked at David, as he quickly took her arm and led her out to their buggy.

Very slowly, and as silently as a mouse, Vernon entered the softly lit bedroom. His eyes searched for his wife, lying so quietly and serenely on their bed. He could make out a tiny bundle being cradled in her arms, being held close to her heart. For some reason, he couldn't will his feet to move.

Beth could see Vernon had entered the room but that he was having difficulty coming closer. She smiled and held out her free arm. "Come here, darling, and meet your son, Frank Harrison Gunn."

Vernon slowly crept up to the edge of the bed and looked down to the bundle that lay protected in the arms of his wife. Returning his stare, was a perfect little piece of humanity, with golden fuzz on the top of his head and blue eyes, the exact color of the Arizona sky, with just a touch of lavender. Most unusual, he thought. Then, he couldn't help smiling. The boy had a dimple right in the center of his chin—Vernon's own. The two men continued staring at one another until the baby smiled and closed his eyes.

"Did you see that?" Vernon asked. "He smiled at me, he really did. And he's got my chin. How did you manage that?" He looked at Beth with amazement.

"Simple. I love yours so much, I guess he was just destined. How do you feel about him, Vernon? Truth."

"I love my son almost as much as I love his mother. He looks like you, darling, and me. He's perfect!" He grinned and then reached tentatively toward the sleeping child. "May I?"

Pleased beyond all measure, Beth held the infant out to his father. Vernon was careful, but seemed relaxed. "When I saw David hold Rosie for the first time, I was overcome with emotion. I wondered how it would feel … and now I know. He is a miracle, Beth. He's a gift straight from God, and I swear to him and to you, I will forever love him, provide for him, and protect him, even with my life. Thank you, angel."

"Thank you, darling, for continuing to be the answer to all my prayers. I love you more than I can possibly convey." Then, the new mother closed her eyes, and with a smile on her lips, she fell fast asleep.

It had been a long day for Ranger Barclay. He was finishing up the tedious business of going through the new Wanted Posters, when his attention was drawn to the last in the stack, and he'd been troubled all morning, since reading it.

It was the arrest notice for Ryann Beaufort. However, there was more information provided. Surely nothing could be added to make any difference at this late date, he thought. That case had to be cold by now. Then one word caught his eye, and made the hairs on the back of his neck stand up—*Doolittle.*

Barclay spent the next several hours going over it all, in his head, and he didn't like the conclusions he was drawing. It didn't make sense, but he had questions … difficult questions that only his friend, Vernon, could answer.

He'd wait until Vernon reported back for duty, out of respect for the man's family. They'd just had a baby boy and he wasn't about to cause the happy couple any trouble at this time—not if he could help it. Any questions he had, could wait.

It was breakfast at the Gunn household and Vernon had fixed his wife bacon and eggs, cooked just the way she liked them.

They were only slightly darker than the ones she cooked, he thought to himself. Smiling proudly, he walked into their bedroom with the tray. He'd seen to it that a rose lay across her napkin. Nice touch, he thought. *Might make them eggs go down a little easier.*

Little Frank was having his breakfast, as well. Vernon couldn't get enough of watching his beautiful wife nurse their son. She resembled a picture he had once seen of the Madonna and her infant. "This is for you, angel. I wish I was a better cook," he stated, shyly.

Beth looked at him with pure love in her eyes. "You're so sweet to do this for me, Vernon. Everything looks delicious. However, Frank has a hearty appetite—just like his pa. It will be a while before I can eat, I'm afraid," she giggled.

"Then, I'll feed you." Picking up the fork, Vernon piled it high with eggs, and slowly brought it to Beth's lips. Only a few fell off and settled on the sheets. "Let me try that again," he said.

Beth placed her hand on top her husband's forearm, to stop his momentum. "No, no, darling. I can wait. But, thank you anyway. Do you have some toast, there?"

"Sure. I guess I can't spill that," he laughed. "What are you going do today?" He spread some blackberry jam over the bread and handed it to his wife.

"Mary said some ladies want to come by and see the baby. It should be fun. Mary is going to arrive early and help me fix my hair. I'm so happy, Vernon.

"Mmmm, this is very good toast, darling."

When Beth's pink tongue came out to lick the jam off her bottom lip, Vernon thought he'd lose control. He yearned to devour that luscious mouth and suck her sweet tongue into his own. *What kind of a man am I? My wife just had a baby!* He turned away briefly and adjusted the front of his trousers.

"I never dared to believe my life could turn out like this, Vernon. After all the hardships I went through, there were times when I almost gave up. Thank you, darling, for taking a chance on me and for catching me every time I fell." She smiled, remembering how they first met.

Vernon turned back around, realizing he was a man who simply loved his wife.

"Don't you mean, every time I knocked you off your feet?" He grinned. "I can't imagine living my life without you and little Frank. I want you to know that if there's any trouble in the future, I'll find a way out. You're never to worry about your past, ever again. Now, having said all that, I think I'll go into the office today and see what trouble I can find to fix. Barclay's a good man but it isn't fair to make him work so many days without a rest. I'll more than likely be home late this evening. If you need me, I'll come a runnin'. Enjoy your day, sweetheart." He kissed his wife and his son, and then promptly left the house.

Mary and Sara arrived precisely on time. Sara wasted no time going outside to visit with Snowball. Mary took the sleeping baby from Beth, and proceeded to change Beth's gown. She brushed and coiled her hair and added just a touch of toilet water behind each ear. Beth wore her mother's pearl comb tucked in her hair. She looked radiant, with the glow of new motherhood.

Mary then proceeded to bathe Frank and make him the sweetest smelling infant in Tucson. She held the baby up for Beth's inspection. "You are aware that little Frank here, is going to be a real heartbreaker. Girls from all over the territory are going to cry their eyes out, when he finally finds the girl of his dreams. Wouldn't it be splendid if Frank chose Rosie? Stranger things have happened, you know."

"Truer words were never spoken," Beth laughed.

Mrs. Jones was the first to arrive. She brought trays of small cakes and cookies, placing them all around the room on pretty little platters. She also made a large crock of lemonade, that her husband volunteered to carry in for her.

"Now, Mrs. Gunn, you're not to lift a finger. That's what I'm here for," the lady beamed.

Robin arrived next, surprising Mary and Beth. Because of her profession, she chose not to mingle with the wives of Tucson, but today, she just had to see the baby. "Robin won't stay long, I promise, but I needed to see you and little Frank and bring you these flowers. They're not much, I know, but I saw them in the window, at the hotel, and I couldn't resist them. May Robin put them in water?"

Mary took the lovely gift and rushed out to the kitchen for the water. She found a beautiful blue glass vase, perfect for the yellow and orange flowers. Bringing them back into the room, she remarked, "These are quite beautiful, Robin. They really dress up the room. It was very thoughtful of you." She smiled at the saloon girl.

Beth always gave some credit to Robin for bringing her and Vernon together; therefore, she was always happy to see her. "Would you like to hold him, Robin?"

"Oh, no. Robin mustn't. It would be frowned upon, I'm sure."

"Frowned upon by whom, young lady?" A loud and commanding voice startled everyone. It could only belong to one woman, and that would be Calliope Bigsby, the Grande Dame of Tucson. "I do the frowning here, in this town, and if I don't find it objectionable, then nobody else will find it so. You want to hold him?"

Robin was scared to death of this dynamic lady, but she swallowed her fear and whispered, "Yes, I'd dearly love to."

"Then pick him up, young woman. Careful not to drop him. Hold his head up."

Then Mrs. Bigsby turned her attention to the new mother. "You look right as rain and smell as good, too," she sniffed. "I've brought a couple of things for you and the boy. They're store bought, on account I don't have the time to make up something at home. Hope that will suffice. What did you name him?"

"Feeling slightly intimidated by her guest, Beth could barely utter a word. "Frank Harrison Gunn," she said, meekly.

"You what?" The older lady almost choked on her words. "Who told you?"

"Told me what, Mrs. Bigsby?"

The older woman's eyes were quickly filling with tears. "My late husband's name was Frank, and my father was named Harrison—only my mother called him Harry. Who told you?" She asked more softly, this time. "You weren't trying to butter up an old lady, were you? It won't work, you know."

"I'm sorry, Mrs. Bigsby, if my baby's name distresses you. It was unintentional, I can assure you. My husband's father was named Frank, Mrs. Bigsby, and *my* deceased father was also named Harrison. That's how we arrived at the two names. I honestly didn't know about your family." She felt her heart tug at the pain she recognized in the old woman's eyes.

Calliope walked over to Robin and straightening her back, she reached out for the baby. Sniffing loudly, she said, "Young woman, don't take advantage of my good nature. I am certain you have had your fair share of holding that child. Hand Frank over."

Robin wouldn't think of arguing with her. Obediently, she stood and allowed the older woman to sit in the comfortable rocker, and gently placed the boy in her waiting arms. Turning back to Beth, she made her excuses.

"Thank you so much, Mrs. Gunn. Robin can't tell you what your friendship means to her. Bless you and the baby." She dipped a small curtsy and left by the back door. She thought it wouldn't be seemly if she was observed leaving this fine young woman's house, by the front door.

Women, whom Beth had never met, started arriving, thanks to the invitations sent out by Mrs. Bigsby. Each one carried a gift. They all wanted to hold the sleeping infant, but after one scathing look from Calliope, they agreed they would return in the next couple of days. The older woman refused to give up custody of the child for even one moment. Beth had to giggle at that. Who would have thought?

Little Becky and her mother came to visit. Her mother was slightly uncomfortable around Beth. She'd been made aware of the discussion her daughter and the schoolmarm had, in class, and now she felt guilty. Little Becky, however, was so excited she couldn't stand still for one minute more. She wanted to see the baby's face. No old lady was going to deter her. She bravely walked up to Mrs. Bigsby and demanded, in a nice way, to see the baby.

"Please, ma'am. You won't let me see." She stamped her little foot and stuck out her lower lip. Then she stared, eyeball to eyeball with the older woman.

A chuckle started to erupt from the back of Calliope's throat. "Well, I'll be. Finally … a girl child in this town, with enough gumption to earn my respect. I like this one. What's your name, child?"

"Becky," she said clearly.

"Well, Becky. How would you like to sit here and rock him

for a spell? You'll get a good look at his face, then."

Little Becky's eyes lit up like a candle. "Oh, may I, ma'am? Thank you ever so much." She held out both her spindly arms to receive baby Frank, and Beth felt her heart jump into her throat.

Noticing the concerned expressions on the faces of the two women, Becky attempted to reassure them. "It's all right. I washed my hands and arms real good before I came. I won't get him dirty."

Calliope did her best not to laugh, as she stood up and nodded for the little girl to take her seat. Very carefully, she positioned the small infant in Becky's lap and kept a firm hand under his head.

"She's polite too," Mrs. Bigsby stated. "I want to get to know this little girl better. Mother, you see that you bring her over to my house, tomorrow after church. It's the big one, you can't miss it."

After a short while, Mrs. Bigsby looked over at Mary. "Well, ladies, it's been long enough. I'm sure Mrs. Gunn needs her rest now, and this boy will be getting hungry soon. Come and take this child and we'll be leaving."

After Becky reluctantly relinquished the baby, Calliope offered her hand to the little girl. "I'm proud to meet you, young lady. See you tomorrow."

Then, like a whirlwind, the intimidating woman was gone, leaving everyone wondering what had happened. They all started to laugh. This had been a fine day.

It wasn't such a fine day for Vernon, however. He knew by the look on his friend's face, that he had discovered the latest Wanted Poster and he obviously wanted some answers.

Ranger Barclay pointed to a chair. "Sit. We've got some serious talkin' to do and it might take a while."

Vernon walked over to the stove and poured himself a cup of strong black coffee.

"You want some?"

Barclay shook his head. "I need to know a few things. I ain't got the stomach for no coffee." Vernon's friend looked like hell. Worry lines were deeply carved in his face and the seriousness of the situation burned in his weary eyes. The fact that he must question his best friend weighed heavily upon him, and he didn't like it one damn bit.

Picking up the most recent poster, he tossed it across the desk to Vernon.

"You seen this? What do you make of it?"

Vernon didn't bother to read it. He knew what it said. "I know that you may not understand the situation my wife was in. I know that I'm in danger of breaking the law. I know all these things, dammit. But I also know, if she hadn't killed that bastard—I would have."

His face turned red with rage. Tossing the offending poster back to Barclay, he stood up and started pacing the room.

"I can't go into all the details with you, Barclay. It's not that I don't think you have the right to know or because I want to keep things secret out of a sense of loyalty. It's just that the horrors my wife endured, while being held captive by that maniac, are so unthinkable … so sick … I'm physically unable to put it all into words." Vernon hung his head, pressing his fingers to the bridge of his nose. He started to weep.

Barclay didn't know what to say, so he sat silently, giving his friend time. He could see the terrible toll it was taking on this strong man, this man he'd admired for so long. It was then he decided what he must do.

Vernon continued. "The senator's son was a monster and I truly do not believe my wife was his first victim. If I have to, I'll go all the way to Richmond and talk to folks, myself. There has to be one woman there, who'll speak up against this man. I'm lucky that Beth survived, and I vow she'll never be threatened by him or his family again."

"What are you gonna do about the warrants—just hide 'em under your desk? You know if I can make the connection, there will be others. What about Doolittle? Does he know anything?"

"Barclay, you don't give yourself enough credit. Besides, you know Doolittle. Hopefully, his brother, back in Richmond, will succeed in not implicating him. That should give us some protection, or at the very least, some time. If I hear that the authorities have made any connection with Tucson, I'm taking my family and heading out for parts unknown."

"Vernon, you know you're throwin' away your career, and I hate to see that. You're one of the best rangers we've got. It's all you've ever wanted to be. You'll be a wanted man; a man with a family, hidin' from the law. That ain't no life for you."

Vernon laughed. "Now, that's where you're wrong, my friend. My wife and child are all I've ever wanted. Yeah, I love being an Arizona Ranger, but it's not my life, not anymore. I've got the scars to prove it could be the end of my life, someday. No, I wouldn't think twice about packing up my family and disappearing."

He had to chuckle to himself. He knew of another family member that had done just that. *Daniel* had to "die" in order for David to regain his family and his freedom. For the first time, he truly understood his brother-in-law.

"What do you plan to do with this information, Barclay?"

"Not a damn thing, Vernon. I never saw that poster and I don't know nothin' about the Doolittle Boardin' House. We never had this discussion and I'll watch your back, friend."

"Thanks," Vernon whispered, past the huge lump in his throat.

"Well, pal, I'm outta' here. You've had a lot of days off, gallivanting around and having babies and such, so I figure you owe me some time off. I'm goin' fishin'."

With that said, The older ranger put on his hat, checked that his six gun was in place, and strode out the door, leaving Vernon to mull over what had transpired over the last half hour. Barclay was a good and trusted friend, indeed. Now, perhaps Vernon would be able to sleep at night.

# CHAPTER FOURTEEN

Motherhood agreed with Beth Gunn. Frank was three months old and thriving. Vernon had never been so content. Beth had bounced back from childbirth in record time and he'd been eager to resume the role of husband and lover.

There had been no more Wanted Posters, and it was his hope that the senator had finally decided that the search for his son's killer was futile. With each passing day, Vernon breathed a little easier.

This day was special. The Gunn family was preparing to ride out to the Williams' spread for a little visit. David had been working hard, keeping the peace in town, and building up his ranch, on his time off. He'd finished Mary's house and the bunkhouses. The barn had been completed, along with all the corrals. From what Vernon had heard, the ranch was impressive, and he and Beth planned to spend the last two weeks of September, there.

Vernon locked up the house, placed Snowball in the wagon, and tied Napoleon to the rear. The cradle was tucked in, along with enough food to feed an army. Beth wouldn't go empty handed, she said. She also bought a doll for Sara, made a soft yellow duck for Rosie, and had sewn two cowboy shirts for the boys. At least, in her opinion, they looked like rowdy cowboy shirts. She bought some sweet smelling toilet water for Mary—Honeysuckle—and Vernon bought a bottle of good Kentucky whiskey for David—to be used for medicinal purposes, naturally. He smiled, knowing he wasn't fooling anyone.

After about three hours of riding, the ranch finally came into view. Vernon stopped on a high ridge to take it all in. It was a right nice spread, just as David had told him. He'd built the houses near the rock bluffs for protection. There was only one way in and one way out of the enclosure. Perched high up, the way it was, they could see clearly in all four directions. No one would be able to sneak up on this ranch, Vernon figured. Indians, Mexicans, or outlaws, would have no chance to penetrate this fortress. He breathed a lot easier seeing how safe David had made his sister's home.

Sure enough, he and Beth had been spotted, while sitting there, gazing out across the land. People came out of everywhere, to greet them. There must have been twenty of them, at least. All were waving a welcome.

"Come on up!" someone shouted.

"Gettup!" Vernon cracked the reins and they started a slow climb. This was amazing. Plenty of mighty fine-looking horseflesh ran in circles behind the corral fencing

"Oh, Vernon, this is so beautiful. I had no idea it would be this grand," Beth exclaimed, as she nearly stood to take it all in.

"David succeeds at whatever he sets his mind to, angel, and my sister may be little, but she has a will of iron. I'm sure she was pushing him all the way. Tenderly, of course," he chuckled.

The twins were the first to approach the wagon. "Welcome, tenderfoot," they cried in unison. Vernon could plainly see that David had also been right about the boys being raised on a ranch. They seemed to have gotten taller and more confident in just the six months they'd been gone.

Mary came running from the house, holding Rosie in her arms. The baby was giggling with all the bouncing around. "Beth, Vernon! Oh I'm so happy you're here!

"Just look at your son! He's grown so big. They grow too fast, if you ask me," Mary lamented, looking at her daughter. "Come on up to the house. I'm dying to show you around. We love it here." That was obvious by her happy glow.

David stood by the gate, waiting for everyone to come up to him. "Bout time, you two. I thought you'd never leave the city. Look around you. This is where you should be livin'. I'm gonna work on you, while yer here, and try to get you to move on out. It's God's country, fer sure." Slapping Vernon on the back he said, "Come on in. It's good to see you, brother."

It was so good to see old friends and family. Beth greeted Mr. and Mrs. Runyon and their beautiful daughter, Lily. They helped work the ranch and had become good friends with Mary and David. In another month, Mr. Albert Kepler would be moving his family to the ranch. He had two boys just a little older than Pete and Travis. It was all very exciting. The way Mary had it figured, they'd be in need of a schoolteacher real soon.

"Wait until you see the sunset, Beth," Mary sighed. "It's very romantic. Isn't it, darling?" She smiled over at David, thinking he was still the most handsome man she had ever seen.

She turned back to Beth and whispered, conspiratorially, "I think you and Vernon should go for a walk this evening and experience it for yourselves. I'll watch Frank for you. There's a small waterfall over in that direction and a grassy area over there." She pointed just beyond the bunkhouses. "It's perfect for a blanket and some star gazing. Enjoy." She winked.

That evening, Beth was ready. With a folded blanket over her arms, she approached Vernon sitting out on the porch. "Vernon, I don't mean to interrupt, dear, but the sunset promises to be glorious this evening and I would like very much to see it from over there, by the waterfall. Walk with me?"

He looked up at her puzzled. Since when did she like sunsets by waterfalls? "David and I are going to take a look at his new stallion and he has two new foals that look promising. Where's Frank?"

Beth stared at this obtuse man. "Mary's watching Frank and I want to see the waterfall at sunset." She shook the blanket at him. "I want you to walk with me." She tapped her foot, impatiently.

"I know that sounds great, but I'm too tuckered out from that long wagon ride to take a walk. How about I walk you over there sometime tomorrow? The boys can show us the way."

Beth threw the blanket down at his feet. "You, Mr. Gunn, have become a very dull fellow and I am not pleased. Maybe I'll just go see the waterfall by myself." She turned on her heel and flounced off in a temper, holding her pert little nose high in the air.

Vernon couldn't see the tears in her eyes.

David slowly shook his head in disbelief. "I don't believe what I just saw. How old are you, anyway? A beautiful woman, clearly in love with you and wantin' yer attentions, asks … no … practically begs fer yer lousy comp'ny, and you tell her you want to go with a man to see a horse? Are you loco? Mary'd dump a bucket of ice-cold water over my head if ever I was to be so slow-witted. What are you waitin' fer, man? Go after yer wife and make her happy." He shoved Vernon out of the chair so forcefully, he nearly fell on his knees.

Finally, regaining his feet and some of his good sense, Vernon stood up and looked down at David. "You mean, she was asking for my *attentions?* Out on a blanket, at sunset, by some damn waterfall? Who's lame idea was that?"

"My wife's—and it ain't no lame idea. What's botherin' you, boy?" David couldn't understand the man's reluctance to make love to his beautiful wife.

Vernon looked rightly chastised. "I've had a lot on my mind, lately, and I guess I've been preoccupied with my job. We've been together a few times, since Frank's birth, and it's been wonderful, but I guess I haven't been very romantic about it. Guess I've got some making up to do." He turned slowly, with his head down, and then asked David. "You have any wine or lemonade that I can take up with me? Might help to soothe a savage beast."

David nodded in agreement and smiled. "Go find Mary. She'll fix you up."

It took a while. The sun was starting to set in the West and he had to admit, the view was amazing from the ranch. Mary had fixed him up good and proper. He was carrying a basket of sweet delights that was sure to make Beth happy. He walked over to the barn, but he didn't see her there.

He hollered, "Beth Gunn. Where are you, darlin'?" She wouldn't have gone far.

There was no reply. He started to get nervous. Walking faster, he headed for that damn waterfall. Had she come across a snake and got snake bit? Or maybe she slipped on a rock and fell down in a ravine. She was delicate and didn't know about the dangers that lurked out here, in the desert, after dark.

"Beth. Angel, where are you. Answer me. I'm sorry." Still, he heard nothing.

*Oh, God*, he thought. What if she came across a coyote or worse? What if she came face to face with the Chiricahuas? With her long, thick, golden hair, she wouldn't stand a chance.

He was running now, listening for the sound of water crashing upon rocks. He didn't even have his six-shooter with him. Being a ranger, he should have known better than to go anywhere, unarmed. *Damn his stupid hide*, he cursed.

"Beth. Oh please, sweetheart. Where are you?"

*Let her be all right,* he prayed.

It was getting dark. The sky had lost its vibrant reds and pinks. The dark purples and indigos of evening were descending upon the rugged rocks. Just then, he thought he heard the slightest tinkle of water splashing.

Vernon ran toward the sound, and suddenly stopped dead in his tracks. He was paralyzed by a heavenly vision slowly emerging from a dark lagoon, the crystal waterfall cascading behind her like a celestial curtain of sparkling diamonds.

With her golden hair, wet and shimmering down her back, falling to below her waist, she slowly arose from the lake. Water droplets clung possessively all about her smooth and luscious body, glittering like the stars in the night sky. As she placed one perfectly sculpted leg in front of the other, Vernon admired the way her plump breasts moved in step. They gently bobbed, making his mouth dry with want. Her nipples stood erect on the perfect alabaster mounds, hard and pebbled from the cool water. This water sprite … this glorious and perfect water goddess … was his wife. Vernon fell to his knees in admiration, humbled by her beauty.

What he didn't realize, she felt much the same way. Beth was humbled by his masculine magnificence. Vernon only had to enter a room and her heart skipped a beat. She was overcome with gratitude that such an admirable man would love her. Of course, she still reveled in her ability to light the flames of his desire. She enjoyed the obvious effect her nudity was having on her husband. He was on his knees, speechless at the sight of her.

Beth ignored his gaze, as she proceeded up onto the rocks, appearing to be unaware of the man feasting his eyes on her naked body. Slowly, she picked up the towel and dabbed at the water droplets beading up over her long legs. Higher and higher she stroked and gently swabbed the golden triangle hidden between her thighs. She thought she heard Vernon groan.

Deliberately, she dragged the towel over her flat stomach and onto her breasts. With each one, she caressed herself, closing her eyes and purring with delight at the feel of the soft towel brushing across her taut nipples. Beth knew what she was doing to her husband and he deserved it. She would make him lust for her, as he had never lusted before.

Her small pink tongue slowly moistened her full lips, as her hair swung loose over her shoulders. She dropped the towel behind her and slowly turned, revealing her backside to Vernon. Gracefully, she bent over to retrieve the towel.

That was all he could stand. Vernon jumped to his feet, leaving the basket on the ground, and ran to his wife's side.

"Oh, angel," he pleaded. "I've been the dumbest cowboy in Arizona. Please forgive my stupidity. I've been selfish and I ignored your needs. I can't tell you how sorry I am." He looked at his wife with his huge green eyes, begging for her absolution.

Still standing, nude and proud, Beth pretended to be annoyed and unmoved by his pleas. She glanced down at her husband, from high upon the rock, from which she had perched. With a small flick of her wrist she showered water from her hair onto his face. She smiled a tiny smile of satisfaction.

"So, what purpose brings you hear? You searching for your wife?" She delighted in the lofty sound of her own voice.

"I thought over what I'd said to you and I realized, I misspoke. I missed you."

She laughed, a deep-throated laugh. "You missed me? Why do I think David shamed you into coming out here to be with me?"

Vernon's face turned red with embarrassment. In a small voice, barely above a whisper, he confessed. "Cause he did."

Vernon appeared close to tears. "He reminded me of what it means to be a husband. I just get so caught up in my work sometimes, that I have trouble tearing my mind away from it all. Please, angel, I promise to do better."

Vernon looked away. "I guess I'll never be the husband David is. It all comes so easy to him." He looked so wretched, Beth decided to put him out of his misery.

She held out her hand and asked for his help down off the rock. Her heart lurched at the feel of his hand on hers. It was so strong and yet, it could be so gentle with her and the baby. The mere touch of his hand caused her heart to beat faster.

"Vernon, will you spread the blanket on the ground? We can sit and talk."

He quickly did as she asked. He also brought the basket over, thinking he could use whatever help he could get. Hopefully, Mary had packed all sorts of goodies.

"I asked Mary to pack me up a few of your favorite things to take to you," he smiled, feeling only slightly guilty in taking all the credit. "Lie down here, darling, and I'll dry your hair."

Beth grinned. "First of all, I want you to know that David was not always the ideal husband. Mary says, that it has taken years and much hardship to mold him into this virtuous husband you now see before you. We've been married less than one year, Vernon. We've *known* each other less than one year. It's only natural that we have some adjusting to do, and I'm aware that I brought a whole wagon full of problems with me. You've done an amazing job in the husband and father department. I just wanted some extra attention this evening. It seems we're never alone and this was our chance. I love you so much, darling."

With that said, she wrapped her delicate arms around his neck and pulled him down to her. Their lips crushed together and the heat of passion flared up between them. They were in need of some serious primal mating.

His lips lightly grazed her ears as he feasted on her face and throat. Her womanly fragrance, the scent that was hers alone, claimed him. He lowered his gaze to her breasts and her cherry pink nipples. He wanted to taste them, take them in his mouth and devour them. He growled with that part of him that was primitive male.

"Vernon, take your clothes off. I want to touch you," Beth commanded.

He was quick to obey. Vernon removed his shirt and stood long enough to unbuckle his belt and pull down his trousers. He forced his boots off, one falling into the lake, but Vernon didn't care. Very quickly, he had disengaged himself from all his clothing.

With his muscles taut, he embraced her, pressing her body next to his, and feeling her warmth go through him. His body trembled with the need to possess her. His physical wants and desires had been too long unfulfilled. He needed to feel his hands upon her skin … all of it … all the parts of her body. He slid his hand down her back and cupped her bottom. It was plump and round and fit him nicely. With a little grin, he gave her just the softest of swats!

"Vernon! Do you think I've been a bad girl?" she asked in all seriousness. "Do I need a spanking?"

Vernon smiled, wickedly. "Yes, my dear. Sometimes you are very, very bad and I must punish you … like this." He brought his hand around to the front of her and touched upon her woman's most sensuous place. He took his finger and lightly flipped her little nubbin.

Beth squealed with excitement. "Oh, yes, husband, I have been bad. Do it again, please," she giggled.

He laughed. His fingers took their time bringing his wife closer and closer to fulfillment. She was very wet and ready for him to make love to her, but he loved pleasuring her with this exquisite torment. He noticed she was beginning to buck and moan, rubbing herself against his hand.

"Slow down, sweetheart. We've got all night and there are many things for us to attend to, before we finish." He felt as if he was going to explode from his own need, but he wanted to make sure that this moment was memorable for Beth.

He nudged himself up against his wife's entrance, weeping with its fragrant nectar. She was so wet and slippery. Oh, how he wanted to taste her … to bury his face there, surrounded in her feminine folds.

"For God's sake, Vernon. Take me. Please," Beth cried out, begging him to take possession of her, arching her back in anticipation.

He was obsessed with his wife. He could not get enough of her. Vernon could hold back no longer. With one hard thrust he was inside his wife's body, surrounded by her warmth. She was slick and tight, just as she had been before the birth of the baby. He marveled at that. He grew harder within her. With a steady, driving rhythm, he plunged himself into her, over and over again. Bare flesh against bare flesh, increased their pleasure.

He kissed her fiercely. His tongue glided like silk across her lips, sending a surge of scorching hot desire through every nerve in her body. Her pliant lips responded to his need, and opened to his tongue.

Beth was whimpering and thrashing about on the blanket, completely caught up in the blinding, white-hot passion of love. She could taste herself on his lips and she reveled in it. As his hands massaged her breasts and as he continued to stroke her, she felt her nerves tighten and the muscles in her womanly place began to quiver. She was about to experience the release that she longed to share with Vernon.

Vernon could tell that his wife was on the verge of exploding. "Give in, darling. Surrender to it. I'll come with you."

He was painfully hard now and the agony of it was exquisite torture. She tightened around him, and he could feel the beginnings of her spasms.

"Yes, Vernon, yes," she cried out in rapture, wild with the need to totally succumb to its lure.

He plunged deep inside her, and shot his seed with explosive power. He growled at his own release. Never had it felt so powerful. He continued to pump, emptying himself, completely.

Beth was laying still, her eyes shut, having been totally ravished. Her breathing slowly returned to normal … and she sighed.

In the faint moonlight, the soft sheen of perspiration gave her body a lustrous glow, creating an ethereal image for Vernon to admire. His wife's body was made to be loved, Vernon thought, and he was just the man to love her. The air around them was still permeated by the scent of their sexual union. It was enough to entice him to take her into his arms, once again, and make love to her a second time.

Vernon reached for her, nibbling on her neck, forcing her to giggle. "Beth, my love. Words fail me. I'm frightened by how much I love you … worship you." He kissed her lips, tickling her bottom lip with just the tip of his moist tongue. "I'm not certain I could continue to live without you or your love, and that's fearsome indeed. It puts me at a great disadvantage, and I'm not used to that. Forgive me if I, on occasion, seem hesitant to get totally immersed in your presence. It's just the foolish act of self-preservation." He buried his nose in the hollow just below her neck and inhaled. Her scent was a drug to him, creating an all-consuming need in him. "Promise, sweetheart, to be patient with me and to love me forever, lest I should perish from this earth."

Beth was overwhelmed by his sincerity. She believed all he said was true. It was an awesome responsibility to hold one's heart in trust. However, it was no burden to promise him her love, for it was already his to do with as he pleased.

"My darling, husband. You think you're incapable of saying romantic things? That was beautiful. But don't you know I feel the same way about you? With every breath I take, your name is written on the air. All my days start with thoughts of you and Frank, and they all end the same. Our love is real, darling. I want us to grow old together. Kiss me and we'll never again speak of our insecurities."

Vernon kissed her, stealing her breath away, and then unable to deny himself any longer, he gently took his wife, again. The two lovers spent the night entangled in each other's arms, their breathing in concert with one another, their hearts beating as one, and totally secure in their unconditional love.

The sun came up early, and the two lovebirds walked slowly back to the ranch house, hand in hand. That fact was not lost on Mary and David. Their little conspiracy to light a fire under the couple had been a success. Met with waving children, on the front porch, Beth felt her face go scarlet. Then she heard the soft wail of a baby's cry.

"Oh, my God … Frank!" She broke free from Vernon's grasp and ran for the house. "How could I have forgotten my baby?" She was fairly hysterical, overcome with the guilt and fear for her child's well being.

"Mary, I'm so sorry. You must think I'm a terrible mother," she shouted, as she ran past on her way to the nursery.

"Slow down, Beth. Everything's fine with little Frank. He's been changed and fed. He's just stretching his lungs a bit," Mary hollered, as she ran after her friend.

Upon reaching the open door of her baby's room, Beth's heart leapt for joy at the happy scene. Lying contentedly upon the big bed, kicking his chubby little legs, was Frank, laughing and cooing as only a three month old baby can do. Little Sara was quietly singing a song she had composed herself, "just for babies", she had said. Beth noticed that the little girl actually had a very pretty voice.

Beth's breasts were full and she was reminded of the fact that she had not nursed her baby for the entire night. "Who nursed Frank?" she asked.

"Rowena, our housekeeper and cook," Mary responded. "She's a wonder. Her child is six months old, so she was happy to step in. She's relieved me, once or twice, with Rosie. Things can happen out on a ranch and you sometimes need an extra helping hand … or whatever." She blushed. "She needed a job and a roof over her head after her husband was killed in a stampede. It was so sad. He never got to see his infant daughter." Mary dabbed at one eye and let out a large sigh before attending to business.

"Get cleaned up and I'll take you down to breakfast and you can thank her for yourself. By the way, you look like a woman that's very much in love with her husband."

Relieved that Frank had been so well taken care of—in spite of her neglect—Beth walked swiftly toward her room to get dressed. She realized she must look dreadful after sleeping and playing with her husband, out of doors, all night.

Beth gasped, when she stood in front of her ladies' mirror. It was much worse than she had expected. *Mary must have gotten a good laugh*, she muttered to herself.

She had red sand stains all over her dress, and several places on her skin were marked as well. Her hair was strewn with twigs and grass, knotted in tangles that might have to be cut out. Her eyes were too lustrous and her lips were still swollen from all those passionate kisses she received from her husband. Her chin had stubble burns from Vernon's whiskers. It was quite obvious, to the most casual observer, how she had spent her evening, and yet, if she had the opportunity to do it all over again … she most definitely would.

Doing the best she could, in a short amount of time, Beth tried to make herself presentable. With Sara holding her hand and chatting all the way, Beth happily went downstairs to enjoy a late breakfast,

"Frank is a wonderful baby, Auntie Beth. He looks like you, but he has Uncle Vernon's chin. Uncle Vernon is a handsome man, isn't he Auntie Beth? Almost as handsome as papa, but not quite."

Beth noticed how Sara had grown up in the few months since they had last been together. How much would the children change by the next time she visited? It was a sobering thought.

"Rosie looks like mama and that makes papa glad. My little dead sister, Ruthie, looked like mama, too." Quite unexpectedly, her happy face fell, recalling her beautiful little sister. "We had a dog named Buster, but we had to leave him in Mizzo ... Uh oh. I'm not 'sposed to say we're from Missouri, 'cause papa's not 'sposed to be here. That's why we changed our names."

Beth had to correct the adorable child. She took her small hands in her own and looked into her precious face. She didn't want to scare her niece, or hurt her feelings, but she needed to gently remind her not to speak of such things.

"Sara, darling. You know how much I love you, don't you?"

The little girl nodded with wide-eyed, innocence.

"I need to remind you not to tell *anyone* of your past life, before coming to Arizona. Can you try to remember that? I know your papa's story and Uncle Vernon knows it too, but you mustn't say anything to another person. Not ever. You mustn't even say you have a new name. They would wonder why. Even if you feel they can be trusted, it's very important that it all remains a secret. Maybe you should pretend you were born in Texas!"

Sara thought for a moment and then piped up. "Can I talk about my dog, Buster and my little dead sister, Ruthie?"

Squeezing Sara tightly, Beth laughed. "Yes darling, talk about Buster all you want, but you might not want to refer to Ruthie as your "dead" sister. I think it might make your mama and papa sad. Just call her your sister, Ruthie. Okay?"

Sara nodded. "Auntie Beth, you're my favorite auntie." She gave Beth a quick kiss, and skipped off to play with her animals—a veritable menagerie.

"I'm your *only* auntie," Beth mused.

# CHAPTER FIFTEEN

Beth and Vernon soon discovered what a wonderful life the Williams' family was now enjoying, and deservedly so. They were truly happy living out here, away from the crowds in town, and they were free to live life on their own terms. They had honest, hard-working ranch hands and good friends, to help out around the place. The twins were growing up more like their pa, everyday, and that was a good thing, Vernon reckoned. Those two could ride better than any ten-year old boys he'd ever seen. They were fearless, but also gentle and seemed to have the ability to talk to a horse and know what the animal was thinking. They had inherited that from their pa, too. His gift with horses was legendary.

Mary absolutely glowed. Vernon loved seeing his sister so radiant. That hadn't always been the case. She'd had a hard life, in her early years, and she was owed some happiness now. With baby Rosie on her hip, Mary tended her gardens with love. She especially enjoyed her roses and was bound and determined to get some bushes started. It was obvious that she loved her home and her beautiful, healthy children. And no one could ignore the way she looked at her husband. She almost lost him once, and she would never, again, take their relationship for granted.

At dinner, David asked his brother-in-law about staying on longer. "Now, tell me the truth, Vernon. Don't you want to stay out here and ferget you ever saw Tucson? There's some good land just over that ridge. You could pick it up at a reasonable price and raise horses with me. Give me some real competition." He laughed. No one seriously competed with David Williams when it came to good horseflesh, and he knew it.

"Mary'd love havin' Beth so close, and I know the children would like it, too. You know, brother, I was told, wearin' a badge is dangerous work." He glanced over at Mary. They'd had this discussion before. "A man never knows which bullet has his name on it. You've got responsibilities now. I know you like bein' a ranger and all, but think about it. You'd have a good life out here."

"Thanks. I'll think on it, some. But don't hold your breath. I've got duties, too, and being a ranger ain't as dangerous as being the sheriff. A town sheriff faces a bullet everyday."

"Yeah, and how many sheriff's have come and gone while you've been there? Hell, the job is so dangerous they couldn't even find someone to replace the last one. Seems to me, that makes you ranger *and* sheriff."

Vernon acknowledged that fact. "Yep, I was for a while, but we just hired a good man. But what you say is true, I guess. So tell me, why are you still the deputy sheriff of Red Rock, if it's so damn dangerous?"

The room got quiet. David thought on it for a spell, before he spoke. "I had to have some way to feed my family and start my ranch. The way I have it figured, after next spring, I should make enough on the sale of the horses to buy some good quality mares, and I'll quit sheriffin'."

Mary nearly jumped out of her seat. It was the first she had heard of this, and it made her immensely happy. Everyday, when her husband pinned on that badge, Mary would worry and fret about his safety. Now, he had given her the answer to her prayers. She ran over to David and threw her arms around his neck and cried with happiness and relief.

Witnessing his sister's reaction to this bit of news, Vernon was shocked into true understanding of the stress his job put on his own wife. He looked into her shimmering blue eyes and knew what he must do. Although she would never ask him to resign, he knew he'd do it for her. He smiled and winked at Beth.

She smiled and winked back. She believed and trusted him to

do the right thing, at the right time. She was confident Vernon would remain safe until then.

"Let's raise a glass," Beth said, looking over at Sara. The little girl held her glass of milk, high in the air, smiling from dimple to dimple.

"Sara, you do the honors. Congratulate your papa on his wise decision."

The little girl beamed. She stood and proclaimed happily, "Papa, 'gratulations on your 'sision. It makes mama and me real happy."

Everyone laughed and applauded.

"Good job, Sara," Beth whispered

Next morning, it was time to head on back to Tucson. Ranger Barclay, while a good ranger, couldn't be expected to hold down the fort, indefinitely. All the womenfolk were crying and promising to visit soon. Sara was sniffling.

"I'll miss you, Auntie Beth and little Frank … You, too, Uncle Vernon."

As the wagon began to pull away, Mary yelled to Beth, "I'll get that piano in six months or so. I'll let you know when it arrives,"

"You do that." Beth had promised to come out and stay for a couple of months and teach Sara voice and piano. The little girl's talent was promising and she certainly loved performing in front of people. Beth wiped her tears and waved until she thought her arm would fall off.

As the ranch grew smaller, no more than a speck on the horizon, Beth was overcome with a sadness she rarely felt these days. She had everything she ever wanted, a fine husband and a healthy baby. But she had been so happy and carefree at the ranch.

That was it. She had been *carefree* for the very first time since before she met that vile man … even before her folks were killed in that horrible fire. Beth couldn't stop the tears that began to overflow her eyes.

Vernon sensed his wife's sadness. He put his strong arm around her, pulled her in close, and kissed the top of her head. "It's all right, angel. I'll bring you back, soon."

The baby started to root around his mother's breast. It was

time for Frank to be fed. Vernon continued to drive the wagon, glancing, now and then, at his son taking nourishment from his mother. In his opinion, there was nothing on earth that was more beautiful than seeing Beth nurse their child. He was in awe of her.

The threesome traveled on in relative silence, simply enjoying being in the company of one another and lost in their own thoughts. Soon they'd be home, all snug and tight in the little house that Beth had grown to love, so very much. She had her flowers and the pretty curtains she'd made herself. She had the lovely dishes that were a gift from Calliope Bigsby, and most of all, she had many good friends there, in Tucson, and she had missed them plenty. Maybe she'd plan that party, now. She was dreaming about the party, when Vernon suddenly pulled back on the reins causing the wagon to shudder to a stop. Beth heard Napoleon snort and whinny in alarm.

"Did you hear that?" Vernon whispered to Beth. "There it is again."

This time, she heard it, too. The report of gunfire … and a lot of it. "What's wrong? Where's it coming from, Vernon?" Beth was frightened. She knew this couldn't be good.

The ranger had already jumped down from the seat, and was running to the rear of the wagon to free Napoleon. In an instant, he'd swung up on the back of the big stallion, struggling to keep him under control.

"Darling, I have to check it out. Someone's in a lot of trouble. Take the extra pistol and don't be afraid to use it. Keep yourself and little Frank safe. Head straight in that direction." He pointed in the opposite direction, away from the gunfire.

"Tucson's just over that rise. Get Barclay. Tell him there's trouble at Scorpion Gulch." He stopped long enough to kiss her sweet lips and murmur, "I love you, angel."

With a nudge from his boot, Napoleon reared, and bounded forward in answer to his master's command. Given his head, the horse could fly. Becoming one with the animal, Vernon tore out across the open desert, and within moments, was gone from view, hidden within the rocks.

The gunfire was getting louder, but traveling in the opposite direction, away from Vernon. "It must be a stage in trouble," he muttered to himself. With hooves flying, he rode as if his hair was on fire, over the rocks, creeks and sandy desert, taking no time to be cautious. Then finally, just as he cleared the rise, he saw the problem, and reined to a halt.

The Butterfield Stage was in trouble, running wild and out of control. The driver looked to have been shot, and his partner was busy firing at six renegades in pursuit. Some of the passengers were firing out of the windows, trying to save their lives.

Vernon, pressed his heals into Napoleon's flanks and charged down the ridge. He surprised the attackers by taking out two of them, almost immediately. The rifleman on top of the coach shot another, right out of his saddle. The situation was changing.

With bullets flying and horses stumbling, it was a fast and furious confrontation. Vernon took bead on another Indian, just as he was aiming for the top of the coach. He fell under its wheels—dead for certain, but not before his bullet struck the rifleman in the back. He slumped forward.

"Go, Napoleon. Get me there!" Vernon shouted at his horse. He had to bring the stage under control quickly, or the travelers were in as much danger of overturning, as they were of being shot.

Napoleon pulled up alongside the front of the coach, allowing Vernon to throw himself off the horse and onto the side of the bench. He crawled up and grabbed the reins securely in hand. He felt a bullet buzz his hair, right along the back of his head, tearing a hole in his favorite hat.

"Shit!" He was mad now. He brought the team of six matched horses under control. He turned the team and was soon able to fire on the renegades, making every bullet count. Within just a few minutes, the attack was over and all the passengers were safe.

Keeping his gun aimed at the two last remaining outlaws, the ranger quickly got them trussed up like a Christmas goose. After a cursory glance at their amigos, Vernon decided they weren't going do anyone any harm, as they looked mostly dead.

Vernon checked the condition of the driver and the shotgun. Unfortunately, the driver was dead from a hole through the back of his head. At least, he never heard the bullet that took his life. His partner had a serious wound to his back, but given the fact that they were so close to Tucson, and good doctorin', the man would probably make it, Vernon reasoned.

"How's everyone back there?" he inquired.

The coach door opened slowly, and a large, very well dressed gentleman stepped out. He held a pistol securely in his hand. His face was flushed with excitement and his eyes shown with determination.

Just as the gentleman turned to offer his assistance, a trim ankle stepped down from the conveyance. It belonged to a magnificent looking woman, wearing the very latest in fashion. Her hair was slightly mussed, but she too, looked grateful to be alive.

Seven other people stepped out into the hot Arizona sun. Vernon noticed that they were all a little tossed about, but with the exception of a nasty scratch on the cheek of a pudgy, bespectacled firearms salesman, no one was seriously hurt.

Vernon offered his handkerchief to the man and said, "Have that scratch looked at proper, when we get into Tucson. You don't want an infection taking your eye."

Hearing horses' hoofs fast approaching, Vernon knew the cavalry had arrived in the guise of Ranger Barclay and the new Sheriff Billings. They were accompanied by a few men, from town, just for good measure.

Looking up at the lawmen, Vernon smiled. "Sure am glad to see you, men. This here stage met with six renegades, as best as I can figure. The passengers were brave and took care of most of 'em. The shotgun is bad wounded, but he ought to make it. The driver's dead. Back over yonder, are three dead Indians and one wounded brave. Two are tied up over there, by that big Saguaro. That has to smart some," he chuckled.

"Did Beth make it back safely?" Vernon asked Barclay.

Barclay hooted. "That's some wife you got there. She wanted to leave Frank with Mrs. Jones, get a horse and ride out with us. She had that pistol you gave her, and she was gonna' ride hell-bent for leather, all to save your worthless hide. She sets a mighty high store in you, Vernon. Gotta treasure a woman like that."

Vernon grinned. "She's special, all right."

The well-dressed gentleman passenger overheard their conversation. "The ranger has it right about that. The love of a good woman is priceless." He glanced at the beautiful woman traveling with him. "A man must do all that is in his power to protect her and keep her happy. Isn't that so, my dear?"

The woman just smiled, saying it all with her eyes.

Vernon nodded in acknowledgement, then ordered everyone back on the stage.

"I'll tie Napoleon to the rear of the coach and I'll drive. Put the wounded man in the back. If you need to make room, one of you can hop up here, with me. We'll be in Tucson in twenty minutes. Sorry for the trouble, folks."

He snapped the reins and the stage lurched forward.

Barclay and Billings rounded up the bodies and the captive outlaws, and tethered their horses together. A catastrophe had been avoided that day and they felt mighty relieved.

Once back in town, Vernon was attacked again … by his lovely and very worried wife. Tears rolled down her chin when she saw him ride in, driving the stagecoach. Running out into the street, she managed to jump up on the running board and get hold of her husband's leg.

"Vernon! Vernon!" she shouted. "Darling, you're back! Are you wounded? Are you hurt? Don't you ever go off like that again!" she scolded.

The gentleman riding inside the coach stuck his head out and observed the happy reunion that was about to take place, and laughed. It was good to see a young couple so obviously in love.

Vernon reached down and put his arm around his wife to secure her to his side. "Beth, you lovely, reckless woman. I'm fine, but you could get yourself hurt jumping up like this," he pointed out. "Hold on 'til I get this team stopped." Secretly, it did his masculine pride good to be met by his woman, in such a manner.

The stage shuddered to a stop and the passengers jumped out as quickly as possible. Tucson looked awfully good to them. One by one, they stood in line to shake the hand of the brave man who had ridden to their rescue. The ranger had saved their lives and they'd be forever in his debt.

Beth was crying tears of happiness. "Trouble sure has a way of finding you out, Mr. Gunn. I was frightened beyond belief. You need to talk to Ranger Barclay. Next time you're in trouble, I want to help. I had your gun, but he ordered me to stay here, in town. You tell him, Vernon. Next time, you tell him I can help." Her bottom lip stuck out in that obstinate pout Vernon loved so much.

"Angel, I hope there won't be a next time, but if there is—I promise, you can help." His green eyes flashed with amusement. Barclay had done exactly the right thing. He'd never allow his wife to go off and fight outlaws, but she didn't have to know that, and he hoped there really wouldn't be a next time.

Beth beamed. "Thank you, darling. I knew you'd understand."

Everyone needed to clean up and rest a spell, before continuing on to San Francisco. They had come a long way. With the exception of one man, they had all come from St. Louis, Missouri. They had proven they were a tough group of travelers. They had to be. The trip was long, arduous, and extremely dangerous under the best of circumstances. This particular group of citizens had been most fortunate with the arrival of Ranger Gunn, and they were relieved to know they were more than half way to their final destination. Their journey would take about twenty-five days, in total. Vernon figured the folks had another nine or ten days of traveling, before reaching San Francisco.

"Darling, let's invite these poor souls home to dinner. They've had a difficult time of it and I know they'll be starting out, at first light. Would you mind, terribly?" Beth asked. She knew that Vernon was anxious to be alone with her and the baby, in their own little house, but she couldn't ignore the haunted looks on the people's faces.

Vernon placed the softest whisper of a kiss upon the tip of her nose. "I think that's a very fine gesture, angel. I'd like to invite Barclay and Sheriff Billings, too, if that would be all right."

"Please do. Tell everyone to be there around six. That should give me enough time to throw something together. It will be simple fare, but there'll be a lot of it. Thank you, dear."

How did she do it, Vernon wondered? His wife had prepared a wonderful dinner for thirteen people, all at the last minute, and cared for their infant son, at the same time. The house was cool and inviting. She'd cut flowers to grace the table and harvested some tomatoes, beans and potatoes. She bought some freshly killed chickens, from a neighbor, and proceeded to fry them up, hot and crispy.

There wasn't time to bake a dessert, so she quickly went to the Hotel Doolittle, in hopes that the cook would have something she could purchase.

"Buy? You want to pay me money for this here, no account pie? Well, I thought I'd just throw it away," Miss Watkins laughingly said. "It's too hot for pie today. If you'll take it off my hands, I'd be beholdin' to you." The cook smiled and winked at Beth. She put the warm pie in Beth's waiting hands and shooed her out of the kitchen. "It's just too hot for pie," Beth heard her mumble, as she stepped of the sidewalk.

"I owe you. Thanks," Beth yelled, over her shoulder, as she ran home with the loveliest berry pie she had ever seen.

It was such a hot day that Beth decided to keep the use of candles and oil lamps to a minimum. She removed all the curtains over the windows and offered individual hand fans for the guests. The hot food was transferred outside to keep the house as cool as possible. She mopped down the floors with cool water and hoped that it would be enough to provide some measure of comfort for their guests.

Heaven chose to send a cool breeze through Tucson, about seven o'clock that evening, making the little house as comfortable as anything Beth could have hoped for, and the food was excellent. Her use of seasonings and peppers were new and well accepted by the weary travelers.

The pretty lady wanted to know Beth's recipe for the chicken, as it was spicy and very flavorful. The distinguished gentleman, accompanying her, had eaten more than his fair share.

Beth learned Mr. Matthew Granger was an attorney out of San Francisco and the lady was his intended, Miss Leticia Brown. She had once been on the stage, back East, and he was very proud of her accomplishments.

"My own mother was a legitimate singer," Beth said. "She sang in Milan, Italy and in France. She gave up singing professionally, however, when she married my father. I don't recall her ever saying she regretted it. My father loved to hear her sing, around the house. I do remember, on several occasions, she sang for special audiences. She once sang for President Jefferson Davis." Beth's face suddenly turned bright pink as she looked at the shocked faces around the table.

"Oh, I am sorry. I'm from Richmond, Virginia, and my mother *did* sing for him. But I'm sure she would have been proud to sing for President Lincoln, if he'd asked."

Miss Brown laughed with merriment. "I like you, Mrs. Gunn. You are priceless. May I call you Beth? I'm a good judge of character and I know you to be an honest and good person. I would have performed for Jeff Davis, too … if he'd asked." She winked and continued to chuckle, good-naturedly.

Mr. Granger stood up and offered his arm to Miss Brown. "Well, my dear, I think it's high time we took our leave and let this fine family get their rest. It was an eventful day for them, as well as for us."

Turning to Vernon, he held out his hand and clasped Vernon's in a firm handshake. "You saved our lives, today, son, and I won't be forgetting it. I'll be eternally grateful. Tucson is a lucky town to have the Gunn family residing in it, making it a safer and more enjoyable place to live. Thank you for your hospitality, sir.

"And Mrs. Gunn, your meal and charming company will not soon be forgotten, either. The ranger is a lucky man."

"I agree," responded Miss Brown. "If you ever find yourselves in San Francisco, please look us up. We'd love to introduce you around. We'll be easy to find, as Matthew is going to be appointed to the Federal bench. Please, bring Frank. I just love babies."

With their promises to keep in touch and their goodbyes said, the last of the guests departed, leaving two very happy, but very exhausted people, to clean up.

"You go and get in bed, sweetheart. Frank will be wanting to be fed again, before you know it. I'll put everything in the sink to soak until morning, and then I'll join you," Vernon offered.

Beth kissed her husband and sighed. "You're my hero. I'm completely tuckered out, and I don't think I could clean up now if you forced me. Hurry up and come to bed, darling." Beth stumbled off to her room.

Vernon blew out all the candles and turned down the lamps. Their home was quiet, now, and they were at peace. He loved walking around the silent rooms in the dark. It allowed a man some time to think. It was amazing how one's life could change so suddenly. A beautiful spitfire of a woman could stumble into your life one day and change it forever. He was a happy man and he prayed that their family would be spared any trouble that might come looking for them.

When he opened his bedroom door, he heard the soft breathing of a woman, fast asleep. He wanted to reach out and touch her, to feel her soft flesh beneath his fingers, but he was not so selfish as to wake her. She'd worked hard today, and had succeeded masterfully. There would be plenty of evenings for him to make love to her, but this evening would not be one of them.

It was autumn in Arizona, but you could barely tell it by looking. The days grew shorter and the morning air was somewhat cooler and fresher, but it still grew stifling in the late afternoon. The Aspens, up in the mountains, were a vivid yellow and the sumac had turned a brilliant red. But typically, the areas that didn't receive adequate rainfall did not produce the glorious fall colors Beth longed to see. There were some Yellow Cottonwoods that had turned golden and she thought they were beautiful, but it wasn't Virginia. It was always so refreshing to feel the first chill of winter upon her cheeks and to smell the crisp clean air. But this was Arizona, her husband's home and the birthplace of her son. Beth was determined to fall in love with its harsh beauty. After all, she had much to be thankful for. Life didn't get much better than it currently was. Everyone was healthy and she was very much in love.

Crime seemed to be taking a holiday of its own. Therefore, there had been no need for Vernon to ride out of Tucson, and that suited him just fine. Friday and Saturday nights brought the usual saloon brawls, and on a rare occasion, he'd have to arrest a man for trying to force himself upon an unwilling woman.

This lull in business allowed Vernon to spend more time with his family. He'd been seriously thinking about moving out closer to David, and trying his hand at raising horses, but it took more money than he had on hand. However, it was something worth looking into. He knew it would thrill Beth. He still liked being a ranger, but it was dangerous work and he had to think about his family now. He was hoping that soon, Beth might be with another child and he'd definitely have to think about moving on.

One frosty morning, while walking back to the shed, old Doolittle found a little black kitten resting in a bed of marigolds. "Well, look'ee here. Yer a cute lil' thing. How'd you like to visit a real nice lady? Maybe she'll let you stay fer a spell." The old man reached down and brought the kitten up to his whiskered cheek. "She's gonna like you, little feller. Yessiree."

And she did. Beth fell in love with Smudge instantly, and so did the baby. Frank was scooting around the house now, trying to get into anything he could find. When he saw the kitten, he giggled and cooed, and immediately tried to put the furry tail in his mouth. The kitten kept the baby entertained for hours.

Over the summer, Beth had added a milk cow, Suzie, and about a dozen chickens to her brood. One rooster took up residence, uninvited, but was allowed to stay, as he had his uses. Snowball was more like a pet than a sheep. She was allowed to come into the house occasionally, and let Frank crawl all over her. She was gentle with the baby and clearly loved the strange little creature.

Every night Vernon made love to his wife. Sometimes it was wild and passionate and at other times, it was slow and tender, but the end result was always the same … most satisfying. Life was just about perfect.

The couple had no way of knowing that trouble was about to explode in Richmond, Virginia. Trouble that would wrap its ugly tentacles around them and threaten to drag them under … and rip their happy lives apart.

# CHAPTER SIXTEEN

*Richmond, VA.*

"I have a brother and he's sick. I have no choice but to sell out. I'm all the family he's got and he needs me. I don't give a damn about your investigation. You can't hold me here. If you thought I done the man in, you'd have arrested me long ago. I've told you and told you, I don't know nothin' about no murder and nothin' about no woman who done it, neither. Now, leave me the hell alone!"

Harry Doolittle was at his wit's end. He no longer had any boarders. The police had seen to that. Life was intolerable. Earlier in the day, he met with the bankers and arranged to sell his beloved boarding house. He didn't care at this point. All he wanted to do was put as much distance between himself and Richmond as he possibly could.

He never regretted, for one instant, helping Ryann, but he never envisioned the relentless pursuit, by the police, for the murderer of that bastard lieutenant. Being as careful as he could, he needed to get to his brother. Horace was not ill, but Harry soon would be, if he didn't get away. The bank promised total confidentiality in the sale of the property. The money would be shipped later, to a bank of Harry's choice. Now, he just needed to pack up what he wanted to take with him, get tickets to a number of different locations—to throw off the detectives—and then head for the Arizona Territory. He was excited and eager to see both his brother and Ryann again. Horace had kept him informed. The letters were all coded and he'd had to read between the lines, but he knew she was well, and that was what was important. He loved the girl.

Senator Price was in town again, inquiring into the progress of the investigation. He realized that money alone wasn't enough to find his son's killer. This woman was devious and obviously no stranger to crimes of this nature. He had first thought that perhaps it was a crime of passion. His son was extremely handsome and heir to a fortune. It would only stand to reason, that a young woman could fall in love with such a man. He assumed his son broke her heart, or at the very least, shattered her dreams of such a match, and of being able to live a privileged life.

But now, the senator was convinced she was a calculating, cold-blooded murderess, and took pleasure in the pain she inflicted on her hapless victims. It was puzzling to him, however, that there was no attempt at extortion—no sign of robbery. Why did she feel the need to kill Mark?

The senator knew his son had a lot of anger in him, ever since suffering a horrendous wound to his skull, at Gettysburg. His personality seemed to change after that. Although mostly recovered, his son no longer felt grateful to be alive. So many young men never walked away from the battlefield, and yet, instead of being happy about his recovery, Mark seemed to resent it, growing angrier and darker by the day. But no matter how he had changed, he certainly didn't deserve to be murdered by some whore!

The senator decided to take a more active approach and not let the police grow lazy in their investigation.

"You've got nothing new to tell me? No new leads? What about Doolittle? You've got witnesses willing to testify they saw him out and about that morning, dragging a large bundle. It could have been my son. I'm telling you … he's the one that hid Mark's body. You're incompetent … all of you! I should have you all replaced."

Captain O'Hara was in no mood to listen to this outsider tell him how to do his job in the investigation of the crime at hand. "Now, look here, Senator. With all due respect, my men have worked harder on your son's murder than on any case I can recall, and I don't appreciate you comin' in here, to my office, and sayin' that they haven't. This has been a hard nut to crack, but I'm not feelin' hopeless about it, yet.

"Only today, we've learned that Doolittle is planning on leaving Richmond. I figure we only have to follow him and see where it leads. He may lead us directly to the woman, or maybe indirectly. But we'll be closer than we are at present.

"I do want to let you know, that we've uncovered a lot of testimony from women who knew your son, shall we say … intimately? He was rough with them, sir, to the point of causing serious injury. Did you know that about him?"

The senator cleared his throat. "I knew that he suffered from some problems due to a war injury he sustained at Gettysburg. I'm sure it was nothing out of the ordinary. What about the woman? Have you talked to her friends? Maybe she resented all Union Officers, being a Reb and all."

"Quite a number of women, and a few men, have come forward to vouch for her character. She was respected and well liked. That's what makes this all so confusing. Where has she gone and why did she run? If she was a victim, herself, why didn't she stay and defend her actions?"

The senator had exhausted his patience. His face grew red with pent up fury. "I've heard enough about her virtues. You sound like she had a bonafide reason to cut my son's throat! For God's sake, man. She allowed him to make love to her and then slit his throat, just to watch him die! I know that's what happened, and I want her caught and punished for her crime. See to it, or I'll see that you're looking for a new job!" He turned and stormed out of the office, leaving Captain O'Hara fuming mad.

"I almost feel sorry for this gal. If the son was anythin' like the father, I can see where he might make the girl so angry she'd take a knife to his throat—just to shut him up!"

Sergeant Donovan scratched his white head. "I think we need to follow the money. Doolittle's pretty smart and he may lead whoever's followin' him, on a wild goose chase. It might be wise to sit back and follow the money trail."

"How we gonna do that? The bank isn't going to tell us where the money is bein' sent."

"No, maybe not, but my sister's husband works at the bank and he would know if a big shipment was goin' out. He could be enticed to watch for a suspicious transaction to occur."

For the first time that day, the captain smiled. "See that it's done, then."

Harry was feeling rather confident that he had done all he could to cover his tracks. He'd made a nice profit on the sale of his boarding house, and now the plan was to hide out, right there, in Richmond, for ten days or so, until the authorities were convinced he'd left town. Then, he'd secretly take a train south to New Orleans. He'd spend some time there asking, very publicly, about buying commercial properties. Then, as in Richmond, he would lay low for a spell.

When he felt the time was right, he would travel to Chicago. He'd always wanted to see that city, and now he'd hide out there for a few weeks and take in the sights. Surely, he'd be able to get lost in a city of that size.

Finally, in about three months time, he'd catch the Butterfield stage and go directly to Tucson. He figured that he'd arrive sometime before the first of February. It would be a long and grueling trip, but if luck were with him, and he could keep his final destination unknown to those in Richmond, it would be worth it. He could finally put all this behind him.

Now, however, first things first. Harry grabbed up his satchel and walked down the street to the train station, where he would buy a ticket to somewhere he never intended to go. Smiling and saying his goodbyes to acquaintances he passed on the street, his heart began to flutter with the excitement of it all. What an adventure he was about to have.

Officer Danny Boyle was briefing Captain O'Hara on the latest developments of the Price case. "This Doolittle has left town, by all indications, sir. I've had a number of people come forward and tell me that they said their farewells, just as he entered the train station. I'm afraid, sir, this may be the end of it. It's impossible to know where he went."

"Nonsense! Nothing's impossible if you don't give up. Sure it is, that the ticket clerk remembers selling him a ticket. Have you questioned him?"

"Yes, sir. He says he sells a lot of tickets and can't possibly remember selling just one."

"Doolittle has a brother somewhere out West. Find him and see what he knows. By the way, son, it's come to my attention that you're planning on weddin' a young woman soon. If you're a smart lad, and I think you are, you'll wait until this case is wrapped up. You might get a promotion out of it, yet." He slapped Danny on the back and pushed him out the open door.

More than a week had passed before Sergeant Donovan reported back to the Captain. "My sister's husband, Albert, told me just this morning, that a very large amount of money has been shipped to the First Capital Bank of Tucson. I'm certain that's where Doolittle went," he said excitedly.

Captain O'Hara was overjoyed at the news. "That's fantastic, Sergeant! Finally, I feel like we got a break in this case. Next time the senator comes down, we'll have something positive to report. Doolittle and this, Ryann Beaufort, may think they're too smart for us, but perseverance usually pays off, and in this instance, it definitely has. Tucson it is! We need to give Doolittle time to get there, about thirty days, I'd estimate. Once there, he'll lead us right to her. We'll have the arrest made there and extradite them both, back here, to be tried by a jury of their peers. Good job, Donovan."

In the soft glow of moonlight, Vernon gazed at his lovely wife, lying naked against his own skin. Her long, lustrous hair resembled a halo shrouding her voluptuous body from his view. Only the angels were worthy to set sight on her magnificence. Her eyes stared into his, shimmering with passion and full of love for him. Her lips were red and slightly swollen from their kisses. Vernon could still taste them on his tongue and could feel her sweet, pink tongue wrestling with his own.

He nestled his face in her hair, inhaling the soft clean fragrance that he found so entrancing. Breathing deep, her scent invaded all his senses, and he felt his passion rise again. His body was beginning to harden with lust for her. She was his obsession and the passage of time had done nothing but increase his need and desire for her.

Her female softness was blatantly arousing to Vernon. She was supple and curvaceous, a feast for his eyes and hands. Beth kept her husband enthralled with her charms. She could be sultry, provocative, and wicked one moment, only to appear to be innocent and demure the next. All her various faces were mesmerizing to Vernon and he yearned for her touch.

He lightly brushed his fingers over Beth's shoulders and trailed down her arms. She felt the familiar rush of pleasure at his touch and made no attempt to move, but continued to lie there, waiting for his desire to build and rise.

Vernon kissed her face, her forehead, and her chin, settling on her moist lips, deepening the kiss. His tongue coaxed her lips to part, and he took possession of her inner mouth, reveling in the smoothness and the sweetness hidden there.

Beth's response was immediate, as she was consumed by a yearning to take this man and claim him for herself. She was wanton. She would be demanding of him this night.

Pulling back from his touch, she put her hands on his chest, feeling the granite hard muscles just below the skin. Stroking his chest, she felt for the masculine nipples hidden there within the curly mass of his sandy colored hair. She bent forward, nipping at them with her teeth. She sucked on them, forcing them to harden like little beans. Her wet tongue licked over the top of the pebbles, as she exhaled warm air softly across them.

Vernon gritted his teeth in painful pleasure. He moaned and tried to move her away from his chest. "Beth …"

Beth looked up at him. "Don't you like this, darling? Or perhaps you would like me to end the torment and move on?"

He could barely speak, "Yes, please move on. I can't stand a lot more of this," he begged. "I need to bury myself inside you."

"Oh, you silly boy. Not yet. My glorious torment has just begun." She smiled wickedly, knowing just what she intended to do to her lover, this night. Her hands drifted down past his waist, entering his most masculine of areas. His erection was huge, and throbbing, forcing Beth to swallow in anticipation. His manhood was incomparable and so deliciously threatening.

"Vernon, I want to make love to you with my hands. You don't mind, do you?" Not waiting for him to answer, she wrapped her slender fingers around his shaft. It felt like sculpted stone encased in the softest velvet. It throbbed beneath her stroking and moved with a life of its own. Yes, Beth loved the feeling of power she derived from coaxing it to swell to capacity. She noticed a sparkling drop of dew forming on the tip, making her mouth water. Groaning with anticipation, she licked at it, marveling in the salty taste of her man.

"Darling, that's enough!" Vernon groaned. "I need to make love to you. I need to have you beneath me. God, Beth, I can't control myself much longer. Now, darling, not later." He was wild with want for his wife and that's just what she was waiting to hear.

Beth tightened her grasp and placed her mouth over the entire engorged tip of his manhood. With the touch of her tongue, she playfully brought him to the edge of insanity. She sucked and licked and sucked some more. She tasted and massaged and stroked him until he was incapable of speech. It was marvelous to play the part of the seductress.

Vernon's heart was pounding, and his head felt as if it was going to explode. His hands were full of firm, round breasts, and his thumbs and fingers pinched and pulled her pink nipples, bringing erotic pleasure to her. Beth and Vernon were past knowing or caring who had control, as each was overcome with their own primal urges. Their desire burned with a white-hot passion that would not be denied.

In sexual desperation, Beth crawled up on top of Vernon. Her feminine parts were weeping for him to enter her. Frantically, she begged for something more. Grinding her hips onto his, he parted her thighs and spread her open in preparation.

"Sweetheart, put me inside you. Ride me. Ride me hard!" He held his erection straight up and his wife willingly, took him inside her, feeling him fill her, as never before. She was impaled on his manhood and it felt divine.

With total abandon, she rode, bucking up and down, causing her breasts to bounce in front of her husband's face. Flames of desire filled his once green eyes. Trembling with excitement, he licked his dry lips, dying for just a taste of her nipples, so beautiful and ripe.

Vernon took his thumb and touched Beth's hidden little nub, causing her to practically explode on contact. He rubbed it gently, in circles and causing a tightening of the muscles in her abdomen. She struggled to contain her emotions. She didn't want this erotic dream to end, just yet. Beth cried out his name.

Once again, it appeared that Vernon had free rein over Beth, but she really didn't mind. He always brought her to paradise in such an explosive and satisfying way. A sensation like warm honey flowed through her body and down over him. He had sent her soaring to enormous heights, as she shuddered her final release, and fell back to earth.

Vernon smiled. Thank God, he whispered, he was afraid he couldn't hold out much longer. Violent spasms seized his own body, as he poured his seed into his wife, sapping himself of all strength. A few more gentle thrusts and he collapsed, weak from pleasure, beneath his very happy wife.

They lay there for several minutes before Beth finally spoke.

"Vernon," she whispered.

"Yes, sweetheart."

"I think this time was special. Did you feel that it was?"

"Yes, precious," he said, lazily. "It was very special. Why ... do you think something miraculous occurred?" Vernon smiled cautiously, knowing what his wife was thinking.

Beth placed her hands on top of her belly and sighed. "I sincerely hope so, darling. I sincerely hope so."

The next morning started off to be the same as any other morning. It was hot, but people were starting to get into the Christmas spirit, nonetheless. It was nearing the end of November, and there was a lot to do, and not much time to do it. Living out in the territory, it was necessary to order things well in advance if they were to be received by the holidays. The telegraph company was doing a big business. Some messages were held up a little longer than they should have been.

Horace Doolittle received a rather obtuse telegram from his brother, Harry. He didn't know if it was good news or bad, so he decided to share it with Ranger Gunn.

Vernon read the coded telegram again. "So, Horace, you know your brother. Does it sound to you like he's fleeing from the law?"

"I can't rightly say. It's a surprise to me that he sold his boardin' house, though. He loved the place, but somethin' made him do it. I'm afeared that someone might follow him here, to us ... to her. You're gonna be in trouble too, Ranger, but I guess you know that."

Vernon's breakfast threatened to come back up. "Yeah, I know. Listen. Don't tell anyone about your brother coming, especially my wife. She really loves him and it would make her happy to see him again, but she's smart, too, and it wouldn't be too difficult for her to put it all together. I don't want her worried about herself or me … or even you—you old codger." Vernon chuckled. "Everything will work out. I'll make certain it does."

"Oh, tarnation. I ain't scared, none. You just see to the Missus, and make sure, if the devil comes a visitin', you get her outta here." Doolittle wasn't smiling. He was deadly serious, and for that, Vernon was grateful. He knew he could trust him to keep their secret.

It was imperative Vernon speak with Ranger Barclay, without delay. He needed to know what to expect. "So you see, trouble's coming, as sure as I'm standing here. I can feel it in my bones and I don't want you caught in the middle. You're a good ranger, and more importantly, you're a good friend. If there comes a time when you're asked how much you knew, I want you to deny it all. You knew nothing, and if you did, you would have notified the authorities in Richmond. I'll not have our troubles fall on you. That clear?"

Barclay nodded. "But I'll make damn sure I'm hard fer them to find. I won't give you up, easily. I know how to evade answerin' questions, and I'll do my level best to protect the two o' you. I really admire Mrs. Gunn, and you know how much I respect you. Hell, I can think of more than one time you saved my rotten hide. Nope, they'll have a hard time gettin' me to talk." With that having been said, the ranger put on his hat and went out the back way, slamming the door behind him.

"That went well," Vernon muttered.

Just then, the front door flew open and a breath of sunshine blew in. Beth stood there, looking radiant in a light blue dress with little pink flowers sewn around the bosom, and was smiling from ear to ear. Frank was playing with his little stuffed kitten, Beth made for him. She placed Frank in his papa's arms and sat in a chair by the desk.

"Paa … Paaap," Frank garbled.

"Did you hear that, darling? Frank has been saying that all morning. He's saying papa. I know that's what he's saying. He's saying papa! Aren't you pleased?" Beth was so excited she could barely contain her enthusiasm. "He's so young and so very smart. He must take after my side of the family." Then she blushed, knowing he couldn't take after Vernon's side. "You know what I mean," she blushed.

"Yes, dear. I know just what you mean, and I completely agree. His good looks come from me!" He grinned broadly, showing his lovely white teeth. He was such a tease.

"Do you think Frank needs his first haircut?" she asked.

"No, I like his curls. They're the color of your hair and I think it looks real nice. Maybe after Christmas."

"Good," she said. "I've been putting it off because it's a milestone in a baby's life. His first haircut proves he's growing up, and I want him to stay a baby for a little while longer."

Frank started chewing on his papa's shirt collar, having lost interest in eating the kitten's ear.

"Well, darling, I don't think you have to worry about that. Before you know it, we'll have another baby for you to cuddle and fuss over. A boy's got to grow up sometime, you know. Now, I don't mean to be contrary, but you need to pack up and take this little heathen out of here, so I can get my work done. There are some problems, down in Tombstone, that I may have to address, so get along with you, woman. I'll see you at suppertime."

Vernon took his free arm and wrapped it around Beth's narrow waist and pulled her to him, squeezing Frank between them. Making lots of smacking and slurping sounds, Vernon kissed his wife long and hard, causing Frank to giggle and squeal with happiness.

"Be gone, wife!"

"Yes, my lord husband!" Beth did a little curtsey and carried a very silly baby with her, both waving bye, bye to papa.

Later in the day, just before Vernon was about to go home, a dusty and exhausted ranger walked in. It had been some time since Vernon had seen Waco Smith and he didn't look like this was purely a social call.

"Howdy, Waco. Pull up a seat. What brings you to Tucson?"

"You got some coffee? I'm damn near done in," Waco growled.

"Sure thing." Vernon grabbed a mug and filled it full of the strong black brew and handed it to his friend. "I heard you've been having some trouble down in Tombstone. What's that got to do with me?"

"Get prepared fer your own troubles. It seems to be spreadin' like wildfire. We bring one gang in and there's two more to take their place. Got word of a big shipment of cash coming to Tucson, from Richmond, Virginia. If we've heard about it, you can bet they've all heard about it. Without us, it'll never make it here."

"From Virginia, you say?"

"Yep. Some old geezer's gonna live here and needs his stash, I reckon. Know anything about that?"

Vernon lied. "Nah, ain't heard nothin'." It had to be Doolittle's brother, Harry. If the rangers had been informed of its arrival, then it wouldn't be hard for anyone else to follow it right straight to Beth. He needed to think. "When is it expected?"

"Bout two weeks. We're supposed to ride out and meet it as it crosses from Texas. Don't think we've gotta' worry too much about the Apache. They don't give a hang about the white man's money. But every damn nasty gang of outlaws between here and Arkansas, will be gunnin' fer it. Kiss yer wife, adios, and meet me in the mornin'. We gotta hit the trail, early." Waco put his empty cup down on the desk and walked out the door. No idle conversation with this man, but Vernon trusted him with his life.

It was a quiet dinner that evening. Vernon told Beth he'd be riding out in the morning, but he didn't tell her about the Richmond connection. After all, what could she do about it, but worry? He knew she would be worried enough about his safety. She always worried when he was gone, but that was natural, he guessed. He always fretted about her welfare, when he was gone.

"Now Beth, darling, I don't want you to go reading more into what I'm going to say, than there is to it, but I've been a thinking. If I don't return before the fifteenth of December, I want you to pack up Frank and have Doolittle or Barclay take you out to David's ranch. I'll talk to both of them before I leave. I know Mary and the children will be very happy to have the two of you for the holidays, and I'd feel better knowing you're not here, in this house, alone. Is that acceptable to you?"

Beth could tell that something was different with this assignment. She also knew better than to second-guess her husband. He knew what he was doing and she trusted him to do it.

"Of course, dear, if you think it's necessary. Is this job very dangerous?" Her large eyes resembled two beautiful, crystal blue pools, and Vernon could see they were filled with fear. She was scared.

He put his arms around her and gave her a reassuring squeeze, then he buried his face in her hair, inhaling slowly. He loved the sweet, feminine smell of her. "No, angel, not particularly dangerous. It just might take some time, that's all, and I don't want to worry about my family spending their Christmas all alone. It's Frank's first, you know." Vernon sighed. He had planned to be here for his son's first Christmas. It would only come once and he didn't plan to miss it.

"Promise you'll do that for me," he insisted, as he looked deep into her eyes.

"Yes, Vernon. I promise." Beth nodded in agreement. "Now, let me help you get ready. What will you need?"

# CHAPTER SEVENTEEN

*Richmond, VA.*

The senator was beside himself with excitement. This was the best news he had heard since his son's tragic and senseless murder. He would catch the very next train to St. Louis, and travel by stage the rest of the way. He'd pay extra, if they could get him there before Christmas. It would be a present to himself. For too long now, he had been consumed with receiving justice. The cold, dead body of his son demanded nothing less.

"Thank you, Captain, and you, Sergeant. I'll not forget this. Mark will be avenged, finally." The old man's eyes unexpectedly filled with tears.

"You didn't know him, of course, but I remember him as a fine and upstanding young man. He was good and had a promising career until … uhmm."

The man cleared his throat before continuing. "It makes no difference, now. He was my only child, my future, and that whore took it all away from me. That will not be allowed to stand. Whatever she has, or whomever she loves … rest assured, gentlemen, I most definitely will take it away. I will leave her with nothing," he spat.

"I'll be accompanied by a U.S. Federal Marshal. We'll make the arrest in Tucson and drag her back here, to Richmond, by the hair of her head, if necessary. I'll see to it that she's convicted of cold-blooded murder. She'll be found to be an evil and heartless viper, preying on our proud men in blue. I won't settle for less, and then, I'll dance for joy as I watch her twitch at the end of a rope. Wish me well, boys." Coming to the end of his tirade, the senator stormed out of Captain O'Hara's office.

"I don't think that man is put together too tightly, Sergeant. Wouldn't want to be the lady in question, that's for sure. Now maybe we can get back to business as usual … prior to *'the crime of the century'*?" he said sarcastically, as he rolled his eyes.

Senator Allenton Price knew how to grease wheels. Whatever he demanded, he received, in short order. He had two marshals accompanying him, and in two days time, he was on the train bound for St. Louis. He was good to his word. He'd be in Tucson before Christmas.

Officer Danny Boyle had been seeing Katie O'Donnell on a regular basis, for a number of months now, and he was eager to ask her to marry him. She had explained to him how Seamus' father was killed in a factory accident, just days after she had arrived from Ireland. They'd been in love for several years and were to have been married. Liam was a nice man and Danny would have approved of him. After he died, Katie had no one to turn to except a woman she had met one evening, outside the Doolittle Boarding House. Her name was Libby McGuire, and she took in single young women—so to speak.

"If it hadn't been for her friendship, I probably would have died on the streets. I knew I was with child before Liam was killed, ya see, and no one would have hired a pregnant Irish girl to do anythin'. She taught me how to keep books, because of me skill with numbers. I liked doin' that and it paid for me room and board."

"How did you end up on the street, fair to starving?" Danny asked.

"She up and disappeared, she did. It was about the same time as that bad lieutenant was murdered. I don't know where she went, but she closed up shop, and that was the last I saw of her.

"It took only a couple of weeks before I spent all the money that I had saved up, and the winter grew so cold. I wasn't able to keep Seamus warm or even fed, for that matter." She blushed. "Ya see, I wasn't eatin' proper and that caused a lack in me milk. We both almost starved, until I met a wonderful Irish constable and he came to me rescue. Did I ever thank ya, Danny?"

"I want you to thank me every day, for the rest of our lives, Katie. In fact, this isn't how I planned it, but it feels right."

He stopped and took hold of Katie's hands, and looked into her lovely, freckled little face. "Will you do me the honor, Katie O'Donnell, of bein' my wife?"

"Oh, Danny!" She jumped up and threw her arms around his neck and started to kiss him all over his blushing face. She didn't care who saw. He had just asked her to marry him and she was going to say … "Aye! Oh, aye, Danny. I'd be proud to marry ya. I love ya so."

They walked hand in hand, down Fourth Street, toward his mother's place. They were to have supper there, again. They didn't need to speak, as each one was contemplating their bright future spent together.

Over supper, conversation returned to the Lieutenant Price murder. Danny asked Katie if she knew the names of any of the other women that had worked for Libby McGuire.

"I would have to think on it. Ryann didn't work for her, if that's what you're gettin' at. They were just vera good friends."

"Katie! You never said that Miss McGuire knew Miss Beaufort! Maybe *she* knows what happened. Maybe Libby knows where she went. Tomorrow, I want a list of all the names of the women you can remember. And this time, Katie, don't leave anything out!" Danny got up abruptly, and left the room.

Not knowing what she had done to cause such an outburst from Danny, Katie looked hurt and perplexed. She glanced over at Mother Boyle, as she was told to call the older woman, hoping for an explanation of just what had happened.

"Don't you never mind him, Katie, darlin'. It's his job and he wants to do well so he can provide for you and little Seamus. He wants to help solve this case and move on to other things. You see … he won't be gettin' married with it hangin' o'er his head like it 'tis. He's not mad at ya, darlin. He's just eager for it all to be over and done with. Now, have some more shepherd's pie. We want to fill ya out some."

Bright and early, the next morning, Katie decided to help Danny with his case. Mother Boyle offered to keep Seamus for the day, allowing Katie to investigate on her own. She knew several of the girls and hoped that most were still on Church Street. She'd ask about Libby and pass the information on to Danny.

Their stories were all the same. One day, Libby was there, helping to keep the girls honest and well fed. She had appointments to keep and places to go. Then, suddenly, one morning, she was nowhere to be found. No appointments were kept and no excuses were provided.

"Shannon, didn't ya think it was odd, her disappearin' like that?" Katie pressed.

"Of course I did. I owed her almost nine dollars and was due to repay it back in just three days. You know how strict she was with loans. You kept her books. What did you find in them?"

Katie thought for a moment. She hadn't really checked the books that closely, at least not recently. She assumed that Libby had closed out her accounts before she left. That's what she would have done. Libby was not sloppy with her bookkeeping. Somethin' smelled bad, and if somethin' smelled bad—as her da would say—it was usually because somethin' was rotten.

"Do ya know if Libby's things are still in her flat?" Katie asked Shannon.

"Oh, sure. She owns the building, you know. We don't have the right to move her things. Why? Do you think something has happened to Libby?" Shannon looked shocked and worried for her friend. All the girls liked Libby and owed her their lives.

"Don't fret. I'm lookin' into it. She probably just took a vacation, after all the scandal when that lieutenant was murdered."

"Oh, don't mention him to me." Shannon's eyes filled with old memories of pain and suffering. "I still have the burns to remind me. He was a cruel one." She spit on the ground. "I sleep better knowin' he's in the ground!"

"You're not the first to be a sayin' somethin' like that. Do ya think his father, the senator, knew what his son was like?"

Shannon shrugged her shoulders with indifference.

"Thank ya, Shannon. You've been a lot of help. How are ya girls gettin' by without Libby to guide ya?"

The girl smiled brightly. "Most of us are doing very well. Libby taught us skills we can use in the shops and public buildings. Only one or two are still on the streets. I work in the library now, and I'm very good at my job," she said proudly. "All thanks to Libby. I hope you find her, Katie."

It took more than an hour for Katie to walk the distance to Libby's residence. She had an apartment in a neat building with shops on the bottom floor. Libby had planned to bring the girls there, to live, just as soon as the renovations were completed.

Katie nodded to the baker as she ascended the stairwell to Libby's private domicile. She knocked on the door several times, but there was no answer. Trying the door handle, she found the door wasn't locked. Looking around the empty hallway, Katie walked in and latched it behind her.

It was dark and damp in the spacious room. She knew instantly that Libby hadn't been home for some time. The dust was thick and the food, lying about on the table, was spoiled. She walked slowly into the bedroom and inspected Libby's clothes.

Libby had lived a modest lifestyle, but she had her fair share of dresses, coats, and other ladies' apparel. It appeared to Katie that Libby hadn't packed anything to take with her. Everything was just as it should be.

"Libby, where are ya?" Katie wondered aloud. "Tis peculiar, your leavin' like this." Suddenly her stomach cringed and a feeling of dread settled over her. This had to be connected with Ryann's disappearance and the murder of the lieutenant, but how?

She couldn't figure it out, but she refused to give up. Libby was her friend, and so was Ryann. There was a mystery here, and she needed to help Danny solve it. This was only the beginning of her search.

That evening, after dinner, Katie told Danny of her venture out in search of some news on Libby's disappearance. At first, he was concerned with her doing something that could be harmful to her safety, but after listening to her, he knew she was on to something important.

"Can you take me with you tomorrow morning? Ma will keep an eye on Seamus, I'm certain. We need to search Libby's buildin' from rafters to cellar, and I'd rather not get the captain involved until we have something solid to show him. He's so relieved at having the senator out of our business, that I'd like to let him enjoy himself for as long as he can."

Katie reached for Danny's hand. "Of course, Danny, but I have a really bad feelin' in me heart that Libby didn't just leave town. Tis' not like her, at all. She was always helpin' people and wasn't afeared o' nothin'. Everyone liked her. She didn't have an enemy in the world."

"Don't borrow trouble, sweetie. We'll find what there is to find, and that'll be that. Maybe she did leave of her own free will. Maybe she took off with Ryann. I just hope she had nothing to do with the murder. Don't worry. We'll get to the bottom of this." He gave her a little peck on her creamy cheek and smiled. Soon, he thought, he'd be able to love her the way he desired. Without trying, she brought his blood to near boiling, but it was important, in their relationship, that he treat her with the respect a man gives to his future wife.

"Now, get some sleep, darlin'. It'll be a full day tomorrow."

"Aye, Danny." Katie smiled, coyly. She knew how he felt about her and she felt just that way about him. Soon, they would share a bed and the life that goes with it.

Katie heard the soft knock at her door. She knew it must be Danny and she had overslept. Seamus was still sound asleep, so she had to be quiet. She dressed as quickly as she could, ran the brush through her flaming curls and tied it back with a yellow ribbon. Danny liked her hair down and tied back, she thought to herself. It could prove to be a long day, but she'd be with him. She smiled.

After they ate their breakfast, the two young people walked, hand in hand, to Libby's building. It was a rather imposing structure and was obviously a good investment for the young woman. Danny could see that she had a very astute mind for business. The shop owners were all in attendance and preparing for their day.

"Can you get us inside, Katie?" Danny inquired.

"Oh, sure. Tis not locked, ya know. Never was. That's what so bogglin'. Why would Libby leave her home and business, and not bother to lock up?" Her forehead wrinkled in thought. "She was always after us girls to watch out for thieves and the like. It's just one o' the things that doesn't make sense. Her rooms are dusty and unlived in, and she left food out, to rot on the table. I can't see that she took any clothes with her. Oh, Danny, I'm so scared." Katie gripped Danny's arm tightly, digging her nails into his flesh.

Standing outside Libby's door, Katie hesitated. "You go in first. I don't like the feelin' it gives me."

Danny nodded, turned the handle, and walked in. Katie was right. There was foul play for sure, in the disappearance of Miss Libby McGuire. He couldn't connect it directly to the crime of Ryann Beaufort, but his gut instinct told him that there was a link, nonetheless. He just needed to find it.

They spent hours in Libby's place. There was nothing amiss that either one could see. That is, until Katie pulled back the quilt, covering the bed. The sheet was missing. Maybe it was to be washed, Katie thought, but Libby was always very orderly, and she knew that she would have made the bed up, straight away.

"Danny! Look at this. Why is the sheet missin'?"

The missing sheet caused a knot to form in the pit of Danny's stomach. More than once, he had seen a dead body wrapped in a sheet. Looking around, he spied a pillow on the windowsill, not precisely in line with all the others. Walking over to the window, he picked it up and discovered a small reticule hidden beneath it.

"Have you seen this before?" he asked Katie, as he held up the bag.

"Certainly. It's Libby's favorite. She almost always had it with her. I don't believe she would have left it behind." Katie started to weep silently. She knew her friend had met with a bad fate.

"I need to talk to the shopkeepers, downstairs. Do you want to go with me or stay here and rest a bit?" Danny hated to leave her, but Katie was in no condition to listen to the serious questions he was going to ask.

"No! I don't want to stay here. I'll go with ya. Maybe I'll be helpful, as they know me. I can do it for Libby."

Katie led the way down the stairs, not being able to endure one more minute in the dark, sad apartment. All the merchants said pretty much the same thing. None had any idea where Miss McGuire had gone. They hadn't seen her for quite some time, and the baker was angry with her.

"Seems like to me the lady could have seen to the completing of the renovations, before gallivanting off on holiday. I still have to empty my water out back, and I was promised a larger storeroom, too. When you find her, you tell her to send the carpenters back!"

Exhausted from the long and most troubling day, Danny thought it was time to return home. He would come back later, if he got any ideas. "Ready to go, darlin'? Don't want ma to wait dinner on us." He turned to look at Katie and was struck by the look of horror on her chalk-white face.

"Danny … we need to go to the cellar. The tools were kept locked up there, and if the carpenters couldn't get to them, they wouldn't work. In the past, they would wait until Libby let them in. They, too, must think she's on holiday, since there have been no complaints. She wouldn't have locked them out. Now, Danny … you must go and look now."

As soon as Katie voiced her fears, Danny knew she was onto something and he was afraid her suspicions would be validated. "Show me, Katie darlin'. Then you come back up here and wait for me, out in the sunshine. You promise?"

She nodded, and took his hand, leading him down the rear stairs and out across the yard, away from the house. She pointed to the pair of doors set in the ground, covering the steps leading down into the root cellar.

"Okay, darlin'. You go on back now. I'll see to this."

Danny patiently waited for her to disappear back inside the house, before he started down the steps. All the hair on the back of his arms stood up. He needed to be prepared for whatever he may find.

It took some minutes before his eyes grew accustomed to the darkness surrounding him. It was as quiet as a tomb—an appropriate analogy, he feared. At first glance, all seemed to be just as it should—until he noticed the scrapes across the hard packed floor. In the faint light filtering in through the open doors, he could clearly see where something had been dragged from the door to the rear corner. Some baskets of vegetables had been turned on their sides, allowing the contents to spread helter-skelter, across the floor. There had been some kind of struggle here, he was sure of it.

Walking gently, so as not to disturb the area, he poked his head around the furthest most set of shelves, and there, on the dirt floor, partially wrapped in a sheet, lay a woman … dead for many months. Danny had never met Libby McGuire, but what he knew about her, made his heart ache, for this was surely that good woman and her death would cause Katie much pain.

Looking from a distance, he noticed her clothing was ripped and had been cast about the small area. No four-legged animal had done this. Partially hidden beneath the ribs, was what appeared to be a U.S. Infantry issued knife. She'd been stabbed in the chest and left to die, here, in the dark and all alone. What kind of a person could commit such a heinous act? A monster, that's clear, Danny thought. Then he recalled the statements from some of the women interviewed in the Mark Price murder investigation. They referred to the lieutenant as a monster.

*What's the connection?* "I know it's right here in front of me! Damn!" Danny stated, aloud. "Tell me, Libby. Help me find out who did this."

He wondered if Ryann had anything to do with this murder, too? Libby was stabbed, just like Mark Price. She was beautiful, and maybe Mark was leaving Ryann for Libby, and Ryann wouldn't stand for it, so she killed them both and left town. That made perfect sense. Not that Katie would believe it for a minute, but he knew a jury would. Ryann was in even bigger trouble than first thought.

The one thing that didn't make any sense, however, was how Ryann obtained the infantry knife? Those were not that easy to come by. It had a serial number engraved on the blade. Maybe he could find out the identity of the soldier to whom it was issued, and that knowledge could help clear up this mystery. But first, he needed to get a lamp or a candle, to get better lighting at the crime scene. He turned and ran up the steps.

Just as he approached the stairs leading up to the apartment, he came face to face with Katie. One look, and she knew he had discovered what she most dreaded.

"She's there, isn't she?" Katie asked, with bated breath.

Danny hurt for the pain he was going to cause. "Yes, my darlin'. She's been gone a good long while, months in fact. I think you should go on out front, and let me do my job."

"I want to see her. She shouldn't be left alone any longer. Hurry back, Danny."

He ran up the stairs and retrieved a small oil lamp and met Katie in the yard, already on her way to the cellar.

"Are you sure you want to go down there?" Danny asked.

She nodded, and followed him down the dark steps.

Danny lit the lamp and the glow filled the room, illuminating every shelf and corner. It was clear to see the signs of the struggle that had occurred there. "Don't touch nothing, Katie. When we leave here, I have to get Captain O'Hara. He's not going to be happy about this."

Katie silently crept to the far back corner and gasped when she saw what was left of her dear friend. "Oh, my God, Libby. Oh, no, no," she cried, as she fell to her knees, sobbing. She held her hand tightly to her chest. It was crushing to see the remains of the lovely young woman, her friend. "Who, Libby? Tell me, who did this to you," she implored.

Danny took notes, and when he thought he'd done all he could do, he gently tried to pull Katie away from her friend. Reluctantly, she stood up, and as she started to turn, her shoe caught on the corner of a basket that had been spilled, at the dead woman's feet.

"Oh, I'm sorry, Danny. I didn't mean to touch anythin'," she gasped.

Danny came over and dislodged her shoe from the small container. Looking down, to make sure she was free, Danny shouted, "Katie, look at that!" He pointed to the flat side of the shelf, closest to Libby. She had tried to scrawl a message. It was obviously written under great duress and probably in her own blood.

The message read; "Price killed".

Libby had named her killer.

It was all too much for Katie. Her legs buckled, as she collapsed where she stood. Danny caught her and carried her up the steps, running all the way to the bakery. With his arms full, Danny hollered for help.

"Put her over here, sir," the baker offered.

Danny laid Katie gently on the floor, out of the way. "Go fetch a constable. Have him bring Captain O'Hara. Got that?"

"Yes sir, right away!" The baker ran out the door screaming and yelling for help.

The authorities carefully inspected the scene. It was agreed that the lady was, indeed, Miss Libby McGuire, and she had been murdered a year earlier, about the very same time

Lieutenant Price was murdered. After taking note of the message the victim had scrolled in her own blood, before she died, it was obvious that her assailant was the lieutenant. Taking into consideration the testimonies of the women who knew him, the captain was fairly certain that Ryann Beaufort killed him in self-defense. He was clearly deranged and a threat to women.

Danny was given credit for cracking the case wide open. It was no longer the open and shut murder case it had been. In fact, Captain O'Hara was now concerned for Miss Beaufort. With the senator seeking vengeance, he wasn't at all certain that she would receive a fair trial without this new information. Someone had to be notified of the discovery … and quickly.

"Boyle, I'm sending you to Tucson. You be ready to leave in the morning. In the meantime, I intend to send a message to the sheriff in Tucson, informing him about our findings. Maybe he'll get it, but in case he doesn't, you've got to tell him that Price was a murderer. I intend to look deeper and see if he's responsible for the disappearance of a few other women, here in town. If you hurry, you'll only be two or three days behind the senator."

Danny nodded. Katie was sitting up with a cool cloth on her eyes. When she heard that Danny would be going to Tucson, she spoke up. "Can I go with Danny, sir? I know Ryann and I was a good friend of Libby's. I also met the lieutenant, and I'll testify, if I have to, to his true personality."

"Yes, yes, go. It may be a good thing to send you along. First thing in the morning, then."

# CHAPTER EIGHTEEN

*Tucson, Arizona Territory*

Vernon had been gone for two weeks and Beth was worried. She hated it when he rode into danger. She knew his job was hazardous before she fell in love with him, but you can't tell your heart who to love and who it shouldn't. She promised to love and support him through the good and the bad, and that's just what she would do. After all, it was only two weeks until Christmas and there was much to do. Keeping busy would help to distract her, and keep her from worrying about Vernon's mission.

Calliope Bigsby, and some of the other influential women of Tucson, were organizing a Christmas pageant for the townsfolk. The children were to be highlighted. The older boys were helping with the scenery, the building of Bethlehem, the nativity, and the gathering of the animals that would be used.

The girls were assembling props and making costumes. The schoolteacher and the pastor of the Christian Church were planning the music. To Beth's utter delight, little Becky was going to be a featured soloist. She suspected that Mrs. Bigsby had some influence in that choice, but that was fine with her. Becky sang like an angel and Calliope clearly loved the child and wanted to see her excel and be happy.

Beth was asked if Frank could be the baby Jesus, but she thought it might be wise to decline. Frank was much like his papa. You couldn't keep the child still or quiet. He was an extremely happy baby, smiling, gurgling, and laughing all the time, but he also had ants in his britches. He was everywhere! Frank was such a wiggle-worm that it was sometimes difficult for Beth to hold on to him. He always wanted down. Other mothers had told her that Frank would be an early walker for sure. Beth was convinced he would skip the walking and go straight to running.

Mary and David had recently been in town to pick up supplies, and told Beth that they would be spending Christmas on the ranch. She and Vernon were invited to come and spend the holiday with them, but Beth knew that Vernon would be tired, and she wanted their first Christmas to be in their own home … just the three of them. She had it all planned.

On December 22nd, they would attend the pageant and then come home and decorate the house with greenery. It wasn't quite the same as what she'd had back in Virginia, but it would be festive and enjoyable and maybe it would prove to be even better.

On the 23rd, Beth planned to be cooking all day, and she was actually looking forward to it. She had invited her special friends to share in their holiday dinner. She never got around to having that party she wanted, so this would be her party.

She invited Horace Doolittle, Mr. and Mrs. Jones, Miss Watkins—the baker, Ranger Barclay, Miss Browning—the schoolmarm, and Robin, from the Fancy Garter. Miss Watkins was a little older than Barclay, but she was single and she might make a friend. Beth knew that Barclay was lonely. Doolittle had a special relationship with Robin, and that was their business. Beth liked Robin. It promised to be a fine evening.

The following day would be Christmas Eve, and Beth planned to be alone with her family and quietly celebrate the birth of the Christ child. In the evening, they would go to church to worship, and return home for cake. She and Vernon would put little Frank to bed and sit cuddling with each other for hours, just staring into the fire, celebrating the joy and the peace that is Christmas.

Beth sighed. *"Oh, Vernon. Please be careful and come home soon. We miss you."* She closed her eyes and prayed silently.

While Frank was taking his nap, Beth took advantage of her

free time to mend one of Vernon's heavy winter shirts. She didn't hear the ruckus starting up out in the street. A sudden loud knock on the door startled her, causing her to drop her mending to the floor, and her heart to jump into her throat.

"I'm coming," she shouted. What on earth could be happening now, she wondered?

A young man, unfamiliar to Beth, looked at her urgently. "Mrs. Gunn?"

"Yes, I'm Mrs. Gunn. Is something wrong?"

"Yes, ma'am. The stage has arrived and Ranger Gunn took a bullet."

All the blood drained from Beth's face. "Oh, no," she screamed. "Is he all right? He isn't … bad?" She felt her legs begin to weaken. Turning to a chair, she sat down for a moment.

"I don't know, ma'am. They just hollered at me to come and fetch you back."

She garnered all her strength and was on her feet running to gather up Frank. He fussed at being disturbed, but settled down once Beth had him securely in her arms, as they rushed from the house. She walked as fast as was prudent, carrying the baby. She needed to get to the doc's house, located just past the Ranger's Office. Tears were staining her cheeks. "Oh, not now," she prayed. "Not now." They'd been through so much together. It wasn't fair that a bullet could take their entire future away, in an instant.

Ranger Barclay was standing outside his office, when he saw Beth, scared out of her wits, carrying little Frank, and practically running down the sidewalk.

"Hey, hey there, Beth," he shouted. "Slow down a mite. Vernon's gonna make it. He's gonna be okay." The ranger reached out to stop her from tearing around the corner and maybe running into somebody.

"What did you say, Barclay?" Beth asked, looking so fragile, he wanted to take her into his arms and comfort her.

"I said, slow down. Vernon's doin' fine. He took a bullet fer me, and it hit him in the thigh. It would've hit me in my dumb old head, but he saved me. He's a real hero, Beth. I owe him," he said, suddenly looking serious. His eyes filled with moisture, but he managed to sniff it away. "We just wanted you to know he was back home. Tarnation! He'll be real angry to think you got all upset over this."

"Thank God," Beth murmured, as she tried to regain control of her breathing. "Can I sit down for a second? I don't feel so well."

"Sure thing. Hand that boy over to me and come inside. There's no hurry. The doc's got some patchin' up to do."

Barclay reached down and took the sleepy baby from her arms. Beth put her head down on her knees. "Is it anything serious, ma'am? Can I get you something?"

"No, I've just been a little dizzy lately. I'll be fine once I see that Vernon is all right." She smiled and closed her eyes for a couple of minutes, taking deep breaths.

The door opened and the old doctor walked out. "I thought I might find you in here, Mrs. Gunn. Vernon's restin' a spell, over at my house. He took a slug to his thigh, but he'll make it. Thing is, I think he could be a bit lame after this. He might always limp some. He don't know it, yet. I wanted to talk to you first, to prepare you. Your attitude will greatly affect how he'll respond to the news that his rangerin' days may be over."

Ranger Barclay looked stunned. "It's all my fault. He told me to watch my back." He hung his head and ran his hands through his thinning hair. "Oh, Beth, fergive me. I'll never be able to face him."

She felt so sorry for Barclay. He was taking the news in a hard way. "Shush, Barclay. Vernon won't feel that way about it, and I'm just glad that his life was spared—yours too. Some things happen, in this life, that are out of our control. This may be one of them."

Beth stood up and placed her hand on Barclay's shoulder—just before she fainted. The next thing she knew, the old doctor was looking into her eyes and wiping her face with a cool cloth.

His wise old eyes were gentle and kind. In a quiet voice, he asked, "Dear, how far along do you think you are?"

Beth felt herself blush. "I'm not sure. I've missed one, maybe two. Could I be with child?"

He smiled. "I couldn't tell you fer certain, but you have all the signs, and I assume you and the ranger are on friendly terms, yes?"

She nodded.

"Well, this'll be one hell of a Christmas present for Vernon."

He laughed and stood up. "I think it's time for you to go on over and see that man, young lady. He can go home now, if he's careful.

"Barclay," the doc hollered. "Will you assist Mrs. Gunn over to my house and return her husband home?"

The ranger stuck his head around the door. "I'd be honored, Doc," he sniffed.

While in a great deal of pain, Vernon was in good spirits. "Shucks, I don't know what all the fuss is about. It's just a little old thing and I'll be as good as new, in a few months." He really didn't believe that he'd be crippled up. He felt too strong.

One thing he knew for sure, he liked being home with his family, and he had decided that this was, definitely, the last bullet he was gonna take for the Arizona Territory. "I'm thinking that I just might turn in my star, Beth. What do you say to that, sweetheart?"

Beth was elated. "Oh, Vernon! I'd love it if you did something less dangerous. I always worry when you leave the house, never knowing what trouble you may face. Will we stay here, in Tucson, or are you thinking about a ranch closer to Mary?"

He laughed. He could always depend on Beth to go straight to the heart of the matter. No beating around the bush for her.

"I'm thinking I might try my hand at raising horses. Napoleon would be a good stud. I just need to find a few really prime mares, and we're on our way." He knew it was harder than that, but it sounded so exciting, he couldn't be bothered with the details.

"I spoke with Barclay this morning," Vernon said. "He said that all of the passengers on the stage, were in one piece and happy to have made it this far. Some of the money was securely deposited in the bank here, waiting for its owner. It seems that old Harry Doolittle sold his boarding house and made quite a killing. Part of that stage money was his. He's moving here, to Tucson, to live with his brother." He waited to see Beth's reaction.

She was pleasantly surprised. "Doo's coming here? Oh that's grand," she said, excitedly. "He was one of my best friends, back home. If he hadn't offered me that room, I would have been out on the street." Her eyes clouded over. "He's done a lot of things to help me, Vernon. I hope he isn't in trouble because of me. You haven't heard anything about, … you know … have you?"

Vernon didn't want to worry his wife, but he didn't like lying to her, either. He decided to take the middle road. "I heard they're still investigating. The senator will not give up. But you knew that, right?"

She nodded.

Reaching up to Beth, from his bed, he pulled her down and kissed her lips and the tip of her pretty nose. "I don't want you to worry. I've sworn to take care of you and little Frank, and I will. No one is going to come here and cause trouble. Believe that, darling." He kissed her a few more times. She tasted so damn good he could hardly stand it, and here he was, stuck in this stupid bed, with a bum leg. Life wasn't always fair.

"That's it! I see Tucson. 'Bout damn time, too!" The senator was tired, hot, and dirty. He was a man consumed by his need to see justice done. He wouldn't rest until he brought the person responsible for the death of his son to trial, and to her ultimate execution. "An eye for an eye," he said.

The two U.S. Marshals, accompanying him, were tired of listening to his tirades, every hour, for the last three weeks. Neither of them had the stomach to arrest a woman, but they were sworn to carry out the law and they would do their best. She was, after all, a cold-blooded killer, no matter her sex.

The trip had been an arduous one and had taken its toll. It had been bitterly cold, and the snow on the plains had been dangerous to cross. Deep and blowing, it slowed them down for days. Food had been dismal, at best. A few of the stage stops had been abandoned due to the problems with the Apaches. Texas was dry, and they had trouble with their team, losing two horses. The final straw came when Mexican bandits attacked the stagecoach. It was fortunate, for the passengers, that the marshals were loaded and ready, and proved to be such excellent marksmen. The hapless travelers took on no injuries, but were thrown around the coach with such force that Senator Price suffered a split lip and a chipped tooth.

"Who'd ever want to live out here in this God forsaken wilderness?" he grumbled. "Once I get back to Washington, I swear, I'll never leave it again," he declared, while watching the city of Tucson, coming closer into view.

Rapping on the roof of the coach, the senator tried to get the attention of the driver. "Stop at the Sheriff's Office. I got business with him."

Barclay was just coming out of the Ranger's Office when he saw the stage race by, not stopping at the Butterfield Office, but continuing on down the street, stopping directly in front of the jail. His curiosity peaked; he stood there and watched from a distance. For some reason, instinct maybe, he had a bad feeling about this.

Two marshals stepped down, followed by a very impressive older gentleman. He was obviously important and appeared to be excited and angry, all at the same time.

*What's going on*, Barclay wondered?

The men remained inside with the sheriff, for more than an hour. Barclay sat out in front, keeping an eye on the office. Eventually, they came out and headed down the sidewalk, their eyes trained on him. He knew, without a doubt, who they were.

"Shit," he muttered, low.

Barclay continued to sit easy, in his chair, with his muddy boots resting on the hitching rail. He tipped his hat back and stared up into the older man's face. "How do? Can I help you gentlemen?" He didn't smile.

The marshals stood silent while the older man thrust a crumpled Wanted Poster in his face. "I am Senator Allenton Price. What do you know about this?"

Barclay slowly perused the old poster. He'd seen it and others like it, many times over the last year. They were vague and filled with venom. Taking his time, he gritted his teeth, wondering what he could do to protect his friends.

"So?"

The senator became furious. "So? That's all you have to say, Ranger? I have reason to believe that this felon is living here, in Tucson, and you haven't done your best at bringing her in. What kind of a ranger are you? I can have your star."

Barclay smiled a slow grin. "You want my star?"

"What I want, you infuriating man, is for you to do your job. Now, tell me where Ryann Beaufort is hiding. I've been waiting a year to lay eyes on the whore that killed my son!"

"Whore!" Barclay shot to his feet and grabbed the senator by his dusty lapels. His face mottled with rage and his dark eyes flashed with anger. "You arrogant, bastard. You got no idea what yer sayin', or who yer sayin' it about. I don't know any Ryann Beaufort, but you will watch yer language durin' yer short stay here, in Tucson. Our women are not whores." He let go, giving the old man a quick shove.

One of the marshals stepped in and held the ranger's arms back. "Do not place your hands on the senator, Ranger." He was coldly polite.

Barclay nodded to the marshal in compliance, while noting the order was issued *after* he had said his piece.

The sheriff instructed the men to go on over to the Capital Arms, clean up and get something to eat. In the meantime, he'd talk to Ranger Barclay and see if they could come up with a person of interest.

The three tired men agreed on a meeting with the sheriff and the ranger, first thing in the morning. The woman would be found, taken into custody, and returned to Richmond for trial. Before departing, the senator warned Barclay. "Don't disappoint me, Ranger. *No one* is beyond my reach."

Barclay told the sheriff that he would think on it and be prepared for the senator's meeting, tomorrow. He told his friend to go back and rest up for the day ahead. Tonight, he had things do to.

Not wanting to look like he was overly concerned for his friends, Barclay paced back and forth inside the privacy of his office. He waited more than an hour before walking leisurely down the street, slowly making his way to Vernon's house. If he were seen, he'd just say he needed to keep Ranger Gunn informed of what was happening around town.

It was almost dark by the time he reached the Gunn's front porch. Barclay didn't want to be the bearer of bad news, but they needed to know of the most recent developments. They might want to leave town under the cover of darkness. He'd help them, if asked. He lightly rapped on the door, not wanting to disturb a sleeping child or a wounded ranger.

Beth answered. "Hello, Barclay. This is a happy surprise. Come on in and rest a spell. Vernon will be awake soon. Can I get you some coffee and a piece of pie?" She was genuinely glad to see him. It made the ranger feel all that much worse.

"Thanks, ma'am." Barclay removed his hat and entered the cozy home of his best friends.

"Uh oh," Beth moaned. "Since when did you start addressing me as, ma'am? That can't be good," she said, half teasing. "Seriously, Barclay. What's going on? Is Vernon in some kind of trouble? Surely you're not here to tell me he has to go out again. He's wounded. He can't sit a horse," she protested. She would simply insist they find someone else to bring in the bad guys.

Fidgeting with the brim of his hat, he didn't know just where to start. "Is Vernon awake, Beth? It's important that I speak with him tonight."

She knew that this was bad news, indeed. Her stomach tensed, preparing her for perhaps the worst news she would ever hear, short of losing Vernon or Frank. "He's dozing off and on, but I'm sure he'll force himself to hear what it is you have to say." She paused. "Barclay … does this news have anything to do with me?" she asked, timidly. Her eyes demanded the truth. She was strong and she could withstand knowing what she was up against.

"Yeah, Beth. I'm afraid it does."

She sat down. So, here it was. It had finally happened. Her tragic past had followed her to Tucson and had found her out, but how, she wondered? She knew she had made a few small mistakes, but how did they know Ryann Beaufort was Elizabeth Gunn? She shook her head in amazement. Richmond was so very far away and there were no pictures of her. She trusted her friends, Harry Doolittle and Libby. They wouldn't identify her—unless they were forced. She paled. Surely they hadn't been threatened by what she'd done. *Oh, God. What all was she responsible for?*

"Beth," Barclay whispered for the third time. "Do I need to go get the doc? You don't look too good. I knew I shouldn't have said nothin' … "

Beth looked up at his sorrowful face. She'd managed to hurt Barclay too, by dragging him into the middle of her troubles, if unwittingly. "No, I'm all right. I'm just a little overcome with the surprise of it. I thought I was safe. Actually, I should thank you. I've lived with this hanging over my head long enough, and it will be a relief to finally face it and have the truth come out. Go on in and see Vernon, but I beg you, don't make it sound as dire as it might be. He's gone through so much already, and I can't bear to see him worry so."

"Sure thing, Beth. But there are some things that will be impossible to hide from him. You'll understand, once you hear what I have to say."

He turned and walked down the short hall to the bedroom. Quietly turning the handle, he peered inside, to see a sleeping man, resting contentedly in his own bed, in his own happy home. "Damn. I really don't want to do this," Barclay growled.

Beth followed the ranger into the room. She closed the door behind her. From across the room, Beth spoke to Vernon. "Vernon, darling. Wake up, dear. Barclay is here and he must speak with you. It's important. Wake up, love."

Vernon stirred, and moaned at the reemergence of his pain. "Hey, pardner. What brings you here at this late hour? The town on fire?" He smiled, trying to make a joke.

Looking as serious as death, Barclay said, "I wish it were. What I got to tell you is worse than the town burnin' ... but that's an idea. Maybe if we set fire to everything, you can get away." He was being sarcastic, but his comment let Vernon know that the problem was most serious.

"Spill it. I'm tired, and I need my wife to come to bed and warm me up a little."

Beth blushed. "Vernon, mind your manners."

"Yes, angel. I stand reprimanded." He smiled at his wife, showing all his love for her, in the twinkle of his eyes. He had a good idea what Barclay was about to say and there wasn't much he could do to spare her that.

"Can I sit, Vernon?" the ranger asked. "This may take a while. We've got a lot to talk about."

Vernon pointed to a chair across the room. "Pull it over here and take your time. We've got all night long to face this thing, if need be."

Beth crawled up on the bed, alongside Vernon. She looked like a frightened doe, but Vernon knew her to be much stronger than she appeared. She grasped his hand with a strength that surprised him. He smiled reassuringly, at her. "Proceed, Ranger," he ordered.

"I've been aware fer some time, that you and Beth have a secret. I needed to decide fer myself, what I'd do if it ever became known publicly. Now, we're on the verge of it doin' just that.

"Today, a stage rode in with its horses all lathered up, havin' been driven hard, and it continued directly on to the sheriff, makin' no stop at the stage line office. Two marshals and a U.S. Senator were on board."

Beth gasped. He was here, in Tucson. This was much worse than she had feared.

Barclay noticed Beth's reaction. He continued, gently. "They wanted to talk to me. They told me how Miss Ryann Beaufort was suspected to be livin' here, in Tucson. They have a sketch of you, Beth. They said she has some connection to the Hotel Doolittle."

"Oh, my God." Beth looked to Vernon. "They've done something to Harry."

Returning her eyes to Barclay, she asked, "Have you talked to Horace about his brother? Does he know anything about him?" It was so like the Beth to be more concerned about the welfare of another, than for her own wellbeing.

"I haven't had the chance. I hightailed it over here as soon as I thought it was safe. You two, need to ride out. Grab what you can … I'll get the rest to you, later. I'm sure David can help you hide."

Vernon thought on it and then shook his head. They couldn't keep running. It was no way to live. "Nope. Don't think we'll be doing that. Beth's right. It's high time we faced this thing, head on. I've known since before I married Beth, that she was wanted for a crime that she admits having committed."

Barclay was stunned by the admission. "You mean … she really *did* murder the senator's son? Oh, hell. I didn't think she'd done it. This changes things, Vernon." He looked perplexed and doubtful as to what he should do.

Beth started to weep silently.

"Not as much as you might think, Barclay. You know my Beth. What would it take to make a good woman, like her, kill a man? Think on it. You can't believe the horrors he put her through, and I can guarantee, if you knew all the facts in the case, you'd help me go and find him—if he were alive—and kill him, everyway possible."

"He was a monster, Barclay," Beth whispered.

"Yeah, maybe he was, but that don't give you the right to cut this throat! God, Beth. Why didn't you go to the authorities? They'd lock him up."

She laughed and rolled her eyes at his comment. "Ha! Don't be naïve, Ranger. That's not the way it works with the rich and powerful. He was a well-respected Army Lieutenant, admired by his commanding officers, as well as the rank and file. He was a war hero, wounded at Gettysburg. His father has been a good and decent senator. I, on the other hand, was orphaned, poor, and pretty. That is *not* an advantage. It makes you vulnerable to unsolicited attention.

"Some offers were innocent, enough. Others were lewd and disgusting. Turn one man down and another was there to take his place. A lot of egos were damaged, resulting in a lot of unfounded rumors and accusations pertaining to my character. If it hadn't been for my landlord, Harry Doolittle, and my best friend, Libby McGuire, I would never have survived the last couple of years."

Beth's hands flew to her cheeks, as a new concern suddenly occurred to her. "Oh, my lord, have the authorities preyed on Libby, as well as Doo?"

"I haven't heard her name mentioned." Barclay looked chastised. "I'm sorry, Beth … Vernon. I didn't know the facts, and yer right, pardner. I'd help you chase down the good-for-nothin' bastard. But we've got a real problem. If the evidence sounds bad to me—so incriminatin', to someone who knows and loves Beth—how's it gonna sound to a jury of strangers? Are you certain you don't want to leave town? You could hide anywhere."

"We didn't manage to hide here, too well." Vernon shook his head. "No, we'll make a stand, here. That all right with you, sweetheart?" He looked at his beautiful wife, knowing her life was in his hands, and rested with his decision. He prayed he was making the right one.

Beth forced a smile. "Yes, darling. This is our home and our friends are here. They won't abandon us. But, Vernon?"

"Yes?"

"I want Mary with me. I know it's silly, but I feel I'll need her if things go wrong."

He nodded. "Barclay, I'd appreciate you riding out to the Williams' ranch, in the next day or so, and get the message to Mary, that Beth would like to see her."

"Sure thing, Vernon. That's the least I can do."

"And Barclay … I don't want you to tell anyone that you had even a hint that Beth, and this Ryann Beaufort, were one and the same. You'll lose your badge, and I don't want that to happen. You're one of the good ones. Got that?"

Barclay snorted. "Sure thing, pardner. You'll lose yer's fer sure, you know that."

"I knew that when I made my decision to love and keep this amazing woman safe. I'm not sorry about that. Besides, with this gimpy leg, I may have to give up my badge, in any case. Just take care of yourself, Barclay I appreciate what you've already done for us. We'll take it from here.

"When are you meeting this illustrious group of gentlemen?"

"First thing in the mornin'. You gonna be there?" Barclay asked.

"No. I need more time to heal. See if you can delay them some. They don't know Beth is the woman they're looking for, do they? And you don't know anything either, right?"

"That's about the size of it, I reckon. I guess it could take four or five days, at least, to follow the nonexistent leads."

Vernon nodded. "That's good. Give us as much time as possible before leading that party to our door. Beth and I need to talk."

Barclay stood and found he was at a loss for words. How do you tell your best friend goodbye? How do you stand by and see his lovely family ripped apart and not do anything to try to stop it? He made a decision. Like hell, he'd lead these men directly to what they were searching for. They'd better be prepared to traipse around the rocks and arroyos of Arizona. And if they were lucky, maybe he could introduce them to Cochise—real close up. The thought of that, made him smile.

"See you tomorrow, Vernon, and don't worry 'bout a thing. It ain't over yet." He nodded and put on his Stetson. "See you at yer Christmas dinner, Beth." He winked, and left the house.

The couple continued to sit, huddled together on the bed, each thinking of what was to come. Vernon could feel his wife tremble in his arms. He wished he could calm her fears.

Frank started to fuss, forcing Beth to get up. Turning to look back at Vernon, she sighed and said, "Well, life's back to normal. Frank gives me hope." She smiled with tears in her eyes, and left to comfort her son.

# CHAPTER NINETEEN

"Damn it, Barclay! You're not taking this seriously," the senator yelled. "Think! What tall, blonde woman arrived here, in the last year? I don't care what name she gave. It's bound to be a phony. There can't have been that many." He was disgusted with the Tucson law enforcement's lack of urgency in this matter. He paced angrily, around the small office.

"Where's the other ranger … Gunn, isn't it?" The senator demanded to know.

"He was shot safeguardin' a stagecoach filled with passengers and money. He saved my life, sir." Barclay's eyes grew dark and cold, throwing daggers back at the old man's watery blue ones.

Nobody said anything for quite a spell, until Barclay broke the silence. "Actually, now that you mention it, I do recall a man, on his way to California. He came through here with a blonde woman on his arm. They were on their way to gettin' hitched. Coulda been her, I reckon." He scratched his chin as if in deep thought. "Or there was that other blonde woman—don't recall her name—got took by some renegades. They found her yeller scalp hangin' on the side of one of them ponies, rounded up at a stage attack. 'Bout six months ago, it was. This is gonna take a considerable amount of time, sir."

"I don't believe it," the old man lamented. "We've come all this way, and I'm certain she's here. I can feel it. She didn't run off and get married and she didn't get herself scalped. She's here, probably living the good life."

Deciding to take another tack with the impudent ranger, Senator Price said, "Look, son. You can't possible know how it can eat at a man, knowing the person, responsible for the death of his only child, is running around free, enjoying life. My son is buried in the ground. His body was so grotesquely deformed, by the time we found him, we had to have a private service. He was well liked and his friends were denied saying their last goodbyes." The old man's eyes filled with tears. "I hope you never know those feelings, but it can kill a man's soul. I know." He took out a handkerchief and blew his nose.

Barclay knew the old man's feelings were sincere. Senator Price felt about his son, exactly the way he described. There was no doubt that he loved the lieutenant very much, even if he was a sick bastard.

"It might be helpful, sir, if you tell me *why* you think your son was murdered. You say he was well liked, even admired. Did he have a wife or a jealous fiancé?"

"Uh, no, no. Mark was too busy with his career. He knew it wouldn't be fair to get married." The senator turned away from Barclay, suddenly refusing to make eye contact.

That surprised the ranger. The older gentleman hadn't turned away from anybody since he stormed into town. The old man had always been direct, even to the point of appearing defiant. He was hiding something important, and Barclay kept poking.

"Fair? Lots of women get hitched to important military officers, sir. It's the man they marry, not the career. Wouldn't you agree?"

"Yes. Under normal circumstances, that would be the case, but you see …"

He turned back around to address the ranger. "Mark was wounded in Gettysburg. Everyone knows about the head wound. It was bad, real bad. I thought I was going to lose him, for a while, but the other wound was near his manhood. It did no permanent damage, but he couldn't believe that it had not. He was unable to perform." The senator struggled with his words. "That is how I know this woman was a whore. He only visited *those* kinds of women, you see. That was his preferred way to receive female pleasure. Don't tell anyone. I would like to guard his dignity."

"Was he ever violent with women?"

No, of course not. Only when the headaches got so bad he couldn't sit a horse, would he take his medicine. The medicine caused him to be short tempered and his personality would change a bit, but he was still a damn fine officer. You can ask any of the men who served under him."

"I'm sure he was, sir." Barclay was getting the old man to reveal much about his beloved son. "What kind of medicine did your son take?"

"He took laudanum. It eased the pain, making it possible for him to continue on with his work. Why are you asking all these question about Mark? You should be asking about that whor … woman."

The ranger smiled. The senator had learned a lesson, in just the short time he'd been here. "I only want to know him, sir. To get a feel fer the kind of person that would take advantage of him. Was he robbed?"

"No. It was crime of passion, pure and simple. It's obvious that she wanted him to love her, and when he refused, I imagine she went insane and cut his throat. She stabbed him in the back, as well. She's violent and a danger to the community. If we don't hang her, then I'll see to it that she's kept in the Richmond Hospital for the Insane. That's where she belongs."

Barclay had to make an effort to relax his fists. This man was talking about one of the nicest and loveliest women he'd ever known. Beth didn't have a violent bone in her entire body. This town would not allow this absurdity to destroy her life.

"All right, sir. I reckon we'll ride out tomorrow and check a few small towns less than a days ride from here. I cain't imagine a woman, that distinctive, could come to town and go unnoticed. She must have moved on. We'll ride south, toward Tombstone. If we don't find her there, we'll ride north toward Winslow. She cain't have gone far, 'less she went to California. I won't be able to help you none, there."

The senator was not happy, but after conferring with the two marshals, he'd brought with him, they all agreed to follow the ranger's advice. They could always come back here and tear the town apart, if needed.

After their little talk, Barclay rode out to David and Mary's ranch. It was sure a pretty place. He was a little envious of them. Stepping down off his horse, Barclay walked slowly up to the front porch. It seemed he was always the bearer of bad news, nowadays.

From inside, the ranger could hear a piano being played in the parlor, and the voice of a little girl, singing like an angel. Yep, he was definitely envious of David Williams. He lightly rapped on the door. Two dogs came running out from under the porch and announced his arrival. "Some watch dogs you are," he chuckled. "You're a tad late."

Mary came to the door. "Well, how do, Ranger Barclay. What brings you to our ranch? Need a good horse?"

Barclay thought for a moment. "As a matter of fact, I could … no, what am I thinkin'?" He silently reprimanded at himself. "I need to speak to you and yer husband, ma'am."

"Oh, no. Has something happened to my brother?"

"No, ma'am, not exactly. But he does need yer help. Can you go find David?"

The tall, good-looking man walked up and filled the open door with his body. "You've found me, Barclay. Come in and take the load off, and tell me what's got you so riled."

The ranger proceeded to tell the Williams' almost everything he knew, leaving out the private details Beth had spoken of. He figured she could tell them, if she wanted them to know.

"Beth needs to speak with Mary. I think she wants to make plans, in the event she's arrested and taken back to Virginia."

"Is it that bad, Barclay? Could she really be arrested and taken away?" Mary asked, as she reached for David's hand.

"I'm gonna be honest with both of you. It's worse than that. If the senator finds out her true identity, she could hang. Yer brother has, more than likely, already lost his badge. It's about as bad as it gets."

David looked at his wife, knowing what they had to do. "Darlin', we'll leave first thing in the mornin'. Get Mrs. Runyon to watch the children, if she's willin'. Have her make up a shoppin' list, a really big one, one that will take us a few days to fill. I'll have John do the same. We'll stay with yer brother's family, while we pick up the 'needed' supplies. It's important everything looks natural.

"Thanks, Barclay, fer comin' all this way. we owe ya."

"No, you don't owe me nothin'." Barclay was quick to explain. "Ranger Gunn took a bullet fer me recently, and it ain't been the first time he's covered my ass. He's the best Arizona Ranger we got, and definitely the best friend a man could have. I owe him. Help him … if you can."

It was good to see Mary and David again, even if the circumstances of their visit were not ideal. For hours, Vernon confided in David. The women played with Frank and tried not to become morose. They both knew what could happen, but chose not to dwell on the dark side. Frank was delightful and Mary was happily surprised when Beth secretly told her she was going to have another baby.

"Please don't say anything to Vernon. He doesn't know and it would only worry him more," Beth pleaded. A faraway look appeared in her eyes. "I hope to have a little girl that looks just like her papa." Her lips curled in a small smile as she glanced down at her slightly rounded tummy.

"Speaking of little girls," Mary interjected, "Sara is chomping at the bit for her Auntie Beth to come out for a few months and give her those voice lessons she promised. She adores you so much, I'm almost jealous. But I intend to get my revenge on you, when you have a little girl. I'll be her favorite Auntie Mary, and I intend to spoil her, immensely."

Beth grew serious. "I have a favorite to ask of you, Mary. Vernon doesn't know what I'm going to say, and I don't want you to tell him, until it can no longer be avoided. If the marshals take me away, I need to know that someone will raise my son. Frank means the world to me, and I can survive anything if I know he's doing well and that he's loved. Vernon may fight you over this, but a man alone can't raise a child properly. And I may have this baby for him to raise, as well. I would rest easier, knowing you will take him."

"Oh, darling. You don't need to ask. David and I will always, *always*, be in Frank's life. Our children adore him and I hope to have another son, someday, and I want them to be best friends, as well as cousins. You rest easy. It will all work out fine. Just don't give up, Beth. If you have the strength and the faith to see it through, it'll all be resolved. I can't tell you of the tremendous fears I had, back in Missouri, and of all the times I wanted to give up. It was David's strength that saw me through. I was horrible to him once, but he never gave up on us. Vernon won't give up on you, either. Neither will David or I. This is just a hiccup in life. You'll see.

"So let's go shopping. David says I must buy everything I think we can possibly use. We need to justify—to anyone noticing our arrival—why it takes us two days to get supplies, and why we're staying away from our ranch so long, at this time of year. Personally, I'd rather think it's David's early Christmas gift to me." She smiled from ear to ear, clearly enjoying the assignment.

David and Vernon finally had their plan in place. They hoped it would not be necessary, for it would be life altering for Vernon and Beth, but David agreed with his brother-in-law that letting Beth be arrested and taken back to Richmond to stand trial, for the murder of a man who should have died on the battlefield, was unacceptable.

"Well, brother," David said, "the wife and I need to start back in the mornin'. We'll have one of the hands get the news everyday. By sendin' in a different man, from time to time, it won't draw undue attention. I'll get things prepared on my end. Don't lose hope, Vernon. I cain't see this thing playin'out in Richmond."

He slapped his brother-in-law on the back, and walked to the door, before stopping to say, "I bought me two exceptional mares, a few weeks back. The problem is, Dollar's just plain tuckered out, and I ain't got the space for no more foals. I was a thinkin' you might want to take 'em off my hands, in a month or two, and give that Napoleon of yers the time of his life. How about it?" His blue eyes twinkled as he gave Vernon a lopsided grin and walked through the door, not pausing for an answer.

The senator and Ranger Barclay returned from their 'little goose chase'—as Senator Price called it—the following day. Barclay had to admit, the man was not a fool.

"I'm looking around Tucson, before we go out again, chasing after some yellow-haired squaw you've heard of, living somewhere up on some mountain, far, far from here. I don't trust you, Ranger. You're hiding something." With that said, the old man turned in a huff and left Barclay wondering what to do next.

The marshals circulated the sketch of Ryann all about town. There were several people that thought she looked familiar, but no one recognized the name. Everyone was sympathetic to the senator, but they just didn't know this woman.

Beth and Vernon kept a low profile. They didn't want to draw attention to themselves and cause people to talk, so it wasn't until the evening of the Christmas pageant, they came out of their seclusion … and it was glorious. The children had done such a great job in the construction of the sets and with the wardrobes. There was a curly headed little imp in the manger; a much wiser choice, Beth thought, than her squirming little bundle of energy. Frank was laughing and pointing at all the decorations and the big, furry animals that had been loaned out for the evening.

"Ca! Ca!" he said.

"Oh, Vernon, he's pointing to the cows and said ca!" He's talking all the time now. Isn't he just the smartest baby you've ever known?" Stars twinkled in her eyes. It had been a long while since Vernon had seen his wife so happy and enjoying herself so freely.

At last, the music portion of the program arrived, and little Becky was the featured angel. As the first chords began to play, she opened her mouth and out drifted the most glorious sound. It was sure to make the angels in heaven weep with envy. Her voice rose higher and higher into the night sky, and not a sound came from those listening. They were all held in awe of this lovely child. As the song came to its conclusion, you could hear a pin drop in the silent church. No one moved. Becky's happy smile quickly disappeared, and was replaced with a look of shear terror. *Had she sung off key? Had she forgotten the words Why didn't they like her?*

Beth recognized it immediately. While the audience was held spellbound by the sheer beauty of what they had witnessed, little Becky was under the impression that she had not done well, and that people didn't like her singing.

Just as the little girl's bottom lip started to quiver, Beth jumped to her feet and started to cheer and applaud loudly, bringing the crowd out of their reverie.

All at once, the entire congregation was on its feet, whistling and cheering for the brave little girl. Becky regained her smile and the evening was saved … except for one minor detail.

Beth had given herself away. Sitting in the shadows, on the

other side of the room, an older and very well dressed gentleman had a perfectly unobstructed view of the lovely, tall, blonde woman, cheering for the little girl. He couldn't take his eyes off her, and his blood began to boil. He could feel it pulsing through his veins. His vision was filled with spots and darkening with fury. The pounding in his head was excruciating. Senator Price took out a crumpled sketch from his vest pocket and compared it. There was no doubt in his mind. *She* was Ryann. She could be no one else.

Leaning over, he whispered to the two U.S. Marshals. They in turn, started asking questions of those in the crowd. Everyone knew Beth Gunn, the ranger's wife. The new schoolmarm had arrived last November to teach the children, but she didn't stay too long, as she married the ranger. Mrs. Gunn was soon with child, but she was well liked and respected, just the same.

"November? It's got to be her. I've got to talk to her. Arrange it," the senator ordered. He could feel his long awaited, satisfaction coming to fulfillment. At last, he would get revenge for his son. Odd though. She didn't look like a whore or a murderess. That pretty face had fooled his son. Well, it wouldn't fool him, he vowed.

The evening was a total success. Everyone said it was the best Christmas Pageant, ever. Calliope was beside herself with pride for little Becky. Becky's ma was so happy, she couldn't stop the tears. The baby Jesus fell asleep in the manger, with his mother insisting that that was not his usual behavior. He was normally a little terror, she professed. Beth had to laugh. Vernon's thigh was aching some, but he was glad to be out of the house and had thoroughly enjoyed seeing all their friends.

As expected, Beth rose early and started cooking at dawn. She'd never had so much to do, in so little time, and she was enjoying every moment. Vernon's main job was to watch and care for Frank.

Her menu was a little ambitious, but she would persevere. She planned a succulent roast beef with gravy, mashed potatoes, and all the trimmings. She had two cakes and three pies to bake, as well as fresh light bread. She had a candy recipe, from her mother and she wanted to do a fruit compote. Hopefully she had everything she needed and the time to get it done. There was still some minor decorating she wanted to finish. Everything had to look and taste perfect. This was a party.

The day was half gone when Barclay came visiting—at least Beth thought he was there for a visit. Without any discussion, he went in to talk to Vernon privately, and left ten minutes later.

"Darling, what did Barclay want? He's not going to miss my dinner party, is he? What will I tell Miss Watkins?" Beth frowned with concern.

Vernon looked distracted, as if he didn't know just what to say to her.

"What's wrong? I can tell you're having trouble finding the right words. You might as well just say it," she insisted.

"Things are happening, honey, and I'm thinking we need to get out of town. You're not safe, here."

Beth looked bewildered. "What are you saying, Vernon? What's happened?"

"Barclay came to warn us. Senator Price has forced himself onto our guest list for tonight's dinner party. It seems he noticed you at the pageant and he's convinced you fit Ryann's description. He's been asking around town and has discovered the date of your arrival. He figures the timeline fits with his son's murder."

Beth had to sit down. She couldn't catch her breath and she was trembling all over. This was bound to happen, but it didn't make it any easier to accept. *What was it Mary had said? Don't give up. Have the strength to see it through*, she repeated to herself.

Vernon reached for Beth's cold hands and lifted them to his lips. He first kissed her palms and then, gently, turning them over, he kissed her knuckles, continuing on up to her delicate wrists. He smiled at her, tenderly.

"Angel, don't fret. Trust in me. I'll protect you and Frank. You're my family, my life, and I'm not about to allow any harm to come to any of us. David and I have made plans. If necessary, we'll put them into action. You, my angel, are not to worry." He kissed her lips.

"Continue with your dinner. It already smells like a slice of heaven and my stomach is grumblin', just at the thought of it. We have good friends that are anxious to come and spend the evening with us. Who cares if one more person shows up? I'll draw him up a chair and fix him a heaping plate. By God, we'll not allow him to upset this party."

The rest of the day was difficult for Beth. She continued on with her plans, but much of the joy had disappeared. No matter how hard she tried, she couldn't dismiss the thought of the lieutenant's father being here, seated at her table. What would she say to him? How would he look at her? It had turned into a nightmare and she couldn't wait for the evening to be over.

Vernon insisted she wear her new dress. It was her Christmas present from him, and he wanted to see her in it. For so long, she'd worn black widow's weeds, and then she was forced to wear larger dresses to conceal her pregnancy. He asked her to wear her glorious, blonde hair down in curls, held back by her mother's pearl comb. Her silky tresses glowed like fields of yellow daisies, glistening in the summer sunshine, and made Vernon feel happy just to gaze upon it.

Beth agreed with her husband. She did look pretty in her lovely white dress with the little blue flowers embroidered, here and there, over the bodice and skirt. A blue sash hugged her tiny waist, bringing out the brilliant color of her eyes. Fine lace trimmed the neckline and cuffs. It was the most elegant dress she'd ever owned, and she loved the fact that Vernon had chosen it for her. She would treasure it, always.

Little Frank had been changed twice and may require a change of clothes for the third time, if he didn't stay out of things. Still, he was adorable. His laugh was infectious and his golden head was covered in a riot of curls. They'd never gotten around to his first haircut. His large round eyes were more lavender than blue, a most unusual color, and stood out from his dark lashes. Beth knew that by the time her son reached manhood, he would be most handsome. As for now, he was her precious baby boy and she was thankful for every day she was able to spend with him.

Finally, all the preparations were complete and awaited the arrival of their guests. Beth's stomach was roiling and she knew she wouldn't be able to eat a bite. She hoped she wouldn't suddenly burst into tears at the table. After having looked about the room for the third time, she heard happy voices approaching the front door. With a last beseeching look at Vernon, she stiffened her spine, forced her head up and plastered a brilliant smile across her face.

"Let's do it," she said.

Vernon nodded. He was extremely proud of his brave and beautiful wife, at that singular moment. It was all he could do to refrain from grabbing her and carrying her off to the bedroom. He laughed to himself. That would surely startle the guests.

Mr. and Mrs. Jones were first through the door, followed closely by Miss Watkins. They were all excited and most happy to be invited to dinner. Miss Watkins brought an enormous tray of Christmas cookies for the "boys", she had said, grinning at Vernon. Everyone knew the ranger had a huge sweet tooth and was partial to her cookies.

Mrs. Jones brought a spectacular centerpiece for the table. "I was hoping you'd have room for this," she said. "I thought it was so beautiful that it needed to be shared amongst friends." She grinned broadly, showing the lovely dimples in her plump cheeks. Beth noticed how pretty the woman was. She must have been a beauty, when she was a young girl.

"Oh thank you, so much. I was so busy with the cooking that I didn't have the time to create a proper centerpiece. I'd planned to just put the roast in the center of the table and hoped no one would notice," Beth giggled. "Now, everything will be perfect," she exclaimed, noticing that Mrs. Jones was beaming with pride.

Miss Watkins asked about Frank. "Where is the prettiest boy in Tucson?"

"Miss Watkins! I'm surprised at you," Beth said in a joking fashion. "Don't you let him hear you say he's pretty. My goodness! He'll find the muddiest puddle he can, and take a good long roll in it, just to prove you wrong. He's a rough and tumble sort of cowpoke, don't you know? And he's just plain tuckered out, I'm afraid." Beth smiled. "He was changed four times before you all arrived and that's tiresome, I guess. I suspect he'll be up soon."

There was another knock at the door and Vernon let Horace Doolittle in, accompanied by his friend, Robin. The old man had never looked so happy. Dressed in an obviously new suit and with a haircut, he was almost handsome. The lady on his arm was dressed demurely and was practically unrecognizable.

Robin wore a dark emerald green dress with no adornments. Her hair was brushed to a high sheen and was coiled upon her head, and with no feathers added. Her face was scrubbed clean and she looked youthful and quite happy. The only decoration she was wearing, was her ecstatic smile. She needed nothing else. Robin, of the Fancy Garter, was a very pretty young woman. Who knew?

The schoolteacher had to send her regrets, as she was told she *must* attend a Christmas Eve dinner with the mayor—for the good of her job. Beth made a mental note to have a talk with her and make sure she wasn't being forced to keep company with the disagreeable man.

Happy chatter soon filled the small house, as everyone seemed to talk at once. The joy of Christmas was felt all around. It was the holidays and good friends had gathered about to celebrate. No one heard, nor did they take notice of the door opening and two men quietly walking in.

Vernon was the first to acknowledge their presence. "Barclay! Come on in, pal. Come in. Make yourself at home." Then he turned his eyes on the senator. It took every bit of will power he had, not to toss the bastard out onto the porch. Gritting his teeth, he addressed the gentleman.

He offered his hand and said, "We don't stand on ceremony in this house, sir. Make yourself at home. All are welcome here." Then, looking around the room, he signaled to Beth to come over and meet the man. No use in trying to ignore him.

"This is my wife, sir, Elizabeth Gunn. *Friends* address her as Beth." His eyes never left the senator's humorless face.

Beth steeled herself and then presented her hand to the handsome older gentleman. It only trembled, slightly. "Sir. Come in and meet our friends."

She led him into the center of the room and addressed her guests. "I would like your attention, please. It is my honor to present to you a most distinguished gentleman. This is Senator Allenton Price, from Virginia. He'll be having dinner with us." Then, still forcing her smile, she turned and fled from the room. Her strength finally running out.

The senator didn't miss the fact that she knew all about him. She'd obviously been informed of his arrival, beforehand, and was prepared. The woman knew his full name and the state he represented. She was cool, he had to admit, and only at the end did her guilt force her to run away and hide from him.

For the remainder of the evening, Senator Price chose to sit back and observe. He watched Ryann's husband and friends interact with her, and with each other. They seemed like a good sort of folks. Given different circumstances, he would enjoy their company, and if he were honest with himself, he would find Mrs. Gunn to be a most likeable young woman. She was undoubtedly beautiful, beyond compare, in fact. Of course, he was aware of that already, but she seemed to be of good breeding and highly intelligent, as well. He would have approved of her being his daughter-in-law—had things turned out differently—and he suddenly realized he was running the risk of softening toward her.

Now that everyone was present, and most of the conversation had run its course, it was time to sit down around the sumptuous table and enjoy the feast Beth had prepared for her friends. It was delicious and surpassed everyone's expectations.

Barclay sat back and forced himself to turn down his third helping of pie. "Beth, if I'd known you could cook like this, I'd have hitched up with you instead of lettin' old Vernon here, win first prize. I always did say, the way to a man's heart is directly through his stomach, and I got the stomach to prove it." He laughed.

Beth smiled. "Thank you, Barclay. That's mighty nice to know. Maybe knowing you appreciate my cooking, will keep my husband in line."

They all laughed.

"You know, Miss Watkins is the baker over at the Hotel Doolittle."

Barclay's eyebrows shot up. "Really? You mean, all them desserts I've been puttin' away, fer the last two years, you've been a bakin', Miss Watkins?"

The shy woman blushed, and looked down toward her lap. She nodded and then whispered, "Yes, Ranger. I make the Brown Betty just for you, knowing it's your favorite."

"Whoopee!" Barclay shouted. "Will you marry me, Miss Watkins?"

Her head shot up, with eyes as round as dinner plates, and she looked scared and shocked, all at the same time. Not knowing what to say, Beth came to her rescue.

"Don't pay this crazy coyote no mind, sweetie. He's in love with your Brown Betty. But he's harmless enough," she teased.

Barclay stopped laughing. He looked at Miss Watkins with new respect, and suddenly, he knew his life had changed forever.

"Miss, may I escort you home after the party? I was joshin' 'bout them desserts. But I'm not joshin' 'bout wantin' to see more o' you, if you'd allow."

The room fell silent. Barclay had shocked them all. Everyone believed him to be a confirmed bachelor, but perhaps they were wrong, for he certainly looked sincere.

Once again, the shy woman nodded and smiled up at the pleasant ranger. "I'd be honored, Mr. Barclay."

Well … enough of these pleasantries, the old senator thought. This cozy, feel-good atmosphere was setting him up. His son still laid buried in the cold ground, unable to enjoy holidays, such as this, and all because of that woman, who appeared to have everything his son was denied. He'd make his excuses soon, and depart this *happy home*. He was envious of what he'd witnessed here, and it was making him angrier by the minute.

While Mrs. Jones helped clear the table, she suggested that Beth play the piano, for she was known to be especially gifted. They could all gather around and sing carols. Applause from everyone, encouraged Beth to play.

It was splendid fun. The men were loud and boisterous, having the time of their lives, being silly, in only the way men can be. The ladies tried to sound more celestial, harmonizing and blending, perfectly. It didn't matter one whit, that they were completely drowned out by the bellowing of the overly enthusiastic men. But as loud as they were, even they couldn't hide the deafening wails of a very unhappy baby boy.

"Oh, no," Beth groaned. "We've finally managed to wake the baby. Give me a moment. I need to attend to him, and I'd like for you all to see him before you leave. Frank so enjoys people making a fuss over him." Quickly, she ran out of the room.

*A baby? What in the hell?* Now the senator was really angry. He stomped over to Vernon and demanded his coat. He'd seen enough. Out of respect for Christmas, he'd wait until the day after, before demanding Mrs. Ryann Elizabeth Gunn be arrested for the cold-blooded murder of his son.

He'd almost made it out the door, when the gurgling laughter caught his attention. Against his own good judgment, he turned to look at the child. Expecting a small newborn, he was surprised to see a little boy of seven or eight months old. Then he noticed the curls, the dimples, and the magnificent lavender eyes, framed by dark lashes. His heart began to beat irregularly in his chest. Weakness overcame him and he felt quite ill. All the color drained from his face.

Vernon saw the sudden change overtake the old man. He thought that he was perhaps having a heart attack. Quickly, he ran to his aid, guiding him to a chair. "Hurry! Get some water for the senator," he shouted. "I believe he's unwell!"

Everyone gathered around to see if there was something they could do. The senator simply sat there, speechless, staring at Frank. The baby smiled at him and held out his chubby little arms, wanting to be taken.

Beth pulled Frank back, not wanting this man to touch her son. "No!" Her voice was too sharp and brittle, and the sound of her reprimand, frightened the baby. His little face screwed up and his bottom lip began to tremble, as a huge tear rolled down his fat cheek.

In a hoarse voice so unlike his own, the older man asked, "Please?" He put out his hands to receive the boy.

Beth had a look of horror on her face, that was not missed by her friends.

"What's going on here?" Mrs. Jones demanded to know. "Just who are you, and what are you *really* doing here, Senator?" she asked with her hands fisted on her broad hips.

He didn't know what to say. Beth couldn't respond. Finally Barclay explained what he could. "The senator's been lookin' fer Beth fer quite some time. They've never met, but they knew someone back in Richmond. This is a very private matter and a difficult one to sort out. I'm certain, bein' very good friends, she'll tell us all about it, later, when it's been resolved. We should probably all depart, now. Miss Watkins, may I still escort you home?"

Wishing each other a Merry Christmas, and thanking Beth for a wonderful feast, her friends all said their goodbyes and left quietly. Something was going on that would adversely impact their friend, and each one vowed to himself, that whatever it was, they would help her. This was Arizona and people stuck together.

The senator sat motionless with his arms out, still waiting for Beth to hand him the child. No one said anything.

With small, hesitant steps, Beth relented and placed her precious son in the old man's arms. He looked down at the child with a sense of wonder and amazement. Bringing the child to his chest, he held on tightly, as if his very life depended upon his hold. The man began to sob.

Miraculously, Frank didn't squirm or fidget, but he was still and comfortable, trusting in this man. He placed his chubby fingers against the man's lips, forcing a slight smile. Frank then opened his mouth showing off his four new teeth, and cooed with satisfaction. It was plain for all to see. He liked this man

The senator, still weeping, rocked the child back and forth in tender arms. He closed his eyes and breathed in the sweet baby scent. After ten minutes or so, Senator Price looked up to the mother and asked, "My grandchild?"

"Yes," she replied quickly.

Before long, Frank had once again, fallen fast asleep. However, this time, he was sleeping in his grandfather's arms.

The time had come for them to talk.

"This boy resembles my late wife, Renee. It was the eyes that gave away his true identity. She, too, was blonde, with curls cascading down her back." He looked at Beth's own beautiful golden hair. "We always hoped to have a daughter resembling her mother, but it was not God's will. Instead, we had a fine son, who took after my side of the family. He was a handsome lad and his mother and I loved him every bit as much as you love your son."

Vernon could no longer keep silent. "Your son was a demon. If you knew what he put my wife through, before he died, you'd perhaps feel differently about him."

Senator Price remained calm. "You don't know anything about Mark. He was good and kind, once. Nothing that my son could have done, would change the way I feel about him. If he was cruel to your wife, then she should have left him, but she did not need to take his life. For that, I will seek justice."

"It was much worse than simply being cruel, sir. He tortured her, threatened to kill her and her friends. He was quite insane! You said he was kind, *once*. You were aware of his dark nature, weren't you?" Vernon said, accusingly.

The senator stopped his rocking and looked directly at Beth. "He was wounded in battle, and it caused him great pain, but that doesn't change the facts of the case. It may be that you exaggerated your claims of his mistreatment of you, yes my dear?"

Beth wanted to be truthful, but for some reason, she said what the old man wanted to hear. "Maybe, just a little."

"Aha! You see? She admits it. She killed him for some other reason. Maybe she's the one that's insane. No matter. The judge will make his decision and it will be final."

Beth was crying, nearing hysteria. "You're evil! You only want revenge. You don't care about justice or doing the right thing. I hate you!" She ran out of the room and slammed the door to her bedroom.

Vernon walked over and retrieved the sleeping child. "You're free to go, sir."

The man stood, but before taking his leave, he had one more thing to say.

"I intend to take that child. I will not allow him to be raised by an unstable woman and a lying stepfather, when his own grandfather is willing to take on the responsibility … And don't even think about leaving town. From this moment on, you and your family will *never* be out of my sight."

Vernon stood still, asking himself, what on earth did they do now?

# CHAPTER TWENTY

Beth tossed and turned for the rest of the night. She cried and whimpered like a wounded animal in her sleep, making it necessary for Vernon to awaken her from her night terrors, more than once. He kept thinking he'd like to have the old man's throat between his hands, squeezing the very life out of him. Finally, dawn peeked in through the curtains and softly lit the pretty little room.

Vernon watched his wife sleep and it broke his heart. He'd promised her that he would keep her safe. He vowed that the past would not be allowed to haunt her present, or take away her future. Now, he was at a loss as what to do. Little Frank was stirring in his cradle. It was a miracle that something so enchanting could come from such a horrific and hellish beginning. Frank was the light he saw shining in his wife's eyes and he'd be damned if he would see that light extinguished. Whatever it took, Vernon's resolve was firm.

He silently crept out of bed. It was Christmas Eve morning. He noticed the baby's eyes were wide open and watching his father. Carefully, Vernon picked up the baby and they vacated the room, leaving mama sleeping, and hopefully, dreaming sweet dreams.

Was that bacon she smelled? Beth sat up, confused. Who'd be cooking breakfast in her kitchen, and where was Frank? She grabbed her wrapper and flew out of the bedroom, in a mild panic. Sitting in his favorite high chair, sat Frank, laughing and trying to feed Smudge his oatmeal. It had never been the baby's favorite food. When he saw his mama, Frank squealed with delight. "Mama," he said, with his little arms reaching for her and his fingers wiggling, wanting to be picked up. "Up."

"Did you hear that, Vernon? He wants, up."

Vernon laughed. "So he's been saying for the last half hour. How do you manage to cook so well, on a stove so old and dilapidated? You should have told me how bad it was. I'll get you a new one from one of those catalogues. You'll have it in six months," he laughed. "Good morning, darling."

With her arms full of Frank, Beth leaned over and kissed her husband, good morning. "Thank you, dear. I love you."

It was a quiet day. Most folks preferred to stay home and prepare quietly for the holiday, with their families. Tonight, most of the townsfolk would walk to the church for Christmas Eve service. They'd sing carols and welcome the birth of the Christ Child, together. The Gunn family didn't speak of the events of the night before, nor did they mention the name of the senator. Today would be spent thinking only good thoughts and dreaming of their future, together. After all, Beth had a secret to tell her husband, tomorrow. She hoped he would be as pleased as she was, hearing the happy news.

The rest of the day was blessedly, uneventful. Dinner was a quiet affair, and while Beth cleaned up, Vernon sat on the floor, playing with his son. It would soon be time to leave for church.

While Beth dressed for the Christmas service, she heard a knock at the door. Who it could be this late in the evening? As she listened at the door, she heard several voices … one was definitely female.

She opened the door and looked out, finding Doolittle, accompanied by a young, redheaded couple, standing on her porch. They looked nice enough. Perhaps they were friends or relatives of his. As they stepped into the light, Beth sucked in her breath.

"Katie! What a wonderful surprise!" She threw her arms around the young woman and dragged her inside. Beth was ecstatic to see her. They hadn't been close friends, but they knew each other through their mutual friend, Libby. It was so good to see a friendly face from home.

"Ryann? I didn't think you'd remember me," the young girl said, awkwardly.

"What nonsense. Of course, I remember you." It felt strange to be called by her former name. "How is everything back in Richmond? How's Libby?" Beth was starved for news from home.

Horace needed to explain a few things. Turning to Vernon, he said, "I know it's Christmas Eve, and you've probably planned on goin' to the church, but this is terrible important. Unfortunately, it's bad news and will be upsettin' to yer missus. But I believe it'll also save her, in the end. Do ya want to talk about it now or later?"

Vernon looked at Beth. "What do you want to do, sweetheart? Your call."

Beth looked at the grave faces standing before her in her parlor. "No matter how important this may be, we will not forget that it is Christmas and miracles occur on Christmas. I'll be taking my child to church, to worship and praise the holy birth. There will be plenty of time for bad news after. You're all welcome to come along, of course." She smiled at them and went to gather up her son, just as if everything was commonplace.

"She's got a wee babe? Oh, how wonderful." Katie clapped her hands together. Looking up at Vernon, she added, "I've got a wee boy, me self. Seamus is his name. I miss him terrible, I do. Mother Boyle is watchin' o'er him, but as Beth done said, tis Christmas." She was close to tears, when Danny put his strong arm around her and cuddled her close for comfort.

"I want to go to church with Ryann," the girl decided.

"Guess I'll go, too." Danny didn't feel as if he had a choice.

Old Doolittle looked slightly amused. "Well, tarnation. I ain't a stayin' here all by myself, so I guess I'll be a goin' with all you fine folks. Bad news'll wait."

The little church was packed to the rafters with sleepy children, excited and tired parents, and the feelings that are peculiar only to Christmas. Goodwill toward all men was the message. A child, born of Mary, had come to save man. The message was the same, but this year it seemed to take on a new relevance.

Vernon noticed the senator sitting in one of the side pews, his eyes never leaving his grandson. Vernon knew this was going to be a fierce battle he may not win, unless he could think of something fast.

When the small group of people gathered back home, Beth put Frank down for the night. Katie wanted to help, feeling sad and missing Seamus. Vernon fixed a pot of coffee and brought out the Christmas Rum cake that Beth had prepared. The men waited for the women to return.

Beth sat down on the settee, next to her husband. She took a long sip of her coffee, loaded with lots of milk and sugar. Vernon always laughed at the way she took her coffee. He said it was more like a fancy dessert than a cup of brew. Clearing her throat, she decided it was time to face reality.

"I know you've all come to tell me bad news. I've had a lot of that, lately. It doesn't get any better, in the delaying of it, so you might as well just come out with it. I won't like it, but what choice do I have?"

Katie took Beth's free hand in her own, and said very quietly, "Libby's dead."

It felt as if a knife stabbed Beth through the heart. Her breath caught and she heard her own cry, as her cup crashed to the floor. "No—not Libby. How?"

Katie was speechless, witnessing her friend's pain.

Danny helped her with more of the information. "Katie's been investigating this case. She knows you're innocent of the charges against you and she set out to prove it. It was Katie that found Libby. She's been dead for almost a year. Even finding the body didn't prove your innocence. I'm embarrassed to say, that I got the wrong impression, myself. It looked as if you may have done her in, once you found out the lieutenant wanted her, over you. Then, in a jealous rage, after you killed Libby, it was possible you finished off the lieutenant, as well. It was motive."

Vernon growled at the red headed man. His fists were clinched and white with rage. "What the hell are you trying to say?" He wanted to rip the man's throat out.

"I'm sayin' that I was mistaken, but that a jury might get the wrong idea if the senator's lawyers present the evidence, in a biased way. And I think we all know that Senator Price will stop at nothin' to get a conviction."

Beth quietly asked, "How did Libby die?"

Katie looked at her with sad eyes. "She was stabbed with an infantry knife, the kind they give to officers. We believe the serial number on it will prove it was issued to the lieutenant."

Beth started to cry in earnest now, her shoulders shaking, her breathing hard to control. "It's all my fault. He threatened me with hurting her and Doo." She looked over at Horace. "Oh, my God. Have your heard from Harry?"

He nodded. "He sold his boarding house and the money has already been deposited in the bank." He looked over at Vernon; silently acknowledging the fact that he knew Vernon had been shot ensuring the stagecoach's arrival with the money. "I expect he'll show up in the next month or so." He smiled sympathetically.

"What made the two of you take this long journey? You could have just telegraphed the news to the Sheriff's Office," Vernon asked the young couple.

"I was ordered by my captain to see that nothin' happens to Ryann. You see, there is no doubt that the senator's son murdered Libby, as she wrote his name in her own blood, just before she died."

Bath gasped. It was too horrible to contemplate.

"She was a strong and determined woman," he continued, "and she wasn't goin' to allow him to continue gettin' away with hurtin' the girls, and especially not Ryann. I wish I'd known her."

"Poor Libby. She was thinking of me, even at the end of her life. How will I ever repay her?" Beth cried.

Vernon smiled at his wife. "By living a good, long and happy life, angel. By giving freely to others and by helping those in need. She knew what she was doing, darling. She sounds as if she was a remarkable young woman … just remember her."

"I need to go to bed, now." Beth was near to collapsing. "Excuse me. Oh, Mr. Boyle and Katie, you're welcome to stay here, with us."

"Won't be necessary, Mrs. Gunn," Doolittle said. "I've got two rooms with their names on 'em, back at the hotel. I'd like to invite you all to come and have Christmas dinner with me, at the Doolittle, tomorrow night. I'd be beholdin' to ya, if you'd come. I get a mite lonesome this time o' year."

Vernon thought about it for a couple of moments, knowing the old man had added that last bit for Beth's sake. He nodded. "Well, we do have to eat, and that's the best invite we've had.

Thanks, Horace." In a very quiet aside, he said, "I think Beth is going to need her friends."

The room was blessedly dark and silent. Beth knew that Vernon was not asleep, but listening to her breathing. "Darling?" she whispered.

"Yes, angel."

"I want to give you your Christmas present now."

Vernon laughed. Rising up on one elbow, he placed his hand on her breast. "Are you sure you feel up to this?" He grinned.

"No, not *that*, silly," she scolded. "I want to tell you something. I'm going to have a baby—your baby. And she's going to be a girl and we'll name her Libby. Merry Christmas."

Vernon was stunned. "A baby? Another baby?" he asked weakly.

"Yes. Don't you want another baby?"

Silence.

Beth sat straight up in bed, "Vernon! Don't you want another baby?" Had she made a mistake about him? Didn't he like being a father?

In the dark, Beth couldn't see the huge smile that crossed Vernon's rugged face. He was elated beyond words. He sat up and took his wife in his arms and kissed her long and hard.

"Happy? Angel, I'm over the moon and struck plumb dumb. Libby … I like that name. Merry Christmas, darling, and thank you."

Several days passed uneventfully. The senator was still lurking around town, watching the Gunn family from a distance. Vernon and Beth made certain that Frank was never left out of their sight. Barclay kept his eyes on the two marshals and the senator, as well. Danny and Katie took turns staying close to the family and to Horace Doolittle. Danny didn't trust the senator.

Senator Price thought it odd that the young red-headed police officer was here, in Tucson. He had telegraphed his investigators in Richmond to poke around and see what they could find out. He wanted to arrest Mrs. Gunn now, and take her back, but the U.S. Marshals were not so eager. They recommended she be tried here, in Tucson. The senator didn't like that idea. He knew that here, she would have an advantage. She'd more than likely get a sympathetic jury.

David Williams and his wife, Mary, came into town, just before the New Year. They said they needed supplies again, but Vernon and Beth knew better. Mary helped Beth pack up Frank's things. The baby was going to take a short trip. Beth had great difficulty stopping the flow of tears falling from her eyes. "I feel so silly. I know Frank will be close by and he'll have so much fun with little Rosie, but I just can't help feeling sorry for myself." She wiped her eyes on her sleeve.

Mary smiled. "If I were in your shoes, I'd be doing much more than letting a few tears escape. I'd be howling at the injustice of it all. Know this, dear, that Frank's in good hands and waiting for his mama and papa to come and claim him."

Beth nodded, feeling a little better. "I think that after all this madness is over, Vernon will be leaving the rangers. He's interested in horses, you know. The thought of moving out closer to you is thrilling and would be the realization of all my dreams. Sometimes I wonder how I got so lucky?"

Mary shook her head and smiled. "You never cease to amaze me, Beth. After all you've gone through, and you're still grateful and amazed at your good fortune. You're a wonder, Elizabeth Gunn, and I'm proud to know you."

That meant a lot to Beth. Mary was a special woman in her own right.

The two friends laughed together and continued packing. It was most important that Frank was well hidden and his things were disguised to look like ordinary supplies, in case they were stopped on their way out of town. Beth knew that the senator would be watching them closely.

"I'm not supposed to mention this, but David contacted Mr. Granger. You remember him."

"Certainly. I write to his wife, Leticia. They're going to have a baby soon. She's so happy. Why did David contact him?"

"As you know, he's a Federal Judge now, and David was hoping that he could do something for you. Maybe he knows someone with as much power as the senator. Don't get your hopes up, but it is a possibility."

"Thank David for me. I need all the help I can get. I won't lose custody of my son, no matter what," Beth said determinedly.

As the Williams' wagon pulled slowly away from Jones Mercantile, Beth's heart was breaking, while she stood, embracing a large, rolled up blanket—large enough to hold a baby boy. Their cargo was precious, and it was necessary that it arrive at the ranch for safekeeping.

Vernon put his arms around Beth and whispered for her ears only, "He'll be fine and it won't be for long, angel. You'll see him, soon."

She silently agreed. "Let's have supper."

Bright and early the next morning, a special stage arrived from San Francisco. To everyone's surprise, Judge Granger was its only passenger. With long and determined steps, he strode straight over to Sheriff Billings' office. He was a no nonsense man with a purpose. Looking around, he spied one of the U.S. Marshals standing across the street, and motioned for the man to join him.

After greetings and introductions were made, he asked to be filled in on the case. David Williams had told him some of the highlights, but he had to know the details, if he was to help his friends.

The marshal told him what he knew and how the senator had his heart set on extraditing Mrs. Gunn back to Virginia, to stand trial. A lot of things had come out about the character of the man's son, but it seemed to make no difference to Senator Price. Even the fact that he now had a grandson, hadn't softened his position against the mother. If anything, it had stiffened his resolve. Now, he was determined to take the child away from her, as well as her freedom.

Judge Granger knew Beth Gunn, and he owed his life to her husband, Ranger Gunn. His wife would be most unhappy with him, if he could not help her friend. He needed to think this through. Senator Price was very powerful and known to be an intelligent and just man. He was admired and respected, so why was he being so unreasonable about this?

"I need to talk to everyone at the same time. There's much that has not yet been discussed and I find it premature to speak of extradition, when she has not yet been arrested. I am aware that there is a price on her head, therefore she is not safe walking the streets of Tucson. She could be grabbed by a bounty hunter, and given the fact that she's wanted dead or alive, she could be in most serious danger.

"Sheriff Billings, I want her brought into protective custody. No one is to speak with her, except me, her husband, or yourself. No lawmen, no senators, no friends. We'll keep her sequestered until I can arrange for a hearing. We'll get to the bottom of this. In the meantime, I need to speak to a list of people." He handed the sheriff a lengthy list. "See to it."

With that, the judge rose and left the office. The marshal felt relief. He liked the young mother and her husband. From everything he had learned about them, they were good people. He liked the senator, as well, but thought he'd lost his objectivity with the grief he'd suffered, over his son's murder. It would be best, for all concerned, for this to come to its conclusion here, and for the senator and the two marshals to return to their homes, in Virginia.

Vernon struggled, as the deputy held his arms behind his back. "No, dammit. You can't take her. I won't let you take her," he yelled, as he fought against his captor. The sheriff was taking Beth away to jail. "You can't do this," he shouted, "She's my wife. For God's sake." Finally, a hard fist landed in his gut, forcing the wind out of his lungs.

"Calm down, Vernon. I don't want to hit you again, but I will if I have to. You're in some trouble too, so stop your fightin'. You can see her later," the deputy growled. "It's for her own good."

Beth walked quietly beside the sheriff. He had always been nice to her, in the past, and she knew that he had his orders. Quite honestly, she was ready to face this. Her biggest concern was the way Vernon was reacting. She knew it was tearing him apart, seeing her being arrested, and she was frightened he would do something that would get him into bigger trouble. He was a ranger, after all, and he'd sworn to uphold the law. She prayed he wouldn't do something foolish.

A few hours after Beth had settled in, Vernon was allowed to see her. He brought her favorite quilt and her own pillow. He filled a tin pitcher with water and brought her flowers to brighten her cell. It was all he could think to do and it broke his heart.

It was plain to see he'd been crying. His eyes were red and swollen; he looked like a tormented man, not the strong and self-confident man that he truly was.

"Beth, I've failed you. I'll never be able to forgive myself."

"No, darling, you're wrong."

Beth rushed toward her husband, and reaching through the bars, she curled her arms around his neck. "You're such a blessing to me. This will end the way it should. Life is unpredictable, but we do the best we can. It's enough to know you will help take care of Frank and see that he is raised in a loving home. I think they will allow me to have this baby before … you know. You must promise to raise her and be happy. She'll need you, when I'm gone."

Vernon felt sick to his stomach, and wasn't certain he could endure this uncertainty. "I can't survive this, even for your sake. I can't see this through to its conclusion. I'm weak, Beth. When it comes to you, I lose myself. I have no desire to live without you. Forgive me, darling. I'm supposed to be lending you strength and making you feel better, and all I've done is make matters worse." He hung his head in despair. His quaking shoulders betrayed his sobs.

Beth forced Vernon to look at her, and smiled. She leaned in and kissed his mouth and his swollen eyes. She let her lips slide over his wet cheeks. She put her finger in his adorable dimple. Oh, how she loved his chin. "Vernon, I will not allow you to do this any longer. Shape up and start being the man I fell in love with." She hoped that by ordering him to buck up, he might find the inner strength needed to continue on. "I have no intention of going back to Richmond, peacefully. It isn't fair and it isn't right that I should be punished, again. I lived through it once, which is more than can be said for poor Libby, and I do not intend to be put through hell a second time. So, are you with me or not?" she asked forcefully. "I intend to fight this."

Vernon smiled through his tears. He knew what she was trying to do. His Beth was amazing and possessed a great deal of strength. He wouldn't let her down again. "Yes, ma'am." He attempted a salute. "If the old man wants war, then by God, we'll bring it to him." He grinned, feeling better already.

"That's my husband. Welcome back, Ranger."

It was three days later before Beth found out that her friend's husband, Judge Granger, was in town and looking into the senator's accusations. She hoped he would be of benefit to her case. The hearing was scheduled for Monday, with all interested parties in attendance. Finally, it was to get underway.

Vernon was surprised at how fast information traveled through Tucson. People he didn't remember, or had never met, came up to him to lend him their support. It was humbling. Beth was popular amongst the folks in town and she had their prayers and best wishes.

Mrs. Bigsby was especially grieved by the situation. She'd gone directly to the senator and pleaded with him to forget the whole matter. He had rebuffed her, telling her to go back and attend to women's business. No one spoke that way to Calliope Bigsby! She would not just disappear. Instead, she decided to kill the senator with womanly kindness. Yes, she knew how to do that. *"The old goat,"* she thought. *"He's never run across a Calliope before, and he'll rue the day he discounted me."*

As the sun rose on that Monday morning in January, the whole town of Tucson was abuzz with the news of the hearing. Everyone wanted to attend, but they were turned away if they could not lend anything to the testimony of the two principal parties. As it was, the little courtroom would be nigh onto bursting. Beth had a lot of supporters, in this town, and they were not about to let her get ridden out on a rail.

The first time Beth saw Judge Granger, was that morning, in the court room. She was amazed and touched by the incredible support she received, from not only her friends, but from folks she didn't even know.

The senator and the two marshals sat apart from the rest, patiently waiting to present their case.

In a loud and powerful voice, Judge Granger banged the gavel.

"Silence! Silence in the courtroom! This is not a trial, but an informal hearing to find if there is just cause to bring Ryann Elizabeth Beaufort Gunn, up on charges of intentional and willful murder of U.S. Army Lieutenant Mark Allenton Price, of Richmond, Virginia. His father, Senator Allenton Price, is seeking to remove Mrs. Gunn from the Arizona Territory and extradite her to the jurisdiction of the alleged crime.

"It will be my decision, and mine alone, as to the outcome of this hearing. I will listen to all those persons having pertinent information on the details of the crime, the character of the defendant, *and* the character of the victim.

"My decision will be final. Is that understood?" He looked directly at the senator. The old man nodded, respectfully.

"Good. Let's proceed.

"Senator, I'll first hear from you. I want you to tell me what you know to be true, concerning the murder of your son. How were you notified and what did you see, firsthand? What did you know about the acquaintances of your son—things of that nature? You must swear to tell the truth."

The distinguished senator rose and came forward, seating himself in a chair, facing outward. "Of course, your honor." He hesitated briefly, putting his words in order. "If I may, sir. I'd like to first tell the court about my son, as I know so little about his actual death, and he is not here to speak for himself. I feel I must let the court know of his true character."

The judge looked at Beth. "Do you object to this man speaking of his son?"

"No, your honor," Beth said just above a whisper.

The senator looked at her and smiled a small and tentative smile. Calliope was right. She was a nice young woman, even under such duress.

"You may continue, Senator."

"Thank you." He took a breath. "Much of what I have to say may first appear to be the ramblings of a distraught father, but I assure you, knowing Mark, as I knew him, is important.

"He was an only child. My wife could never have more; so naturally, he was the apple of our eye. He was a beautiful child, happy and highly intelligent, very much like my grandson." He glanced over toward Beth. "He loved his mother greatly and sought to please her. As he grew, so did his appreciation for life and his desire to excel. He was first in his graduation class at West Point. All who knew him respected him. Mark loved to laugh and have a good time. Women admired his good nature and his fondness for dancing. There was nothing he couldn't do well. He was a remarkable young man, incapable of inflicting the kind of pain and misery of which he is accused.

"I have signed letters and statements, from his field commanders and the enlisted men under him, extolling his virtues and his many acts of bravery during combat. He was compassionate. He never left a wounded man behind, if he could reach him. Once, he gave a wounded corporal his own horse, in order to make an escape from imminent capture. Mark ran away on foot. Time and time again, he proved himself to be a man of honor and a man of great courage.

"Now, he lies dead in the ground, his name besmirched and sullied by that woman." He pointed his finger directly at Beth.

"You bastard!" Vernon yelled, as he jumped up from his seat.

The gavel cracked upon the desk. "Silence! I'll not have you disrupting these procedures, Ranger Gunn. If you cannot control your outbursts, I'll have you removed for the remainder of our time. Is that understood?"

Still standing, reprimanded by the judge and fearful of ejection, Vernon quietly nodded his head. "Yes sir. Sorry, sir." He sat back down, where his wife promptly grasped his hand.

"How did you find out about the death of your son, sir?" the judge inquired.

"I received a telegram. I was in Washington, at the time. The police had discovered his body." The old man stopped for a moment, in order to compose himself. It was difficult recalling those painful days.

"He was found in an alleyway, and had been stabbed in the back. His throat had been cut." The senator's empty gaze was haunting, as if he was seeing his son's body lying lifeless in the alley. "He had been there for several days." His voice trailed off, as he felt the abandonment of his son.

"The authorities weren't making much progress in their search for the murderer, so I hired my own investigators. They questioned a great number of people. The name, Ryann Beaufort, kept coming up as a known associate of Mark's. The name was found amongst his personal items, and he had mentioned, to several officers, that he needed to bring Ryann Beaufort to heel. I assumed, along with the investigators, that the name, Ryann, was a man's name. We lost three very important months looking for a man. A couple of infantrymen had been overheard discussing Mark's intent on romancing a beautiful blonde woman with a most unusual name. Her name was, Ryann. That changed everything.

"From that moment, the search has turned up much about her. She was orphaned and has lived on her own, from an early age. One can only guess *how* she earned her keep. She was also known to keep friends with other women of questionable virtue."

Danny Boyle stiffened. The senator was talking about women like his Katie, and the old man didn't know anything of their circumstances. Worse yet, he didn't seem to care.

"When the investigation led the authorities to the Doolittle Boarding House, we were able to make a connection with Tucson. Your Hotel Doolittle belongs to Harry Doolittle's brother, Horace. He's been knowingly giving her sanction. I expect him to face charges at some point" he stated firmly.

There was much whispering and muttering, in low voices, among the people gathered inside the courthouse. No one agreed with anything the old man was saying. It was obvious he was mad.

"Do you have anymore to add, Senator, before I allow Mrs. Gunn to speak?"

"Only that my son was a decorated war hero, wounded at Gettysburg, and still he loved serving his country. He didn't deserve to die this way." His eyes were filled with genuine tears.

Judge Granger could feel the gentleman's pain. He, too, was going to be a father, and he already loved his child to the point of madness.

"Mrs. Gunn, I'd like to hear from you now. Please rise and come forward. You make take your seat, Senator."

Once Beth was seated, she looked up at her friend, the judge. She knew she would not receive preferential treatment, but she was confident that he would be fair in his decision. She could not hope for more.

"Start at the beginning, Mrs. Gunn. Is your rightful and legal name, Ryann Beaufort?"

"Yes, your honor. I was christened, Ryann Elizabeth Beaufort. My father was a physician and my mother was a world-renowned singer. I was born in Richmond, Virginia and lived my entire life there, until a year ago, last November, when I fled to Tucson."

"You say you fled. Why was that necessary, Mrs. Gunn?"

"Because I had killed a man and I was in no physical shape to stand trial."

The shocked gasps of disbelief in the small courtroom, were

deafening. No one could imagine Beth hurting anyone.

The senator stood up. "You see? She confesses her guilt. She admits to killing Mark," he screamed at the judge.

"Sit down, sir, or I will have you removed. I will not tell you again."

Looking back at Beth, the judge asked, "You must have had help leaving Richmond. Who aided you?"

"I'd rather not say, sir. He just provided me with medical care and a railway ticket."

"How did you meet Lieutenant Price?"

"I'd seen him around. Being single and on my own, many men approached me. I never went with them. Originally, just after the fire that killed my parents, I got a job giving voice lessons to the colonel's daughter, at Fort Clark. I may have seen him there, but if I did, I don't recall it. I then worked at the hospital, and Mr. Doolittle gave me a small room that I could afford. That was my life. Once in a while, I would go along with girlfriends to small parties. That's when I first saw the lieutenant.

"He was tall and quite handsome. All the girls were giddy over him. As I never went out with gentlemen, I refused his offer to see me home. After that initial meeting, he would run into me on my way home from the hospital, or the library, and offer to escort me back to the Doolittle. Again, each and every time, I refused his attentions.

"One evening, my dearest friend—" Beth's voice hitched, as she uncontrollably let go of a sob. The courtroom had no choice but to wait for her to regain her composure.

"Sorry," she apologized. "My most beloved friend, Libby McGuire," she stated loudly, feeling that Libby deserved to be recognized distinctly, by all in this room, "begged me to accompany her to Fort Clark, for the biggest dance of the year. She loaned me a beautiful dress and put up my hair. She remarked how we both looked too magnificent for ordinary men." Beth chuckled at the memory.

"It was a glorious evening. We danced with every soldier and officer there. At the end of the evening, Lieutenant Price insisted on seeing me home. I had danced two dances with the officer, throughout the entire evening, but I still refused his escort. Libby was waiting for me. Over my protests, he took my arm and led me to his carriage, where he politely, but firmly, insisted he return me home.

"The next evening, he was waiting for me in the lobby of the Doolittle, once again demanding that he escort me. He was under the illusion that we were seeing each other. He'd say nice, complimentary things one minute and then he'd say something unbelievably vile, scaring me, the next. When I got angry and insisted that I did not want to see him again, he became abusive, and physically hurt me."

"That's a lie!" the senator shouted.

Rapping the gavel loudly, the judge decried, "I'll have no more of that, sir." Looking at Beth, he smiled and asked her to continue.

Suddenly, becoming shy, Beth didn't know what to say. She couldn't bring herself to tell half the town her most intimate secrets, the things she had revealed to her husband. "He hurt me, sir. He held me captive, for days. He beat me and … and did other things." She spoke barely over a whisper. Judge Granger had to lean in to hear her clearly.

It was obvious she wasn't going to say anything else without being prodded. The judge then asked her why she didn't have him arrested or at least tell others about him, if she was so frightened?

"I tried several times. A major, at Fort Clark, ordered him to behave properly or leave me alone. But, he was handsome and a war hero. No one believed that I was in any danger. Only Doo saw the evidence of my condition."

Horace stood up and shouted, "That's right. My brother wrote me about the beatin's and how scared he was fer her."

"Sit down, Mr. Doolittle. You'll get your turn," the judge ordered. "Continue, Mrs. Gunn."

"Toward the end, he abducted me and kept me hidden for days. He tied me up and starved me. Doolittle saved me and took me home. When the lieutenant discovered I had made my escape, he threatened to hurt my friends, if I didn't fully cooperate. I believed him.

"I tried to leave town, but he discovered my plan and swore he was going to kill me. I was terrified, and so after he beat me, I managed to stab him in the back with a little pen knife, belonging to my father. He actually laughed at me, and said he would take care of me after he took care of Doolittle. I couldn't allow that to happen, so I grabbed the knife, he had pulled out and tossed to the floor, and I sliced his throat."

Not a sound was heard in the room. Beth forced herself to looked at the senator and found him glaring, venomously, at her. Pure hatred consumed him. He truly wanted to see her dead.

"Ahem," the judge cleared his throat. It was inconceivable to think that this pretty young woman could sit here and admit to cutting a man's throat.

"That's all I have to say, sir." Beth was done, now and forever more. She would never mention this again, to anyone. It was finished. She stood up and went back to her seat.

The judge was somewhat taken aback. "You have not been dismissed, Mrs. Gunn. If what you say is true, then it doesn't leave the court much latitude in its findings. Won't you say anything else in your defense?" He was practically begging Beth to say something to justify her taking a man's life.

"No, sir. Nothing else." She sat as if frozen. He could tell she had shut down.

Judge Granger then asked the bystanders if anyone of them could add anything to the picture, either for the prosecution or the defense?

Danny, Horace, Katie, and even Calliope, bless her heart, wanted to add their own testimony. Calliope said she was an excellent judge of human character and had *never* been proven wrong. "Had she?" she asked the audience. Shaking their heads, everyone agreed—no, she had not.

"That girl is incapable of cruelty, I tell you."

She looked sympathetically toward the old senator. "Allen, listen to me. She couldn't have done what you think. She may have killed him, but I know she must have had her reasons, and I surmise you have your doubts. She's given you a grandson, Allen. Live for him. I'll help you." She spoke that last part, softly, and then smiled in his direction.

"Thank you, Mrs. Bigsby. Your opinion will be dully noted. Next I'll hear from Horace Doolittle."

"I know her as well as I know my own face. Harry, my brother, filled all his letters 'bout her. He loves her as if she was his own child. He wrote and told me how she started sneakin' in, keepin' her face covered. One time he saw her, and he barely recognized her. She denied that she'd been beaten, but he knew better. He had seen the lieutenant force her into his carriage, more than once. She told him she was gonna leave Richmond. She even bought herself a ticket. When she disappeared fer a week, he got real scared, and was able to follow that mad man back to a shack in the hills, where he found her all tied up. Harry cut her loose." Horace curled his finger at the judge, wanting him to draw closer. What he needed to say was for the judge's ears only.

"She was naked, sir … not a stitch, and her body was covered with wounds." He clicked his tongue and wagged his head, from side to side, in disbelief of his own words.

The judge was visibly shocked at what he'd heard. "Since this in an informal hearing, I will take this hearsay into consideration. Officer Danny Boyle? You wanted to add something?"

"Yes, sir, I do. "I've been working this case for a year, sir. I've talked to upwards of a hundred people, and there was always one constant remark, I'd hear, when I asked women about Officer Price. They'd say he was a handsome one and a very cruel one. He liked to make women scream and he enjoyed hurtin' them. It got so bad, that he had to pay for his pleasures. Even then, he was turned down, more often than not. He was a bad one, they said.

"His men loved him and they would follow him anywhere. As frightened as the women were of him, his men were just that filled with admiration of him. It was as if he was two people."

"Is that all, Officer Boyle?"

"Almost, sir. My fiancé and I discovered the body of Miss Libby McGuire. It was gruesome to be sure. Her death had occurred right around the time of the lieutenant's own murder. He carried through with his threats of killing Miss Beaufort's—I mean, Mrs. Gunn's friend, Libby. There is no doubt that Mr. Doolittle would have been next."

Voices rumbled throughout the courthouse.

"We have no proof of that, Officer Boyle. You may take your seat.

"It seems as if there's a lot of information available to me, but there is still no concrete proof that Mrs. Gunn's very life was endangered. We don't know for certain, that she didn't kill Miss

McGuire over the loss of Lieutenant Price's love and affection. We cannot …

"Stop! Sir."

The judge looked incensed that someone would yell at him while he was delivering his closing remarks. "Young woman. You had better have a very good reason for this interruption, or I will find you in contempt of interrupting me!"

"Oh, I'm so sorry, your highness, but I cannot let ya go thinkin' that Miss Ryann is guilty of doin' such an awful thing." Katie's brogue was more evident now that she was so nervous. "I saw with me very own eyes, that Miss Libby wrote in her own blood, the name of her killer … and it was Lieutenant Price. She wrote he killed her."

"Who are you?" the judge demanded to know.

"Your highness," she curtsied, "I'm Danny Boyle's intended, Katie O'Donnell, from Ireland." Giggles permeated throughout the courtroom. Even the judge had some difficulty remaining serious.

"I knew both Ryann and Libby. I found the body, I did," she said proudly. "Danny says, I helped to crack the case." Then, her freckled little face sobered, "It was just awful, sir. Libby was a dear one, she was. She helped all of us girls, down and out on our luck. She didn't like the lieutenant and she tried to warn Ryann about him, but he got to her, first."

"Thank you, Miss O'Donnell. What you had to add was very important, indeed, and I rule that young Officer Boyle is lucky to have such a smart and brave young woman, for his future wife." He smiled at Danny, wanting to laugh out loud. He would never be bored with this pretty young lass in his life.

"Now, I am going to retire and think about all that I have heard today. I need to wire the authorities in Richmond. This is a most sad and bitter case, and I feel that no matter how I decide, hearts will be broken. I promise you all, that I will do my level best to look at this case from a most unbiased point of view, and try to be Solomon in my findings. We'll meet back here, tomorrow morning, at ten o'clock. Thank you all."

The hearing was at a close. Everyone went home, but none would get much sleep, this night.

# CHAPTER TWENTY-ONE

Vernon took Beth back to their home, to rest. She was weak from the emotional stress of having to relive the horrors she suffered, at the hand of Mark Price. Thankfully, Judge Granger had been gentle with her and was understanding. Thank God, he thought, for the testimony of Katie and Danny. If it hadn't been for the two of them, he wasn't sure how things would turn out. Now, he was confident that Beth would go free.

"Vernon," Beth said, softly, "I want to know that you're going to be okay, if things don't turn out the way we want them to. You must be strong for our children. I've made up my mind that no matter the outcome, I'll make the best of it. You must too."

His wife humbled him. Vernon pulled her close to him, eager to feel her skin beneath his fingers. As he massaged her back in slow and comforting circles, he released the buttons on her dress. He nuzzled her neck and took in the feminine fragrance that was hers, alone. He would be able to identify her in the dark, just by her sweet, sweet smell. His fingers found the pins that held her hair high upon her head. One by one, he released them and let them drop to the floor, allowing her heavy, golden mane to fall in a thick cascade, past her waist. Her hair was truly magnificent.

"I have no intention of getting along without you, my love. My life is worthless without you in it." He kissed her neck, her tiny little ears, and continued down her throat to the tops of her creamy breasts. "Now, come with me. This is how I want to spend our evening, together."

Almost reverently, he took her by the hand, leading her slowly into their bedroom, and shut the door, keeping the rest of the world at bay. Tonight, would be spent in each other's arms, as lovers, as man and wife. This was the way their lives would be, forever more … if he had anything to say about it. This was not the end of them.

The winter sun shone brightly, heralding a new day, and perhaps the last happy day of their lives, together. Vernon had gotten virtually no sleep, while Beth willed herself to sleep for the sake of her baby. Neither could force down a bite of breakfast. After feeding the stock, Vernon escorted his wife over to the Hotel Doolittle. He thought it might be nice to spend the hour, before going back to the courthouse, with friends.

"I don't think you should fret about it, overmuch, Ryann. It's bound to be a bonnie day, much better than yesterday. I've got a feelin' and I'm seldom wrong." Katie said, cheerfully. "I know that we'll all be celebratin', tonight."

Horace was trying to be optimistic, as well. "I could tell by the judge's face that he believed all of us. He's a right smart one. He'll make the right decision."

"Well, if he doesn't, don't block the door. I'm taking my bride out of there, and not stopping til Tucson is only a memory," Vernon declared.

"No, Vernon!" Beth insisted. "I won't have you doing anything of the sort. Whatever happens … happens. It's all in the hands of fate."

"That's what you think, angel. My middle name is Fate!" He was serious. While he was lying in bed, the night before, he'd come up with a plan to get Beth out of town and hide her in some Indian dugouts in the hills. It wouldn't be comfortable, but they'd be together, until he and David could come up with something better. Napoleon was saddled and tied behind the courthouse steps.

The big clock, in the town square, struck ten. The small group of friends started across the street, together, to the courthouse and to Judge Granger. All were filled with apprehension, but they were committed to stick by Beth Gunn and her husband. It was possible for the judge to decide either way.

Vernon said a silent prayer.

After all were seated, Beth noticed Calliope was sitting directly behind the senator. It was odd, she thought, but she knew Calliope was a good and honest woman and whatever she had decided to do, was fine with Beth.

The gavel cracked upon the table, bringing everyone to attention.

Judge Granger wasted no time in taking his seat. After shuffling a few papers, he looked up at the anxious faces, all directed at him.

"I don't mind telling you all, that I got very little sleep last night. There is something about this particular case that just doesn't settle well with me. Before I pronounce my final decision, I would like to request something of the esteemed senator."

Turning toward the older man, the judge asked, "I respect you, sir. Your reputation for honesty and loyalty is beyond reproach. I know you to be a thoughtful man, slow to anger, and a methodical thinker, never accepting something just because everyone else does. That is precisely the problem I have in this case. The evidence against your son is overwhelming. So many women who knew him, all say the same thing. He was cruel and dangerous. He threatened their well-being and in some instances, their very lives. It is obvious that he is guilty of committing the most ultimate act of cruelty. The authorities in Richmond have deemed him guilty of Miss Libby McGuire's homicide.

"My final question to you, sir, is this: How can your opinion of your son's character and temperament be so contrary to the opinion of all others? Were you not aware of his violent and unusual proclivities?"

Senator Allenton Price stood slowly, looking far older than his actual years. The court proceedings had been difficult for him, and listening to the testimonies of good people, hearing what they had to say about his son, had taken its toll. His anger was gone. He appeared to be a shell of the man, he had been before. Beth noticed the two marshals were not present in the room, today. He had released them. Before speaking, the tired old man glanced over his shoulder and gave a weak smile to

Calliope.

"You can do this, Allen," she murmured, low.

He nodded. "I need to first apologize to this court, to you, sir … but most of all, to the Gunn family. I have done Mrs. Gunn a terrible disservice. In my zeal to correct a wrong, in my misguided sense of fatherly love, I almost succeeded in punishing a lovely young woman, already hurt and terrorized by my family. I can never make up for that. But what I'd like to do, if I may, is explain a little bit about my son, Mark … *not* Lieutenant Price.

"Mark had all the virtues I told you about, yesterday. I did not lie about that. He was a loving and gentle son, a good man, and I was very proud of him. He continued to grow and became a leader of men. Then one horrible morning, in an open wheat field in Gettysburg, Pennsylvania, he was most grievously wounded. His skull was split wide open and he was not expected to live. But somehow, a miracle occurred, and he did survive; only he suffered the most horrendous headaches one can imagine. They were blinding and, at times, he begged to die. He had also suffered a slight wound to his groin, but it had no real lasting effects. However, in Mark's sickened mind, he was unable to have a normal relationship with a woman. It was false, but that's what he believed, just the same.

"He could only get through the day with massive doses of laudanum, and sometimes he mixed it with alcohol. At first, it allowed him to sleep, but then his body seemed to thrive on it. He didn't feel drugged or slow witted. Quite the contrary, his abilities were enhanced. He was a good officer and his men loved him. It allowed him to once again, take charge.

"I took great relief from the way he seemed to be returning to his old self. He was never short tempered around me, and he seemed to be genuinely happy, once again. I could see glimpses of my son, emerging from the darkness.

That is, until about a year and a half ago, when a young maid, working for me, was often seen crying. I don't get too involved in ladies' matters, relying on my housekeeper to see to it. Then the girl simply vanished. I thought she quit. Her mother came to visit me a month or so later. She hadn't seen her daughter for weeks, but knew her daughter had been seeing my son. She had the letters to prove it. Letters in my son's distinctive hand.

They were not love letters, as one would expect, but letters full of threats and promising great cruelty. She was frightened of my son.

"I hadn't believed the girl. She was obviously hysterical. I told the mother that I would look into the matter, and I did. I demanded my son tell me all he knew. He didn't recall the girl at all. That was good enough for me. Six months later, her body was found buried in the stable yard afforded the officers at Fort Clark. Once again, I chose to ignore it, attributing it to a simple coincidence. But now, after hearing all this, I know my son had access to that stable. I believe he may have murdered her. God forgive him." The old man hung his head and closed his eyes for a moment.

"As God is my witness, I think it was the injury and the laudanum that caused my son to react in such a way. I've heard that severe head wounds often times create psychological disorders. My son did not do those terrible crimes, but Lieutenant Price may have."

The hearing was over, but not the pain.

# CHAPTER TWENTY-TWO

It wasn't a time for celebration, but it was a time to give thanks, and to be surrounded by good friends, Beth thought. She stood quietly. "Please, everyone. You're all invited to come back to our home for refreshments. I would like to thank you for your support and ask for your assistance in putting this nightmare behind us."

The courtroom emptied out, leaving the senator sitting alone. Calliope had been the last to leave. He was a pathetic figure, lost and alone. It would be necessary for him to make arrangements to go back to Washington, in the morning. Slowly, he too, finally exited the building.

The women headed to the kitchen to assist Beth in fixing the light fare, she had offered. Katie, Mrs. Jones, Miss Watkins, and even the Grande Dame of Tucson, Calliope Bigsby, pitched in. They chattered like magpies, cheering the hearts of all who heard them. The outcome had been as they all predicted.

"I told you, you had nothin' to fear, Ryann," Katie said enthusiastically.

"Katie, you literally saved my life, but I have one more favor to ask of you. Since I left Richmond, I've been known as Beth. It would be less confusing for everyone, if you'd call me Beth, too.

"That would be me pleasure, *Beth*. It's such a bonnie name." Katie smiled radiantly.

"Now, let's get this food on the table. I hear the men approachin'," Mrs. Jones announced. She carried in the bread tray and the platter of scrambled eggs.

Beth grabbed the ham and Katie took in the fried potatoes and onions. That left a pie and muffins for Miss Watkins, and the pot of hot steaming coffee, for Calliope.

"Hurrah!" the men all exclaimed. They were famished, as all of their appetites had returned. No one had eaten anything, that morning—but that was then, and this was now.

"Dig in, fellas!" Vernon ordered.

A knock on the door brought everyone to attention. "Who could that be?" Beth asked.

Vernon walked over and opened the door, surprised to see the senator standing there, hat in hand. "Yes, Senator?" He stood squarely, blocking the entrance to his home.

In a hoarse voice, so unlike the once loud and boisterous senator, the old man asked, "May I come in, Mr. Gunn? If you would allow, I'd like to take one last look at my grandson." He waited for an answer.

Vernon just stood there, immovable, the muscles in his jaw clenching, when a woman's voice came from behind him.

"Senator, you may come inside." It was Beth's voice.

Calliope walked up to stand beside her. Katie stood just slightly behind.

"What is it you wish, Senator?" She was polite, but distant, to the man who had hunted her for so long. The man who had wanted to see her hang, and had wanted to steal her child. Yes, Beth kept her distance.

"Madam, I would like to see the boy, one last time, before I return home. I promise never to bother your household again, or to ever set eyes on my grandson, again."

Calliope walked over to Senator Price and placed one of her bejeweled hands on his arm in support. She smiled up at him and nodded ever so slightly. He patted her hand and waited for Beth's response.

After thinking the matter over, carefully, Beth said, "No. I don't think so, Senator."

Calliope was mildly shocked. She didn't expect Beth to be so hurtful with the man. Even some of her friends were a little surprised. Vernon was relieved.

The old man's eyes watered up, but he nodded, accepting her decision. He deserved nothing more. He knew he'd brought this all on himself. It was his due. As he turned toward the door, and started to walk away, Beth stopped him.

"Sir, you refer to Frank as your grandson, but a true grandfather would not disappoint his grandchild by seeing him only once in a great while. He would not be satisfied, being excluded from that child's life. No. If you are promising me, to never see Frank again, then I must refuse you. However, if you want a relationship with my son, and if you promise to see him as often as you can, while he's growing up, I'd take your request into consideration. If you're willing to teach him the things that only a grandfather can teach his grandson, and share with him the knowledge of your vast experiences, then I would say yes to you." Beth looked directly at the senator. She was quite serious and he knew she was giving him his chance.

"Well? Do you want to be a true grandfather, good and proper … or just a stranger on a piece of paper?"

He couldn't believe his ears. This lovely woman had offered him more than he'd ever hoped. He could no longer keep his emotions at bay. Tears ran over the old man's noble cheeks, as he found himself taken aback. Overcome with gratitude, the old politician was speechless, for the very first time. He could only nod at the beautiful young woman.

"Well, then … that's that." Beth held out her hand to the repentant man. He gratefully accepted it and smiled up at her through his tears.

"Please, call me Allen. I'd like nothing better than to move here, to Tucson, at the end of my term. Would that be acceptable to everyone?" he asked Beth.

"That's better than acceptable, Allen. Frank will benefit from having his grandfather close by." Beth noticed that Calliope was smiling broadly. Evidently, she also approved of the move. *Could there be a romance brewing*, Beth wondered?

Vernon spoke up. "Unfortunately, you both have forgotten one minor detail. Frank isn't here."

"What?" The senator was shocked. "Where is he? I know he hasn't left the house." His eyes darted to the floor, as he felt the guilt of what he had done to this family. His money had bought people to spy on them continuously.

Looking a little sheepish, Vernon answered. "I snuck him outta' town, in a wagon."

"You what? How did you get away with it? I had men watching this house and all your friends, too." The senator wasn't angry, just really surprised that Vernon had gotten the better of him.

Vernon's eyes sparkled with victory. It felt good to win. "We packed him in a crate of dry goods, going out in a wagon, heading for a ranch I know. I couldn't sit back and let you take our son."

"I understand, Vernon, and I'm truly sorry. I hope I can make it up to you, someday."

"Well, then. I think, right after we eat, we ride out and claim that boy and bring him home. What do you say, Senator?"

He laughed with joy. "I say, call me Allen, son. And I also say, we leave only *after* we help the ladies with the dishes."

Everybody laughed at that remark and agreed to the arrangements. It looked as if everything was going to work out between the little family and the senator. Life was going to be just fine, after all.

As they celebrated in the parlor, only Doolittle heard the knock at the door. It was only Ranger Barclay, but he walked in with great authority.

"Hello, ever'one. I've a few important announcements to make."

Walking over to Vernon, he pulled out a piece of paper. "This here, is a letter of commendation, to be given to Ranger Vernon Gunn fer work exemplifyin' the best attributes of an Arizona Ranger. With uncommon skill and bravery, he saved the lives of seven people on the Butterfield Stagecoach Line, while under extreme fire. In addition, he saved the life of a fellow ranger." Barclay cleared his throat, and smiled at Vernon. "It was during this daring rescue, that he was seriously wounded, himself.

"He protected and preserved the entire payroll for the town of Butte, Arizona. Without his courage and gallantry, the whole town would've suffered. These acts of heroism and great courage under duress are to be rewarded.

"Please accept this bank draft, in the amount of five hundred dollars, from the grateful citizens of Butte, Arizona." He handed the draft to Vernon, who was standing with his mouth hanging wide open.

Everyone applauded.

"Say somethin', pardner," Barclay coaxed.

Thinking for a moment, Vernon said, "This is a surprise, indeed. Up to this point, I was so poor, I didn't have the money to buy hay for a nightmare." They all chuckled. "Now, I have the start of a little nest egg. Eventually, I want to buy a ranch and raise horses. I've promised Beth, that I've taken my last bullet for Arizona. Course, Arizona may not want a gimpy ranger, no how. Thanks, Barclay."

Barclay was still standing in the middle of the room. He once again, cleared his throat. "I have somethin' more to say."

"It is with deep sorrow and regret, that I order you, Vernon Gunn, on orders from the Arizona Rangers' Command, to hand over yer badge. As you are well aware, you've been on probation fer the last several months, continuin' fer another several months. You deliberately and knowin'ly hid important information concernin' a wanted fugitive." Barclay lowered his voice and his eyes, with embarrassment.

"Sorry Beth," he murmured, quietly.

"It's been decided that yer commission is to be terminated, immediately," he lowered his voice, considerably. "However ... out of consideration for yer exemplary record, the Arizona Territory wishes to thank you fer yer service and present you with a bank draft in the amount of sixty dollars, to help you while yer lookin' fer other employment." He handed Vernon another draft.

Everyone was silent. This had been some day.

Vernon looked at the check and started to laugh. As he laughed, the others caught his humor and joined him, laughing loudly and boisterously. He looked at all his friends, old and new, and said, "It's nothin' personal, simply justice ... Arizona Justice!" And they all laughed some more.

Finally, Beth announced it was time. "Let's go get our boy!"

## THE END

# ABOUT THE AUTHOR

ALICE ADDY has always been in love with historical romances. Many of her tales spring from stories told to her in her childhood. She proudly claims a famous Missouri bushwhacker as her great-great grandfather, and her overactive imagination fills in the rest of the story.

Collecting American antiques also fills her hours, along with her passion for gardening. Colorful flowers and blossoming trees often times find their way into her novels. She believes in setting a beautiful scene for her beloved characters. Readers will also notice her love for children and animals in her books. Hopefully, they will make you laugh, and they may even cause you to shed a few tears, but always, always … her stories will have a happy ending.

Soon, she hopes to travel extensively throughout the Southwest and the Northern plains. Maybe she will see you, there.

You can visit her website: **www.aliceaddy.com**

25513159R00180

Made in the USA
Charleston, SC
05 January 2014